RIFT

By Andrea Cremer

NIGHTSHADE

WOLFSBANE

BLOODROSE

ANDREA CREMER

RIFT

PHILOMEL BOOKS

AN IMPRINT OF PENGUIN GROUP (USA) INC.

PHILOMEL BOOKS

A division of Penguin Young Readers Group.
Published by The Penguin Group. Penguin Group (USA) Inc.,
375 Hudson Street, New York, NY 10014, U.S.A. Penguin Group (Canada),
90 Eglinton Avenue East, Suite 700, Toronto, Ontario M4P 2Y3, Canada
(a division of Pearson Penguin Canada Inc.). Penguin Books Ltd, 80 Strand,
London WC2R 0RL, England. Penguin Ireland, 25 St. Stephen's Green,
Dublin 2, Ireland (a division of Penguin Books Ltd). Penguin Group (Australia),
250 Camberwell Road, Camberwell, Victoria 3124, Australia (a division
of Pearson Australia Group Pty Ltd). Penguin Books India Pvt Ltd, 11 Community
Centre, Panchsheel Park, New Delhi—110 017, India. Penguin Group (NZ),
67 Apollo Drive, Rosedale, Auckland 0632, New Zealand (a division of Pearson
New Zealand Ltd). Penguin Books (South Africa) (Pty) Ltd, 24 Sturdee Avenue,
Rosebank, Johannesburg 2196, South Africa. Penguin Books Ltd,
Registered Offices: 80 Strand, London WC2R 0RL, England.

Published simultaneously in Canada. Printed in the United States of America.
Edited by Jill Santopolo. Design by Amy Wu. Text set in 10.25-point Apolline Regular.

Library of Congress Cataloging-in-Publication Data
Cremer, Andrea R. Rift : a Nightshade novel / Andrea Cremer. p. cm.— (Nightshade)
Summary: Sixteen-year-old Lady Ember Morrow fulfills a family obligation
by joining her friend Alistair in the Conatus Guard and begins training
to help with the order's true mission, to seek out and stop evildoers and their
unnatural creations.   [1. Knights and knighthood—Fiction. 2. Apprentices—Fiction.
3. Sex role—Fiction. 4. Supernatural—Fiction. 5. Middle Ages—Fiction. 6. Scotland—
History—1057–1603—Fiction.] I. Title. PZ7.C86385Rif 2012
[Fic]—dc23   2011042237

ISBN 978-0-399-25613-4
1 3 5 7 9 10 8 6 4 2

For Jill
To adventures, past and future

A Templar Knight is truly a fearless knight, and secure on every side, for his soul is protected by the armor of faith, just as his body is protected by the armor of steel. He is thus doubly armed, and need fear neither demons nor men.

—Bernard de Clairvaux, c. 1135,
De Laude Novae Militae—In Praise of the New Knighthood

ONE

EMBER BROUGHT HER sword down without warning and her aim was true. Her blade whistled through the air, hitting its mark and smoothly halving her adversary.

Her enemy might only have been a kirtle she'd outgrown and put to use by stuffing it with straw. Even so, the kirtle now lay in pieces, and bits of golden debris floated in the air around Ember as if celebrating her victory. With a yelp of joy she twirled around, brandishing her sword.

She held up the blade, letting its surface catch the sunlight. She was pleased, not only because she'd destroyed her poppet but also because her success meant she'd given her weapon the care it needed. Her sword was bright and sharp. The blade showed no signs of rust though she had to keep it hidden in the small niche she'd dug in this hollow, where it couldn't be fully protected from the elements.

Ember brought the sword up once more and swung it down in a broad arc as her body turned, following the path of the blade. The effortless stroke ended abruptly when her sword met resistance. The sound of steel on steel rang in her ears a moment before the shock of impact jolted up her arm.

"I thought I'd find you here." The familiar voice made Ember's shriek of horror transform to one of delight. Though his clothing had changed, Alistair Hart had not. His ebony curls still shone in the sun and his eyes still rivaled the spring sky.

She began to lower her sword, but Alistair stepped forward. His blade rasped, pressing into hers and forcing her to push back.

He smiled at her. "Tsk. Don't lower your defenses, Em. Is that how you'd respond to an ambush?"

"But—" Ember's brow knit together. She couldn't believe he was here.

"We'll have a proper reunion after you've shown me that you've been practicing," Alistair said, glancing at the remnants of the poppet. "It's a bit more of a challenge when your adversary can fight back."

His blue eyes shone with mirth that made Ember want to laugh, but she gritted her teeth. With a twist of her wrist she knocked Alistair's sword away and struck. He dodged, deftly wielding his blade to parry her swing. Ember met his blow and pushed their swords up so she could aim a kick at Alistair's stomach. Catching her sudden movement, Alistair tried to jump back but not quickly enough. He grunted as her heel dug into his gut.

Doubling over, he stumbled away. Ember cried out, dropping her sword.

"Oh, Alistair, I'm sorry." She ran to him. "I got carried away."

His shoulders were shaking and she gripped them, leaning down in hopes of peering at his face. "I didn't mean to hurt you."

When he looked up, grinning, she stomped her foot. His body shook not with pain, but with laughter.

"You're horrid." Ember's cheeks were hot with embarrassment. "I thought I'd hurt you."

"Only my ego, sweet Ember," Alistair said, still laughing. "Fortunately my stomach can withstand a gentle kick."

Ember winced at the word *gentle*. She certainly hadn't meant to be gentle.

"I'm impressed," Alistair continued. "You have been practicing."

Though she wanted to stay cross with him, Ember couldn't help but smile. "I have . . . If I don't sneak out to this hollow, I'll be forced to spin. I hate spinning."

Her fingers twitched at the thought. She didn't mind the calluses that made her hands rough from gripping her sword's hilt, but she resented the blisters that covered her fingers after the tedium of carding wool and pulling thread from a wheel. With a sigh, Ember turned to rescue her blade from the dirt where she'd dropped it, but Alistair took her arm and pulled her back.

"Have you forgotten already?" he asked with an impish smile. "Now that you've proven yourself, it's time to welcome me home."

Ember laughed and threw herself into his open arms. He crushed her into his chest, so she couldn't draw a breath, but Ember didn't care. She had missed Alistair every day since he'd left the marches. He was the only person who would know to look for Ember in the hidden glen. The only person she trusted with her secrets. The one who'd secreted a sword into her possession and helped her learn how to use it. In this last year, his absence had meant she had no sparring partner and no one to reassure her that wishing of a life of adventure wasn't a silly dream for a girl.

He laughed and spun her around so quickly that her feet swished through the air. "Ah, I've missed you, Em."

Ember wriggled against him until she was able to gulp in air. The question pounding in her veins rushed out. "Have you come to take me away?"

Alistair buried his face in the crown of her hair. "Did you have doubts? I keep my promises."

"But my father—" Ember tried to pull free, but Alistair's arms were tight around her body, holding her close.

"There are some powers in this world that even your father must answer to," Alistair told her. "And I'm here representing one of them."

Though he seemed reluctant to let her go, Ember managed to

wrestle herself out of Alistair's embrace. "It's wonderful that they sent you."

"It was decided that things would be easier if I were to come," he said. "For all of us." He reached out, letting his fingers rest on her cheek. "After today things will be better. Forever."

Ember nodded, though the lingering touch of his hand felt strange. Her mind was working too quickly to give the gesture much thought. Even with Alistair returned, she wouldn't believe that her father would let her leave his home, be free of his rule, until she was well away from the family estate.

When Alistair had left his own father's manor—only an hour on foot from Ember's home—to join Conatus, Ember had been delighted to receive word that he'd been chosen to serve in their elite Guard. He'd always bested his brothers in combat. He'd made his preference known, and not many would give up the comforts of domesticity for a life of war, even the sacred war of the Church. But Alistair was the third son of a noble, which meant his father's fortunes would pass to his elder brothers. Though he could have sought the hand of an heiress, Alistair claimed he'd prefer living by his sword than winning his fortune through a marriage.

Ember's situation was the reverse. She was the ideal fiancée for someone in Alistair's position. He'd even jested that they could marry to please their families. But two things kept Ember from ever considering that course. First, she knew marrying Alistair wouldn't please her father. He had an eye on husbands who would extend his holdings in France or Scotland. Alistair might be noble in name, but he brought nothing to the table that would gain her father's favor: no inheritance, no land of his own.

Second, and much more pressing, was the protest of her spirit. She was certain she'd suffocate trapped in a manor as some lord's wife. Even as a girl she'd longed to escape the monotony of spinning, weaving, and needlework. She'd been plagued by jealousy as Alistair and his brothers learned swordplay and horsemanship while she and Agnes were cooped up in the manor. Alistair had become her closest friend and confidant because of his willingness to thwart convention, stealing away to meet her in the hollow so she could at least have a taste of martial training.

Ember ached for a life where she could live by her sword and her courage. A life unavailable to the daughter of a nobleman. Except for this single possibility. Her father's debt to Conatus meant that she might be called to serve at Tearmunn. In what capacity she couldn't know. Even with her obligations to Conatus she might still be destined for a politically expedient union.

Her hopes were futile. Ember knew as much. But over the past year she'd too often allowed herself to imagine otherwise. Alistair's letters had encouraged her dreaming, hinting that joining the order would forever alter her life's path.

No work could be greater than the sacred duties of Conatus, he'd written. But what was that work? Despite his reassurances she still found herself doubting that she'd have a place within this strange order. Perhaps she'd been a girl who played with swords and slaughtered straw dolls, but now she was a woman. And women warriors were aberrations, creatures of legend but not the world she inhabited. Though it might be at the ends of the earth, Tearmunn was still of this world, and that meant she had to live as women did. As a wife. As a mother.

But now Alistair had returned, as he'd promised. Her pulse jumped at the thought that her daydreams of another life might be realized. With opposing currents of hope and fear sloshing against each other in her mind, Ember clambered up the grassy bank after Alistair.

Alistair's horse, a glossy bay mare, was gorging itself on the spring-green shoots that appeared in thick tufts throughout the pasture. The horse blew out in annoyance at having such a lovely meal interrupted when Alistair took up the reins. They started across the green fields toward the tall manor that loomed over the glen. The mare snorted, craning her neck in an attempt to snatch another mouthful of the grass.

"She's beautiful," Ember said, looking over the long lines of the mare's form.

"Her name is Alkippe. The horses at Tearmunn are exceptional," he told her. "Everything there is exceptional."

"And they haven't made a monk of you?" she asked, easily falling into their old pattern of teasing each other about romance. Alistair had always boasted that one day no woman would resist his knightly charm. Ember had countered that no man could ever have charm enough to make her want to marry.

Expecting Alistair's laughter, the suddenly harsh cut of his mouth startled her. "Of course not," he said. "Conatus may be an arm of the church, but we're not a monastery."

"I was only making fun," Ember said. "Your letters spoke of taking vows."

"The vows are of loyalty." Alistair's pace quickened. "Not chastity."

"But you said as a knight of Conatus you can't marry," she argued. "And that you continue the work of the Templars—who were chaste, were they not?"

The words left her mouth and Ember's heart became tight as a fist when she remembered that the Templars had been disbanded and many tortured and burned because of charges they'd broken their vows.

Alarmed, she murmured, "I shouldn't have jested about something so serious."

He grimaced. "You don't understand the function of the vows. They exist only because of the danger . . . Never mind. You'll learn the truth of this soon enough yourself. Now our task is to deal with your father."

Ember fell silent, lost in her own thoughts about the strange world that Alistair had called home for the past year. The world that was intended to be her home too.

"Are you so worried about my prospects for marriage?" Alistair smiled and tried to take her hand.

Ember shied away. She'd missed him, but twining their fingers wasn't something they had ever been in the habit of doing. He frowned when Ember pulled her hand back, causing a twinge in her chest that made her regret her choice. She quickly took his hand, squeezing, and was pleased when he smiled.

"You know I don't bother with such things," she said. "My father and mother have their plans. I have others. We shall see who wins the day."

Her words carried courage that Ember didn't feel. In truth she'd fled her house that morning in a desperate attempt to keep her mind occupied, just as she had every morning since her sixteenth birthday passed. Fear that an emissary from Conatus would never arrive, that her hopes wouldn't be fulfilled, had rendered her sleepless night after night.

"We shall." Alistair's tone grew serious. He halted, covering her hand with both of his. "Your arrival at Conatus is considered a harbinger of the order's future. One way or the other."

He dropped her hand, but only after briefly raising her fingers to his lips. An unpleasant shiver coursed through Ember. The flood of happiness filling her at Alistair's return was seeping away, leaving a cold foreboding in its wake. Why was he acting so strange? Touching her too often and in ways that were unbefitting of their friendship.

"How can that be?" Ember asked, hoping to avoid more awkward interactions. If she kept Alistair talking about his life at Tearmunn, perhaps it would make things more comfortable between them.

"You're the daughter of a noble," he said.

"You're of noble birth," she countered. "Wasn't your arrival equally auspicious?"

He shook his head. "I went to Tearmunn voluntarily. You are being called because your life is owed to Conatus."

Ember went quiet. Though she had no memory of it, the story never failed to unsettle her. When her mother's labor pains began, the birth hadn't progressed as it should. Death hovered over mother and unborn child. The sudden arrival of an extraordinary healer—a woman trained by Conatus—had offered salvation. But miracles came with a price. And the price named was the infant girl when she reached her sixteenth year.

Growing up with this memory following her like a shadow had been strange. That she was pledged to Conatus hadn't been hidden from her, but whenever it was mentioned, her mother fretted and her father roared. Even lacking her own memory of the event, Ember felt as though the circumstances of her birth had left her only loosely tethered to this world. That her survival had been a mistake, leaving her with a half-formed and chaotic soul. And that was why she wanted things she wasn't meant to have and dreamed impossible dreams. Because her very existence was ephemeral. Unintended.

As the manor rose before them, its hulking shape looming over the fields owned by her father and worked by his peasants, Ember's heart dropped like a stone in a well. Alistair had fallen silent, as lost in his thoughts as she'd been in her own. Ember wondered if her friend's outward confidence belied his own doubts.

A groomsman intercepted them in the courtyard, taking Alistair's horse and leading the animal to the stables.

"Your father is in the great hall," Alistair told her as they passed through the manor's tall oak doors. "With quite a feast prepared."

"He was hoping to impress Conatus," Ember said. "And he's likely disappointed that he's spent a fortune only to have young Alistair Hart appear to collect me."

"Not only me," he said with a quirk of his lips that might have been a smile or a grimace.

"Someone else is here?" Ember could hear her father's booming voice as they approached the great hall. He was using the expansive tone Ember knew meant he wanted to convey his importance.

Alistair leaned close, whispering, "Someone more intimidating than young Master Hart. Though I'm loath to admit such a man lives. But in truth, it is someone your father would be less likely to dismiss."

Curiosity brimming, Ember walked as quickly as she could without running. The hall was bursting with color, scent, and sound. Lord Edmund Morrow sat in a carved wooden chair, taller than its counterparts. A long table was overspread by silver platters laden with roasted pheasant, venison, and suckling pig. Wooden bowls were close to toppling under the weight of sweetbreads, piping hot fish stew, and savory pottage. Servants scurried about the hall, refilling empty glasses with crimson wine and amber cider.

Despite her pattering heart, Ember's stomach rumbled. This feast was far greater than even the Christmas celebration her father had thrown. Was he so concerned about his reputation with Conatus? After all, hadn't he spoken of them as a strange, isolated sect that had little to do with the world of court and kings?

Ember's mother, Lady Ossia Morrow, sat to the left of her husband. She was dressed in one of her finest gowns of ebony silk. Her hair was pulled into an intricate knot and adorned with gems. Ember's sister, Agnes, sat to her mother's left. She was also dressed in a favorite gown of rose and cream silks. Her eyes were downcast as she picked through the meats on her plate.

The other guests at the meal were warriors—the men-at-arms who served Lord Morrow. Burly and riled up by an excess of food and drink, they toasted and jostled each other, making the most of this unexpected bounty.

The only person in the room Ember didn't recognize was the man sitting at her father's right hand. Unlike the other revelers, the stranger's demeanor was stiff. Both uneasy and wary. Even though he was seated, Ember could tell he was a great deal taller than her father.

Catching sight of the new arrivals, Ember's mother extended her hands. "Alistair! You found her."

Edmund jabbed the tip of his knife at them. "Good lad, Alistair. As for you, errant girl, you might have taken a moment to don appropriate attire for this feast honoring our guests."

Ember glanced down at her plain and rumpled gown, its hem covered with dirt. "I was walking in the pasture," she said, cheeks warming with blood.

"Agnes, take your sister and help her make herself presentable," her father said. He glanced at the tall man on his right.

Agnes began to rise, but the stranger frowned. "There's no need for your daughter to adorn herself."

He waved for Agnes to return to her seat, but she hovered, uncertain what to do. When her father's eyes narrowed, she stood and scurried to Ember's side.

"You might hail from the wild north, good knight," Edmund answered him. "But I expect my daughter to act as befits her station, not as some peasant girl who runs around with straw in her hair."

Ember reached up, gingerly running her hands over her tangled locks. Blushing more deeply, she picked several pieces of straw from her hair. The stranger watched her closely, and Ember thought he might be on the verge of smiling. Her embarrassment melted into irritation. Was seeing her scolded like a child so entertaining to this man?

Still holding her gaze, the knight stood up. He was at least a head taller than her father and even a bit taller than Alistair. Ember glanced at the younger man beside her. Both knights of Conatus had dark hair, but where Alistair had curls as glossy as a raven's wing, the stranger's smooth hair was shorn so it fell just below his ears and had a rich color, like a tree's bark after rain.

She looked away from him only when Agnes took her hand. "Come, sister. I think the green silk gown would be a fine choice."

"Hold!" The knight's booming call stopped Ember from following her sister. Before her father could speak again, the stranger said to Ember, "My lady Morrow, I am Barrow Hess. Lord Hart and I have come to escort you to the Conatus keep of Tearmunn in Glen Shiel."

Ember freed her hand from Agnes's tight grip and dropped into a curtsy. "I understand, my lord."

"Are you prepared to leave now?" Barrow asked her. "We've already enjoyed too much of your father's generous hospitality. If you are amenable, we would take food for the journey and leave within the hour."

Beside Barrow, Ember's father began to sputter. Her mother gasped in horror. Agnes grasped Ember's arm, as if that gesture alone would keep her in their father's house.

Ember looked from her father to the tall knight. "I—"

"What sort of insult is this?" Edmund jumped up, squaring his shoulders. "I prepare a feast for you and you can't be bothered to share in it."

Barrow gave him a measured look. "I've eaten my fill, Lord Morrow. This gesture was a rich gift, but unnecessary. Lord Hart and I are here only to collect what you owe Conatus. Now that your daughter is here, we should be on our way."

A chill crept over Ember's skin. *What you owe.* Was that all she meant to Conatus? A debt to be paid?

She felt even colder when Alistair stepped forward, gaining her father's attention.

"The Circle bade me remind you, Lord Morrow," Alistair said slowly. "One life for another. These are the terms."

Agnes's fingers dug into Ember's skin, but Ember didn't flinch nor did she speak, even when her sister began to cry softly.

Their father paled. "Mercenaries you are. Cruel and demanding."

"One life for another," Alistair said again. His gaze fell upon Ember's mother. Ossia's lip quivered, but she laid her hand atop her husband's.

"You cannot forswear your oath, my lord," she murmured.

Edmund snatched his hand from hers and stood. "No. I shall not forswear myself. But I shall journey north with you. We all shall."

Agnes threw a pleading look at her mother and sniffled. "But my wedding . . ."

Ossia nodded, turning to her husband. "My lord, our daughter is but a month from her sea journey."

"Her trunks can be packed by servants." Edmund snorted. "She needn't be here. Our house travels to Tearmunn on the morrow."

Barrow coughed. "Lord Morrow. My orders are to bring the younger lady Morrow to Conatus today."

"Tomorrow is as good as today." Edmund glowered at the knight. "You shall not further offend me by refusing to share this feast and spend the night as guests in my home. We will leave at dawn."

"If you insist on making this journey north," Barrow said, with a slight shake of his head, "we will depart within the hour."

Edmund's face purpled. "You dare to command me in my own house."

His warriors ruffled at the exchange. Ember felt as though someone had grabbed her by the throat when she saw several of her father's men reach for their weapons. She could feel Agnes trembling.

"Father, please." Ember started forward, but Alistair put up his hand, signaling for her to keep still.

"Just wait," he murmured.

"I do not command you," Barrow told her father quietly. "But I will not fail in my own duties. I take your daughter to Tearmunn today. If you travel with us, you will already slow our progress. Three riders would make the trip quickly. The entourage you seem to be suggesting will make our journey longer by days. Delay is simply untenable."

Ember was holding her breath, her gaze locked on Barrow. He towered over her father with shoulders set, face calm but unyielding. She couldn't look away from him. No man had ever spoken thus to her father. Without fear. Without apology. Her pulse rippled with anticipation. It was marvelous.

Ember's father puffed up his chest. "I will not suffer this humiliation. Nor will I send my daughter off on a horse with two men like some common woman. She shall arrive at Tearmunn with her maids and her belongings."

Barrow glanced at Ember. "The lady alone will return with us today. You may send her things to the north as you wish. There is no place for her maids at Tearmunn."

"Enough!" Edmund brought his fist down on the table, the force of the blow toppling several platters and overturning cups. "I will hear no more of this."

"Perhaps we can resolve our differences another way," Barrow said quietly.

Red-faced and huffing with fury, Edmund scowled. "And what way would that be?"

"Pick your best men." Barrow waved at the cluster of warriors in the hall. "If they can defeat me in combat, we'll depart tomorrow."

Edmund squinted at Barrow. "Did you say *men*?"

The warriors guffawed, trading grins. Edmund raised his hands and the hall fell silent.

All traces of Ember's father's rage had been wiped away. With a hearty laugh, he said, "I'm tempted to hold you to your words, knight. And guarantee myself victory."

"I didn't misspeak, my lord," Barrow answered without hesitation. "Your best men. Name them."

The chortling of Lord Morrow's men quieted and soon became angry rumbles.

"A bold challenge," Edmund said, his smile hard. His gaze swept over his men. "Hugh! Gordon! Felix!"

Ember drew closer to her sister as the three warriors eased their bulk from their chairs. Her father had picked well. Not only were these his most seasoned knights, but they were among Ember's least favorite. Hugh wasn't horrible, but when she was a girl, his scarred face and missing teeth had frightened her. Gordon and Felix had a habit of leering at Ember and her sister when they passed in the hall. Even worse, Felix had a reputation for cruelty to both the manor's servants and his hunting dogs. These men would fight hard and, if given the chance, wouldn't hesitate to seriously injure Barrow out of spite.

Barrow nodded at the three men. "My lords, choose your weapons." He turned to Ember's mother. "My lady, I would not sully your home with combat. Might we move into the courtyard?"

Ossia nodded, taking her husband's arm. Edmund led his wife from the room, beckoning his chosen champions to follow.

The buzz of anticipation in the hall broke into a low roar. The men-at-arms surged after their lord, leaving the hall and barreling to the courtyard. Alistair hung back, offering his body as a barrier between the rabble of men and Ember and Agnes.

Watching the tide of warriors ebb from the room, Ember jumped in surprise when a low voice, very close, said, "I apologize for this spectacle, Lady Morrow. I hope I haven't given offense."

Barrow had appeared suddenly out of the mob, standing at her shoulder. She looked up and found him searching her face intently. What he was looking for she couldn't say, but her own gaze was caught in the dark blue-gray of his eyes, their shade like that of a storm-ridden sea. Unable to find her voice, Ember simply shook her head.

"Are you sure this is necessary?" Alistair asked Barrow.

"Lord Morrow is in need of a lesson," Barrow answered.

Alistair frowned. "Perhaps. But Ember's father will like us even less afterward, which will hardly please the Circle. Also, I know those men. You're in for a dirty fight."

"Don't worry about me." A smile flickered over Barrow's mouth. He shrugged off his cloak and handed it to Alistair.

Alistair sighed, muttering, "I wonder if Kael could have avoided a fight."

"Your mentor in the Guard?" Ember asked, remembering the name from one of Alistair's letters.

"Yes," he said. "He has a lighter touch than Barrow—but our commander didn't think a cheerful countenance would persuade Lord Morrow."

"Your commander is probably right," Ember said, and Alistair's only answer was a rough laugh.

As Ember and her sister hurried to match the long strides of the two Conatus knights, Agnes whispered, "How horrible! Can't you stop this?"

Ember glanced at her. "How could I stop this?"

"They're fighting over you," Agnes said. "Alistair has been our friend since we were children. Plead your cause to him. Surely he'll convince Lord Hess to release you from Father's promise. You were but a babe and our father was desperate. This burden shouldn't fall to you."

Gritting her teeth, Ember said, "You know how dear you are to me, Agnes. But I have no desire to be released. I want to go with them."

Agnes sighed. "You say that now, but what do you know of Conatus?"

Ember pulled her gaze away from her sister's worried face, frustrated by the truth in her words. Conatus was shrouded in mystery—

an order of knights sanctioned by the Church, but one whose tasks were known only to its members.

"You told me that Alistair's letters spoke of vows." Agnes stared at Alistair's back as she spoke. "Vows wherein you would forsake a life of your own."

"My life now is not my own," Ember hissed through her teeth. "If I stay here, I am but Father's to give to whatsoever noble he chooses."

A mewling sound of sorrow emerged from Agnes's throat and Ember put her arm around her sister.

"Forgive me, Agnes," Ember said, cringing at her own thoughtlessness. "I should not say such things."

"I know you look upon marriage with scorn." Agnes kept her eyes on the floor as they walked. "But it is only because you haven't been struck by love's arrow."

Ember would have snorted, but she'd already hurt Agnes enough. "I hope you find the love you seek in France."

Agnes glanced up, but at Alistair rather than Ember. "So do I."

Bright sunlight made Ember squint as they emerged into the courtyard. Her father's warriors had already formed a ring in the open space. Within the circle Hugh, Gordon, and Felix brandished their weapons. Hugh bore a short sword and had a shield strapped to his left arm. Gordon carried a halberd and Felix a spiked mace.

Lord Morrow's men stepped aside to let Barrow enter the ring. Alistair led Ember and Agnes to a nearby slope where their parents stood, overlooking the ring. Barrow had drawn his sword. Unlike Hugh's thick, squat blade, Barrow's sword was sleek and curving. The men about to fight bore as much resemblance to one another as their weapons did. Like Ember's father, the three warriors he had chosen to face Barrow were thickly muscled with an impressive girth of chest and shoulders. Their hulking bodies were built like piles of large stones. By contrast Barrow was tall and lean, his form drawn in long, taut lines.

Barrow searched the courtyard until he found Edmund. "My lord?"

"Whoever does not fall or does not yield," Edmund shouted. "My men or this knight of Conatus shall be declared the victor!"

Brutish hollering rose from the ring of warriors. Agnes shuddered, pleading with her sister once more: "How can you bear this, Ember?"

Ember barely heard her sister's question. Her blood was roaring in her ears, her heart drumming heavy against her ribs. Her hands moved restlessly, fists clenching and unclenching. She wished she could hold her sword, even if only to mimic the exhilarating match that was playing out before her.

Barrow raised his sword in salute to his trio of adversaries. They grunted and shrugged in reply. Hugh and Felix exchanged grins, signaling their anticipation of an easy win.

As the warriors around them roared for blood, the men within the ring began to move. Barrow kept his sword low, watching his opponents. Gordon bellowed, rushing at Barrow, his halberd aimed to impale. Barrow sidestepped, letting Gordon's spring carry him past the point of attack. As Gordon blew by him, Barrow twisted and brought the flat of his sword down on Gordon's skull. The crack of steel on bone made Agnes shriek.

"I can't watch!" She buried her face in Ember's shoulder. Ember didn't blink. It was as if she could feel Barrow's muscles tensing and exploding into action as he fought. Her body hummed with his strength and grace. She'd never felt more alive.

Gordon crumpled and lay unmoving. With Barrow's back turned, Felix and Hugh were already on the attack. Felix leapt at the knight, swinging his mace in a broad arc, while Hugh darted around their adversary, keeping his shield up but his sword low.

Barrow dove, rolling in the dirt as Felix's mace whistled past his ear. Hugh struck as Barrow lay on his back, but the knight managed to kick Hugh in the stomach with both feet. As Barrow sprang to his feet, Felix brought his mace around. A cry of warning rose in Ember's throat, but Conatus's champion spun around, his blade sweeping up to meet Felix's mace mid-blow. Metal clanged as they struck over and over.

Recovering from having the breath kicked out of his lungs, Hugh scrambled from the dirt to rejoin the fight. He tossed aside his shield and threw himself at Barrow's unguarded back. As Felix swung his mace, Barrow dropped to the ground flat as a board. Hugh tripped over Barrow and fell forward. Bone crunched, and a groan rose from the circled warriors when Felix's spiked mace buried itself in Hugh's shoulder.

Hugh screamed as Felix swore and wrenched his weapon free. Blood poured from Hugh's wound and his left arm hung limply at his side. Barrow had already rolled away from them and was on his feet again. Without pause he darted toward Felix, his curved blade flicking through the air. Gashes began to appear on Felix's arms and shoulders. Felix winced, stumbling back. With a strangled cry he wheeled around, flailing as Barrow continued his relentless strikes. Felix's shirt was in tatters, his chest covered with cuts that looked like whiplashes. Breathing hard, he dropped to one knee. Only then did Barrow's blade pause.

"I yield," Felix rasped, his head bowed.

Barrow nodded. He turned to face Hugh, who though bleeding and groaning in pain was still standing in the ring.

"Do you yield?" Barrow asked him.

Hugh spat on the ground just short of Barrow's feet, but he nodded. As Barrow sheathed his sword and turned to leave the ring, Hugh began to laugh. Felix had risen from the dirt, his eyes bulging with outrage. Without a battle cry, Felix lunged at Barrow, bringing his mace around in a high arc so it would smash into Barrow's skull.

In a movement eerily similar to Felix's submission, Barrow pivoted and dropped to one knee, but his hand was moving, sliding his blade from its sheath and slashing the air. He easily met Felix's swing, but Barrow hadn't aimed his blow to block Felix's attack. A shriek pierced the air as Felix's mace and his forearm dropped to the ground, hewn from his body by Barrow's sword.

Felix fell to the ground, still screaming and holding the bloody stump of his arm. Without looking back at the fallen warrior, Barrow left the ring. He didn't break stride until he stood before Ember. The slight incline upon which she stood put them face-to-face, and she found she couldn't breathe.

Ember stared at the tall knight. Every muscle in her body was taut as if she'd been in the ring herself. Her gaze lingered on his arms, his chest, the muscles of his thighs. Ember had seen dozens of men fight in her sixteen years at her father's estate. She'd never seen anyone move the way Barrow had.

Though she couldn't fathom why she would merit such a gesture, Barrow bowed to her.

"My lady."

She was still shaking when he turned to her father and said, "We leave for Tearmunn in an hour."

Edmund Morrow, pale with rage, answered. "An hour."

TWO

EMBER WATCHED AS servants carried another chest laden with gowns from the room she'd shared with her sister all of her life.

"I'm afraid Father has given me some of your dresses," Ember told Agnes, who was seated beside her at the foot of the bed. "I don't remember having so many."

Agnes laughed and took Ember's hand. "The dresses are yours. Most of mine have been packed for France."

"You shouldn't have to travel with us," Ember said, frowning. "Not now. You've been ill lately. This journey will do you no good."

"I can bear it if it means our parting is delayed." Agnes offered her sister a weak smile. She paused and then said very quietly, "I envy you."

Ember frowned. "Envy me? Sister, I go into an unknown that offers no prospects for marriage or all those things you crave. You've been asking me to find a way out of this obligation."

"I know I have." A gentle blush painted Agnes's cheeks. "And I do fear the place that claims you. But . . . you go with Alistair."

"It will be a comfort to have a friend at Tearmunn," Ember mused. "Perhaps he'll keep me from making a fool of myself—" She stopped when she noticed the way Agnes was watching her and the way her sister's eyes were glistening. "Agnes? Are you ill again?"

Though Agnes had always been the more delicate of the two

sisters, lately she'd been subject to fits of weeping without provocation.

Agnes shook her head, swiping the tears from her cheeks. "I'm well enough."

"Don't envy me," Ember said, taking her sister's hand. "For I'm likely to be a scullery maid to these mysterious knights, while you will soon be a countess wrapped in silk and dripping with jewels."

Agnes didn't answer, but kept her eyes downcast. Another tear slid over her pale skin.

"And you know the Count de La Marche is said to be very handsome," Ember teased. "You are surely the fortunate sister."

"I wish . . . ," Agnes murmured.

Ember squeezed Agnes's fingers. "Do you not wish to go to France? I'll support you if you want to beg Father to release you from this betrothal."

Agnes shook her head, pulling her hand away from Ember's grasp. Agnes reached up and touched the brooch pinned to her gown.

"A husband who sends such lovely gifts will no doubt dote on you," Ember said, hoping to cheer her sister.

With a soft, choking sob Agnes covered the brooch with her palm, pressing it to her chest. "This gift was not from the count."

"Then who—" Ember's question was cut off by someone clearing his throat.

Barrow stood just inside the door to the sisters' room.

Agnes jumped up and curtsied. She quietly excused herself, hurrying from the room.

Ember sighed and rose from the bed.

"I didn't mean to scare away your sister," Barrow said as he quickly surveyed the room.

"You didn't," Ember told him. "She hasn't been well of late."

"It's a shame your father insists that she accompany us." He frowned. "That anyone but you travel north, in truth."

She smiled weakly. "I'm sorry for that."

"I came to see if there were more chests," Barrow told her. "If there are, we'll need another wagon."

"I believe those were the last." Ember laughed. "And I would be happy enough to accompany you without my family or the chests."

Barrow came closer, his gaze curious and intent. Ember stiffened, feeling her pulse quicken with his scrutiny.

"I believe that," he said. "And I would have argued about the burden of this caravan he's put together had I not maimed one of his men."

Ember swallowed hard, remembering the blood and the screams as Felix fell to the ground. "That was no fault of your own."

In the pause after she spoke, Barrow watched her face, just as he had in the courtyard. Ember's skin felt warm and her fingers began to shake, but she refused to break his gaze.

At last he said, "I'm glad you understand that."

Barrow sighed, and when he pulled his eyes from hers, Ember was struck by a strange sensation of loss.

"I've come to take my leave, Lady Morrow," he told her. "Once the caravan is prepared, I'll travel ahead of your family. We were expected at Tearmunn much sooner than will now be the case. I need to inform the Circle of this delay and of your family's imminent arrival."

The warmth of her blood had vanished. Her hands felt clammy. "You won't be with us?"

He turned to face her and seeing the fear in her eyes said, "Lord Hart will be with you to ensure there are no further delays."

Ember looked at the floor. She didn't want to speak ill of Alistair, but she knew her father would see him only as the childhood play-mate of his daughters. It was Barrow her father now feared. With the knight absent she wondered if she'd be traveling north at all.

She drew a startled breath when Barrow's fingers lightly touched her face, lifting her chin so she would meet his gaze. His blue-gray eyes were hard as steel.

"You father knows that should he further hamper your arrival, he will lose much more than one man's sword arm."

Barrow's fingers were barely touching her, but the light contact could have been an iron brand. Ember didn't dare move nor breathe. All she could think about was the way his hand burned into her skin but with a fire that didn't cause pain, just an awareness of her flesh and her blood, alive with sensation, like nothing she'd ever known.

"You're strong, Lady Morrow," Barrow said quietly. "I can see it in your face. In the way you carry yourself. No matter how he tries to rule you, your father cannot break you. And soon enough you will be free of him."

Her breath came quickly. How had this knight known the hope that had lain hidden in her heart? How could he so easily speak the words she had longed for, but feared? That she was destined for something greater than the life her father planned for her, the life her dear sister was about to begin.

Barrow stepped back, letting his hand fall to his side, and once again Ember felt a tightness in her chest, a knot of sadness and regret.

He smiled and the knot loosened a bit.

"We will meet again soon." After a curt bow, he left Ember alone.

She closed her eyes, holding fast to his words. *You're strong, Lady Morrow.*

Now, more than ever, she was determined to prove those words true.

Ember found Agnes with Alistair in the courtyard. The caravan of wagons, mounted warriors, and a char branlant for the three ladies awaited Lord Morrow's order to depart.

"You must inform me if you fall ill," Alistair was saying to Agnes. "We can pause to rest."

Agnes smiled but shook her head. "I'll not keep my sister from her adventure. Though I still can't understand why she longs for a life in the north."

"Where the men are wild and the beasts are monsters?" Alistair laughed.

"I've always wanted to see a fire-breathing sheep," Ember said drily. "Will we be leaving soon?"

"Your father is readying his mount," Alistair told her.

"It's a shame you couldn't stay for a few days," Agnes said. "You're so near your own family's estate yet unable to visit them."

"Another time," he said. "And I've had word from them that all is well. My parents oversee their manor as always, though it must be different without us."

"And what of your brothers?" Agnes asked.

"Robert is at court, hopefully not getting into trouble," Alistair said. "You know what a mess the succession has been. He hopes to gain favor for our family with the king . . . whoever that might be."

There was a catch in Agnes's voice when she asked, "And Henry?"

Alistair looked away but answered. "Henry is building a new manor in Yorkshire. He and the lady Howard expect to take residence there next summer after they are married."

Agnes's cheeks went slightly gray. She nodded and said, "I think I should prefer to wait in the carriage."

"Of course, my lady." Alistair helped Agnes into the char branlant, then turned to Ember, offering his hand.

"No." Ember stepped back. "I don't want to be shut up in that box until I have to be."

Alistair laughed. "I don't blame you. It's much more pleasant to ride in the open, particularly given the roads we'll be taking."

"Wonderful," Ember muttered.

"But I think you're about to be put into the box." Alistair looked over her shoulder. Ember turned to see her father sitting atop his black destrier, barking orders to servants and warriors.

Her mother emerged from the manor, worried lines creasing her face.

"I would that this cursed journey be over before it has began," Ossia murmured as Alistair helped her into the char branlant. "Come, Ember, your father will be cross if you dally."

Ember sighed and took Alistair's hand as she climbed into the carriage.

THREE

THE WARRIOR SISTERS were fighting again, but their fury remained a secret between them. Hushed voices belied the tension that boiled in the air of their shared quarters. Still fuming, Eira turned her back on Cian and gazed out the slit of a window that gleamed in the otherwise dreary stone wall.

Cian looked at her sister's tight shoulders and sighed. "There's nothing to be done."

"I can't accept that," Eira said, not turning around. "And I refuse to believe that your heart rests easily."

"Of course it doesn't," Cian said. "That doesn't change our lot. I won't tire myself trying to draw blood from a stone."

Eira whirled, giving her sister a cold smile. "Our adversaries are not stone. And they will bleed."

Cian drew a hissing breath. "Hush, sister. Your jest is too costly."

"Our sacrifice is too costly." Eira ran her palms over the heavy brocade of her dress. "Look at this farce."

"I think you look lovely." Cian's teasing smile earned her a withering stare from Eira. "Italian silks are difficult to come by—you should be grateful for such luxurious gifts from our benefactors."

"It is not a gift, it is a costume through which our lies are bought," Eira said. "I tire of playing the puppet for the abbot and the nobles."

"Their visits are rare," Cian said.

Eira tugged the lacings of her gown free and then set to work unbuttoning the tight sleeves. "Not rare enough. And each time they appear, they ask for more."

Cian pursed her lips as Eira shed her overgown and shimmied out of her kirtle, leaving only a linen chemise. Eira breathed in relief as she traded the cumbersome women's clothing for sturdy chausses, over which she pulled on the Conatus tabard. The sturdy black wool fell to the middle of her thighs. The embroidered silver compass rose—the symbol of their order—spread the width of her chest, setting off a subtle shimmer against the dark expanse of fabric.

"I simply wish to be truthful in our affairs," Eira said as she buckled her belt and reached for her scabbard.

"The truth could destroy us," Cian said quietly. "I prefer wearing a dress to burning at the stake. You know the fate of the Templars as well as I."

"If we deny who we are, we'll destroy ourselves," Eira said. Steel hissed as she drew her sword. The blade gleamed when she held it up to the sliver of pale light. "The Church needs us more than we need them. And we're far more powerful than the Templars ever were."

"But we exist as a legacy of the Templars, and just as quickly we could be condemned as heretics." Cian let her own gown slide to the floor. "Conatus exists in secret, and therein is a source of our power. The Church and nobles legitimize our existence, helping to keep us hidden. We couldn't serve the world as we must without their aid."

"Couldn't we?" Eira snorted, gazing at her blade. "Our so-called benefactors spend so much time engrossed in their own conceits, we hardly merit their attention. The Circle cowers when it should command."

Cian looked up from belting her own tabard. "Command whom? We are servants of the earth, not kings of it."

Eira sheathed her sword, shaking her head. "I'm speaking out of turn. Of course you're right. We serve the world as we should."

"I don't blame you for being frustrated, Eira," Cian said. "But we have so much more than many others born to our lot."

"You wish me to be grateful that I'm not a swineherd's wife?" Eira laughed.

"Or a nun?" Cian smiled.

"We're little more than nuns." Eira's laughter faded. "We've given up as much as any man or woman who's taken holy vows."

"Says she who declares love as nothing more than a fool's errand," Cian said, assessing her sister with a sly gaze. "Has a gallant young knight captured your elusive heart? Barrow perhaps? He's very handsome—though given the way he fights, I'd wager he's akin to a wild boar in bed."

She waited for Eira to throw her a chiding glance and remind her that the men of the Guard were supposedly as chaste as its women, and maybe she'd even laugh, but Eira only scowled.

"Don't be ridiculous. Love *is* a fool's errand, and I've no time to worry over which of the Guard are handsome or ugly. I only care how skilled they are with a blade," Eira said. "But my view of love is shared by few. How many do we lose because of the Church's edict— men and women alike?"

"The Church again." Cian frowned. "I wish you would leave your anger, sister. The edict doesn't dissuade the Guard from seeking love. Your enemies are elsewhere and much more dangerous than the abbot."

"It dissuades women," Eira said. "We are here only because the plague left us orphans."

"And the Church took us in," Cian continued, raising her eyebrows. "Father Michael saved us and brought us to Conatus."

"Father Michael serves God and Conatus. He understands what would happen if we didn't exist." Eira glared at her sister. "The abbot only serves his coffers."

"And the abbot is not the Church," Cian said. "He's simply a greedy man, though a powerful one."

"I know that's true." Eira's shoulders slumped. "Still, I can't bear much more of him."

"But now he's gone and we can get back to our business," Cian said. "Come now. We can't be late for the ceremony."

Eira ran her hands through her long copper-colored waves. "I'll have to leave it down, I suppose."

"Yes, you will. We don't have time to braid our hair," Cian said, shaking her own unbound strawberry-blond locks. "Just be grateful the nobles haven't given us those headdresses the Spanish noble-women currently favor. They're horrid."

Eira shuddered. "I'd sooner wear a net full of live pixies on my head."

"That we could arrange." Cian grinned. "But they'd pull all your hair out."

"And then I'd have to wear a headdress," Eira said with a rueful smile. "I can't win."

"No, sister," Cian said, glancing over her shoulder as she passed through the doorway. "You probably can't."

Eira hesitated after Cian disappeared into the hall. Her fingers wrapped around her sword's hilt, its shape familiar and reassuring in her hand. It had been the same for twenty years. From the day she and Cian were called to join the Guard, they'd been asked to disguise themselves. When the nobles or church officials visited the stronghold, they were forced to dress and act as the other women did. Even after they had been invited to join the Circle, they could not exert their authority in the presence of strangers. Instead they followed when they would usually lead, submitted when they would rule.

Twenty years, Eira thought. *It wears thin. There must be another way.*

One of the carriage wheels dropped into a deep rut in the mud-slick road, making the vehicle lurch. Agnes gasped and clung to her mother while Ember leaned forward, trying once again to catch a glimpse of the countryside. It wasn't much of a road they were following, but likely a cattle drovers' track. Despite the well-built structure of the carriage, the horses labored hard to drag it forward across the rough terrain. Ember braced herself against the door, pressing her face against the small slit where cool, mist-filled air poured in.

"Stop fussing, Ember," Ossia Morrow said, stroking Agnes's cheek. From her sister's perpetual cowering, Ember thought, one wouldn't have guessed that Agnes with her pale skin and flaxen hair was the older of the two girls. Yet she boasted eighteen years to Ember's sixteen.

Ember forced herself to sit up straight, though she longed to be free of the armored carriage that bore them from her father's lowland manor to the solitary fortress of Tearmunn. The trip had been infuriatingly slow, and time was working against them. Ember was required to be present at Tearmunn on this Oestara—the spring equinox that followed her sixteenth birthday. The roads in the south had been choked with pilgrims making their way to cathedrals and holy sites for Easter. Though they'd stepped aside for the char branlant and its entourage of horsemen, there were still enough travelers filling the roads to hinder their party's progress. No doubt some of the pilgrims had taken extra time clearing the road, stealing a few more moments to gawk at the company of knights who escorted them—both serving to ward off bandits and to signal to the outside world the gravity of this trip. Ember was sure that villagers' whispers filled the air long after they'd passed.

She wished her father hadn't insisted upon making the journey. If Alistair and Barrow had been her only companions, she was certain she would have had a mount of her own. Ember's presence riding alongside two men would have given the pilgrims even greater cause to gossip, which would have delighted her. She would have ridden beside Barrow. Instead she was a prisoner in the dark carriage with only her whimpering sister and dour mother as company.

Agnes cried out and almost jumped into her mother's lap when there was a sharp rapping on the carriage door.

"Peace, dear ladies." Alistair's cheerful voice was only slightly muffled by the barrier. "We've reached the north end of Glen Shiel and we've just spotted Tearmunn and Loch Duich beyond."

Ember resisted the urge to clap in delight, knowing her mother would chasten her. She waited until her mother deigned to answer, "Thank you, Alistair."

Ember swallowed a sigh, envious that Alistair had spent the trip out of doors astride his mount. Even with the constant rain chasing their party, Ember would have preferred enduring the elements to her confinement.

"At last this wretched trip is over." Ossia wrung her hands, eyeing Ember. "Though if all goes as we expect, we'll return on the morrow."

Ember didn't respond. Her hopes and those of her family diverged with no hope of reconciliation.

"Only if Mackenzie is present." Agnes worried at the brooch on her cloak while Ember frowned. Agnes had grown deeply attached to what Ember had assumed was a love token sent from France by her betrothed. Ember had even been tempted to steal it and hide it, only to see if Agnes could survive a day without it. But Agnes had confessed the brooch wasn't a gift from her betrothed. Whom could it be from?

Since they'd departed her father's house, Ember hadn't been able to speak to her sister alone. She worried over Agnes's persistent gray pallor and frequent sickness.

"Father said he must pay his respects to Mackenzie given he's the clan leader nearest Tearmunn," Agnes continued, trying to keep the conversation pleasant.

"Of course, of course," Ossia said. "But surely Mackenzie will be there."

Ember's mother wore an increasingly sour expression. She hated travel, being happiest in her own manor, directing the activities of the kitchen. Much to Ember's despair, her mother believed that carding wool, spinning yarn, and occasionally embroidering were delightful ways to while away the hours and insisted her daughters spend their time doing the same.

"If Mackenzie is there, his son will be too." Agnes's gaze settled on Ember, and worry crept over her face. "I suspect Father hopes a match will be made."

Ember gave her sister a tolerant smile and went back to musing about her future—one that she hoped wouldn't involve matches of any sort. The carriage jolted again and Agnes groaned, clutching her stomach.

"We're nearly there." Ossia took Agnes's trembling hand. Agnes nodded, her face pale.

Ember's insides had begun to churn as well, but it had nothing to do with their transport's inability to manage the poor conditions of the road. Soon they would arrive at the Conatus stronghold at Tearmunn, and on the morrow her fate would be decided. Ember closed her eyes, offering a silent prayer that the knights would find a purpose for her other than marrying a son of Mackenzie.

"Are you unwell also?" Her mother's question snapped Ember's eyes open.

"No," Ember said.

Ossia smiled, turning back to still-whimpering Agnes. Ember watched her sister with concern, increasingly anxious that Agnes's distress was the result of much more than a dyspeptic stomach.

An hour later the carriage rocking ceased and its door was flung open to reveal the ruddy, bearded face of Ember's father. Though he didn't look as ill as Agnes, he was obviously in a foul temper as he reached for his wife's hand.

"My lady." With his aid, Ossia carefully descended from the char branlant. Ember let Agnes exit second, despite the fact that she was desperate to throw herself from the close confines of the carriage. Agnes kept a handkerchief pressed to her mouth as she leaned heavily onto her father. She gave a small cry when the horses, restless and eager to be free of their harness, whinnied loudly and began pawing at the earth.

"There, there, lass," he said. When Agnes was safely in her mother's care, he turned to Ember.

"Ember." His voice offered none of the coaxing tone with which he'd addressed her sister.

Though she didn't want or need to, Ember took his proffered hand, allowing him to assist her out of the carriage. She'd done enough to incur her father's wrath of late and had no desire to provoke him further. The moment Ember's feet touched the ground, her father turned away, moving to join his wife and elder daughter.

"I don't think Agnes will do well when she's sent to France." Alistair approached Ember. "Sea voyages can be much worse than overland travel."

Ember laughed, but guilt made her offer an excuse for her sister. "It's not entirely her fault. The roads were awful." Her mind returned to the way Agnes clutched the brooch. How often she seemed close to tears. What was Agnes keeping from her?

"That's because they're rarely used." Alistair's words broke through her thoughts. "Tearmunn is at the ends of the earth because we don't encourage nor do we want visitors."

The ends of the earth, Ember thought with a shiver born of fear and excitement, *and it's to be my new home.*

Alistair was watching her, only half hiding his smile. "First impressions?"

Ember frowned at him in confusion.

"The fortress?" he asked.

Having been so relieved to be free of the carriage box, Ember hadn't bothered to take in her surroundings. Now she turned and

gasped. The carriage had stopped outside of an immense stone structure that lay nestled against the steep hillsides of Glen Shiel. Spikes
of sunlight pierced through the heavy gray skies, making patches of
water sparkle on the backdrop to the fortress, Loch Duich, for a few
moments before they disappeared again, leaving the waters dark and
secretive.

Tearmunn itself was an imposing, solitary stronghold, its gray
stone form as bleak as the skies that hung low above it. The outer
walls of the keep shielded the inner buildings of the fortress from
view. From below, Ember spotted archers keeping watch from their
perches along the top of the walls.

"Why did we stop here?" she asked, watching as her family
climbed up a steep path to Tearmunn's gates.

"Outside travelers must enter on foot," Alistair said. "The carriage must remain here until it's inspected."

"Inspected for what?" she asked.

"I can't say until you're one of us," he said, offering his arm. "But
that will be soon enough."

"I hope so," she said, lightly grasping his elbow.

Alistair cast a sidelong glance at her as they started up the path.
"I've done all I can."

"And for that I'm indebted to you," she said. "But my father—"

"Your father will find his influence is far less here than amongst
the nobles," he said.

Ember didn't answer. Her long skirts made the climb tricky. The
fabric near her feet was quickly darkened by mud. She imagined that
Agnes and her mother must be going mad at the indignation of trek-
king through the muck. She didn't want to imagine what her father's
reaction would be.

She wasn't at all surprised to find him awaiting Alistair as they
passed through Tearmunn's gates, his face a thundercloud.

"What sort of barbarians are your people?" He shook his fist in

Alistair's face. "I came here in good faith to fulfill my debt and this is the way I'm treated."

Alistair bowed before Edmund. "My apologies, Lord Morrow. I realize the climb was inconvenient, but all visitors must enter the keep on foot."

"Ridiculous!"

"Just arrived and already raging?" A rotund man, whose squat face was capped by carrot-red hair striped with silver, strode toward Edmund, arms outstretched.

"There he is!" Edmund's sour mood vanished as he embraced the other man. "You old rascal, it's good to see you."

"And you, Lord Morrow," the red-haired man said.

Edmund drew his wife forward. "My lady Morrow, let me introduce to you Lord Mackenzie."

Ember's mother curtsied. "My lord."

Mackenzie grabbed the startled woman and noisily kissed her cheeks. "Fine woman indeed. Welcome to the wild north."

Ossia spluttered, her face flaming.

Ember waited for her father to erupt into curses, but he roared with laughter. "Never change, do you?"

Mackenzie shrugged. "Why would I?" He surveyed Agnes and Ember like they were prize cattle. "Who else have you brought for me to kiss?"

Edmund laughed again. "My daughters, Agnes and Ember."

Ember stopped holding her breath when Mackenzie didn't make good on his kissing pronouncement, but she guessed she wasn't nearly as relieved as Agnes, who was clinging to the sleeve of their mother's dress.

"Fine lasses." Mackenzie raised a brow. "Not married?"

"My elder daughter, Agnes, is betrothed to the Count of La Marche." Edmund beamed while Agnes blushed and clasped the brooch on her cloak.

"And this one?" Mackenzie's gaze fell on Ember. "The auburn-headed girl?"

Ember knew better than to speak, but she desperately wanted to give this uninvited spectator a lashing with her tongue.

"Ember is the reason we've been called here," Edmund said. "I owe a debt to Conatus."

"Don't we all," Mackenzie said. "Have no fear, my friend. It's likely they'll train the girl as a healer and keep her nearby."

His voice dropped to a wheedling note as he glanced at Ember once more. "My son Gavin is in need of a wife."

"Is he now?" Though it came out as a question, Ember was certain that her father was already well aware that Mackenzie had a bachelor son. She wondered if Gavin had found time to grow a belly as large as his father's.

"After the ceremony we'll talk," Mackenzie said, smacking Edmund on the shoulder. "Our holdings are close enough to Tearmunn that your Ember could serve Conatus and a husband."

Ember wanted to scream. This plot would undermine all her hopes for what coming to Tearmunn could mean. Agnes was smiling at her encouragingly and Ember was working so hard to keep her temper in check that she jumped when Alistair's voice was suddenly in her ear.

"I'll steal you away before that can happen," he whispered.

Her anger died in a giggle. "My savior."

"Of course," he said. "Would you expect anything less?"

She shook her head, now happy to ignore her father and Mackenzie as they lamented things like taxes and English encroachment.

"Besides," Alistair went on, "it won't come to that. Haven't I promised?"

"I know," she said, but despite Alistair's confidence, she had a hard time believing he could hold as much sway over her fate as he boasted. He'd only arrived at Conatus in the previous year.

Alistair raised his voice so everyone could hear him. "Pardon the interruption, my lords, but I'm to escort Lord Morrow and his family to their quarters."

Mackenzie nodded. "Of course. We'll speak again soon, Morrow."

"Indeed we shall." Her father fell into step alongside her as Alistair led them through the courtyard.

"Perhaps we'll find a suitable home for you in this debacle after all." He smiled at her, but Ember saw only the calculations of his mind and no thought for her happiness in the expression.

"Yes, Father," she said, knowing that any argument would earn her a cuff from her father's hand and a disapproving gaze from her mother.

As Lord Morrow began to recite the desirable traits of the Mackenzie clan and the wealth of their landholdings, Ember let her gaze wander around the keep. The thick outer walls enclosed a broad courtyard bustling with activity. They passed the stables first, the sharp, sweet scents of hay and grain filling the air. She pinched her nose as they walked by the tannery, but her eyes were drawn in fascination to the mysterious glow and shock of sparks from the smithy. It was almost as large as the stables, and Ember was startled to see women among the well-muscled, leather-aproned blacksmiths.

Following her gaze, Edmund snorted. "Bloody Amazons. We must get you away from this place as soon as a marriage can be arranged. I'm a man of my word and I've brought you here as promised, but I won't have Conatus twisting your mind. Religious orders have a strange way about them."

"Yes, Father," Ember said again, but her hopes were expanding by the moment. This place, hidden from the eyes of the world in the wilderness of the Scottish highlands, had set itself apart from society and its rules. It offered the only escape Ember might find from her father's designs on her life.

"That's the barracks." Alistair glanced over his shoulder, gesturing to a squat building on their right. "The quarters of the Guard."

Ember smiled when he winked at her.

"The kitchen is straight ahead and, of course, you'll be staying in the manor," he continued, leading them to a larger building to their left. "The guest quarters are here as is the great hall, where the ceremony will be held tomorrow morning."

Ember peered into the kitchen as they passed it. Fires roared in the massive ovens as servants shaped loaves, turned spits, and trussed game birds. Ember's mouth began to water as the savory odors spilled over them.

Alistair must have seen the hunger on her face, because he said, "The great feast will be held tomorrow evening, but tonight servants will bring repast to your quarters."

"We thank you, Alistair," Ossia said. "Our journey has left us weary and much in need of refreshment."

"Of course, my lady," Alistair said. "We are here to serve you."

Alistair led them into the manor, a building far more appealing than the austere barracks. The Romanesque stone walls of the great house featured friezes of ancient battle scenes and great adventures of classic mythology. The interior of the building welcomed them with walls covered in intricately carved dark wood.

"Watch your step as we ascend the stairs to your quarters," Alistair said. "The fourth step is horribly wobbly. It will soon be fixed, but alas, not during your stay."

"Humph." Edmund scowled as he tested the broken step and found it unbalanced indeed.

The room in which Alistair left them was small but well appointed. Ember wandered immediately to the windows, which offered a view across the courtyard and over the expanse of the loch. Despite the unfamiliar setting, she felt oddly at peace—a sentiment not shared by her family. Ossia was crooning over Agnes, who still complained of an upset stomach.

Edmund paced around the room. "We'll sup, we'll sleep, and tomorrow this nonsense will be over."

Ember bowed her head and then returned to her watch from the windowsill. She took a deep breath, willing that tomorrow didn't bring an end to her stay at Tearmunn, but instead a new beginning.

FOUR

TIME HAD SLIPPED through Ember's fingers, forcing her through the halls at a breathless pace. Her family had departed much earlier, as her father had hoped to speak further with Lord Mackenzie prior to the ceremony. Her mother and sister being absent, Ember was left to her own devices and she'd spent far too much time gazing out of the room's narrow window at two figures sparring in the practice fields below. A tall, broad-shouldered knight was evenly matched by a lanky, quick rival. She was breathless as she watched them battle. Every time she thought one was about to best the other, the faltering soldier would feint, roll, or twist in a way Ember thought impossible, rebalancing the fight once again.

Though certain she must be imagining it, given the great distance from her window to the field below, the sounds of their battle rang in Ember's head. Even more far-fetched, Ember couldn't stop herself from believing that she knew the taller warrior. His strong, confident movements, the twist of his waist and set of his shoulders: it was Barrow. She was sure of it.

But that very notion was ridiculous. She'd met him only once and though she'd watched him fight, it hardly meant she could recognize him from this sort of distance. Not to mention that his face was hidden by a steel helm.

Whistles of air chased their blades, punctuated by the sudden staccato whenever their weapons met. Ember pressed her face against the window, trying to see them more clearly but mostly wanting to confirm her suspicion that it was Barrow she watched. As the knights dove, leapt, and circled each other, she felt as though she witnessed not some savage exercise but an unending macabre dance defined by exceptional skill and wicked grace. She made a game of pretending she was Barrow's opponent, thinking of how she would strike and dodge, imagining the type of blade she'd wield if she were a knight. How magnificent it would be to master skills that matched his. It was a daydream both impossible and wonderful. She hadn't realized how long she'd been watching them until the church bells began to peal, signaling the start of the ceremony.

She feared a late arrival so much that she'd forgotten Alistair's warning about the loose step as she raced down the stairs. The stone wobbled and jerked under her weight, twisting her foot and turning her speed against her. She pitched forward, tumbling over the stone staircase until she landed in a heap in the central corridor.

"Em, I thought you'd gotten lost. I was about to go hunting for you in the guest quarters, but it seems you were merely perfecting your entrance."

She rolled onto her side to see Alistair leaning over her. His coal-black locks grazed his cheekbones, which were softened by the dimples that framed his grin.

"Ugh." She'd attempted to break her fall by landing on the heels of her hands. Raising her palms to examine them, she was relieved to see that the smooth stone floor hadn't left her with open cuts or scrapes, but she could already feel the bruises forming.

Alistair's smile vanished. "Are you injured?"

She shook her head, though she wasn't convinced she'd escaped unscathed. But she wasn't willing to entertain the thought that she'd be limping into the ceremony. Fragility was the last impression she wanted to make when she was presented to the Circle.

Alistair extended his hands, but she waved him away.

"I'm fine," she said, ignoring the fact that she was still a tangle of limbs and fabric. Her cloak, finely woven wool the gray of morning mist, a gift from her sister to wear at the ceremony, was twisted through her legs and prevented her from standing.

Alistair pushed his own cloak back over one shoulder, revealing the belted tunic and leather trousers he wore beneath. She caught sight of the long sword that hung in a scabbard at his side. Her mind flashed to the sparring knights and she wondered if Alistair had met either of them on the practice field—and how he'd fared against them.

He folded his arms and sniffed the air, feigning contempt. "Too good for help as always, I see."

"Hold your tongue," she said.

As Ember leaned forward to unbind her legs, heavy footsteps reached her ears. She fumbled with the long cloak, desperate to be on her feet before anyone else arrived. Having Alistair see her like this was one thing, but anyone else . . .

"What's this?"

She gritted her teeth, not looking up at the questioner, whose voice was already lighting with mirth.

"She took a spill down the stairs," Alistair said. Ember threw him a venomous glance.

The man Alistair had spoken to looked at her, arching an eyebrow. "Is this the young lass you've been jabbering about for the past year? Is she that eager for her calling? I've never considered whether you'd get to the ceremony faster rolling instead of walking, but I'm game to find out. Would you like to start over from the very top of the staircase?"

"Hold your tongue, Kael, and show some respect for Lady Morrow," Alistair said while Ember finally kicked herself free of the cloak. "It's not her fault no one's bothered to fix that step."

"Of course, Alistair." Kael's blue eyes were dancing beneath his wheat-blond fringe of hair. "My lady, I meant no offense."

He winked at Ember before wiggling his eyebrows. She rolled

over, horrified by the flood of crimson into her cheeks, and tried to regain some semblance of dignity.

"We've been so eager to meet you after all the praise our Alistair has heaped upon you." Kael offered a sweeping bow, all the while grinning at Alistair. "But what of your champion? Didn't you catch the lass when she fell?"

"She was on the ground before I got here," Alistair protested. "I would have caught her if I'd had the chance."

Now on her feet, Ember shot a glare at Alistair. "You would not. I'll have no man catching me."

"Feisty as ever." Alistair laughed and elbowed Kael. "What did I tell you? She was made for Conatus."

"Now that everyone is vertical, let's see to proper introductions," Kael said. "I'm Kael MacRath, a knight of the Guard."

Ember's training set in and she dropped into a curtsy. "Ember Morrow. It's an honor, Lord MacRath."

Kael chuckled. "I can't remember the last time anyone addressed me as Lord MacRath. It's Kael, please."

Ember blushed again and gave him a shy smile. "Then you must call me Ember."

He smiled, but his brow furrowed. "An unusual name."

"My mother named me," Ember said, shifting her weight uneasily. Her father always went into a fury when she tried to inquire about the circumstances of her birth. "I don't know very much— only that the midwife said neither I nor my mother would survive, but a healer from Conatus came to our manor and saved us both. My mother said the healer took the tiny embers of life I clung to and breathed them into a fire."

Kael's rapt attention unnerved her further, so she said, "My sister, Agnes, has a proper Christian name as chosen by my father."

"Your sister, Agnes?" Kael glanced at Alistair. "Isn't she—"

"What are you doing here anyway?" Alistair asked, cutting off his question. "Shouldn't you already be in the hall?"

"We were sparring." Kael gestured to his mud-covered boots. "You know Barrow—anything to avoid a ceremony. In truth he would have stayed away, but I thought it best that we make an appearance."

Barrow? Ember's cheeks were burning, but they went cold when a tall, helmeted figure appeared in the hall. While watching the battle below her window, she'd wanted nothing more than to discover she had recognized Barrow. But now that he approached, she was apprehensive.

"Dallying, Kael?" Barrow asked as he approached them. "You were the one who insisted we quit the field. I thought we daren't miss the solemn occasion."

Though Ember couldn't see his face beneath the steel helm guarding his forehead, nose, and cheeks, his quiet, deep voice unsettled her very bones. Despite coming upon Kael and Alistair's laughter, Barrow did not sound amused. Encountering him here, after she'd fallen and suffered Alistair's teasing, the very idea that she'd ever be a match for Barrow in sword fight seemed so silly it made her bones ache.

Barrow's pitch-black cloak covered his broad shoulders, sleek as night, making her even more embarrassed about the crumpled fabric of her own cloak. Ember tried to restore some air of dignity, standing as straight as she could and inclining her head to the warrior. He didn't acknowledge the gesture, glaring at Kael instead. Beside her, Alistair straightened up, eyeing Barrow warily.

Kael shrugged, jerking his chin at Ember. "Our guest of honor is practicing acrobatics on the way to the ceremony."

Alistair laughed, which earned him a stern look from Barrow before he glanced at Ember.

"It's good to see you again, Lady Morrow. I trust your journey was without incident," Barrow said. "The Circle will be awaiting your arrival."

Keeping her head ducked, Ember shouldered Alistair aside, murmuring, "Of course." She had no idea if Barrow had heard her, but she felt blood draining from her face. She was already up against enough today. She didn't need any of the Guard to think poorly of her, but especially not Barrow.

Ember tried to ignore the sound of Kael's laughter as he continued to speak with Barrow. The swift scuffle of feet announced Alistair's presence at her side.

"You should have let me help you up. We'd already be in the hall with the others," he whispered. "Now Barrow thinks we're fools and I'll never hear the end of it from Kael."

She didn't answer him, miffed at his words but feeling he was right. It made her fists clench.

He wasn't finished. "Why do you have to be so stubborn?"

"I'm sorry," she said. She didn't want to anger him, but it was hard to make a sincere apology as they approached the great hall and fear began to creep like frost over her skin.

Alistair touched Ember's arm, flashing her a smile that told her he was satisfied by the exchange even if she was still irked.

The warmth in his eyes broke through her nerves, drawing a question from her she'd been trying to ignore. "You said I'll be tested. What if I fail? I know nothing about what's expected of me."

"You won't," Alistair said. "I know you belong with us. Have faith and a little patience. I'm so sorry I can't say more, but it's forbidden."

"I know, but—" Ember bowed her head. "If I fail, will I be sent home?"

With a frustrated grunt, Alistair said, "I can tell you nothing more than this: the test isn't one you can fail. It shows where you belong."

His words brought Ember up short. She turned to stare at him. "Where I belong?"

"Yes." He kept walking and she hurried to catch him. "And I shouldn't have said even that much."

"Is that how you became part of the Guard?" she asked.

"I've said too much." He kept his voice stern, but the corner of his mouth turned up and Ember knew she'd guessed correctly.

Alistair stopped, taking her shoulders and turning her to face him. "I swear, Em, this is where you're meant to be. You've always known it. I know it. We'll be together."

Ember gave him a weak smile. "Perhaps." But her hope had drained away.

"Are you ready?" he asked.

They approached the doors to the great hall, which today stood open, waiting for her. Ember's mind was turning faster than a spinning wheel, but she nodded.

"Godspeed, Em," he whispered.

She managed a soft reply, despite her closing throat. "Godspeed, my friend."

They entered the immense space. Sunlight speared through the intricate stained glass windows blazing amid the dark walls, filling the room with a riot of bright colors. Most striking of all was the impossible broad and tall living tree at the center of the room. Its twisting branches, covered in deep green needles, served as a canopy for the room. The tree's scent spilled through the air, warm and alive. Ember knew the tree was somehow special, or important, or both.

The great hall exceeded its name. A smile pulled at Ember's mouth as she imagined her father's sour face when he laid eyes on a chamber much finer than the hall of his own manor.

Visitors milled about in the gallery above the open space, where the other initiates already stood waiting, uneasy. Unlike Ember, these young men and women had arrived at Conatus due to misfortune, or so Alistair had told her. Conatus drew its members from those for whom there wasn't a place in the world. Some came seeking charity and decided to stay. Others, like Alistair, sought fortune when it had been denied elsewhere. But cases like his were rare, and today Ember was the sole initiate to be called from a noble family.

A cloud of whispers filled the hall as Ember hurried to take her place beside her peers. Alistair had moved away from her, though she could still see him out of the corner of her eye as he joined the Guard.

She was here as a pledge of Conatus. But her presence was only the first step. Next came the trial.

Where I belong, Ember thought. If the reward was her true place of belonging, she was willing to endure any trial. She hoped she could.

Her heart began to pound. The girl on her left was trembling. The boy to her right stood with eyes shut tight, lips whispering a feverish prayer.

A gray-haired priest came to the center of the hall, stopping in front of them. "I am Father Michael."

He smiled kindly at each of them. "'We have many members in one body, and all members have not the same office.' So wrote Saint Paul in his letter to the Romans. Your presence here today signifies your desire to serve in the body of Conatus and thus perform a holy office."

From the door behind them, Ember heard the sound of approaching feet. Six people, four men and two women, walked past the line of initiates and formed a half circle around Father Michael.

"Before you join this body, that office must be determined," the priest said. He nodded to the men and women standing beside and behind him. "The six who stand before you are the Circle—called from within Conatus to lead us, chosen because each has excelled in his or her office."

Ember looked at the members of the Circle while the priest spoke. It was like gazing into a strange mirror, a reflection of some possible future. Six initiates on the cusp of adulthood, six elders: veterans of Conatus. Ember's eyes were drawn to the two women in the group. She could guess their identity from Alistair's letters: the sisters, Cian and Eira. Ember was surprised that they wore their hair long and loose. Their bright, cascading tresses offered a blatant contrast to the black tabard of the Guard. Rather than making them appear softer and more feminine, their untamed hair gave the sisters a wild appearance—like the Amazons of legend or the pagan queen Boadicea, all stories Ember had gobbled up as a child, searching for any sign that a girl could find her way to the warrior's life. No longer were tales of old Ember's only hope. The living, breathing example of what she longed to be stood before her now. Alistair had written that everyone in Conatus referred to them as "the sisters" rather than as individuals and that some even whispered of them as "the weird sisters" in snide tones. Indulging her fascination with their history, Alistair had explained that the sisters had been orphaned together and inseparable since they'd arrived in the keep. They'd won their place in the Circle by virtue of their courage and prowess in the field. Within Conatus, the sisters were as legendary as any warrior of history or myth.

". . . we are blessed by their guidance." Father Michael was still speaking. "Two souls to represent each major office of our order."

He paused, gesturing to the two men in cowled robes who stood on his left: "Knowledge."

Stretching his hand and pointing behind him, the priest acknowledged the next two men—both dressed in the simple garb of commoners. "Craft."

Father Michael extended his hand to the two sisters, who stood on his right. "War."

War. Ember drew a quick breath, wondering what war was being waged here. She knew of the ongoing war between England and France but not of any holy war on behalf of the Church. Another possibility was the squabble over the Scottish throne, which could turn deadly at any time. And wasn't the church divided against itself because of the papal schism? Her heart stuttered. Was Conatus simply acting under orders of the pope in Rome or Avignon to secure a specific outcome? For whom would she fight if she became a soldier in this order?

"Any role undertaken at Tearmunn falls under one of these three offices," Father Michael said. "Today your task is to find the office of your true calling."

Despite her harried speculations, Ember focused on the priest's calm voice.

A true calling. Where I belong. This must be something more than petty politics.

"Look there," Father Michael said, pointing to the wall on his left. "Beyond that door you will find three rooms. Each room contains another door. You must choose the room that best reflects your heart. Pass through the door in that room. You may not turn back once the choice has been made. To ensure that you have been truthful in searching your soul to find your office among us, you will face a trial on the other side of the door you have chosen. Should you fail this test, you are not meant to serve here."

Ember barely stopped herself from flinching. She could fail. She could be sent away. Alistair had lied to her.

"Go now." The door to which Father Michael gestured was a simple portal of dark wood, neither ominous nor welcoming. "Make your choice."

In a single-file line the pledges turned and walked to the door. Ember was the third to pass through. On the other side of the door was an oval antechamber split by three archways. Like her companions, Ember hesitated in the small room. She turned with a start when the door to the great hall was closed forcefully behind them. And locked.

FIVE

EMBER AND THE OTHER pledges huddled in a tight cluster like chicks who'd lost their mother hen. No one spoke. Each initiate understood that this was a solitary endeavor and conversation would only serve to muddy any clarity of mind one might have for the task at hand.

Glancing at each of the arched portals in turn, Ember couldn't see what lay inside the chambers. As the others made their own choices, Ember decided to investigate the room to her left, drawn there by the subtle hint of candlelight from within. She sensed two of the pledges trailing behind her. She looked over her shoulder and saw the rest of the group drifting into the other rooms.

When Ember passed through the archway, the sight awaiting her stole her breath. The room's vaulted ceiling stretched toward the heavens. Each wall, each nook, each crevice of the room was bursting with scrolls or bound volumes. Ember stumbled forward, mesmerized by the sight of so much collected scholarship. In addition to the works that were strewn on the walls, massive tomes lay open on table throughout the room. She tentatively came forward to peer at the open volumes, marveling at the illuminated texts. The pages were a riot of colors that rivaled those of stained glass; their exquisite artistry could have been wrought by the hand of angels.

The only space in the room not covered by bound volumes or tightly rolled scrolls was a narrow door in the far wall.

Sneaking a look at the girl and boy who had joined her in this room, Ember saw that they were breathless with anticipation. The girl dropped to the floor with a book the size of her torso wedged onto her lap while the boy scrambled up a ladder to explore the highest reaches of scroll-laden shelves. Ember continued to wander through the room. It would take several lifetimes to absorb the writings contained within this single room. Ember wondered if this room was Tearmunn's library but suspected that even this enormous collection was only a taste of the boundless knowledge the clerics of Conatus had at their fingertips.

Though she was tempted to read a few pages, curiosity drew Ember back to the archway. She glanced back at her companions, but they were both lost in reading and gave no sign of ever wanting to leave the room.

What had Father Michael said? *Each room contains another door. You must choose the room that best reflects your heart. Pass through the door in that room. You may not turn back once the choice has been made.*

As wonderful as the room of books had been, Ember wasn't willing to choose a door without seeing all three of her options. She went to the central room and was surprised to find herself alone in the chamber. This room lacked the striking architecture of the first. Rather than a high vaulted ceiling, the chamber had a somber, plain design. Several long tables were arranged in straight lines at the center of the room. Upon inspecting the tables, Ember found they were covered with maps. The charts didn't simply show the land's features and its cities, but also were filled with notes and symbols: arrows suggesting movement, sites marked off for significance. As she compared the maps, Ember realized they were as much history lesson as navigational. Here was the progression of the Peloponnesian War. There she could follow the action of Alexander the Great's movements through Asia. Another map showed the Norman invasion of England.

War. The center room depicted the office of war. Ember's pulse quickened, her mind alert as she pored over the charts. The patterns on the maps were fascinating to her. Puzzles of the past waiting to be solved. Why this army's success while the greater force had floundered? Why this path of invasion when the sea route might have offered a faster course?

Ember pulled herself away from the charts to examine the walls. One wall was covered with the tools of war. Swords of all lengths were suspended in the air. Double-bladed axes, cudgels, quarterstaffs, and flails were there along with an abundance of weapons she couldn't name.

Her eyes wandered back to the charts and then flicked to the wall of weapons. This was the contradiction of war—strategy partnered with brutality. She shivered and walked across the room so she could gaze at the opposite wall, where she found yet another contradiction. Mirroring the weaponry were images so beautiful Ember felt her throat tighten. Paintings lined the wall, filling the space from floor to ceiling. The scenes depicted varied widely: here Ember found Greeks spilling out of the Trojan horse, there she watched as Judith lifted the head of Holofernes in triumph. Though many of the paintings were severe in their violence, others were sublime. Ember's eyes stung as she gazed at a portrait of a young woman tearing her hair as she mourned a fallen warrior and her heartbeat quickened when she found a painting of a Templar taking his vows.

The paintings rendered vividly the third aspect of war. Not only a practice of mind and body, this office was also one of the heart. Within these frames she found courage, sorrow, sacrifice, and hope.

Ember paused, closing her eyes and letting the collection of the room sink into her memory. When she opened her eyes, she was looking at the door set in the chamber's far wall. A part of her was tempted to run to it, flinging it open and casting her lot with this room of battling impulses. Of beauty and horror.

She forced herself to turn her back on the beckoning door. There was no going back once her choice had been made. She passed a boy on her way out of the room and wondered whether he would choose the door she'd walked away from.

The first impression made by the third room was one of scent rather than sight. The mixture of odors was so intense and confusing that Ember had to pause and regain her bearings. The temperature in this room was markedly higher than in the previous chambers. The reason for the difference was easy to find. A blisteringly hot forge squatted in the center of the room. The fire within its bowels roared despite the absence of a blacksmith to stoke its flames.

Unlike the first two rooms, this chamber was a perfect circle. Ember walked to the edge, and while she kept her distance from the forge, sweat was soon beading on her forehead. In the ring around the blazing fire, she found the tools and crafts of master artisans. She paused amid the stringent scents of a tanner's work, marveling at the skill it must take to create one piece of leather armor that seemed as tough as steel while another was softer than silk. As she continued, her nose crinkled not because of a foul stench, but in distaste. She quickly passed a spinning wheel and several looms. While she could appreciate the fine clothing and marvelous tapestries spread along-side the weaver's tools, she had too many memories of sitting with her mother and Agnes forced into the monotony of spinning to want to linger here.

Ember walked past a chandler's wares and barrels of all sizes created by a cooper. Of all the rooms this one offered the widest variety of sights and scents. The office of craft encompassed many liveli-hoods should she choose the door in this room. She watched as a girl brushed by her, hurrying to the door. She turned, giving Ember a shy smile before she disappeared and the door closed after her. Despite the many possibilities presented by this room, Ember knew it wasn't what she desired.

Making her way to the antechamber, Ember felt as though a fist had closed around her heart. She looked at the archways that led to the room brimming with scrolls and the one leading to war. Which should she choose?

The first room promised a world of secrets revealed. A life of learning—a rare and precious vocation, one she wished she could share with Agnes. Ember's sister would happily stay forever in such a room. The second would be exactly as it appeared: unpredictable, dangerous, filled with contradiction. Though immersing oneself in the arcane wasn't without risk, a scholar's life would be filled with a much subtler danger than the overt costs of war. She knew what her family would want. Her mother and sister would be relieved that she was sequestered with scribes. Her father might hope that she could continue her studies while still becoming the wife of Gavin Mackenzie. If she surrendered to Lord Morrow's will, she might even be able to spend time with Agnes. It wasn't unheard of for sisters to spend a season or more in each other's home, particularly after the birth of a child. Would it be worth choosing the room full of books so she could keep Agnes in her life?

Though the risk to her body might be less by her choosing the first room, the risk to her spirit was too great. The hope Ember held dear, that she'd imagined might be made real through her father's debt to Conatus, was that she could have a life where she wouldn't be caged. And marriage would leave her tethered to a husband and his manor for the rest of her life.

Ember drew a long breath and turned to the center room. She walked swiftly beneath the archway, past the chart-covered tables. The door in the far wall of the room was plain and narrow. It waited for her. Without pause, Ember grasped the handle and flung the door open.

"This is my choice," she murmured, and stepped into darkness.

Blinking to let her eyes adjust to the much dimmer light, Ember discerned that she had entered some sort of passageway.

Ember gave a startled cry as a hand on her shoulder turned her around. Her fear became embarrassment as she found herself looking up at Barrow.

"You've made your choice, but now you must be tried," he told her. "Come with me."

She couldn't read his expression, try as she might to draw some hint of what was to come from within his storm-gray eyes.

"Where are we going?" she asked.

He didn't answer, and the brief thrill she'd felt at seeing him became sullen resentment. The corridor widened, and Ember saw a row of figures lining each side of the hall. Her pulse thundered in her ears as she realized that they were the members of the Guard standing at attention. They watched solemnly as she passed them, twelve on each side of her, though Alistair, Kael, and Barrow were the only three warriors she knew. Why were all of the Guard assembled here? And what were they waiting for her to do?

At the end of the row of knights, Alistair stepped forward and fell into step beside Ember. His mischievous smile eased her mind a bit.

"Good choice, Em," he whispered, and she smiled at him.

Barrow stopped, turning stony eyes on Alistair. "Return to your place. She isn't finished."

Alistair ignored him, leaning closer to Ember. "Don't worry. We've all done it."

"Alistair. Stop." Barrow took a step toward him. "You know this isn't permitted."

Alistair scowled at the tall knight.

"Why are you interrupting the trial?" Barrow gave him a stern look.

"Only offering to accompany my friend as long as I'm able," Alistair told him curtly.

The chill covering Ember intensified. Alistair's words suggested that at some point, he wouldn't be able to remain with her—wherever they were going. And Barrow seemed to think Alistair shouldn't be with her at all.

Barrow stiffened but didn't offer further objection. He turned his eyes on Ember.

"Follow us."

Alistair placed his hand on her elbow, walking beside her as Barrow led them from the hall. Ember caught several gazes from the two rows of knights from the corner of her eye. Everyone was watching her. Wherever she was going, whatever was about to happen, it was important. It was important to all of them.

Ember shuddered and Alistair squeezed her arm. "Ember, I swear that—"

"Enough, Alistair!" Barrow had turned to face them.

Alistair glared at the taller knight. "What harm could it do if I explain what's happening? You must understand that Ember is different. She has no—"

His words were cut off when Barrow shoved him away from Ember. "If she is to be one of us, there can be no exceptions."

"You don't know her like I do. I only want to ensure—" Alistair snarled at him.

"I said, enough." Barrow nodded at Kael, who while watching the exchange slunk from his place in the line of soldiers and came to stand beside Alistair. "You will remain here with the others."

Alistair blanched but upon feeling Kael's hand on his shoulder followed his mentor back into the row of knights.

Barrow didn't say anything to Ember but simply turned and continued along the corridor. She hurried to keep up with him, her heart racing as much from the angry set of Barrow's shoulders as from anticipation of whatever lay ahead. She also felt the sting of Alistair's words. Did he believe she was too weak to live by the rules of the Guard? Part of her was resentful of his poor opinion of her, but another part worried about what could make him so afraid for her.

Barrow stopped when they reached another door at the end of the corridor.

"I leave you here," Barrow said, reaching beneath his cloak. "Take these and use them as you see fit."

He handed Ember a lantern and a dagger. The short, thick blade was coated in a viscous, bile-colored liquid that gave off a pungent odor.

The door groaned in protest when Barrow pulled it open. All Ember could see were the first three stone steps in a staircase that spiraled down.

"That is your path," Barrow said.

Ember looked up into the knight's steel-gray eyes but found no hint of his feelings there, only a steady gaze. Dozens of questions swirled in her mind, but she already knew they would be asked to no avail. She forced herself to nod and began to descend the stairs. She'd barely stepped into the darkness when the door closed behind her, making her gasp. Her heart stuttered when she heard the door's lock click into place. The only way now was forward, into the darkness.

With the lantern in her left hand and the dagger gripped in her right, Ember moved down the steps. The darkness closed around her while the candle in the lantern bobbed and winked in her trembling grasp. She could see very little, only what was revealed by the pale cloud of light cast by the lantern—the stairs' tight coil, the rough stone walls. Her descent wasn't long, and she soon found herself at the bottom of the staircase. The darkness hadn't abated, and she walked cautiously, trying to identify her surroundings. The air was musty and full of a damp chill.

Shapes began to appear at the edge of her lantern's sphere. Tall and rounded, the objects rose from the floor to the low ceiling.

Ember reached out, running her hands over the wooden casks. The wine cellar. She was in the wine cellar.

Ember didn't know whether to laugh or scream because this could be nothing other than some sort of joke meant to frighten her for the entertainment of the more seasoned knights. Poor Alistair, no wonder he'd tried to warn her. He'd only been attempting to save her from this humiliation.

She had imagined Barrow's stern face and made a silent promise to herself to one day trick him into an equally embarrassing predicament when something turned her away from the wine casks.

Had there been a noise?

Her vengeful musings had captured most of her attention, but at the edge of her mind she'd sensed something. A wheezing sound. The hard-won breath of a sick man.

Ember raised her lantern, keeping her back to the wooden casks. She stayed very still, listening so hard her temple began to throb. The darkness remained silent. She cursed her heart, which was pounding against her ribs.

Her eyes widened. There it was again. This time accompanied by a scuffling sound. Feet dragging over the floor. The thick wet drawing of breath.

"Who's there?" Ember kept her tight grip on the dagger and took a step forward.

Something came whistling from the blackness beyond her lamp's glow. A clay jug cracked into her wrist. She cried out, dropping the lantern. It didn't go out when it hit the ground but rolled away, letting shadows pour over her. The jug smashed against the floor and beer spilled around her feet.

The shuffling became scuttling. The wheeze a cough. A hunched figure lurched at her.

Ember cried out again, falling back against the wine casks. The thing was reaching toward her. Whether it was a man or a woman, she couldn't tell. It stood on two legs, but its skin was gray and in some places torn away; it flapped like loose cloth when the creature moved. It was staring at her, but it had no eyes. Only black pits that were somehow full of hunger.

And the smell. Terror was all that kept Ember from retching. The thing reeked of spoiled meat and worse. With each cough and ragged breath it seemed the creature was choking on its own putrefying lungs.

It gaped at her, swaggering forward. She didn't know if it was trying to speak. Its mouth opened and closed, and sloppy, gibbering sounds emerged. It leaned over her and she couldn't move. A maggot dropped from the rotting flesh of its jaw and squirmed over Ember's cheek. She screamed. She could see its teeth. See how sharp they were.

The instinct to survive freed Ember's body from fear's paralysis. She dropped to her knees, crawling across the floor toward the lantern. She reached the flickering lamp and rolled over, thrusting the light up toward the thing, which had followed and was already bending over her. It moaned, clawed hands covering its face as if the light were painful. As it backed away from her outstretched arm, Ember scrambled to her feet.

The creature scuttled into the shadows, its labored breathing faster now, its groans frustrated. It wanted her. Ember knew the light would only keep it at bay for a short while. She had to find a way out of the cellar. Keeping her back to the wine casks, she began to move along their length. She held the lantern away from her body, creating a barrier of light between herself and the thing. She could hear it moving with her, following her.

Without warning it lunged, a thick, bubbling scream pouring out of its throat. Ember swung the lantern at the creature. It flinched, flinging one arm up to protect its face even as it reached for her throat with its other hand. With the thing half-blinded, Ember struck at it with her dagger. But she quickly discovered that fighting this beast was nothing like attacking her lifeless straw targets, much less her playful battles with Alistair. The creature feinted from her unskilled hand, the blade catching in the tattered rags that hung from the monster's skin.

Ember stumbled back as it attacked with renewed fury. Its arms flailed, one at last knocking away the lantern, and this time the glass shattered upon hitting the floor. The candle snuffed out and Ember was plunged into darkness. She sobbed, gripping the dagger in both hands. Slowly she moved back, sliding each foot along the ground.

She couldn't see the creature, but she could smell it and hear it. She knew it was only a few feet in front of her. She knew it would attack again.

The rustle of its shredded clothes reached her ears a moment before the thing hit her, knocking her to the floor. She was on her back. Its hands were on her shoulders, holding her down. She felt the rush of its hot, putrid-sweet breath on her face. She choked on the rotted air as she thrust the dagger up with both arms, using every ounce of strength she could muster.

The dagger hit its mark, tearing flesh and crunching through bone. The thing's gargling screech became a whine. Its body jerked and then went still, all its weight dropping against her.

Ember shoved the creature's limp form off and rolled over onto her hands and feet. She gasped, gulping air as if there would never be enough of it. Then she began to sob. Her muscles trembled as she tried to stand, but her legs wouldn't support her.

Another groan reached her ears. Ember bowed her head, closing her eyes, waiting for the creature to overpower her. But no other sound followed. No scuffling. No wheezing.

She looked up and saw light where there had been none. A river of sunshine poured down a straight, narrow staircase different from the spiraling steps by which she'd entered the cellar. Fighting for control of her trembling limbs, she crawled to the base of the stairs.

SIX

EMBER HALF RAN, half climbed up the stone steps. Her hands were shaking, but she refused to let go of the dagger as she pulled herself forward. The creature's blood painted her pale skin crimson, warm red liquid sliding from her fingers to her wrists.

She staggered through the doorway at the top of the stairs. Warmth and light surrounded her, pressing back the nightmare of the cellar. She whirled, raising the dagger to strike, when she heard the door shut and lock.

A figure in a cowled brown robe raised his hands. "Peace, Lady Morrow. You're safe now."

Ember recognized the weathered-face priest from the ceremony.

"God bless you, my child," Father Michael said. He touched her forehead, making the shape of the cross. Water dripped down her brow. "You have completed your ordeal."

"Father." Ember fell to her knees, her voice rasping. She finally unclenched her fingers from the dagger, which clattered onto the stone floor. "That thing . . . I don't understand what happened."

Father Michael bent down, retrieving the weapon and depositing it beneath the folds of his robe. "We see but a poor reflection as in a mirror, but we shall see face-to-face. Where you have known in part, now you shall know fully." The priest reached out, helping her to her feet. Ember recognized his words as scripture but could make no sense of their meaning.

He took her arm, leading her away from the closed door and the horror it hid. As shock loosened its grip on her senses, Ember lifted her face to the light that streamed in through tall windows. The stained glass transformed sunbeams, washing the dark wood of the walls in gem-like tones. Father Michael guided her from the small antechamber into a long, narrow room filled with rows of wooden benches. At the far end of the room, an altar was stationed beneath another stained glass window, this one large and round. Suspended within the bright colors was an angel, his face proud and unyielding, his hands bearing fiery swords.

"My namesake," the priest said, looking up at the window with a brief smile. "The archangel Michael who cast Lucifer out of heaven."

Ember simply nodded as they passed from the chapel into another, smaller space that held a table and chairs and a simple wooden pallet.

"My humble quarters." Father Michael gestured for her to sit. A cup of steaming liquid sat on the table and the priest pushed it in front of Ember when she settled into her chair.

"A simple herbal tonic," he said. "It will calm your nerves and your spirit."

Ember took the cup in her hands, sniffing before she took a sip. She recognized chamomile, lavender, and mint. When she drank, the tonic chased lingering chills from her body.

"Where are the other initiates?" she asked. "Didn't they have trials?"

He smiled kindly. "Yes. A trial awaited each of the pledges. But you alone chose the office of war, which requires a more dangerous and frightening ordeal than that of knowledge or craft. I'm here because I wanted to offer you assurance that such a trial was necessary and to be certain that, having faced the darkness, you are still fixed upon this path."

Ember didn't know what to say, so she settled for drinking more of the tonic.

"You have many more questions, I'm sure," Father Michael said. "And I will now do my best to answer them."

He seemed prepared to speak to her fears, so Ember waited and listened.

"What happened in the cellar was the means by which you will know the purpose of Conatus," he said. "And the tasks of the Guard in particular."

He crossed the room, hands clasped at his back. "We seek to emulate Michael's work. To drive evil from the earth."

Ember took another draught of the tonic. "That creature in the cellar. It was evil . . . unnatural."

He nodded.

"What was it?" she asked.

"A revenant," the priest told her. "The foul pet of a necromancer."

"One who raises the dead?" Ember asked. "Can someone truly wield such power?"

Father Michael sighed. "While it is often creatures of darkness you will face, in truth it is their masters we must thwart: those who draw evil into our world to feed their hunger for power."

"Who are they?" Ember's mind reeled. She knew of witches' curses and mischievous spirits but only in the way that children fear what hides in shadow.

"They have many names, none of which I suspect are true: wizards, witches, sorcerers, magicians. There are few who find a way to draw the dark, but enough to manifest evils that harm many," he said. "Our work here is to seek them out and quell their evildoing."

"How do you find them?" she asked.

"Sadly, it is often following in the wake of violence left by their minions." Father Michael bowed his head. "We are hunters chasing a trail of blood. By the grace of God, I would we had the means to set snares and stop them before they wreak havoc on innocents."

Ember sat quietly, letting his words sink in.

Father Michael watched her. "Now a choice belongs to you, Lady Morrow."

"And what is my choice?" she asked.

"We ask none to serve against his or her will," the priest said. "Our work, continuing the war waged by Michael and God's army against the rising darkness, is too dangerous and too vital to be done with doubt or hesitation. If you give your life to the Conatus Guard, you forsake all else. The comforts of family and the flesh will be denied you. Your body, your will, and your spirit shall belong to us and to this fight. But the war is not only waged by sword. You saw the other rooms, but chose war. I ask you now to affirm your choice, lest in doubt you balk in your service, putting our cause at risk."

Ember met the priest's kind gaze, finding no judgment, hope, or expectation, only kindness and patience. She could walk away from the violence she'd chosen by walking through war's doorway. The stink of death that pursued her in the cellar would be forgotten.

It had been horrible, yes, but something else as well. Ember shivered with the thrill of it. She'd been pitched into darkness to face an unnameable terror. And she'd won. Her blood sang with that knowledge.

"How did you come to fight these creatures?" she asked.

Father Michael leaned back in his chair. "You know of the Templars. The knights of faith, born out of the Crusades and sanctioned by the pope himself."

Ember nodded though unease slithered over her limbs, muting some of her excitement. Talk of the Templars offered no comfort. It had been nearly one hundred years since those knights, however renowned, had met a terrible end. An end filled with betrayals. Sins punished by fire.

"But they are no more," Ember said quietly.

The priest shook his head slowly. "When the servant grows too strong, too willful to offer his master obeisance, the master will sometimes destroy the servant to save himself."

Her eyes widened; it was more than a little startling to hear a priest suggest that the Templars had become more powerful than the pope.

At the sight of her shocked face, Father Michael laughed. "You think I blaspheme, child?"

She blushed, looking at her hands, which were folded yet trembling on the table's surface.

"Do not fear, Lady Morrow," he said. "I do not speak ill of the Holy Father, only of the nature of power. A nature that does not lend itself to sharing."

When she didn't reply, Father Michael said, "Conatus was born within the Templar order. Where the knights pursued the conquest of the Holy Land, our small contingent confronted the secrets of the arcane, the mysteries beyond the veil."

Ember swallowed the thickness in her throat. She had so many questions but no idea how to voice them. Their shapes remained unwieldy in her mind.

The priest's gaze was sympathetic. "The Church teaches of evil spirits, of darkness and the craft of witches and sorcerers."

Ember nodded, hardly able to draw a breath in her eagerness to hear the story.

"The Crusades offered the means by which we might tap into the very font of that knowledge and harness it for good," he said.

"Why?" Ember frowned.

"Conatus emerged when a few of the knights learned the secrets and wisdom of our Saracen counterparts," he said.

Ember jolted upright in her seat. "The heathens?"

The priest held up his hand. "What makes our order unique is that we place the value of good over evil. The pope himself agreed."

"I don't understand," she said.

"Encounters in the East did not always end in bloodshed," Father Michael answered. "And we've learned a great deal from the holy texts of our adversaries. For example, did you know that King Solomon had the power to command devils?"

Ember barely stopped herself from laughing. Only the calm, serious eyes of Father Michael choked off the mirth trying to rise in her throat.

He held her gaze. "'He subjected the wind to him, so that it blew softly at his bidding wherever he directed it, and the devils too, among whom were builders and diverse others and bound with chains.'"

"What words do you speak?" She frowned.

"Those of the holy text of our adversaries in the East," he said. "One that contains many mysteries of which we must learn."

Ember's frown deepened. "What mysteries?"

"Perhaps you think of spirits, demons, and witches as frightening tales spun for children?" He stood up, clasping his hands behind his back. "I trust that your trial in the cellar made you see the truth."

Ember's pulse began to thrum again. Father Michael was right. Hadn't she just faced an unfathomable horror in the darkness below? The revenant had been a creature of nightmares, not anything she would have believed part of creation except for her life-and-death struggle with it. This was the war. And it was incredible.

"King Solomon, in his wisdom, could harness dark forces without letting them corrupt him." Father Michael paced beside her. "But his spirit was a rare thing. We know that from some other place, some dark place, monstrous beings thrive. Sometimes the beasts steal into our world, corrupting everything they touch. Some arrive of their own free will, hunting poor souls who stray across their path. But others are summoned at the will and power of the prideful wizard, witch, or sorcerer who believes himself able to command the dark."

The priest stopped in front of Ember, leaning down so his gaze pierced into her. "The wandering evil is the prey we hunt and slay. But the true mission of Conatus is to find those evildoers who will-fully bring these monsters into our world."

"You hunt witches?" She watched Father Michael in amazement. He smiled. "Among other things.

"The affairs of men are filled with blood, violence, and sin." Father Michael straightened, turning partly away from her. "That cannot be helped, for we are a fallen people in need of redemption. But to invite more darkness, unnatural evil, into our midst—that is a sin greater than any other. It must be stopped. Conatus serves that purpose."

"And the Church?" Ember asked, remembering the fate of the Templars.

Father Michael nodded. "When the Templars were disbanded, and many of their number executed for heresy, Conatus was unharmed, but hidden. The Church knows that our work in the mys-teries of the spirit world remains essential. We deal not in the world of men, but the world of darkness and demons. Our war is endless, and our enemy cannot be allowed to go unchecked. And we do not sojourn alone. The evil we fight overspreads the world. Our allies do as well. Lukasz joined us as a token of goodwill from our brothers in the East. And we benefit from the continued studies of our counter-parts in the Holy Land."

Ember was shaking her head. "Are you saying you still rely on the knowledge of the Saracens?"

"Any wisdom that lights the darkness we face cannot be ignored, no matter the source," he said. "The libraries of our sometime ene-mies boast stores of knowledge far older and broader than any found in Christendom. The roots of our order lie in the Holy Land. Did you recognize the tree in the great hall?"

"No," Ember said. "But it's beautiful."

"An exceptional tree with an exceptional purpose," Father Michael told her. "That tree was carried by Templars from the Holy Land and planted here over one hundred years ago. It is a cedar of Lebanon. Each year we renew our fealty to serving the earth and seeking knowledge of its mysteries and sharing that knowledge with our brothers and sisters of Conatus near and far. The tree is the symbol of that commitment."

Ember spoke carefully. "The pope knows of this?" She couldn't believe the Church would condone friendship with enemies of their faith. Too many wars had been fought to separate Christendom from nonbelievers.

"Whom of the three popes do you mean?" His blunt question made Ember gasp. He smiled wryly before continuing. "While in name we serve the Church, our work is not like that of any other order."

Father Michael's gaze shifted away. "There are some elements of Conatus that remain hidden, even from its mightiest benefactors. Particularly when the Church is at war with itself."

Ember went very still.

"I am a man of the cloth, Lady Morrow," he said. "I can only offer you my assurance that my role here is to ensure that our order serves the greater work of God. Even if we may not be able to reveal the extent of that work to my superiors."

"Are you not afraid such secrets will be discovered?" she asked.

He nodded. "It's a constant danger. No matter how necessary our work, if the Church believes its authority here to be questioned or waning, our fate would be the same as that of the Templars. That is the reason we seclude ourselves in the wilds of Scotland, why we rarely engage in the affairs of kingdoms or of men in general. Our lives are apart. And we take the orders of holy men and women, forsaking the comforts of flesh and family in our service. By freely placing such restrictions on our actions and our lives, the Church is reassured that our strength is tempered, our pride kept in check. We must demonstrate submissiveness and humility so that our purpose may be fulfilled."

"I understand," Ember said softly. What she understood even more was that the dangers of serving Conatus ranged far beyond the existence of monsters and the expectation that she would fight them. This place housed secrets and encouraged practices that could easily be deemed heretical.

Father Michael watched emotions play across her face. "The risks are many."

Ember couldn't pretend she wasn't afraid. To flee would mean a safe and comfortable marriage that would please her father. She would provide grandchildren that would delight her mother. She would never fear death at the hands of a monster or the fires reserved for traitors of the faith.

But something within Ember stirred, restless and yearning toward the unknown. She'd gone into the cellar armed with a dagger, not the sword familiar to her. She'd faced a creature beyond her imagining. And she had survived.

To stay meant she would continue to battle with nightmares, but she would also be granted the ability and knowledge to defeat them. The secrets of Conatus would be her own. It was power she had never dreamed of, and its allure was intoxicating.

Father Michael asked, "What say you, child?"

"I have been called," she said, if a bit unsteadily. She cleared her throat before she finished. "And I will serve."

"And so you shall." He took her hands in his, helping her rise. "Come with me, Lady Morrow."

He led her from his simple quarters back into the chapel. Ember followed the priest dumbly, caught in a daze by her own words. She'd committed herself to Conatus, to the Guard, and some small part of her mind was screaming at her stupidity. How would she survive here? But another, deeper voice—one that she believed was her spirit—whispered that her choice was the right choice, the only choice. To know of the existence of evil, true evil that corrupted the world, had forever altered her heart and mind. If she had chosen a different path, she wouldn't have slept another night. Her head would have been restless as she thought only of the horrors that might be creeping outside her door, waiting to rend her flesh. She would not live a life as the hunted; she would be the hunter.

Father Michael took her through a rear exit in the chapel and across the courtyard to the barracks. The structure resembled the manor but on a smaller scale.

"This is your home now, Lady Morrow," the priest told her. "Your new companions will be waiting for you in the hall."

Ember left Father Michael at the barracks' entrance. As he'd told her, the Guard who had been lining the corridor that led to her trial were assembled, waiting for her.

"Novice!" A booming voice demanded attention. Ember's gaze fell on the speaker. He was an impossibly tall man, nearly seven feet in height, his hair and eyes dark as freshly turned earth. Though it was the first time she'd seen him, Ember had no doubt as to the man's identity: Lukasz, commander of the Guard. Alistair spoke of him with near reverence. The knight's sharp features, hooked nose, and bright eyes made it clear why Alistair called him "the Falcon." He was distinct from the warriors in appearance and demeanor. Unlike most of those residing in the keep, Lukasz hailed from kingdoms in the eastern reaches of Christendom, bearing with him an air of experience and worldliness that both intimidated and fascinated Ember. Power rolled off his shoulders as he moved through the room, his piercing gaze at last falling on her.

She shivered when he said, "Step forward."

Ember had never felt more alone as she stood, a solitary figure, while the twenty-some number that made up the full Guard formed a ring around her.

Lukasz drew a claymore from its sheath, which was strapped across his back. The sword was taller than Ember, and she knew one sweep of the knight's thick-muscled arm would easily cleave her in two, as it had undoubtedly already done to many of Lukasz's foes.

He pointed the blade at her. Ember clenched her fists, forcing her shrieking muscles to remain still. Every inch of her being was screaming to jump back from the sword, even to flee from the room.

"Who has claimed this girl and will bear the burden of guiding her steps?" Lukasz asked.

His words didn't come as a surprise. Alistair had explained that Ember would have a mentor, a seasoned warrior to train her as she rose from novice to a full member of the Guard. Of course, that had all been speculation. Now that she stood with the knights of Conatus and had chosen to become one of them, the haze of astonishment that had surrounded her bled away. She wouldn't be going back to her father's manor. She would not marry Lord Mackenzie's son.

Ember let her eyes slip over the half circle of knights facing her. One of these warriors would be at her side day after day, teaching her to fight. She shivered, wishing that Kael MacRath weren't already Alistair's mentor. Though she'd only just met him, his cheerful demeanor was much less frightening than the hardened faces staring at her now. Glancing to her right, Ember met the gaze of a woman whose piercing blue eyes seemed at war with her mouth, one side of which was pulling up as if in amusement. Unlike the wild, loose tresses of Eira and Cian, this woman's muddy-brown hair was pulled up in a severe knot. As the sole woman Ember had spotted among the Guard besides the sisters, she could only assume this must be Sorcha—who according to Alistair was as ferocious as any man on the battlefield. As Ember held her gaze, Sorcha's half smile broke into a full grin, which Ember found herself responding to with an uncertain smile. Sorcha's open expression was confident, if a bit mischievous.

It must be her, Ember thought with relief. For her mentor to be the only woman of the Guard was reassuring. As much as she'd hoped with all her being to be a part of it, this was a man's world and Ember knew she'd need wisdom and experience like Sorcha's if she were to succeed. Ember began to breathe a little easier. Though Sorcha's expression was crafty as a wildcat's, Ember thought wiliness and courage must have made her the warrior Alistair claimed she was.

Sorcha winked at her, and Ember almost giggled but managed to keep still. The warrior woman had taken a step forward when shouts filled the room, turning all attention to the doorway.

Lukasz frowned, shaking his head. His height allowed him to see past the ring of Guards to whoever had entered the room. "You shouldn't be here, Lord Morrow. We're in the midst of our own ceremony. Only members of the Guard may be present."

"And that's why I'm here! I found your priest and he claimed my daughter passed some sort of trial. This madness must end." Ember's stomach twisted when her father pushed his way into the circle, glaring at her. "I only beg for reason. Surely there has been an error."

His eyes were bright with outrage. "Ember, your mother and sister beg you to reconsider. As do I."

"For what reason?" she asked, her temper flaring. Not only was her father still denying what she'd always wanted, but she was also humiliated that he would confront her about it with the entire Guard assembled to witness his outburst.

"For every reason!" He lunged forward, gripping her arms. "You would throw your life away to drink blood with the rest of these brutes?"

"Is that what you think we do here?" Kael asked, grinning. "How flattering."

He'd stepped from the ring of knights and came to stand beside Ember. Alistair mimicked his mentor's actions, taking up a post at Kael's shoulder. Ember started when Barrow materialized at her back, glowering at her father.

Her father paled, glancing around at the rest of the Guard. "Forgive me. Of course I give you nothing but honor for your sacrifice, but this is my daughter. She's just a child and doesn't understand the cost."

"Is this true?" Barrow's question was directed not at her father, but to Ember.

"No." Ember pulled out of her father's grasp, holding the gray-eyed knight's stern gaze. "This is my choice. I belong with the Guard."

Barrow's mouth twitched like he was about to smile, but her father's mirthless laugh shattered the moment.

"You are a woman, not a warrior," Edmund said, glaring at Ember. "You should honor your family with a marriage suiting your rank and children to carry on your legacy, not the mischief and bloodshed that you'll find here."

From behind him, Sorcha snorted.

"Agnes will give you grandchildren, Father," Ember said. "Leave me be." She almost added "please" but worried it would make her sound weak. If she could have begged him to leave, she would have, but members of the Guard didn't beg . . . at least she didn't think they did.

Ignoring her, Ember's father whirled, thrusting his fist at Sorcha. "How did you bewitch my daughter? Only you could have requested her to serve you."

Sorcha's hand went to her sword hilt. "That's quite an accusation, my lord. I would be more careful of your tongue. I would remind you that two of the Guard, both women, now belong to the Circle. You are indebted to Conatus. This is the price required."

Edmund's eyes bulged. His face was a bright shade of red slowly ebbing into violet. Ember wanted to shout her fury at him, but she was loath to act like a temperamental child before her new companions.

"Peace, Lord Morrow." Barrow stepped in front of her father, breaking his line of sight to Sorcha. "It was not Sorcha who chose Ember."

"Then who?" her father said, his clenched fists trembling. "Who dares claim my daughter as a squire?"

"I do," Barrow said.

Ember gaped at him while Sorcha clapped her hand over her mouth. Ember couldn't tell if it was from shock or if she was laughing and trying to hide it.

The mottled hues painting Edmund's face drained away, leaving his skin sallow. "But why? Why would you choose a girl to serve you?"

"That is a matter for the Guard and the Guard alone," Barrow said.

Edmund choked and spluttered, staring at Barrow in disbelief.

"You have your answer, my lord," Barrow said. "Leave us now or you will be taken from these quarters by force."

Glaring at Barrow for a moment longer, Edmund finally bowed his head. To question Barrow's statement would be to challenge his honor—a foolish act for any man. Edmund turned away, passing Ember as he moved to the door.

"Foolish girl," he hissed under his breath. "I swear you've not heard the end of this."

When he left the room, Kael closed the chamber doors, barring them with a stout length of wood.

"I'd say that's enough interruptions for today." He grinned at her.

Ember's stomach churned with a mixture of embarrassment, relief, and lingering fear. Her father was a proud and powerful man. If he believed he could still bring her back from the Guard, he would keep after it like hounds after a fox.

Sorcha laughed, slapping Barrow on the shoulder.

"Show me your tongue, my lord," she said. "I didn't know it was forked."

Barrow offered her a fleeting smile. "The man outstepped his place, as he has a habit of doing too often. He needed to be reminded of it . . . again."

A tightness overtook Ember's chest. Barrow had been lying. For a brief moment she'd believed that the most feared warrior of Conatus had chosen her as his apprentice, proving beyond any doubt that she was destined for a life with the Guard, but it had only been a ruse. She turned away, not wanting the others to see her cheeks burn. By giving her back to the others, Ember was now facing Alistair. He watched her face and his eyes narrowed. He stepped beside her, leaning down to whisper.

"What ails you?"

Every buried fear, nagging doubt planted beneath her skin by her family surfaced. If Barrow doubted her place among the Guard, perhaps she didn't belong here. What if her father was right? She couldn't bear it.

Alistair touched her shoulder, drawing her slightly apart from the others and peering at her face in concern. "Ember?"

Ember managed to choke out her confession. "Barrow didn't want me."

Something about her words made Alistair stiffen.

"Of course not," he said. "And why would you desire otherwise? He's too brutal to guide an initiate. And it's better for you to be trained by a woman—Sorcha has been wanting a squire, and no man would have a woman try to teach him swordplay."

His words stung Ember more than Barrow's lie. Did he think so little of her? When he'd given her a sword and taught her to use it, had it only been in fun?

Sorcha was still laughing. "You're caught in your own web now, my friend. You'll have to take her on or her father will cry foul."

"Surely you jest." Alistair snorted. "Barrow has no call for an apprentice."

"Do you know me so well, boy?" Barrow's eyebrows went up.

Alistair scowled at the word *boy,* but he inclined his head in reluctant acknowledgment of Barrow's station. "Forgive me, my lord. Ember is a dear friend. I only spoke out of concern for her well-being."

"Do you fear I would offer an initiate of the Guard ill treatment?" Barrow asked.

"I—" Alistair struggled, glancing around the room to find all gazes upon him. "I meant no insult. Sorcha had claimed Ember, so it seems right that she would be the one to train her."

"Politics outweigh intent," Sorcha said, smiling at Alistair. "You'll find that is often the case, even when it comes to the Guard. We value our swords, but we know they can't always win the day."

"Bearing in mind that young Alistair is still serving as squire to Kael, I have decided it follows that I should lay claim to this girl," Barrow said. "We'll complete your training together."

Alistair's face darkened as he listened to Barrow. "You'll remain Ember's mentor, then?"

Ember couldn't understand Alistair's glowering when she was ready to shout for joy. Not only was she going to join the Guard, but her life would be training side by side with her best friend.

Barrow was still considering Alistair's statement. He turned to Ember. She straightened up, hoping that all traces of embarrassment had vanished from her face.

"If the girl will have me," he said, "I would be honored to train her."

She started at his words. Accept the training of Barrow Hess? What madness would keep her from agreeing? Well, what madness other than an instinctive fear of Barrow's ferocious reputation. She wondered if she could make it through a round on the practice field against him. But he'd just said it meant that she and Alistair would train together. Having Kael's laughter and Alistair's friendship to offset Barrow's stern demeanor would be reassuring as she found her place among the Guard. No doubt she'd have to endure an inordinate amount of teasing from Kael and Alistair, but it would be worth it.

Barrow continued, keeping his gaze on Ember though she thought he spoke for Alistair's benefit. "Ember comes from a landed family with great influence. Even the Circle must sometimes concede to the will of the nobles. We cannot show signs of doubt before them. If Edmund Morrow objects to women fighting in the Guard, it will only fortify his case should we place Ember in Sorcha's care. If he were to take his complaint to the other nobles, it could cause great trouble."

Alistair nodded, but he glared at Barrow before casting his gaze on Sorcha.

"I agree," Sorcha said. "I withdraw my claim on the girl. Let her be trained by Barrow."

Barrow drew his sword, laid the blade flat on his palms, and dropped to one knee before Ember. Her blood roared in her veins.

"To fight, to lead, and to teach are the roles of the Guard," he said, holding her in his gaze. "The first two obligations I have fulfilled. I am indebted to my order to meet the last. I have no great knowledge to impart nor do I believe myself a wise teacher, but it would be my honor to guide you."

Ember reached out, letting her fingertips rest on the flat of the blade. "And I would be honored to serve you, my lord."

Behind her, Ember heard Alistair expel a hissing breath.

Kael chortled. "Barrow, my friend, you know how to stir up a hornet's nest. Wait till Father Michael hears about this!"

Barrow rose, nodding at Ember before flashing a smile at Kael.

"Father Michael speaks well of peacemakers. Let him now make peace."

While the knights of Conatus swarmed around her, Ember accepted their hearty congratulations and words of welcome with forced smiles. She couldn't help but wonder what sort of battle her call to the Guard would spark.

SEVEN

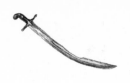

CIAN SAT ON THE EDGE of the bed while Eira finished binding her hair up and then fastened her heavy riding cloak.

"You'll be missed at the feast," Cian said.

"The nobles won't care if one of the weird sisters fails to appear at dinner," Eira said.

Cian winced at her sister's use of the foul name that dogged their steps. Catching sight of Cian's frown, Eira laughed coldly.

"You know I speak the truth."

"Even so." Cian shrugged. "You mustn't let them chase you away."

"They aren't chasing me anywhere," Eira said. "It's a night of power. We need someone to keep an eye on the villages in the glen in case an aspiring sorcerer attempts to draw on that power."

Cian gave a reluctant nod. "Would you like me to join you?"

"No," Eira said. "I'm abandoning you to a different type of watch, sister. I think Lord Morrow is of a mind to abduct his daughter and deliver her to Mackenzie's son. Such is the gossip of the day."

"It wouldn't be the first time a marriage began with kidnapping." Cian rose, crossing the room to the window. As members of the Circle they no longer resided in the barracks but shared quarters in the manor. Though darkness covered the valley, Cian spotted winking lights one by one breaking through the black veil. Gatherings would take place up and down the glen to honor the turn of winter to spring, darkness to light. And Eira was right to worry about what might take place at a few such meetings. It was their life's work to watch and to worry.

"I'd be more concerned if the other party were any other but Mackenzie," Eira said. "He knows enough to prevent any foolishness. Mackenzie wants our protection more than a wealthy daughter-in-law."

Cian laughed. "Do you think he'll set Lord Morrow's mind at ease?"

"Edmund Morrow will soon be back in the lowlands and no longer a concern of ours." Eira pulled the hood of her cloak up, casting a shadow over her face.

"Do you think he'll forget his younger daughter so quickly?" Cian turned away from the window to gaze at her sister.

"She is no longer his daughter," Eira said. "She is one of us. You and I know what that means, even if he doesn't."

Without another word Eira left the room.

"And even if *she* doesn't," Cian murmured to no one but herself.

Most of Ember's triumph was pecked away through dinner by her mother's constant lamenting and her sister's pathetic sniffling. It had been like this all day. She'd returned to the guest quarters to collect her belongings only to be beset by a dissonant chorus composed of her father's curses, her mother's pleas, and her sister's sobs. After what had seemed like the longest hours of her life, they'd returned to the manor hall for the feast as a family but with none of the warmth one hoped for among kin. Her father had refused to sit with them, instead seeking a place beside Lord Mackenzie. No doubt he was conniving a way to see her married to the highland lord's son, despite the day's events. Ember could only hope his pleas would fall on deaf ears. She glanced frequently across the room, hoping to spy evidence that her father wasn't making any progress toward his goal. From his reddened face and the sour turn of his mouth it seemed his efforts were being frustrated.

Even with this reassurance, Ember was finding it difficult to enjoy the feast. Her family had been seated at a table of honor not far from the head table, where members of the Circle sat. Alistair and the rest of the Guard were gathered at their own long table, and Ember wished she could join them. At that table her presence would be welcomed. Currently she felt much like a guest at her own funeral. But since it was the last time she'd spend with her family for the foreseeable future, she felt obligated to remain at their side.

"Surely you can't want this?" Ember's mother asked for the third time. "If you don't want to live in the highlands after your father's debt to Conatus is paid, I'm certain we can find a husband for you other than Mackenzie's son. I'll speak with your father."

Ember ignored her, trying to enjoy the decadent feast spread before her. The heavy wooden board was laden with foods welcoming spring. Nests were filled with hard-cooked eggs, an accompaniment to roasted pheasant and suckling pig. Wine breads, bursting with preserved fruits, forecast the ripeness of summer berries to come. She was about to tuck into a crock of fish stew scented with savory herbs when her father's shouts roared through the hall.

"Am I not lord of my own house?" Edmund's fist swept across the table, sending platters of food sailing. Slabs of meat smacked onto the floor while vegetables rolled underfoot.

Lord Mackenzie rose, trying to calm her father. "Sit down, my lord."

"I will not!" Edmund's face matched the beets that were now staining the floor.

Ember sat frozen in horror. Her father's anger was obvious, but so was how deeply he'd sunk into his wine cup. In his rage he waved his arms, swaying unsteadily as his glare swept the room.

"This place is cursed, I tell you!" he cried, stumbling toward his family. He pointed an accusing finger at Ember. "A den of iniquity that has stolen my daughter to bend her to their will."

Ember had been so focused on her father's ranting that she hadn't noticed others moving nearby. Father Michael walked calmly to the center of the room.

"Lord Morrow, do not speak of evil here," he said. "Your child has been called to a higher purpose, God's purpose."

"No!" Edmund stumbled forward, knocking the priest aside. "Yer . . . no man of . . . of . . . God. There's . . . there's . . . no true Church wi'in these . . . walls. Your lies . . . all . . . yer . . . lies . . ."

Her father's words began to slur as his voice became hoarse. She could no longer make sense of his rambling, only picking out a few words as he shook his fists in the air, shouting.

". . . devil's snare . . . heathens . . ."

"You know not of what you speak," Father Michael said, bowing his head and making the sign of the cross. "Stop this wicked speech."

"Tricked!" Edmund cried out. Ember shrank into her chair as he came toward her, pointing an accusing finger. "No daughter of mine will become a witch."

Sensing a presence behind her, she drew a quick breath when she turned to see Barrow standing over her. His stance wasn't aggressive, but he looked as immovable as an oak tree.

"You'll find no witches here, my lord," he said, offering her father a cold smile. Ember shuddered when his hand rested on her shoulder. A strange sensation curled from the point where his fingers touched her, sliding over her skin and snatching her breath.

Another tall figure loomed before her father, blocking his path to the table.

Edmund Morrow lurched into Lukasz's immense form. The knight grasped her father's arms, steering him away from Ember.

"Seek your bed, my lord," Lukasz said, giving her father no choice in the matter as he pushed him to the door. "Before you do any further harm."

Ossia Morrow rose, pale and trembling. She didn't look at her younger daughter when she spoke.

"Agnes, we must see to your father." Ember's mother made a much more dignified exit from the hall.

Ember watched her mother disappear into the hall and her heart pinched with grief. Despite their disapproval, she'd still hoped to part from her family on good terms. Now it seemed only bitterness would mark their farewell.

A soft touch turned Ember's gaze. Agnes's slender fingers grasped hers shakily.

"I shall miss you," Agnes whispered.

For the first time that day, Ember's resolve cracked. She grabbed Agnes, pulling her into a fierce embrace. "I wish you every happiness, Agnes."

Agnes flinched at Ember's words. She kissed Ember's cheek and hurried after their mother, leaving Ember to sit alone. The scene having ended, conversation returned to its low din. Servants appeared to clean up the rubble of food and broken dishes Ember's father had left in his wake. She twisted her hands together, unsure of what to say or do now that her family had abandoned her. Without the storm of her father's rage commanding her attention, her mind began to reel. He'd obviously been drunk, but his furious cries had unsettled her. Of course he would be angry about losing her match to Mackenzie's son, but he'd voiced fears about trickery and curses. How much did her father know about the secrets of Conatus? His shrieks echoed in her mind, making her shiver.

"It's over now." A chair scraped over the stone floor as Alistair pulled up a seat next to her. "They'll be gone in the morning."

He smiled at her, but she couldn't return the mirthful gleam in his eye. A heavy weight pressed into her chest. The jubilation of being freed from her father's will felt hollow now in the wake of his outburst. Her family, despite how she'd thought them burdensome, had always cared for her. Now they were gone and she faced a world filled with dangers she couldn't imagine.

"No daughter of mine will become a witch."

Father Michael seemed a good man, but if the work of Conatus was kept secret from the Church, did that mean it was somehow wicked?

Weariness settled over her like a winter cloak. Barrow, whose hand still rested on her shoulder, must have felt her sigh.

"You should rest," he said. The pressure of his touch stirred something deep inside her. She wanted to take his hand in hers and feel its warmth.

Alistair stood up. "I can show you to your room."

"No," Barrow said. Grasping her arms lightly, he helped Ember rise. "I am her mentor and as such my task begins now. I will introduce her to life as one of the Guard."

Alistair opened his mouth to protest but was interrupted when Kael appeared. The blond warrior slung his arm around Alistair's shoulders. "Come, good squire. Help me settle a wager. Did I not slay four foes single-handedly two nights ago?"

Before Alistair could answer, Kael pulled him around, dragging him back to the Guard's table.

Barrow strode from the hall. Ember stared after him for a moment until she realized he meant for her to follow. She nearly crashed into him as she hurried into the corridor, where he stood waiting for her with the barest hint of a smile. It was one of his most frequent expressions, and it both intrigued and puzzled her.

He didn't give her the chance to speak, but simply turned and led her through the torch-lit manor until they reached its outer doors. Given Barrow's height, Ember had to match each of his long strides with two of her own. His silence pressed down on her. She wondered if he regretted offering to train her and perhaps now saw her only as a burden. After her father's behavior at the feast, she wouldn't have been surprised if he expected her to be nothing more than a spoiled noble's daughter.

Soon they were crossing the dark courtyard to the barracks. In the darkness its squat, stone shape was lonely and foreboding. He turned sharply right instead, leading her up a narrow staircase that she hadn't noticed on her prior visit. The second level of the barracks featured a long hall lined with wooden doors.

"Our cells," Barrow said.

Ember glanced at him, wondering at the use of the word *cell* for their quarters. Perhaps this life would differ little from that of a nun.

"You're likely to find them simple," he continued. "But they serve our purpose well."

"It's fine," she said.

He led her to the very end of the hallway, stopping at the final door on the right. She spotted another staircase descending from this side of the corridor.

Barrow followed her gaze. "These stairs lead through the armory and are the closest to the rear exit that opens onto the practice field."

He gestured for her to open the door they'd stopped in front of. "This will be your room."

Ember turned the iron handle and the door swung inward, revealing an austere, rectangular space. Her cell contained a narrow pallet. The lip of a brass chamber pot peeked out from beneath the wooden frame. A simple writing table and chair sat under the room's only window. Three objects sat on the table: a candlestick, a clay pitcher, and a basin. A tall wardrobe was half hidden by the open door.

"You'll find the clothing you need there." Barrow waved in the direction of the wardrobe. Then he coughed, looking away from her. "The belongings you brought with you from your father's house are being stored in the manor. You'll have no need of them here . . . nor does your cell offer space to keep them."

Ember thought of the trunk filled with dresses that her mother had insisted she bring. The more Ember considered their journey, and the conversations leading up to it, up to the very morning she'd been called to the Guard, the more Ember saw how deeply each of her father's words and deeds had been full of contradiction . . . and how all of it had been tinged with fear.

"In the event that you must dress as befits your former station," Barrow was saying, "you will have a room in the manor where you can make ready. I should give you fair warning that even the dress you wear now will be gone when you return to your cell tomorrow night."

"What do you mean?" Ember asked.

Barrow frowned. "I think it best if I leave it to Sorcha to explain this to you. I have no experience to share."

Ember wanted to ask further, but Barrow's stern manner didn't seem to welcome questions.

Barrow went to the table and picked up the candlestick before slipping back into the hallway. A moment later he reappeared, having lit the candle from one of the corridor's lanterns, and returned it to its place on the table. "I'll bid you good night then, Lady Morrow." He closed the door as he left, not waiting for her answer.

The cloud-covered sky rendered her cell very dark. The single candle offered a subtle gleam as she moved to the wardrobe to search for nightclothes. Upon opening the wardrobe, Ember was greeted by unfamiliar garb. No kirtles, brocade, or even simple wool dresses lay within. Instead she found a pair of hose so fine she thought they must be silk, linen chemises, leather *chausses*, and the tabard worn by the Guard. She ran her fingers over supple leather breeches. She'd never worn anything like them. The clothing of the Guard was the clothing of men. The thought of dressing in their manner was both strange and exciting. On the highest shelf she found sleeping shirts, though like the rest of the wardrobe's contents they were new and not those she'd brought from home.

Ember shed her gown and kirtle, trading her chemise for one of the sleeping shirts. She folded her clothes and left them at the foot of the wardrobe where they could be easily collected. The floor chilled her bare feet and she scurried to the pallet. She blew out the candle before lying down. Without the help of the slender flame, the room surrendered to darkness. Ember shivered, pulling the scratchy wool blanket over her, thankful that the pallet was filled with a soft material, likely feathers or down, and not straw.

Damp cold crept beneath her blanket and Ember considered digging her cloak out from the pile of clothing and wearing it for additional warmth. But if, as Barrow had said, the clothes she'd worn today would be gone tomorrow, then she'd be better off adjusting to her new living conditions as quickly as possible. She missed Agnes, with whom she'd shared a bed at their father's house. Her sister's giggles and whispers late into the night would have been as welcome in this lonely cell as her warmth.

Thoughts of her sister made Ember feel even colder. With each day of the journey, and tonight at the feast, Agnes seemed to grow more ill and sorrowful. Ember was certain her sister was hiding something. The only regret she felt was that she wouldn't be able to help Agnes as she prepared for her wedding.

Ember curled into a ball and waited for the wool blanket to trap her body heat, cocooning her away from the chill of her cell. As her mind drifted, she couldn't help but remember the warmth of thick furs and fine cloth that covered her in her father's house.

"The past," she murmured, only half awake. "The past is no more."

She had begun to drift away from the world when quiet knocking brought her back. She slipped from her bed, the cold floor on her bare feet making her draw a hissing breath. Another knock came and when Ember opened the door, Barrow's tall frame loomed before her.

"Barrow," she whispered, the sight of him shocking her heartbeat into a frenzy.

He took a step back, as if the sight of her made him unsure of himself. Ember glanced down. Her nightshirt fit loosely and its neckline was askew, leaving one of her shoulders bare. And he'd easily glimpse her pale legs from the knees down.

Heat crept up the back of her neck. Giving a quick shake of his head like someone trying to clear his own befuddlement, Barrow moved out of the doorway to reveal another figure standing at his back.

"You have a visitor," he said softly.

"Oh, Ember." Agnes rushed forward, throwing her arms around Ember.

"I'll be waiting outside and will escort you back to the manor when you're ready, Lady Morrow," Barrow told Agnes, and closed the door.

Agnes was clinging to Ember, who held her sister tight. She was embarrassed that her eyes had begun to sting with tears, but having her sister close was such a comfort, and their sudden parting at dinner hadn't been the type of good-bye Ember had hoped for.

"Thank you for coming," Ember said. "My heart was broken after the day our family had."

Agnes let Ember go, and though her face was tear-stricken, her eyes were tight with guilt.

"What's wrong?" Ember asked.

"Father sent me," Agnes murmured, casting her gaze downward.

Ember turned her back on Agnes and crossed the room to sit on the bed.

"But, Ember." Agnes's voice quivered. "I did want to come myself.

I swear. I already miss you terribly and we haven't even been parted a day."

Ember couldn't bite back her anger. "Why did Father send you?"

"Only to ask you to reconsider." Agnes scurried to the bed, taking Ember's hands.

"He knows I can't leave. And even if I could, I don't want to," Ember snarled, though it felt like stones were slowly being piled on her chest. It wasn't Agnes's fault that their father wouldn't accept Ember's determination to have a life of her own.

Agnes squeezed Ember's fingers. "You don't have to. Father only asks . . . no, pleads for you to make a different choice. One that doesn't cut you off from your family."

Ember sat quietly, looking into her sister's reddened eyes.

"I know you don't want to surrender to Father's will," Agnes said. "But what of me? Of Mother?"

"What would you have me do?" Ember whispered.

"Couldn't you serve Conatus some other way?" Agnes asked. "Must you become a warrior?"

Ember gritted her teeth. "Father's only concern is that he's still able to marry me off."

"You're right," Agnes agreed, surprising Ember. "But I would wish the joys of marriage and motherhood upon my sister. Joys we could share."

Ember pulled her hands free of Agnes's grip with a sigh. "Agnes, you are so dear to me, but you've never understood who I am."

"Do you really want to be like Father's men?" Agnes frowned. "Those horrid brutes?"

Ember thought of the Guard standing around her, welcoming her to their ranks. She remembered the terrible beauty of Barrow and Kael battling on the practice field. Most of all, she recalled the pure exhilaration of fighting alone, of opposing a true foe, and of winning.

She'd never felt such joy and she wouldn't give that up. Not even for her sister.

"The Conatus Guard are nothing like Father's men," Ember said quietly. She focused a piercing gaze on Agnes. "But you know that. You saw Barrow fight them."

When Ember said Barrow's name, a smile formed on her lips.

Agnes bowed her head. "Tearmunn serves a noble purpose. I won't deny that. But surely you needn't fight—"

"I do," Ember interrupted. "I will miss you every day, Agnes. But this is what I've longed for, always. There is no other choice for me."

She smiled gently at Agnes. "Imagine how you felt when you learned you were to marry—how happy you were. That is how happy I am."

Agnes made a choking sound that became a sob. She didn't speak, only nodded. Rather unsteadily, Agnes rose and moved to the door. Before she opened it, she looked over her shoulder.

"I wish you well, sister," Agnes told her. She paused, lowering her voice. "Would that I had the happiness you think I do."

Ember stood up. "Agnes—"

But Agnes shook her head, opened the door, and slipped out, leaving Ember alone. She stood still for a few minutes and stared at the door while an emptiness made her feel cold to her very bones. Rather numbly, Ember lay down and pulled the wool blanket up her chin. She let a restless sleep take her, not knowing if it would bring sweet dreams of the future or nightmares.

EIGHT

MORNING LIGHT WOKE Ember just before a knock came
on her door. She sat up, breathless, not remembering where she was.
The knock came again, more insistent this time.

"Ember!"

It was Alistair's voice that jarred her memory. She scrambled out
of bed, panicked that she might already be late for her first day with
the Guard. She bit her lip, not wanting to cry out as her feet touched
the icy floor.

"I'm awake," she called.

The door opened and Alistair's head poked in. "Hungry?"

Ember smiled at the sight of her friend's familiar grin. "I am."

"Get dressed and come to the hall," he said. "You'll need your
strength."

Then he was gone. Ember had no idea what the day might bring.
She only hoped she could meet any challenges thrown her way. She
took the pitcher from the table, grimacing when she saw the thin
layer of ice covering the water inside. Cracking open the ice with her
fingers, she poured the water into the basin. She squealed a little as
she splashed the freezing water over her face, but she hoped not so
loudly that anyone heard.

Dressing would be her first adventure of the day. She had just
pulled on her hose and had one leg in her leather breeches when
another knock came at the door.

"I'm almost ready, Alistair," she called.

But the face that appeared when the door opened was not Alistair's.

"And I'm sure he can't wait to see you." Sorcha smiled.

Ember had been on one foot preparing to draw up the other leg of her breeches and nearly fell over.

Sorcha laughed. "I'm here because Barrow thought you might need some assistance with your clothes."

"Really, I'm doing fine," Ember said, quickly pulling on the chausses. "You startled me."

"Mmmm." Sorcha came into the room. She was holding a long, narrow band of cloth in her hands. "I'm sure. That's not what I'm here for. Breeches are easy."

Ember frowned as she tied the laces of her chausses to her cotton braies. "And shirts are hard?" It was odd, but not unpleasant, to have layers of fabric wrapped around her legs rather than the broad press of skirts.

Sorcha laughed again. "Not really. But you'll want something more than a shirt. Trust me. Take your nightclothes off."

Ember pulled her sleeping shirt over her head.

"Now lift your arms," Sorcha said.

"Why?" Ember asked, though she complied.

"You'll see." Sorcha began winding soft fabric around Ember's body, starting just below her armpits. Sorcha kept the fabric tight, which bound Ember's breasts firmly to her chest, considerably flattening her curves. The wrapping stopped in line with Ember's lower ribs.

"When you practice doing this yourself, be certain you've bound the cloth tightly enough," Sorcha said. "You don't want it coming apart when you're in the middle of a fight."

Ember watched as Sorcha forced the end of the band beneath the wrapped fabric and over again, holding it in place.

"It's an extra step, but a necessary one," Sorcha said. "There's a reason the Amazons cut off the breast on the side of their bow drawing arm. Our extra flesh can get in the way of a warrior's tasks. And if not that, your breasts will simply ache if left free."

"Thank you," Ember said, grateful for Sorcha's matter-of-fact approach to this rather intimate lesson. It left Ember wondering if she would have been better off if Sorcha had claimed her rather than Barrow. Yet she was keenly aware of the way her pulse quickened at the thought of being near him.

"You're welcome," Sorcha was saying. "I think you'll find this remedy much preferable to amputation."

She waited while Ember donned a linen shirt and then the Conatus tabard, belting it low on her hips. Sorcha nodded her approval.

"It suits you," she said with a smile. "And soon you'll have a weapon or two to hang from your belt."

Ember returned her smile nervously. The idea of weapons was thrilling, but intimidating. Having faced the revenant, she knew that all her mock fighting was nothing compared to the real thing.

She followed Sorcha out of her cell and down the back stairwell. Her mind, already full of weapons, manifested them before her eyes as she reached the first floor. The armory's walls glinted with the steel that covered them. Ember gazed at a tapestry of death with fear and wonder. One wall was filled with swords, ranging from those the length of her arm to others that appeared to be twice her height. Some had curved blades, some straight, and some had wicked serrated edges. Another wall featured battle-axes of all sizes and yet another spears and polearms.

"Anything catch your fancy?" Sorcha asked.

Ember bit her lip. "How . . . how will I know what I should use?"

"Don't be afraid," Sorcha said. "You'll find your arms without trouble."

They passed through the armory door and into the main hall. Sorcha settled at a table where Alistair sat with Kael and Barrow. Breakfast consisted of a fresh loaf of bread, still warm from the oven, and a brick of hard cheese. Barrow sat quietly, though he glanced at Sorcha, who gave a quick nod before reaching for the loaf. Kael was also silent, but the dark circles under his eyes left Ember guessing that he'd celebrated a bit too much at last night's feast.

Alistair shifted in his seat, glancing around the table uneasily.

"Did you sleep well?" he asked Ember.

"Yes," she said.

They fell into an awkward silence as she ate her breakfast. When she pushed her plate away, Barrow stood up.

"If you're finished, we should be on our way," he said. "Come with me, my lady."

Ember scrambled out of her chair, waved a brief good-bye to Alistair, and hurried after Barrow, whose long strides had already carried him out of the hall.

As she walked beside the tall warrior, she said, "If I am to serve you, my lord, it seems strange that you should address me so formally."

"You would have me use your Christian name?" Barrow asked.

"My name is Ember," she said. "And I would be called so, my lord."

Barrow nodded. "Then do me the same courtesy."

"But I am your servant," she said.

He gave a slight shake of his head. "I am your teacher, but you serve Conatus, not me. I have no desire for your deference. In battle we fight together, as companions."

"Yes, Barrow," she said, dropping her gaze as she blushed.

Ember heard his quiet laugh.

"Is my name so unpleasant?" he asked.

She kept her eyes away from his. "No, my l—Barrow."

The heat in her cheeks flared. His name wasn't the problem, but her sense of place remained uneasy. Barrow's reputation and stern demeanor intimidated her. Keeping him distant felt safer than to think of herself as his companion. In the recesses of her mind, Ember knew she was trying to deny something else. A much more troubling feeling. When she was with Barrow, she wanted to study him, to learn everything about him. She didn't want to indulge in a childish fascination with her mentor, but despite her intentions, Ember knew her gaze kept finding its way to Barrow's face, hoping to meet his dark gray eyes.

Barrow suddenly spoke, and she looked away, embarrassed. "Tell me what you thought of your first revenant."

She shuddered as it dawned on her that "first" implied there were more of those hideous things to come.

"I think the smell is the worst part," Barrow continued. "Don't you?"

When she looked at him, she thought he was about to laugh. It made his eyes light up like a storm cloud full of lightning.

"The worst part was that it seemed as though it wanted to eat me," she said.

Barrow did laugh then. "It certainly did want to eat you. Revenants can only survive by eating the flesh of the living. You would have been a tender morsel indeed."

"I'm flattered you think so." Ember frowned at the comment, unsure if it could be taken as a compliment.

He caught the sharpness of her tone and his voice softened. "Have I offended you, Ember?"

She thought to hold her tongue, but words poured out unchecked. "I was thrown into that pit with no warning, given a weapon I didn't know how to use."

"You weren't thrown," Barrow said. "You walked in of your own volition. And you used the weapon ably."

"It was cruel," she said.

"It was necessary," he told her. "Without the test we cannot determine if an initiate was truly called to our purpose."

"You would have let me die," she said. "I could have failed and filled that creature's belly."

"No," Barrow said. "You were watched at all times. Had your life been in danger, you would have been saved. You fought well enough that we never had to intervene."

"But if the test was to survive—"

"The test wasn't of your fighting skills," he said, "but of your mind and spirit. The true test was given by Father Michael, after you knew the truth of our work."

"But what if the revenant had overpowered me?" she asked, startled by his words.

"It's happened many times." He shrugged. "We had to help Alistair escape from the hobgoblins loosed on him."

Ember stopped mid-stride and Barrow wheeled around, watching her.

"He didn't kill them?" she asked. This news was more than surprising. In all of her letters from Alistair he'd spoken only of adventure and triumph and never of struggles . . . or failure.

"No," Barrow said. "But in his defense, hobgoblins are fast, deceptive, and don't go for the kill. They're playful creatures, more interested in maiming than murder. We intervened when one had Alistair pinned and the other was about to suck out his eyeballs."

Ember clapped a hand over her mouth.

"So you see." He walked toward her. "It isn't a test of strength, but will. Now your training will begin. You'll learn to use the weapons and skills required to best any evil you're sent to face. Alistair would dispatch the foes that overcame him a year ago within minutes. As will you, soon enough."

Beneath her hand, Ember's mouth crinkled in a smile. Though

she felt for her friend's plight, she found it reassuring that in her first trial, she'd been more successful than Alistair.

"Come, Ember," Barrow said. "Your day has only just begun."

She balked, wondering what could be awaiting her. "Very well."

"Have no fear." Barrow was smiling at her. "I won't ask you to face another creature today."

"I—" Ember grimaced, worried she'd shown too much fear. Already she felt as though she should be ready to fight whenever asked, without doubt. Without hesitation. Barrow was watching her.

"I knew you'd do well," he said, surprising her. "I can see you're already anticipating the work ahead, the dangers. It suits you. From the moment I saw you in your father's hall, it was clear you belong with us." He took her shoulder in a light grasp before moving down the corridor.

Ember's heart twisted beneath her ribs and stole her breath. Pushing aside the strange sensation, she followed Barrow through the manor and out into the courtyard. Her mouth was full of questions, but she bit her tongue. Better to let the answers come to her than to chase after them like an impatient child.

The chill of the day was shoved aside by the heat of the smithy. While their assistant stoked the fires, steadying the temperatures of the forges, craftsmen and craftswomen kept up a steady rhythm of pounding hammers. A chorus of clanging metal filled the air as shields and swords were born. The air shimmered with the power of the raging fires.

"This way," Barrow said, leading Ember past the line of blacksmiths. The labor was carved into their bodies, reshaping their limbs into thick, sweat-covered muscles as they bent and curved metals to their will.

The workplace of the metalsmiths was large. At least a dozen men and women were bent over anvils or raining hammer blows down onto iron and steel. Red-hot metal sizzled and steam clouds filled the already smoky air as blades were bathed in icy water.

Barrow stopped midway through the smithy, bowing before a figure whose body was pure, hard sinew. Ember was startled when she realized the blacksmith, whose hair was clipped close to the skull, was a woman. Her leather apron was mottled with burn marks.

"Good morning, Barrow." She returned his bow.

"Morag." Barrow smiled. "I've brought you our young initiate. She is in need of a tool with which to do her work."

Morag turned appraising eyes on Ember. "She passed her trial?"

Without pause, Morag began an inspection of Ember's form, asking the girl to hold her arms over her, then out to her sides. She took time to grip Ember's shoulders, her upper and lower arms.

"She did," Barrow said while Ember stood as straight as she could. She let herself be stretched and prodded, determined to endure the assessment without complaint. The smoke was making her eyes burn, but she forced herself to meet Morag's gaze without blinking. Her eyes began to water.

The burly artisan chortled. "Strong spirit. You'll have your hands full with this one, Barrow. I wonder if you're up to the task."

Ember looked at Morag sharply, finding it difficult to believe that she'd call Barrow's skill into question.

But Barrow simply smiled. "Time will tell."

Morag grinned at him. "It will indeed." She took Ember's wrist and led her to a stool very close to the roaring flames of the forge.

"Sit here," she instructed. "Be as still as you can."

Morag moved to a nearby workbench. She emptied the contents of several pouches and glass jars into a mortar and then ground the mixture together with a pestle. She carried the mortar to Ember's side.

"Do not take your eyes from the flames," she whispered. "Let them speak to you."

The fire was so close Ember felt her skin heating up and feared it would soon burn, but she didn't dare move. Morag flung a handful of fine powder into the flames, causing it to flare up and spew lavender plumes of smoke. Ember coughed as she took in lungfuls of the bizarrely colored air. It smelled of moss and heather and tasted like licorice root.

"Keep breathing," Barrow said from behind her.

She wanted to beat her chest and clear her lungs of the smoke, but she sucked in another deep breath even as her eyes watered. The flames kept up a furious dance before her, the colors of the sunset darkening to the violet of twilight. Her vision swam and she swayed on the stool, nearly sliding off it. She rubbed her eyes, struggling to see through her tears.

Morag caught Ember's wrists in her hands, pulling them away from her face. "Nay, lass. Ye must see. Look into the flames."

But there were no longer flames to see. Through still-watery eyes Ember gazed into a midnight sky, starless and eternal. Somewhere very far away she heard a crooning melody. The voice sounded strangely like Morag's but was so distant Ember thought it couldn't possibly be her singing. A subtle gleam cut the darkness. The moon, a bright globe, shimmered into substance, the solitary object in the heavens. As she watched, darkness slowly covered its gleaming surface. She could still see the lingering outline of the full moon, but the encroaching shadow left only a slender crescent to light the sky. Crimson drops slid along its curve before plummeting to the earth.

Ember reached into the sky and the bloodred tears splashed onto her hand, sizzling as they made contact with her skin.

"Ember!" Strong hands gripped her shoulders, jerking her back from the fire and wrenching her out of the vision.

Barrow kept her balanced against his body as she began to cough again. Morag handed him a damp cloth, soaked in some kind of astringent that stung Ember's hand when he bound it around her scorched skin.

"You're supposed to look into the flames, not touch them." He shook his head, but he was smiling.

Ember opened her mouth to protest but only managed more coughing. She was still a bit dizzy. She put her hand to her forehead, closing her eyes, and hoped the smithy would soon stop spinning.

"Here, lass, drink this." Morag crouched before her, holding a bucket and a ladle filled with springwater.

"Thank you." Ember gulped the cool water, grateful that she was able to breathe steadily again.

Barrow watched as she took a few more ladlefuls of water. When Ember straightened, unnerved that she'd been leaning all her weight against Barrow for several minutes, he simply nodded at her. "Are you well again?"

"Yes," she said, though her legs were a bit shaky. "I think so." She didn't object when Barrow pulled the stool away from the forge and eased her down onto it.

His gaze returned to Morag.

"What did ye see, Ember?" she asked the girl.

Ember's mouth twisted as she wondered what she was supposed to see. Her vision didn't make sense, and as she tried to describe it, she felt foolish.

"I saw the moon," she said.

"What sort of moon?" Morag asked, seemingly unsurprised by Ember's words.

"First it was a full moon," Ember said. "Then the full moon was covered in shadow, leaving only its crescent form."

"Was there anything else?" Morag's eyes had grown thoughtful.

"It . . ." Ember glanced at Barrow, who, like Morag, appeared nonplussed by the strange vision. "It cried tears of blood."

Barrow's brow went up, which sent heat running up Ember's cheeks. It was a silly thing to say.

Morag laughed. "Well, then. There was no mistake in your calling."

Ember looked at her, startled.

Barrow shifted his stance, his speculative gaze giving way to a pensive one. "I had no doubts."

"I never suggested *you* did," Morag said. "But there was talk."

"Too much," Barrow said. "Foolish and dangerous."

Ember knew he was defending her against the sort of gossip she'd always hated and wanted to thank him, but her mind was still fixed on the bleeding moon and what it could mean.

"Soon, lass." Morag smiled at Ember, taking in her puzzled expression. "I'll devote a night and day to this. Come back to me on the morrow."

"Are we done then?" Barrow's mood had soured.

"Aye," she said.

"You have our thanks." He looked at Ember. "The day is still young. Is your head clear enough for work?"

She sprang up, happy that she didn't stumble despite the fact that her vision blurred at the sudden movement. "Of course."

Barrow was already weaving his way through the maze of forges and clouds of sparks. Ember kept her eyes on his back, still needing a point of focus. The heady incense lingered, muddying her senses.

Ember blinked in the bright light of day as they emerged from the cave-like smithy.

Barrow eyed her carefully. "We'll get you some water before training."

She thought about protesting, wanting to deny any weakness, but realized how foolhardy that lie would be. "Thank you."

As he led the way up the slow incline toward the barracks, Ember cast a sidelong glance at the tall knight.

"What did you see when you looked into the fire?"

He grimaced, and she wondered if perhaps the question was too personal. Her desire to know how unusual her vision had been made her wait rather than retract the query.

Readjusting the sword at his waist, Barrow glanced at her. "I saw a lion crouched in the darkness. When it struck, its claws became a single curved blade."

"That must have been frightening." Ember's eyes moved over the saber that he always carried.

Following her gaze, Barrow said, "It was more than frightening. When I came out of the vision, I'd gained a long, bleeding gash across my chest."

"How is that possible?" Ember asked.

"You'll find the impossible to be possible more often than not the longer you're with us," Barrow told her. He paused for a moment before saying, "My blade is known as a shamshir. It's a weapon of the Persians, and its name means 'curved like a lion's claw.'"

Ember found it difficult to suppress her disbelief at Barrow's story. Her skepticism must have shown on her face because Barrow stopped walking and turned to face her. Without giving explanation, he unbuckled his sword belt, handing it to her. The blade was surprisingly light in her hands. Even more shocking was the sight of Barrow stripping off his tabard and undershirt to reveal his bare chest.

His fingers traced the single diagonal gash that stretched from just below his right shoulder to his left lower abdomen. Heat prickled along her skin, but she knew it wasn't from the smithy. The image of Barrow's torso etched into her mind. The contours of his body could have been carved from stone. The dark scar slashing across his flesh reminded Ember that this was a man before her, built of muscle, bone, and blood. Her fingers twitched, full of the desire to trace the deep crimson line and linger on his skin. The vivid thoughts startled Ember and she pulled her gaze off him.

"I will never lie to you, Ember." He didn't wait for her to answer, but she heard the rustle of fabric as he quickly dressed again. She handed over his sword belt but remained quiet, her mind awash with questions. His words made her blush as much as the memory of his bare chest.

"No two visions are the same. The weapons are crafted precisely for the one who will wield them." Barrow buckled the belt low on his hips. "We'll see what Morag has for you tomorrow. But it's not only a weapon that you'll need."

She tilted her head, watching him curiously.

His smile broadened. "Come with me, lass."

NINE

AS THEY CROSSED the courtyard, passing the manor and moving in the direction of the barracks, Ember struggled with Barrow's taciturn manner. Would it be so difficult to simply explain to her where they were going and what the shape of her day would be? Making it worse, the tall knight seemed to take some perverse delight in watching her puzzle over her new life. She was beginning to look forward to the opportunity to spar with him, no matter how much of a novice she'd be on the training field. Giving Barrow one good knock with a mace would be worth it.

Ember was playing out this imagined confrontation, in which she managed to kick Barrow in the chest and send him sprawling, when the real Barrow's voice intruded on her musing.

"We're not going to the barracks, Ember."

She hadn't noticed that he'd abruptly changed direction, walking away from the barracks' entrance toward the far end of the courtyard. Her blood went icy when she realized he was heading toward the practice fields where she'd spotted him sparring with Kael. Her daydream took a wicked turn, where suddenly she imagined Barrow drawing his sword and smiling cruelly at her.

"Be careful what you wish for." He raised the wickedly curved blade.

"Ember!" Barrow was suddenly standing in front of her, both of his hands resting on her shoulders.

She shook her head. "I'm sorry."

"Is your brain still addled by Morag's incense?" He searched her face with concern. "If you need water or rest, you must tell me."

"No." She pulled out of his grip. "I'm fine. Lead on."

His eyes were doubtful, and Ember swore silently that she'd keep her overactive mind in check.

"Very well." He took her past the barracks but bypassed the practice fields as well, to which Ember's emotions had a lurching reaction of disappointment edged with relief.

"Ho, Barrow!" A lanky boy was waving at her companion. The boy set aside his pitchfork and came to meet them.

"Well met, Ian." Barrow clapped him on the shoulder. "How's their mood this morning?"

Ian laughed. "Restless. The spring air puts the spark of life in 'em like nothing else."

"Glad to hear it," Barrow said. He gestured to Ember. "Ian, this is Lady Morrow. She's just joined our ranks."

Ian gave her a lopsided grin. "So I've heard. Welcome, my lady."

"Ian is apprenticed to the master of the stables," Barrow told her. "Which means he's here day and night, should you need anything."

"It's true that I'm a slave to these beasts." Ian bowed his head, but Ember saw him grinning.

"These beasts are better than most men." Barrow laughed.

"That they are," Ian said. "That they are."

Barrow led Ember into the stable while Ian returned to forking through a mound of hay. The stables were spacious and airy. Sweet and musty scents mingled in each breath Ember drew. As they walked the wide path between the stalls, snorts and whickers sounded. Heads stretched over the stall doors and large eyes kept watch over them. A sudden banging against wood accompanied by a bellow made Ember jump.

The bellow came again.

"I see you, Toshach," Barrow called. "Have patience."

Ember saw a finely shaped head with ears flicking back and forth reaching over the barrier. The animal resembled a living shadow. In the dim light of the stable its black coat revealed a violet undertone. The horse tossed its mane and snorted, fixing them with a startlingly intelligent gaze.

Barrow glanced at her. "I suppose introductions are in order."

Ember followed him to where the horse continued to bow its strong neck, straining to be free of its confines.

"Easy." Barrow went to the horse confidently. The dark creature blew into Barrow's outstretched hand and bent forward when the knight reached up to scratch behind the horse's ears.

"Ember, meet a dear friend," Barrow said. "He's called Toshach."

She edged forward, looking up at the horse's large head. "He's yours?"

At the sound of her voice, Toshach abandoned the bliss of having his ears scratched and snorted. The giant head moved toward her. Ember turned up her palms and let the horse take in her scent. He mouthed at her fingers playfully and then tossed his head, not finding a treat hidden for him within her grasp.

Barrow nodded his approval. "He likes you. And to answer your question, I could hardly call a creature with this one's spirit mine. But we fight together. I owe him my life many times over."

Ember watched as Barrow returned to greeting the horse. Having satisfied his curiosity over who this new visitor was, Toshach gave his full attention to the knight, pressing his huge head against Barrow's shoulder. The horse banged against the stall door again.

"All in good time, my friend." Barrow laughed. "We must find Ember a suitable mount first."

Ember's heart seemed to flip in her chest. Of course she'd expected she'd ride, but she'd never had a horse of her own. Her sister, Agnes, was afraid of horses, and Ember had endured the effects of that fear by spending far too much time in carriages that kept Agnes at a distance from the huge beasts.

"Take a walk to the far end of the stables," Barrow said, nodding toward the long stall-lined building she had yet to explore. "All the claimed horses are here, but those without riders have stalls in the back of the building. I'll find you shortly."

"What am I supposed to do?" she asked.

Barrow's attention was focused on Toshach, who had made a game of trying to steal the knight's cloak.

He didn't look at her when he said, "It will become clear to you as it happens."

Ember almost stomped her foot as she turned to walk away from her teacher, but she knew it wouldn't do any good. Barrow's idea of instruction apparently pivoted on frustrating her and forcing her to figure everything out for herself. Stewing in her own temper, she was vaguely aware of horses watching her as she moved down the long hall, feeling aimless. Perhaps she'd be better off finding Ian and asking him what she was supposed to do. She was about to turn around to seek out the stable hand when a brief, high-pitched whinny sounded so close it made Ember trip over her own feet.

Regaining her balance, Ember whirled to see liquid brown eyes fixed on her. The horse's gaze was sharp and bright; its head was tilted and bobbed as it watched her. The horse snorted and chomped its teeth. Ember couldn't shake the sense that it was laughing at her.

With her hands on her hips, Ember faced the horse.

"You think it's funny to frighten someone?" she asked, somewhat surprised she was speaking to the horse. "What if I'd fallen?"

The horse flicked its ears at her and suddenly bowed its head. Ember laughed, taking a few steps toward it. The horse glanced at her, then made a deeper bow, straining down over the door of its stall. When Ember was close enough, the horse blew out a long breath, pushing its velvet-soft nose against the back of her hand.

"Very well," Ember said, and began to stroke the horse's nose. "You're forgiven."

The horse lifted its head and looked directly into her eyes. Its coat had been groomed to a burnished gleam, an ocher that resembled Ember's own fiery tresses. The horse had no markings that she could see, just this rich shade, deep as a sunset, coloring the beast from head to tail.

"You're a lovely one, eh?" she whispered, taking the horse's face between her hands. The horse stood very still, happily accepting Ember's light fingers on its nose, ears, and neck. "Do you have a name?"

"It's Caber."

Ember jumped back at the sound of Barrow's voice. He'd approached quietly, not drawing her notice. Now he was watching her, a look of surprise and interest playing over his face.

A sharp snort drew Ember's gaze back to the horse. Caber glared at Barrow for a moment and then threw a pleading look at Ember. Without thinking, Ember went to the horse and resumed stroking its soft nose. Caber whickered his pleasure, sparing Barrow a stern glance before pressing his head against Ember.

She sensed when Barrow moved beside her but kept her gaze on Caber. A low sound came from Barrow's throat, followed by words:

"I wasn't expecting this."

"Is something wrong?" Ember looked at him, and Caber snorted.

Barrow shook his head, smiling at the horse. "Don't worry, boy, I'm not going to take her from you."

He looked at Ember. "How much experience do you have with horses?"

Though she briefly considered lying, Ember said, "Very little."

"I thought as much." He reached out to touch Caber's bowed

neck. Ember winced at his easy dismissal of her skills as a horseman. "Though I'm sure through no fault of your own."

"My sister fears horses," Ember said. "And my father thought it best to keep both of his daughters away from the stables."

"Foolish that." Barrow snorted, sounding very much like Toshach when he did so. "Horses can help a man when little else will save him."

Caber nosed Ember's shoulder, then decided to chew on the braid that ringed her head.

"Stop that!" Ember jerked her head back and swatted Caber's nose. The horse snorted and backed away, but a moment later he was inching back toward her, head bowed in apology again.

"Good," Barrow said, watching as she let the horse make his apology and then began to pet him again. "You'll have to be firm with him. Caber's young and a stallion. He doesn't have a rider because his temper makes him difficult to handle. And he's thrown not a few young men who thought themselves better riders than they were. If you don't pay attention, he'll have you halfway to England before you tug on the reins."

Ember's hands dropped from the horse's neck and Caber whinnied in protest.

"You're giving me a stallion?" she asked. Caber was beautiful and she was drawn to the horse, but it seemed foolish to pick a horse beyond her skill.

"I'm not giving you anything. The horse chooses its rider," Barrow said. "Any other way and you'll find an ill fit. Caber wishes to serve you. He's a good horse—but very spirited."

"He's incredible," Ember said. "I'm just not certain I can—"

"You'll learn." Barrow cut her off and moved to open the stall door. "Starting now."

TEN

EMBER HAD TO CHIDE CABER several times as she led the stallion from the stable. Eager to be free of his stall, Caber was skittish, tossing his head and nearly treading on her heels. Barrow kept a close eye on the way she interacted with the horse, never interfering, but Ember sensed that he was wary of her losing control of the large animal and ready to jump in should she need his aid. Ember was determined not to let that happen.

They encountered Ian in the paddock. The young apprentice gave a low whistle when he saw Ember leading Caber but offered no further comment.

Barrow went back for Toshach, reappearing a few minutes later with the glossy black steed. The stallion danced from side to side like a roiling thundercloud ready to burst into storm.

Ember watched the two horses snort and paw at the earth, impatient to be on their way. They were an exquisite pair: Caber bright as the sunrise, Toshach darker than the night sky. Yet the longer she looked, Ember realized the horses weren't what she'd expected.

Ian noticed her frown. "Is something wrong, my lady?"

Though she didn't mean for her words to be critical, Ember still felt nervous when she said, "They aren't warhorses."

"I assure you they do not fail in combat." The furrow in Ian's brow made Ember regret speaking up.

"She only means they aren't the elephants her father uses in tournaments," Barrow told Ian.

Ember laughed, thinking of how her father would react to having his prize steeds described as elephants, and quickly nodded. "They're more beautiful than any horses I've laid eyes on."

Her gaze traveled over the sleek, gleaming bodies of the stallions. Their curving necks stretched perfectly into strong backs and hard flanks. Their firm, slender legs tapered to almost delicate-looking ankles. The horses struck her as simply too lovely, too graceful for war.

Taking full advantage of her admiration, Caber tossed his proud head and whinnied.

"Careful, Ember. That horse already thinks well enough of himself as it is."

She smiled, patting Caber's neck.

"We don't fight in heavy armor," Barrow continued. "And our tasks require speed and agility over strength. These coursers better serve our purpose than a destrier could."

Ian took hold of Toshach while Barrow retrieved the horses' tack. Despite his feisty mood, Ember was managing Caber rather well. Her pleasure at that small triumph drained away when she encountered the next challenge. Abashed, she admitted to Barrow that she had no idea how to prepare the horse for her first ride.

Ian offered to saddle and bridle Caber, but Barrow waved him away.

"This horse is your responsibility," the knight told her. "There will be no one to help you when we're in the field."

Barrow was patient as he taught her how to properly tack up the stallion. He tested the girth, reminding her that it would loosen when bearing her weight. When she'd finished saddling the horse, Barrow made her take the equipment off and start over again: this time without his instruction. Caber craned his neck to watch them, his ears flicking in curiosity as his saddle was placed on his back only to be removed and placed again. When she'd gone through the process five times and was cursing her teacher under her breath, Barrow pronounced her ready for an actual ride. He turned around only to find that Ian had saddled Toshach during the lesson.

"He would have run off without you if I hadn't kept him busy." Ian handed Barrow the reins.

Ember hoisted herself into the saddle, settling on Caber's back. The stallion began to move immediately, sidestepping and tossing his head.

"Don't let him forget you're there," Barrow said. "And keep him in check. He'll bolt right out from under you if you let him."

Ember nodded, gritting her teeth as she shortened her reins. She could feel the stallion's power, churning like white water beneath her.

"Are you ready?" Barrow was astride Toshach. The black stallion pranced incessantly, lifting his front legs as though he wanted to rear.

"Yes." Though her heart was flying, Ember's smile stretched wide. Caber's excitement, his energy, seemed to flow into her very limbs.

Barrow returned her smile. In the quick flash of teeth Ember understood that it wasn't just the horses that longed to race from Tearmunn. On the back of his steed Barrow moved with supreme grace. Even with Toshach's fitful prancing, horse and rider flowed together. With a motion she could barely detect, Barrow started Toshach forward at a trot. Caber kept pace beside the other stallion while Ember maintained a firm grasp on the reins. Barrow was holding Toshach back as well. Both horses wanted to run.

"Hold up!" The call came from near the barracks. Barrow reined Toshach with a sign, wheeling the horse around. With a snort of protest, Caber relented as Ember turned him.

Alistair waved and Kael shouted, "Why did you put the poor girl on that demon? Are you trying to kill her?"

Barrow shook his head. "Ignore him. He was kicked and had a

broken rib as a result, but it was his own foolishness, not Caber, that led to the kicking."

Ember half smiled, knowing Caber could have bitten someone's finger off and she'd still feel lucky to ride him.

"We thought you two might be interested in seeing some more action," Kael said. "The real kind."

"There's a problem in Cornwall," Alistair said. "We're leaving now."

Ember tightened her grip on the reins. "When will you return?" As much as she was adjusting quickly to her new home, the thought of the only familiar face being long absent unnerved her.

Kael shrugged. "Depends on what we're dealing with. But if all goes well, before dinner."

Ember stared at him. She must have heard wrong—a journey to Cornwall would take days, not hours.

"Thanks for the offer," Barrow said. "But she's not ready."

Ember winced at his curt answer.

"That's not what the sisters say," Kael told him. "They said she's a natural. They were watching the trial."

"She has talent," Barrow replied. "But we'll be in the field soon enough. Today we'll ride."

"You and your horses." Kael snorted. He turned falsely mournful eyes on Alistair. "I'm afraid we've been cruelly rebuffed."

"And my heart aches because of it." Alistair winked at Ember.

"Save your laments for the south." Barrow was already turning Toshach around. "At least Cornwall will be warm."

Alistair held her gaze for a moment longer. "I'll see you tonight, Ember."

"But you're going to Cornwall," she said, and then felt a bit dizzy when she remembered Morag's description of the magic wielded by Conatus's clerics. Would Alistair and Kael truly be in Cornwall and return in the same day?

"And I'm sorry you're not coming," he said. "Barrow's right. The weather will be much more pleasant in the south."

"Ember!" She turned in the saddle to see Barrow waiting for her, Toshach dancing beneath him.

When she looked back, Alistair was walking away, waving to her. She lifted her hand briefly before reining Caber in the opposite direction.

Her mind was more agitated than Caber, but Barrow wasn't in a talking mood. As soon as she reached him, he set out at a faster pace. The swift trot took them across the courtyard and out of Tearmunn's gates. The horses easily mastered the steep path from the keep into Glen Shiel. Ember could feel the tension in Caber's muscles. The quick, steady pace of their trot was irritating him.

"When we hit the valley floor, we'll follow the river to Loch Duich," Barrow said. "They'll want to open up, but I'm keeping it to a canter for now. Don't give Caber his head."

Ember nodded and Barrow urged Toshach forward. The black stallion leapt ahead, shaking the reins when Barrow kept him from reaching a full gallop. Caber rolled into a canter, keeping close to Toshach. Ember felt Caber champing at the bit, wanting to get control away from her. His ears were up, turned toward her, and she knew the horse was testing her, wondering if his rider matched him in cleverness and skill. She kept a firm hold on the reins, letting her body flow with the easy rocking of Caber's gait. The stallion snorted a few times, shaking his head, rolling his eyes back, but soon he seemed to settle into contentment as they loped alongside the river. Barrow turned to look at her, smiling when he saw her keeping pace just behind Toshach. He gave Toshach a bit more rein and the dark stallion surged ahead, the canter giving way to a gallop.

Caber tried to burst into a flat run, but Ember held him back. Though he snorted and tugged at the reins, she forced him to speed up gradually. Only when she was sure he was acting with her assent did Ember free the stallion to fly after Toshach.

Barrow glanced back again and Ember offered him a thin smile. It wasn't only her mount testing her; her teacher was too. She leaned forward, letting Caber race ahead to close the distance between them. When Caber was neck and neck with Toshach, eager to leap ahead, Ember reined him in, working to keep perfect pace, stride for stride with Barrow's mount.

They rode that way for half an hour. Barrow would make subtle changes in speed followed by sudden shifts in their pace. Each time Ember adjusted accordingly, never letting Barrow catch her off guard. She was becoming appreciative of Caber's sensibilities. He was sensitive to her mood; his ears were always turned toward her, waiting for a whispered word of encouragement, a click of her tongue urging speed. And she was constantly aware of him. She understood when he wanted to run, the difference between a toss of the head that was frustrated and one that was joyful. She knew to stroke his neck to praise him and the firm tone needed to hold his attention.

When they reached the shores of Loch Duich, Barrow reined Toshach in, bringing them to a trot and then to a walk. Having had their run, the horses were happy enough to take up an easy pace along the lake.

"It seems fighting isn't the only thing you have a natural talent for," Barrow said.

"Thank you." Ember spoke briefly, not wanting to reveal how breathless she was. The ride had been exhilarating, but also hard work. The muscles in her arms, back, and thighs were tight coils, hot and strained from the effort of this riding lesson. Still, proving herself to Barrow had been worth it. And the thrill of riding itself was something she never could have anticipated.

Ember leaned over, resting her cheek against Caber's mane.

"You're a good match." Barrow paused to let the horses drink from the lake.

Ember loosened the reins so Caber could reach the water. "We are." She patted his neck, finding it damp from the run.

The sky above was heavy with clouds. Streams of mist reached down, finger-like, to grasp the hillsides, which had just begun to glow with the green of spring.

"The loch borders Tearmunn to the west and north. The hills of the glen guard us from the east and south. You'll have passed the village on your journey to the keep," Barrow said.

"I couldn't see anything." Ember's face scrunched up at the memory. "I was with my mother and sister in the carriage."

Barrow looked like he wanted to laugh, but he continued: "The village sits below Tearmunn on the northeastern shore of the loch. They supply us with livestock and trade goods in exchange for our protection."

"Do they know about Conatus . . . why it exists?" Ember turned in the saddle, squinting to see the cluster of buildings squatting on the valley floor to the north.

"No," Barrow told her. "They believe us to be knights of a normal variety. The fewer that know our true purpose, the safer we are. If you make visits to the village, it cannot be as a member of the Guard. The sight of a woman dressed as you are would stir suspicion. If you want to travel there, we can make arrangements."

He patted Toshach's shoulder. "We'll take rides out of the keep so you can gain the skills required for battle astride a horse, but we'll also ride so you'll come to know the land. This is your home now."

Wind lashed Ember's cheeks as she gazed over the rough, gray waters of the lake. She turned, searching the landscape behind her and finding jagged hills. Some were covered in pine; others were bare but would soon blush with heather. Tearmunn lay nestled in a place both severe and beautiful. A gust of wind made the surface of the lake shiver, and Ember thought she heard a cry carried on the cold air.

Without a command from Barrow, Toshach raised his head and began to move on.

"Barrow!" Ember had turned in her saddle. The sound of the cry was closer now. She peered along the shoreline, seeking the source of the keening. A small figure hurtled toward them, flailing its arms.

He reined in, brows lifting in question.

"Look!" She pointed at the runner.

"A villager?" Barrow wheeled Toshach around. His voice grew soft in a way that made Ember's breath catch. "A child."

He gave a shout and Toshach reared, striking the air with his hooves. Then they were away, gliding beside the lake. Without the splashes of water thrown up by the stallion, Ember might have believed Toshach's hooves weren't touching the ground at all.

Caber threw his head up, prancing in a circle. With a whisper Ember let him run. Caber tore up the ground, flying over the shore. The wind screamed around Ember, pulling tears from her eyes. But she laughed as her heart matched the rhythm of Caber's pounding hooves.

Though she couldn't imagine being anything but terrified of two riders bearing down at full gallop, when the child saw that they were coming, he ran even faster. As they drew close, Ember saw that the small boy was about six or seven. He was still waving his hands, and dark liquid spurted into the air with the motion.

They were almost on top of the boy when Barrow reined Toshach in. The knight leapt from the saddle and ran to the boy. Caber snorted and pranced, making it awkward for Ember to dismount. She stumbled away from the horse and found Barrow kneeling in front of the child. He was holding the boy's left wrist in his hand. The child had a bloody knife clutched in his other hand. Barrow examined the boy's left hand, and Ember's stomach lurched when she saw blood pouring from two stumps where his ring finger and pinky had been.

"It took them! It took them!" The boy's cries were ragged. "They're drowned!"

"What's your name, child?" Barrow asked gently, then glanced at Ember. "There are bands of clean linen in my saddlebags. Get some so we can bind this wound."

"Gordon," Ember heard the boy say as she rifled through the pack strapped to Toshach's saddle. Both the horses were restless, moving skittishly on the shore, their ears up and swiveling as if straining to hear approaching danger.

"That's a strong name for a strong lad," Barrow told the child. "And you must be strong, for you've been fighting. Is that not so?"

"You're one of them, aren't you?" Gordon's eyes were wide as he looked at Barrow. "One of the knights from the keep. My da says you protect us."

"Your da told you the truth," Barrow answered. "Tell me what happened."

Gordon wailed and Barrow murmured in a voice too low for Ember to hear, but a moment later the child's cries quieted.

Ember returned to them with the bands of linen.

"Who did this to you?" she asked Gordon.

Gordon blanched, his eyes sweeping the rough water. "I had to. It took them. It would have taken me."

Frowning, Ember reached for the boy's wounded hand. Gordon sucked in his breath but didn't cry out as she began to bind his wound.

"You cut off your fingers," Barrow said hoarsely, and the boy nodded.

Bile rose in Ember's throat. "Why would you do that?"

"I had to!" Tears ran down Gordon's pale cheeks.

"Did the beast come from the loch?" Barrow asked.

Ember looked at him sharply. *What beast?*

Gordon sniffled. "We didn't know. We didn't see it come out of the water. Mackie thought it was a loose horse and we'd get a reward if we brought it back to the village. But it was a kelpie!"

Barrow gritted his teeth, swearing. "How many of your friends did it take?"

"Mackie and John," Gordon sobbed. "They couldn't get their knives out it time. It took them under and I ran away."

"You did the right thing, Gordon," Barrow said. "You were clever and brave."

"Clever and brave?" Ember wanted to shove Barrow into the loch. Why was he going on about bravery when this child was bleeding all over the shore?

Barrow cut a sharp look at her, making her bite her tongue. "The children were hunted by a water horse. It's a bad omen that one would prey on a village neighboring Tearmunn. It's as if the darkness wanted to taunt us."

"A water horse?" Ember shivered, glancing at the gray waters of the loch. "But they . . ." She'd been about to say that water horses only existed in stories meant to keep children from playing too close to lakes and rivers, but her mind choked off her words. She couldn't cling to the beliefs that had shaped her life prior to arriving at Tearmunn. She'd already faced a revenant. If Barrow said water horses were real, she had no choice but to believe him.

She crouched beside Gordon. "Why did you cut yourself?"

Even through his tears, Gordon eyed her as if she were a fool. "Everyone knows that once you touch a kelpie, you stick to it. That's why the others drowned. They didn't remember their knives."

"As I told you," Barrow said. "You're a clever lad and a brave one. I'll need you to be brave again. Can you do that?"

Gordon looked into Barrow's face and nodded.

"The kelpie will be angry that you escaped," Barrow continued. "It will want to hunt you. If it comes for you, we can kill it and your village will be out of danger."

Ember's brow knit together. "You aren't seriously going to use Gordon as bait?"

Barrow stood up and took her by the shoulders. "You are here to watch and learn. We have no choice but to lure the creature with Gordon's blood. If we don't, it will carry more villagers to their deaths beneath the waves."

Gordon was eyeing Barrow's saber. "You'll kill it with that?" He pointed to the sword.

"I will." Barrow smiled grimly. He turned to Ember. "I need you to hold the horses—they'll want to bolt when the kelpie comes, and we need them to get us home."

Ember glared at him. "You don't think I can fight."

"You're a fine fighter, Lady Morrow," Barrow snapped. "You're also impetuous and bullheaded. You don't have proper training or a weapon."

"I have my dagger," she argued.

"Stay with the horses," Barrow said grimly. "I'll not tell you again."

She swallowed her next retort but stomped back to the horses, who were tossing their heads and whinnying their anxiety. Taking the reins firmly, Ember watched as Barrow led Gordon to the water's edge. Her blood went cold when Barrow unwrapped the bloodied linens from the boy's hand. Gordon stretched his arm out over the water and his blood spilled into the lake.

Holding her breath, Ember watched the surface of the loch, which despite the blustery gale had gone eerily still. Gordon was also standing perfectly still while Barrow crouched behind a boulder on the loch's edge. Barrow was right. The boy was incredibly brave.

A movement in the water drew Ember's gaze. The ripple was subtle, but slowly it stretched out over the gray surface like a dark ribbon unfurling. The shadow moved swiftly toward the shore, its shape undulating like that of a serpent.

Toshach and Caber whinnied, fighting to pull free. Ember held them in check, trying to soothe them. The creature's head broke the surface of the water. At first it appeared to be reptilian, like she'd pictured a dragon, but as it rose, dripping, its features changed. What had been serpent-like became equine. Gordon began to tremble but didn't flee as a black horse with a coat that shone like sealskin stood facing the boy in the shallows of the loch.

The real horses panicked. They began to squeal and dragged Ember back several steps. She fought to keep hold of the reins. The water horse turned its head to gaze at the frightened mounts. Its eyes were like burning coals. Ember gasped when she saw two pale objects hanging from its dark mane. Gordon's severed fingers were still clinging to the kelpie.

With the beast's attention turned to Toshach and Caber, Barrow hurled himself atop the boulder and leapt from the rock. The kelpie, sensing danger, wheeled to face the flying knight. When it pranced, the loch's water frothed around its legs. The water horse reared, but Barrow's saber was already slicing down. The curved blade passed through the kelpie's neck as if it were made of air. Barrow crashed into the water, rolling over and finding his feet again. He whirled to face the beast once more.

Ember gasped when the kelpie struck out with its hooves. Wicked hooked talons protruded from its slime-covered legs. Barrow jumped back, but not quickly enough. The kelpie's claws tore through his tabard and shirt, slicing into his abdomen.

Large flaps of cloth dropped to the beach, leaving his flesh exposed, and Ember cried out at the sight of blood pouring out of his skin.

"Keep the child safe!" he shouted, not looking at them.

Though she knew he wanted her to stay away, Ember couldn't stand by while Barrow fought. Her blood drummed in her veins, its beat spurring her to act.

"Stay back and stay quiet," Ember told the boy, pushing him

behind her. As Barrow continued to dodge the water horse's attack, Ember drew her dagger. Taking aim, she hurled the blade at the kelpie with all the force she could muster.

The creature screeched when the dagger buried itself in the dark hide of its flank. It whirled to face the new attacker, giving Barrow the opportunity to strike. He pivoted, bringing his saber down in a broad arc.

For a moment Ember thought the kelpie had transformed itself into a spirit as a means of defense, that Barrow's blade had only cut through air and not flesh. But the water horse didn't turn on him. Its head tipped forward, cleanly severed from its neck, and fell to the water with a splash. A moment later the kelpie's body crumbled, becoming a heap of seaweed and foam on the shore.

Gordon gave a whoop and ran over to Barrow. "You did it!"

Barrow nodded, laughing when the boy threw his arms around the knight's broad shoulders. "Without your help I would surely have failed. Yours and the lady Morrow's."

The look he gave her was stern. "I asked you to keep out of the fight."

Ember set her shoulders, defiant. "You're wounded. I thought I could help and I did."

"Yes, you did," Barrow said, wincing as he touched the gashes in his abdomen. The torn flesh wrapped around his lower back like a wicked girdle. "I'm indebted to you for ignoring my order. Though I'd prefer you didn't make a habit of that."

Ember laughed, but her smile faded when Barrow dropped roughly onto the stone-covered shore.

"How badly are you hurt?" she asked, kneeling beside him.

"The wound isn't deep," he told her. "But water horses have venomous claws."

Ember's mouth went dry.

Seeing her distress, Barrow smiled wryly. "Don't mourn me yet.

There's a salve in Toshach's saddlebag that will stop the spread of the poison. I'll need you to get it. The linen bag tied with blue ribbon."

Ember ran to Toshach and rifled through the saddlebag. She was surprised at the number of parcels Barrow carried with him. Was there a remedy for every injury here? And who had made them?

She found the linen bag and returned to Barrow's side. He was using his shredded shirt to stop the blood flow.

"Take the jar out and rub the salve into the wound when I take away this cloth."

Ember nodded; her heart had climbed into her throat, making it impossible to speak.

She was vaguely aware of Gordon perched beside her, watching with fascination as she pulled the clay jar from the bag, opened it, and scooped out a mixture that looked like yellow clay but made her fingertips tingle.

"Do it now." Barrow removed the tattered cloth and bright red blood seeped down his skin. He drew a sharp breath when she began to spread the salve over the gashes.

"I'm sorry," she whispered.

"Don't be. It has to penetrate the wound, so you mustn't worry about hurting me." He was propped on his elbows, watching as she scooped more salve from the jar.

Her fingers moved over his abdomen, running across hard muscle between the claw marks. Her pulse jumped wildly each time she touched him, especially when her hand brushed over the depression close to his hip where his skin disappeared beneath the fabric of his trousers.

Suddenly his hand was over hers, pulling it away.

"That's enough." His voice was rough, and he wouldn't meet her eyes. "Thank you."

He stood up and bound the wound with the remnants of his shirt and tabard.

Without looking at Ember, he said to Gordon, "And now it's time to get you home."

He wrapped the boy's hand in the linen bandages once more.

"I have to take him to the village," he said, finally returning her puzzled gaze. "Ride to Tearmunn and tell them to send a cleric to meet me. They'll want to question him further."

"I could ride with you," she protested.

"The villagers can't see you like this." His eyes traveled over her garb. "It will raise suspicion."

"But—" She gave Gordon a pointed glance.

"He won't say anything," Barrow assured her, taking Toshach's reins from her hand. He lifted Gordon onto Toshach's back and then swung into the saddle behind the boy. "I'll speak to you again soon. Tomorrow we'll begin your training in earnest."

Without bidding her farewell, Barrow nudged Toshach into a trot.

As they rode away, she heard Gordon's excited voice. "Can I be a knight too?"

Ember mounted Caber and turned the stallion toward Tearmunn, cursing Barrow's orders under her breath. With bitterness lingering on her tongue, she glanced at the pile of seaweed and foam. A glint of silver caught her eye. Her dagger. She jumped down to retrieve the weapon.

Hadn't she been quick in thought and deed, coming to Barrow's aid when he needed her most? Ember thought as she cleaned the blade of debris. She couldn't help but feel that he'd been eager to get away from her. That he'd been repulsed by her touch.

Ember sheathed her dagger, mounted, and put her heels to Caber's sides. As the horse leapt into a gallop, she swore she would yet prove her worthiness not just to Barrow but to all of Conatus.

ELEVEN

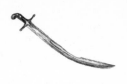

DUSK CHASED THE TWO riders as they rode through the gates of Tearmunn. Eira rested her fingertips against the window, watching as the horses passed beneath her.

"We made the right decision," she murmured. "We should never bend to the will of the nobles."

Cian crossed the room and peered over her sister's shoulder. "Is that Barrow?"

"And one of the clerics," Eira said. "Barrow took Lady Morrow out riding today. And word came from the village that they saved a child from a water horse. A cleric went to interrogate the boy after Ember returned to the keep."

"A kelpie in Loch Duich?" Cian frowned. "That's troubling. And must have been quite the surprise for Ember on her first day out."

"She looks no worse for it." Eira smiled. "I spoke with her in the barracks this afternoon. I daresay she seems happier. The girl holds much promise."

"That's not surprising. How happy were we after our first fight? I remember thinking I was like a daughter of the Morrigan. Immortal and invincible." Cian turned away, moving to a table covered in scrolls. "Have you looked through these?"

Eira didn't take her eyes off the courtyard. "Yes."

"What do you make of the reports?" Cian looked at her sister, but Eira continued to gaze out the window. "Eira?"

"It's as we suspected," Eira said. "Something is amiss in our realm. Reports from the German principalities are particularly disturbing. Why the sudden rise in incidents?"

Cian picked up a scroll, carefully unrolling it. "We should send an advance patrol to the Black Forest. Perhaps they'll uncover some answers."

Eira was smiling when she faced her sister. "Make sure she goes with them."

"The lady Morrow?" Cian frowned. "She hasn't even received her weapon yet. We can't send her into the field."

"She must go," Eira told her.

"Why?" Cian asked.

Eira crossed the space between them, taking her sister's hands. "That girl is the key to our future. If she has the skill I believe she does, she'll preserve our legacy among the Guard. If we don't ensure it, the abbot will do his best to keep women from serving as knights."

Cian sighed. "But she could fail . . . or worse. We don't know what's causing these disturbances. We can't send her blind against her foes."

"You saw how quickly she dealt with the revenant," Eira said. "Bearing no training, she excelled in the trial. She possesses strength of body and spirit and a quick mind. The sooner we put her in the field, the better."

Before Cian could protest further, Eira raised her hand.

"I'll speak to Lukasz tonight," Eira told Cian. "If he disagrees with me, I'll let it go."

Cian gritted her teeth but forced herself to nod. Lukasz respected Eira—she'd been the one to bring him from the eastern kingdoms to join their ranks at Tearmunn. No matter what his doubts, he would defer to Eira's preference.

"I won't be at dinner," Eira said. "I want to scout the villages of the glen until dawn. If this darkness is indeed stirring locally, it will only show itself at night."

Cian gripped Eira's hands tight. "Alone? Again?"

"If the darkness is spreading in the east, it will soon reach our shores," Eira said. "I won't be caught unawares. At the first sign that a new evil festers here, we must move against it."

"You're a member of the Circle now," Cian said. "An adviser. Let the Guard patrol as is intended."

"Joining the Circle doesn't remove us from the Guard. We've only earned more work on behalf of Conatus." Eira pulled away from Cian, reaching for her cloak. "The task of patrolling is mine if I choose it. I won't hide behind these walls waiting for the enemy to storm our gates."

Cian's shoulders slumped with the knowledge that she'd never win this argument. "Very well. Don't be reckless. If you do find something, report it to the Circle. Don't try to deal with it alone."

Eira threw a withering glance at her sister, strapping on her sword belt as she left their room.

After her sister was gone, Cian took up Eira's post at the window. Twilight bathed the courtyard in deep indigo. Shadows slid over the group, transforming the familiar shapes of servants into strange, lurking forms. Cian turned from the window with a shudder. Eira was right. Something was coming—something that caused a raw foreboding to settle beneath her ribs. And it was changing things between her and her sister.

When they'd simply been fighting with the Guard, they'd rarely argued. Since they had been appointed to the Circle, the divisions between the two had grown ever wider. While Cian wanted to prepare, to defend, and to preserve Conatus, Eira sometimes acted as though she wanted to rule it. She seemed almost eager for the threat to manifest.

Cian watched her sister's behavior with growing apprehension, sensing that darkness was approaching not only from outside but from within. That this threat was real, Cian had no doubt. The only question was how soon it would be scratching at their door. Or, as she secretly feared, how soon it would reveal where it lay hidden in their midst.

TWELVE

EMBER WAS SURPRISED she could move at all. Her first day as one of the Guard had left her with twisted, throbbing muscles, which now made their objections to the afternoon's abuse known in the form of unceasing aches. And while the time spent on horseback had been thrilling, the moment she'd left the saddle her thighs had gone to quivering mush, leaving her to totter back to her quarters. She forced herself to keep a pleasant manner through dinner.

Even as a novice, Ember could tell the mood in the barracks was somber. Her companions ate quickly, speaking very little. Kael and Alistair hadn't yet returned from their mission. Ember had been eager to tell her friend about the water horse and perhaps gain his sympathy about Barrow's gruffness with her. Her mentor had returned to the keep and joined her at dinner, though he seemed completely oblivious to her sour mood, and when she'd asked Barrow about their absence, he'd laughed.

"Kael is always overly optimistic about how quickly he can complete a mission. They'll be back late tonight. You needn't fear for your friend."

Though she'd wanted to ask more, she straightened up and fell silent when Lukasz loomed over Barrow's shoulder.

"I need to speak with you," the commander said. He nodded a greeting to Ember and then stood, waiting.

Barrow looked at her. "You should seek your bed. You'll rise early tomorrow and it will be a long day."

Ember knew she was being dismissed and didn't dare object. But she bristled with curiosity, wishing she could linger and listen to the warriors' conversation. She bid the men good night and made the slow, shockingly painful climb to her cell on the second floor.

Once cloistered in her cell, she shed her clothing one piece at a time, wincing with each movement. She groaned when she pulled her long nightshirt over her head and stumbled to her pallet. Lying down hurt in a way Ember didn't think was possible. But her body was merciful as it surrendered to pure exhaustion and carried her out of consciousness.

She didn't know how much time had passed when the creak of her cell door caused her to stir. A small sound, the light shuffle of feet on the stone floor, made her breath catch. Something was in her room.

Still half gripped in the haze of sleep, Ember battled against panic. The revenant's gaping mouth and empty eyes haunted her.

What if she hadn't killed it? What if such creatures couldn't be killed? Could it be here now, seeking vengeance for the pain she'd inflicted on it?

A pungent scent filled the room, but it wasn't the stench of rotting flesh that had clung to the revenant. She forced herself to breathe, to wrestle rational thoughts out of fear's grip.

Ember rolled out of bed and was on her feet in an instant. Her aching muscles shrieked their objections, but she held her dagger low. Her threatening stance was met by a familiar laugh.

"Are you really going to gut me, Em?" Alistair asked.

Ember let out her breath and set the dagger aside. "What were you thinking? I could have killed you."

"I didn't know you were sleeping with a dagger under your pillow," he said. "But it's a good idea. You never know."

"Why are you sneaking into my cell at this hour?" Ember sank onto her bed, stretching her sore muscles. The sudden movement of being startled awake had brought on a fresh wave of aches.

"We just returned from our mission." Alistair sat beside her.

"The trip to Cornwall?" Ember said sourly, unconvinced that Kael and Alistair weren't having a joke at her expense.

"That's the one," he said. "Aren't you relieved to see me alive?"

Ember didn't take the bait. "You've been fighting for a year, haven't you? I'm sure you can hold your own."

"I'm so grateful for your faith in me, Lady Morrow." Though seated, he bent over in a mock bow.

"What are you doing here?" Now that she was fully awake, Ember couldn't ignore that her muscles hurt even more than when she'd climbed into bed.

"I know what the first few days with the Guard are like," Alistair said. "I brought you something." Warm tendrils rose from the wooden bowl cupped in his hands.

"What is it?" she asking, taking it from him.

"An elixir infused with willow bark and honey," he said. "It won't take away all of the pain, but it will make the morning much more bearable."

"Thank you." She took a sip of the concoction. Her face scrunched up at the taste, but she drank more. Anything to ease her sore limbs was worth it.

"Of course," he said. "It does get easier. Your body will learn how to meet every demand you make of it."

"I hope my body isn't a slow student." She laughed, wincing as the muscles of her chest and stomach objected.

"Has he been too hard on you?" Alistair asked.

"No," she said. "I'm just soft. It's Father's fault. He cooped me up in his castle to be a lady. Barrow has to remake me into a warrior."

Alistair shifted closer to her. "I still can't believe you're being trained by that brute. They should make an exception for your circumstance."

She set the bowl down and drew away from him. Barrow could be stern, but he was hardly a brute. She'd seen the almost childlike joy on his face when they'd raced along Loch Duich. The only thing she was sure of about Barrow was that she knew very little about the man he was. She wondered if anyone did.

"No," Ember said. "That's the last thing I want. Barrow's exactly the teacher I need. He won't let me be anything less than the warrior I must be if I'm to survive."

"I'm sorry, Em," he said quickly. "I'm only concerned for you. I have no doubts about your skill."

"Thank you."

"And what of your mind?" Alistair asked. "What you've learned today—you're not afraid?"

"Of course I'm afraid," she said. "That the world is full of such terror . . . such evil. But I wouldn't know of the danger and then run from it. What good would that do?"

Alistair touched her cheek. "Such spirit. Had you been born a man, you would have led armies and made other men tremble."

She turned her face away from his hand. "Perhaps I still shall. I'm here, aren't I? And, if memory serves, I'm not the one who needed to be rescued from my test."

Alistair fell silent and Ember cursed her temper.

"Who told you?" he asked. "Was it Barrow?"

"I'm sorry," she murmured. "I'm tired and my mouth makes complaint for my broken body. Please forget what I said."

He laughed softly, though there was a rough edge to the sound. "Anything serious, though? Have you strained a muscle?"

"I don't think so," she said, wishing he would leave so she could let sleep take away her pain.

She jumped when Alistair touched her arm. "Don't be afraid. I just want to make sure you aren't hurt."

Ember tried to relax as Alistair's fingers probed her upper arms, shoulders, and neck. His touch was gentle, but it sent a creeping sensation along her skin.

"I'm fine," she said, trying to pull away. "There's no need for this."

His arm slipped around her waist. "Shhh." His other hand was stroking her cheek.

"Alistair, what are you doing?" Her question came out shaking.

"What we've always wanted," he whispered. Then he turned her in his arms, pressing his mouth against hers.

Panic surged through Ember's limbs. She went rigid against him, but Alistair took no notice. His tongue thrust between her lips.

She shoved him away with a hiss. "Stop!" Despite her shock, she kept her voice low. She had no idea what had gotten into her friend, but she didn't want the rest of the Guard to burst in on them.

"What's wrong?" Alistair tried to pull her against him again.

"Why are you doing this?" She put her hands against his chest, keeping him at bay.

"Don't you see, Em?" Alistair sounded confused and hurt. "We can be together now."

Ember's skin had grown very cold. "We're together in the Guard. We'll fight side by side."

"And at night I'll warm your bed. I'll worship your body." There was a fever in his voice that made Ember's stomach turn.

"No." Ember pushed against him, forcing him to move farther away from her. "Our vows. Father Michael said they're all that protects us from the Church's intrusion. From the fate of the Templars."

"The vows mean nothing." He spit out the words. "Don't you see? We take the vows to pacify the Church and the nobles. They dare not cross us for they too greatly fear the evils we face each day, but they don't know what happens behind these walls. Father Michael keeps our secrets. He understands we are but men. We fight the encroaching darkness and then do as we please."

"You can't be serious," she said.

His laugh was quiet, but horrible. "Are you really such a child? Do you believe men as brutal and hardened as those in the Guard would forgo pleasures of the flesh?"

Now Ember thought she would vomit.

He went on. "They find lovers where they will and when they will. The vows merely protect us."

Ember curled up against the wall. Alistair crawled toward her. His voice became soft, coaxing.

"I'm sorry, Em. I didn't mean to frighten you. I thought you understood. You needn't be afraid. I'm here to protect you."

She didn't answer. She couldn't. How could his words be true? What about Father Michael's warning? Did the Guard simply laugh behind the old priest's back?

Alistair brushed her hair out of her face. "I haven't sought a lover. I waited for you. Not just this year, but all my life. I've always wanted you, Ember. We belong together. You must know that. Fate brought us both to Conatus and to the Guard. How can we deny what was meant to be?"

He started to put his arms around her, but Ember shrank back.

"That isn't why I'm here," she said.

"Em," Alistair began.

"No." She snatched the dagger from the table beside her bed, holding it between their bodies. "I was called to the Guard to be a warrior. Not your concubine."

He glared at the dagger and then at her. "And what of us? You must have known that I've loved you since we were children. You've done nothing to discourage my affections."

"Get out!" Ember stood up, keeping the dagger pointed at him. She was startled and enraged by his claims. Of course they'd been close as children, but Ember hadn't felt anything other than sisterly love for Alistair. She couldn't believe she'd done anything to make him think otherwise.

"Don't do this, Em," Alistair said, though he backed toward the door. He voice went soft again. "Please. Just listen to me."

"Leave me alone." She gripped the dagger so tightly it shook in her hand. "If you value our friendship, you will never speak of this again."

Alistair's shoulders slumped, but he quietly left her room.

Ember wasn't sure how long she stood there. The chill of the room crept up her limbs and the trembling in her hand soon overtook her whole body. She didn't care when the dagger slipped from her grasp, clattering on the stone floor.

THIRTEEN

THE MORNING WASN'T as torturous as she'd expected. Ember glanced at the empty bowl of tea on her table, wincing from guilt at the reminder of Alistair's thoughtful gesture. Guilt was chased away by frustration and then rage as she remembered how free he'd been with his hands. The crush of his mouth on hers had bruised her lips. How could he make such presumptions about her feelings?

In all their years together he'd never tried to push their relationship beyond friendship, except to concoct ridiculous plans about eloping with her. She turned his words over in her mind.

We can be together now. What we've always wanted.

Though she wished it weren't so, Ember couldn't claim he'd never raised this idea before. He'd constantly sworn his affection for her. Jested that they should be married. Had his teasing masked the true desires of his heart?

Her chest tightened. Perhaps she'd been too hard on him. Alistair had been so loyal, so dear to her. If he did love her as he'd claimed, then her words must have battered his heart. Ember's sigh was long, full of the weariness of her body and spirit. She would try to mend anything broken between herself and Alistair, but she had to do so in a way that didn't encourage him. She loved Alistair, but as a brother, not as a lover.

Much to her relief, and surprise, only Barrow was waiting for her in the barracks' main hall. She sat beside him, happily accepting the bowl of steaming porridge he pushed in front of her.

"Where is everyone?" she asked.

Barrow leaned back in his chair; lines of concern appeared at the corners of his eyes. "Lukasz called a meeting. There's been some news."

Ember put her spoon down. "Shouldn't we be there as well?"

"He discussed the matter with me last night," he said. "We have other work to focus on today."

She returned to eating, her poor mood worsening at the lack of inclusion. Despite the praise she'd received after her trial, Ember still felt like an outsider, like she was being kept away from the real purpose of the Guard. She took a few more bites of the porridge and set her spoon down again. When she rose, Barrow frowned.

"You've barely eaten."

"I'm not hungry this morning," she said.

He studied her face. "Are you ill?"

"No." She avoided meeting his eyes. "Just eager to begin the day."

Barrow stood up and servants appeared to clear the table. "If I know Morag, she'll have worked nonstop to have your weapon ready. We'll head to the smithy first."

Ember didn't answer but simply followed Barrow out of the barracks. She felt restless, battered by her fitful night after Alistair's appearance and her deepening uncertainty about her place in Conatus. Too many questions left unanswered, too many secrets whispered behind closed doors.

When they stepped into the courtyard, Ember looked over her shoulder, her gaze wandering toward the stables.

She turned back with a sigh, only to find Barrow watching her with a knowing smile. "I won't keep him from you long."

Ember returned his smile stiffly. She was too unsettled to seek a bond with the knight over their shared love of riding. The one person she'd fully trusted here had been scheming, manipulating her path to serve his own desires. Alistair's confession—no matter how well intentioned—only felt like a betrayal. It stung in her chest and made her bristle against any friendliness Barrow showed.

Though the sun had risen only a short while ago, the smithy was already alive with its craft. Barrow led Ember, stopping only when he'd reached Morag's forge. The blacksmith was stoking the fire.

She greeted Barrow without looking up. "Good morning, my lord."

"Morag." Barrow leaned against the workbench. "Do you have something for us?"

Morag straightened with a smile. "Nothing for you, but something for the lady."

Ember sidled past Barrow, curiosity edging out her ill temper. What could have manifested from her strange visions of a double moon?

From a lower shelf of her workbench Morag withdrew two leather objects.

"It's a good thing I apprenticed for two years with a Chinese blade master," the blacksmith said as she gripped a leather-wrapped handle. From within the slipcover appeared a weapon like none Ember had ever seen. Morag extended the strange piece to her. Her fingers closed around the handle and she held the weapon up to examine it. Connected to the handgrip was a bright silver ring, a perfectly circular blade with a diameter slightly wider than her face. A crescent blade with sharp, gleaming points projected from the leather grip into the center of the ring.

"Two moons," Ember whispered. The weapon was light in her hand. She moved her arm up and down slowly, marveling at how natural it felt to hold something so foreign to her.

Barrow stepped closer. "What a strange thing."

"Not everyone must fight with a massive hunk of steel." Morag snickered. "This weapon will play to her strengths."

"What is it?" Ember asked, turning the piece over so its bright surface reflected the leaping flames in the forge.

"A variation on a weapon of the Far East, the wheel of wind and fire," Morag said. "Your vision pointed to a wheel for combat, but a wheel of two moons."

The blacksmith cast a sidelong glance at Ember. "But its origins are naught. This weapon belongs to you. It shall not serve you until you give it a name."

"A name?"

Morag nodded. "The name invokes the blade's power. As the one who'll wield the blade, the name comes from you, lass."

The blacksmith handed Ember a second leather case, identical to the first. "Wheels are wielded in pairs. They are tools of beauty and devastation. Graceful and lethal."

Ember closed her eyes. She could see the full moon and the crescent sliver. Tears of blood rained from the night sky. "Silence and Sorrow."

Hearing Barrow expel a slow, even breath, Ember glanced at him to find he was nodding.

"Fine names," Morag said solemnly.

Gazing at the blades' mirror-like surface, Ember thought she caught a glimpse of the moonlight and crimson tears—as if her vision were captured within the very steel.

Ember broke out of her reverie, eyes narrowing. "These are weapons of the East?"

"China," Morag told her.

"And you've followed the overland route that distance?" Ember asked. "As the spice merchants do?"

Morag laughed. "I couldn't spare the time. If I took a caravan to the East anytime I needed to make inquiries about their weaponry, I would never forge a blade of my own."

"But you said you could craft these wheels because you apprenticed there," Ember said.

Morag looked at Barrow sharply. "She doesn't know?"

"Later," Barrow said, putting a hand on Ember's shoulder. "Let's give you a chance to test these blades."

"Hold, knight." Morag laughed. "You lot are always too eager to skip the rote lesson for the sake of letting your blades fly. The girl should know our magic."

Barrow smiled with chagrin. "Very well. Teach on, Morag."

With a snort, Morag turned to Ember. "The vows of Conatus require that we submit to the will of this earth. We are the shield that pushes back corruption that would taint God's creation."

Ember nodded and Barrow took up the story: "The Crusades taught the Church that we aren't alone in this battle against darkness. The Templars were born to seize the Holy Land for Christians—but Conatus was born of the Templars for a purpose altogether different."

"Father Michael said we learned from the Saracens," Ember said quietly. "That we share our wisdom."

"Our sometime enemies in the mortal war prove our allies when we fight for that which is immortal," Barrow said. "And we rely on constant correspondence to increase our skills."

"I understand the reasoning behind this cooperation," Ember answered. "But Morag spoke of an apprenticeship without a journey."

Morag smiled. "Not without a journey, lass, but a journey other than what you imagined. You were called to the Guard, but there are other gifts that bind our numbers to Conatus. The clerics have uncovered some of the earth's greatest secrets. Secrets that render the impossible possible. That make a journey to the Orient take only a moment rather than months."

"How can that be?" Ember asked breathlessly.

Barrow shifted the sword at his waist and coughed.

Morag glanced at him. "Your companion is eager to train you. And here I'll agree that you must see the magic at work to truly understand it."

Barrow bowed deeply to Morag. "We are, as ever, indebted to your skill."

The blacksmith inclined her head.

"Thank you," Ember said as she returned the first wheel to its slipcover and discovered that the two cases were designed to hook onto her belt. With the weapons hanging comfortably at her side, she hurried to catch Barrow, who had already made his way back to the courtyard.

Her irritation bubbled over when she fell in step beside him. "What did she mean?"

Barrow didn't answer, only walked more quickly in the direction of the practice fields.

"When will I see this wonder?" Ember asked. "Will I travel to the Orient?"

He stopped, returning her hard gaze without flinching. He didn't speak, and a moment later it was Ember who pulled her eyes away.

"You are one of us," Barrow said quietly. "But you are here to learn, not trot off to sate your appetite for travel. And I am to teach you. Trust that I will meet that task."

Ember kept her head bowed, following when Barrow continued on his path. But after a few steps she came to a halting stop. She couldn't be certain if it was shock or outrage traveling over Barrow's face when he realized she wasn't following and wheeled around.

"I am here to serve." She forced herself to speak calmly. "But not to be led around because my own ignorance blinds me. You are my teacher. You've just said this yourself. Give me the knowledge I seek."

His brow furrowed as he walked slowly toward her. He looked her up and down.

"Have I truly angered you this much?"

Ember frowned, thinking her words hadn't been that harsh. Then she noticed him looking at her hands. Unbeknownst even to her, they'd clenched into tight fists at her sides, bloodless and shaking. It took a surprising amount of will for her to pry her own fingers free of their furious pose. She closed her eyes and took a deep breath.

"I—" She didn't want to look at Barrow. This outburst had nothing to do with him or her impatience with her schooling in the ways of the Guard. Tears that had begun to burn beneath her eyelids made her squeeze them closed so none could escape.

"Perhaps you're right," Barrow murmured. "If you have questions, I'll hear them. My desire was only not to delay your training. You'll need your weapon sooner than you might think."

Ember hoped that her tears were gone when she forced her eyes open. She was about to apologize when Barrow turned away from her, waving for her to follow him. He swung around, no longer heading toward the practice field but instead toward the stable. Her spirit surged at the possibility of another outing with Caber, but she kept silent, regretful of her rash words. Barrow had done nothing to deserve her childish temper. She was lucky he'd taken her disrespectful tone in stride. Part of her wondered why he hadn't simply sent her back to the barracks with some punishment to carry out—like scrubbing the floors or, worse, emptying all the chamber pots.

Instead of punishment Ember received what felt like a reward for her complaints. Barrow seemed thoughtful, his only words to her when they reached the stable: "Ready your mount."

Caber snorted and immediately began banging his hooves against the stall when he saw Ember approaching. She fondly patted his soft nose, laughing when he tried once again to chew on the ring of braids that crowned her head.

When she led the horse from the stable, fully tacked and ready for the ride, Barrow was waiting with Toshach. He remained silent as he swung into the saddle, leaving Ember to guess that she was expected to do the same. Toshach was already heading for the gates at a fast clip when Ember mounted Caber. The young stallion tossed his head, impatient to follow.

Barrow didn't look back to see if she had managed to get herself into the saddle. Ember hadn't quite caught him when he passed through the gate, Toshach's pace steadily increasing. When he hit the valley floor and Toshach broke into a gallop, Ember began to wonder if this ride wasn't intended as some kind of punishment after all, one in which Barrow would force her to ride hard without any aid should she lose control of Caber. She leaned forward, letting Caber leap into a flat run. He stretched out, flowing over the ground like a gale in pursuit of Toshach.

The path Barrow took led in the opposite direction from their previous day's ride. Toshach tore through the glen. Soon Tearmunn was a speck and Loch Duich a shadow in the distance. They rode east for an hour. The clouds had broken through the night and sunlight filled the glen with the impish gleam of spring. Ember found the pace exhilarating, smiling as the sun warmed her back and the wind pulled strands of hair free of the braid to tickle her cheeks. Caber reveled in their speed as well, giving a whinny of triumph when he finally caught Toshach. Barrow still didn't look over his shoulder, but the slight tilt of his head made Ember smile, knowing he was fully aware of her approach.

Toshach began to slow, first to a canter and then to a trot as Barrow turned his mount south. With the horses blowing hard, they began to climb the hillside, leaving the open valley for the cover of trees. Though Ember couldn't make out any path, Barrow kept Toshach moving forward. They wove through the dense pines, their path twisting but leading steadily upward. Sunlight battled the trees' heavy shadows, its golden blades periodically splitting the darkness to mark their progress.

Now that her attention wasn't captivated by the thrill of Caber's strength and speed, Ember found herself waiting for some acknowledgment from Barrow. The forest around them was unnervingly quiet. The pine trees surrounding them rose straight and solemn like pillars of a temple. Her own breath seemed blasphemously loud.

Ember was chewing on her lip, fighting the impulse to speak and quell her anxiety, when a new sound drew her attention. At first she thought it was wind rustling through the trees. But the sound was steadier than the rise and fall of fickle spring gusts. And it was growing louder. Her head cocked to the side, Ember concentrated on the noise, trying to discern its source.

Barrow reined in Toshach and dismounted. He turned to look at her for the first time since they'd left Tearmunn.

"We'll leave the horses here," he said. "Don't worry. Toshach knows this place well. They won't wander."

He gave no further explanation but watched her, waiting. Ember slid out of the saddle. She murmured her thanks to Caber, taking a moment to stroke his bowed neck and convey her reluctance to part from him.

During the ride Ember had forgotten the new additions to her wardrobe, but now that she was walking, the wheels beat rhythmically against her hips. Their presence was oddly comforting, since she still had no idea how to wield them. As she followed Barrow up a gentle rise, the persistent sound grew in intensity to a quiet roar. Ember had guessed what the cause of the rushing noise was by the time the waterfall came into view, but she wasn't prepared for the sight that met her eyes.

Her breath caught at the web of white water that cut through stone. The stream didn't throw itself from a sheer precipice to strike a pool far below. Instead the water had wound its way between ancient rock, splitting into three rivulets and glistening like enormous threads of spider silk.

Barrow carefully made his way between the jutting rocks, descending until he reached the place where the falls settled into a narrow stream that wound its way toward the glen's floor. He paused at the edge of the brook and then beckoned for Ember to join him. It only took a few steps for her to understand why he'd taken so much time in the descent. Though the drop wasn't steep, the stones beneath her feet were slick, waiting for an opportunity to catch her off guard and turn her ankle.

When she reached Barrow's side at the bottom of the falls, she asked, "Why have you brought me here?"

"You were distracted this morning, and angry," he told her. "That's not an ideal disposition to bring into your first bout of training."

Ember looked away; even the mention of her irritability made it roll beneath her skin.

"In the Guard you'll see things more terrible than any man or woman should witness," Barrow said. "It can lead to distraction . . . and despair."

He was speaking softly and with kindness. A child forced to hew off his own fingers. The kelpie's claws dripping slime as they shredded Barrow's tabard, seeking flesh. Barrow thought her erratic mood was a result of the fight . . . of fear and uncertainty. She almost laughed. That she'd fought that creature and won was one of the only things sustaining her sense of place. Her heart was the beast she couldn't tame.

Barrow crouched, laying his palm on the water's surface. "It helps if you can find a place that brings you peace. Make it your own, share it with no one. Go there when you need solace. If you can't fight the demons that seek to conquer your spirit, you will not survive among us."

"Share it with no one?" Ember asked with a sidelong glance.

"Being that I'm your teacher, I've made an exception." Barrow looked up at her. "You'll need time to become familiar with the valley. I found this place many years ago, shortly after I joined the Guard. This slope, this brook—they're almost as helpful a friend as Toshach. You're welcome to come here until you find such a place of your own."

Ember tilted her head, regarding him curiously. "I had a place like this at home. Somewhere I could hide from the world . . . though it was mostly to hide from my father."

"I don't blame you for that." He smiled. "I would appreciate it if you didn't reveal it to any others in the Guard."

She did laugh then. "Of course not. I'm honored that you've brought me here."

Spotting a thick, fallen tree, Ember climbed up on it and let her legs dangle.

"Ember, I want you to know that among the Guard you have friends," Barrow said, his eyes back on the water. "Our lives are hard and we may seem equally hard as people. But we live and die for one another. We are more closely bonded than any others . . . at least that's what I've found."

Ember sat quietly. When Barrow spoke of the Guard, it was with quiet intensity. A question stirred within her, but it was one she was afraid to ask.

They find lovers where they will and when they will.

What did Barrow mean when he invoked the bonds of the Guard?

She had to know if Alistair had handed her lies in the hopes that he'd sway her.

"Barrow—" The thickness in her throat made her voice crack. Barrow looked at her, his brows raised in surprise.

"The Guard . . ." She dropped her gaze to the forest floor, not wanting to meet Barrow's eyes when she put this question to him. "Are they truly chaste?"

For the longest moments Ember thought she'd ever experienced, the only answer that came was the babble of the brook as it made its way along the hillside. Then Barrow began to laugh.

FOURTEEN

EMBER JUMPED DOWN from the log and, squaring off with Barrow, folded her arms across her chest. He was still laughing as she glared at him.

She opened her mouth to speak, but Barrow shook his head.

"I'm sorry, Ember." He drew a shaking breath and managed to quell his mirth. "It's just that when you started to speak, I thought you were about to confess something horrible to me. Your face had no color whatsoever."

"You think my question was funny?" Ember snapped. "Excuse me for taking the vows I spoke with some level of solemnity."

A smile hopped on and off Barrow's mouth, but he managed to keep from laughing again. "Of course, you're right. You surprised me, that's all."

Despite her flare of anger, Ember remained desperate for an answer. "Well?"

"Well what?" Barrow didn't bother to fight off his smile this time.

Ember stamped her foot and then cursed herself for stamping her foot because it made Barrow chuckle.

"You know what!" she blurted.

His smile faded. "Why are you asking this?"

"I heard rumors," she said lamely. "I only want to know if they are true."

"You should be wary of rumors. Particularly those regarding who's been visiting whose bed." His eyes grew distant and lost the spark of laughter. "But the answer to your question is: sometimes."

"Sometimes?" Beneath her arms, Ember felt her heartbeat speeding up though she couldn't pinpoint the source of her nerves.

Barrow shrugged. "It's a matter of choice. The only true restriction on one's personal relationships is that they may not interfere with our service to the Guard. And love is an interfering thing by its nature, so some of us choose to avoid its entanglements altogether."

"Is it really that simple?" Ember asked, frowning.

"We study the ways of this world's finest warriors so that we may enhance our own skills. Our models are those we find in history, not the dictates of the Church," Barrow said.

"History?"

"Think of the champions of Sparta," he answered.

Ember nodded. "Few would compare."

"We know that they prized love for one another—physical as well as the loyalty of friendship—and it bore no ill consequences for them in battle," Barrow said.

"But what of the vow?" Ember grew more confused by the minute. Had her outrage at Alistair been unreasonable? If it was, why did her stomach still churn when she thought of his words and his attempt to persuade her into his bed?

Barrow stood up, pacing to the edge of the stream. "The vow has its place. And most of the Guard adhere to it, for safety's sake."

"Safety's sake?" Ember followed his path, gazing into the rippling water.

"We may fight only by leave of the Church and the nobles," he said. "The restraints we put on our own lives to serve the cause render us less threatening to them. By acting the part of monks, we offer them the semblance of servitude."

"So it's all an act?" Ember said bitterly. "The vow means nothing?"

Barrow turned suddenly, looking into her eyes. "Does it mean nothing to you?"

She gazed at him and slowly shook her head. What she'd given up had in turn granted her freedom. She thought of Caber's pounding hooves and the wind tugging at her hair.

"It means everything," she said.

"As it does to many of us, but the vow is about service to the order, not the choices of the individual," he said. "I only suggest that you not judge those who have fallen under love's spell despite their vows. Pride is an empty cup."

Ember blushed. Love's spell—was that what had drawn Alistair to her? Perhaps she'd been too harsh. Her shock had overwhelmed any kindness merited by their long friendship.

Barrow was watching her with narrowed eyes. "Again I ask, Ember, is there something that troubles you beyond the rumors—which are indeed more than rumors—about some of the Guard?"

She flinched, not wanting to incur Barrow's ill will toward Alistair, especially now that she was doubting her initial reaction to his advances.

She looked at Barrow. "What about you?"

"What about me?" He pulled a smooth stone from the streambed.

"Do you have a lover?" Ember paused, thinking of his comment about the Spartans, and suddenly gasped. "Is it Kael?"

Barrow dropped the stone. It plunked into the water and rapidly sank. "Is that what you think?"

Ember worried she'd offended him, but when he faced her, one corner of his mouth was crinkled in amusement.

"I'm not Kael's lover, though I love him like a brother," Barrow said. "As much as I admire the Spartans, I prefer the company of women in my bed."

At that moment Ember wanted nothing more than to kick Barrow in the shin and run away. She couldn't fathom why she'd have such a childish reaction to the calm conversation that she'd instigated. She also couldn't bear the sudden hot stinging in her eyes. She turned away, bending down to place her palms against the stream's surface so he couldn't see her face.

Barrow continued, "I mean only if such were the case. I have no lover."

Ember caught her breath, but she didn't want to look at him. She still didn't understand why her emotions veered wildly from one moment to the next.

"Why not?" she asked.

"One of the reasons that Kael and some others take lovers among the Guard is that it can be kept secret. With women it's a much greater risk," Barrow said.

"Why?"

Barrow coughed. "Because I wouldn't shame a maid by giving her a bastard child."

"Oh." Ember blushed again. Of course that was a risk, and if Barrow fathered a child, he'd likely be forced out of the Guard and into marriage. Father Michael had spoken of this very thing when she'd been called to the Guard.

"And while some noblewomen find dalliances with warriors a welcome distraction from their older husbands, I'm not flattered by such offers." Barrow shifted his sword on his hip.

Though it all made sense, Ember remained unsettled. "Do you not care about the vow? If you wanted a lover, would you take one?"

"I don't know," he said, giving her a half smile. "I've never had to make that choice. I believe in the vows I made. And I honor them, but I don't believe love is a sin. I keep the vow because it lends me focus and strength in battle. I simply don't begrudge the happiness of those who follow a different path."

Ember finally rose from her crouch, facing Barrow. Her heart skipped a beat when she met his eyes. To her chagrin, she once again found her gaze moving over the hard angles of his jaw and chin, the shape of his lips. It was no wonder noblewomen had tried to coax this warrior into their beds. The thought made her want to find a new target for her dagger.

Barrow's expression changed, as if a cloud had passed over his face.

"If . . . if there is someone you wish to share your bed with . . ." His words carried an edge. "Sorcha could help you. There are herbs that reduce the chance you'll become with child."

She was so taken aback that it took her a moment to answer. "No!"

Her exclamation brought bewilderment to his eyes and she blushed.

"I mean . . . there is no one. That isn't why I asked." She kept her gaze on the waterfall, thinking that her mind felt too much like the tumbling river.

After an unbearable space of silence, Barrow cleared his throat. "We should make our way back to the keep. You still need to get some practice in with those weapons Morag crafted for you."

Ember was grateful he turned his back because she was certain her own shock at the audacity of her examination and speculation about Barrow's would-be lovers was written clearly on her face. Why would she even ponder such things? As her mentor, Barrow deserved her respect, and instead her mind drummed up fodder worthy only of gossiping, shrewish wives.

Shame-filled, Ember kept her distance as they made the

slippery climb back up the falls. Barrow gave a short whistle, and a moment later Toshach and Caber appeared from within the forest's shadows.

Ember watched as Barrow spoke softly to his horse and then swung into the saddle. She cringed when he noticed him scrutinizing her.

"I still believe you're keeping something from me, Ember," he said. "Your every move bespeaks worry. If you have other questions, you'd best ask them before we return to Tearmunn."

She shook her head as she tightened Caber's girth. "It's nothing."

He sighed. "I won't press you, but I'd be lying if I claimed not to be saddened that I've not yet earned your trust."

With a cluck of Barrow's tongue Toshach was off at a trot, leaving Ember to stare after him, startled by his words. She cursed under her breath as she swung into the saddle. Urging Caber into a swift gait, she sought to catch him.

"Barrow!"

He pulled up at the edge of the forest. Toshach pranced, snorting and jerking at the reins.

Barrow patted the stallion's neck. "What is it? He's ready for a good run and I'm of a mind to let him go."

Caber had picked up Toshach's restlessness. Ember struggled to keep him checked.

"You have it," she said through gritted teeth. The stallion was strong and he wanted to take the bit from her.

"I have what?" Barrow raised an eyebrow as he watched her fighting for control of her steed.

"My trust . . . gah!" Caber sprang forward, leaping onto the moor. He set out at a dead run, the bit firmly grasped in his teeth.

Ember righted herself in the saddle and hauled back on the reins. Despite throwing all her strength into the effort, Caber was aflame with his own power and paid her no heed. He bolted across the sodden ground, tearing up earth in great clods that flew out behind him. The wind burned Ember's face and made her eyes water, blinding her. She could hear Barrow's shouts at her back and the thunder of Toshach's hooves as he chased her.

Caber ran as if the hordes of hell pursued him. Ember shouted, pleading with the stallion to slow. He ignored her, plunging on with a shrill whinny. At her wits' end, Ember dropped the reins, throwing her body against Caber's neck. She reached forward, grasping the bridle on either side of his mouth, and gave it a sharp jerk. At the same moment she shouted with all the breath in her lungs, "Stop!"

Startled by her shout and the new leverage against the bridle, Caber abruptly pulled up. His hooves slid along the wet ground, sending a shower of grass and soil in a cascade around them. While the horse had stopped, Ember did not. She catapulted over his neck and head, crashing to the ground on her back. The impact knocked her breath away. Stunned by the earth's blow, she didn't move but stared up at the flat, gray sky.

As she waited for air to fill her lungs again, Ember heard Barrow pull up. Curses spewed from his mouth as he berated Caber for his unbidden race toward home. Ember rolled onto her side. She knew she'd bruise but could sense no serious injury as she gingerly sat up. She finally drew a long breath, only to be horrified that it entered and left her as a shaking sob.

Tears streamed down her face. She wept angrily, rubbing at her traitorous eyes. First Alistair, and now she'd made a fool of herself by letting Caber run wild. How could she be a warrior if she couldn't even control her own horse?

She hid her face in her palms when Barrow approached.

"Ember!" He knelt beside her. "Are you hurt?"

She tried to say no, but all that came out was a sob. Barrow's face paled as he searched for signs of injury, while she carried on—a mess of shaking muscles and salty tears.

After a few minutes Barrow rocked back on his heels.

"Hush, little one." He put his hands on her shoulders. "There's no harm here. You've gotten a shock, that's all."

His gentle tone made her wail and shake her head. "Caber . . . I couldn't . . ."

Hearing his name, Caber walked over, nosing her with a soft whicker.

"He apologizes." Barrow laughed. "And there's no shame in it. I'd bet my life there's no rider who hasn't let a spirited horse get out from under him. When I was training Toshach, I doubt there was a night I went to bed without bruises. It's simply the price you pay for finding a mount who isn't a broken-down nag or a fat, spoiled palfrey."

Ember looked at him through bleary eyes. She sniffled, grateful for his consolation but horrified that she'd fallen to pieces in front of him.

"Ember." He leaned close, speaking softly. "What ails you?"

His face was etched with concern, and his questioning gaze finally drew a confession from her.

"Alistair—" she whispered.

"What of him?" Barrow kept his tone even, but his eyes narrowed.

She told him everything about the previous night. Alistair's profession of love, his desire for her bed, his claims about the freedom of love, and even lust, among the Guard. Her words came out as quickly as her tears. While she spoke, he listened intently, occasionally nodding, but he didn't interrupt her or question her. When she finally stopped and drew a ragged breath, Barrow spoke.

"He is a coward and a cur." His hands clenched into fists, leaving his knuckles bloodless.

Ember was taken aback by the cold fury in his voice. "But Alistair has always been my friend. Perhaps I've done wrong by him . . . After all, you said yourself that love is not a sin."

"If I'd known the source of your query, I would have chosen

other words," Barrow said, grinding his teeth. "Love is not a sin. What Alistair did is not love but only served his own desires."

She wiped lingering tears from her cheeks, relieved that she was no longer carrying last night inside her.

"If he loved you, he would have told you of this plan before you took your vows," Barrow said. "He should have asked your father to marry you."

Ember shuddered. She didn't want to marry Alistair or anyone else. She suddenly wondered if Alistair had chosen this deceitful route to her bed because he'd known she would refuse or at least protest any offer of marriage he made.

"I'll take this up with Lukasz." Barrow helped her to her feet.

"Please don't," she said. "Alistair knows his feelings are unrequited. He made a mistake, but I don't want it to cost him his place in the Guard."

"He should not go unpunished for this offense," Barrow said.

"My rejection is punishment enough." Ember sighed, remembering the broken look on Alistair's face when she'd shoved him away. As much as she was still furious at him, she was also brokenhearted over their ruined friendship. "He may have kept his feelings for me a secret, but I believe them to be genuine. I've hurt him deeply by refusing him. He was my friend, and I am sorry for that hurt."

Barrow frowned, but nodded. "If you truly wish it, I'll keep your confidence. I am honored that you've shared this secret with me."

"Thank you," Ember said.

"But if he doesn't respect your choice . . ." Barrow's voice became close to a growl. "I will not let it pass."

She didn't know what to say to that. Instead she turned to Caber, taking his face in her hands. "You will not steal the bit from me again."

He blew softly against her neck and she stroked his velvety nose.

"That's a good lass." The menace in Barrow's words had given way to warmth. "Are you ready to ride again?"

In answer Ember swung into her saddle. Caber twisted his head to look at her, flicking his ears back and forth in question. It might have simply been that he'd gotten the run out of his system, but the horse's gaze seemed full of concern for her welfare.

"I'm fine," she said to the horse. "But no more racing."

"Aye." Barrow took Toshach ahead at an easy canter.

As they steadily made their way home, Ember withdrew into her thoughts. She watched Barrow's lean, straight back as they flowed over the hills, the horses carrying their riders along in smooth, graceful strides. Though her confession had come as a relief, she worried about its consequences. Would Barrow tell Lukasz about Alistair despite her plea?

For his own part, Barrow kept Toshach in the lead rather than riding beside her or slowing so that they could carry on a conversation. He'd been kind to her in many ways today. The watchfulness of his eyes and his gentle words had been a balm to her stinging heart. But it also threw her feelings awry. He'd spoken of leniency when it came to bending the Guard's vow to accommodate love—yet his fury at Alistair's actions had been sudden and unrestrained. She wasn't sure what that meant. She forced her eyes off him when she realized she was entranced by the way the wind whipped through his hair and the strong set of his shoulders. Gazing at his form, his easy command of Toshach, and the way the mist left dark streaks in his brown hair sent a shiver over her skin that did nothing other than to unsettle her further. When she'd begun training with Barrow, she'd admired but feared him. That fear had slowly eroded and was being replaced by . . . what?

Ember shook away her unwanted musings as the horses crested a hill and the keep came into sight. No matter what the mystery of her own shifting sensibilities, when she returned to the Guard's quarters, she would no longer have the solace of time alone with her mentor. Her afternoon respite was about to end, leaving her to return to her duties. And to face Alistair.

FIFTEEN

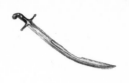

EIRA AND CIAN WERE sparring when the messenger arrived, red-faced and breathless. Though he was bent over and panting, the sisters didn't pause from their fight.

With a move Eira should have known to anticipate, Cian feigned a misstep. Eira moved to strike as her sister seemed to stumble, but as Eira brought her sword down Cian suddenly crouched, springing up with a twist, landing behind Eira. Using the momentum of Eira's swing to her advantage, Cian aimed a kick at Eira's low back, sending her sister sprawling.

"That trick works every time." Cian offered Eira her hand.

"One of these days you'll actually fall," Eira said, standing up with a groan. Sheathing her sword, she turned her attention to the messenger, who had finally caught his breath. "What news?"

"Pardon me, Lady Eira." The messenger bowed deeply. He was little more than a boy, bearing a grimy face and a nervous disposition. "But I'm not quite sure, as the message I was given . . . came from a source unknown to me."

"What do you mean?" Cian asked, sweeping her sword through the air in leisurely arcs.

Eira didn't blame her sister for giving the messenger only half of her attention. The boy was obviously new to his post, and she thought his strange words nothing more than a reflection of his inexperience.

His face twisted with worry, the messenger reached into his coat pocket and withdrew a small bit of parchment.

Eira took the paper, read it, and looked at him sharply. "Who gave this to you?"

Catching the harshness of her sister's question, Cian returned her sword to its scabbard. "What's wrong?"

"Who gave this to you?" Eira repeated, taking a menacing step toward the messenger.

The boy put his hands up pleadingly. "Apologies, my lady. He was a stranger in a cloak. I didn't see his face. I was riding in the forest and he appeared on the road, startling my horse. I nearly fell from the saddle."

He blushed at this admission but continued. "I thought at first he was a bandit intent on robbing me, but he held out this parchment and said, 'Your masters are needed.' He disappeared into the forest before I could question him."

"What does the note say?" Cian asked, seeing Eira's furrowed brow.

Wordlessly, Eira handed her sister the parchment. Three words had been scratched in ink onto the paper's surface.

Dorusduain is gone.

"The village is gone?" Cian frowned. "How can that be?"

"Did you investigate this claim?" Eira asked the messenger.

He hung his head. "No, my lady. Pardon me, but I'm training to be a scribe, not a warrior. I was afraid to go."

Cian patted his shoulder. "No harm done, lad. You'd best leave this to the Guard, though I'd be surprised if it were more than a hoax. You did right in bringing this note to us; now go and find a meal."

The boy smiled gratefully and scurried off toward the manor.

"Why would anyone jest about a village disappearing?" Eira asked Cian. "If that's even what the note's meaning is."

"I don't know," Cian answered. "But it must be false. Dorusduain is small, but villages don't simply go missing. I suppose we should give this to Lukasz and he'll send a scouting party."

Eira began to nod but then said, "Or we could go ourselves."

Cian laughed, but her sister remained stone-faced.

"We should go," Eira said slowly. "Now. We have no obligations for the rest of the day. Dorusduain isn't far. We would be back not long after nightfall."

Shaking her head, Cian muttered, "This is work for the Guard."

"We still belong to the Guard," Eira countered. "Serving in the Circle may draw us from the field, but it doesn't mean we can't return should we so choose."

When Cian fixed a dubious gaze on her, Eira said, "When was the last time we rode out together? Don't you miss it?"

"I miss time spent with you," Cian answered. "I'd much rather hunt trolls than listen to Thomas discuss the state of the treasury."

Eira offered her a slight smile. Since they'd joined the Circle, their hours were increasingly spent on matters bureaucratic and political. Eira knew her sister well enough to be certain that Cian longed to be away from the keep and into a good fight as much as Eira did.

Watching Cian's resolve waver, Eira said, "If we tell Lukasz, it's time wasted while a scouting party is formed. And if it *is* a hoax, that's even more of a waste for the Guard. We can be on our way in a few minutes."

A smile twitched across Cian's mouth. "It isn't a very long way to Dorusduain, is it?"

Without answering, Eira turned and walked quickly to the stables, knowing Cian would be right at her heels. They saddled their horses, two mares with coats like mist. Their horses were sisters too, foaled from the same mare: Geal for Eira and Liath for Cian. The sisters' abrupt arrival in the stables earned a few curious glances from Ian the stable hand. He was respectful—or wary—enough to refrain from asking any questions.

Soon enough they passed through Tearmunn's gates and brought their horses to a gallop. The sisters didn't bother with the main road. They'd spent enough years exploring Glen Shiel's terrain to know the drovers' paths and game trails that cut a journey's time in half. Having been cooped in the stable as their riders were in the keep, the horses were eager to run.

Giving Geal free rein, Eira mused that she and Cian should be tired of running after all these years. They'd been running since they were small girls. At first they ran from a town overcome by plague. A town filled with more dead than living, including their own dead parents. The sisters had continued running. They dashed from place to place, knowing that quick hands and quicker feet would win them a meal and spare them the lash or a dungeon. Through luck or fate, the one time Eira and Cian weren't fast enough they'd been stealing loaves from the large open kitchens of a monastery. The rough handling of the burly, red-faced baker who'd dragged them before the monastery's abbot didn't prepare them for the priest's sympathy or his kindness. Not seeing two thieves like the baker, the abbot saw Eira and Cian's dirty faces and tattered clothing as an opportunity for charity. He fed the girls and offered hot water to rub months of grime from their skin and a bed to sleep in instead of the forest floor. The next day he changed their lives forever by sending them to serve Conatus.

At Tearmunn the sisters still ran, but with a new purpose. Now they chased monsters—creatures more frightening than any they'd imagined when they'd been huddled together, cold and hungry, in the dark. But Conatus taught them to fight, not fear, the wicked things that lived in the dark. The sisters grew tall, grew strong, and grew ferocious.

Eira sighed. A warrior's reward after two decades of battle should not be a seat at a council table where one's bones ached and muscles went weak as porridge. She recognized the honor of being called to the Circle and the rarity of a woman serving in the role, but the endless squabbling over expenses and ridiculous accommodations to keep Abbot Crichton happy had become nearly intolerable.

Riding eastward, Eira thought she could feel the pressure of the low, swollen clouds weighing on her shoulders. She'd believed this unplanned scouting trip would free her mind of frustration. Instead resentment seeped through her veins. Her thoughts turned over and over on themselves as the day wore on.

By the time Eira pulled up her horse, Geal, sullenness festered beneath her skin. She almost failed to hear Cian murmur, "Do you feel that?"

Tucked into the foothills and blanketed by forest, the village of Dorusduain had always been quiet. But today the sisters came upon unnatural silence. No languid sounds of cows being milked or soft footfalls of villagers going about their day.

Eira nodded at Cian.

"Something's wrong." Cian nudged her mount forward. Geal's and Liath's ears were up, alert and flicking back and forth. As they passed beneath the cover of trees along the small path that led into the village, Liath squealed and reared.

Keeping her seat, Cian reined in the mare and attempted to calm her. Geal pranced and snorted, her eyes rolling wildly so the whites showed.

With soothing whispers, Eira carefully slid from Geal's back. "We should leave them here."

"And if we need to run?" Cian asked as Liath shied.

"Our feet will carry us back to the horses quickly enough," Eira answered.

They led the skittish horses to the edge of the forest, where the beasts became noticeably calmer. Eira tethered the mares to a fallen tree and the sisters returned to the path. As they moved beneath the forest canopy, Eira noticed that the silence wasn't simply the absence of human noise. She couldn't detect the song of a single bird or the buzz of an insect. The air was void of sound. The rasp of steel when Cian drew her sword was so deafening in contrast to the stillness around them it made Eira jump. Then she drew her sword as well.

The gloom of the woods broke when they reached the meadow in which the village squatted. Though the sky remained overcast, the thatch-roofed stone huts could have been bathed in sunlight compared to the nets of shadow cast by the trees along the path. Despite the brightness of the open space, Eira shuddered.

The village lay still. No chickens pecked the ground for seeds or insects. No children chased each other around the houses while their mothers patched worn clothes.

Eira and Cian exchanged a glance before moving farther into the village.

"We should check the houses," Eira said. "I'll go in while you keep watch."

Cian nodded.

Ducking into the closest house, while Cian stood with her back to the open door, Eira crept forward. The hut was empty, but while she wouldn't have described what she found as signs of a struggle, she did see what looked like disruption. A knife lay on the floor. The table near it held a loaf of bread only partly sliced. Embers from a cooking fire still glowed in the hearth.

"Is anyone there?" Cian called to Eira.

Eira emerged from the hut, shaking her head.

"I'll check the next house," Cian said, already moving.

They moved through the village methodically, searching every house for signs of people or what had happened but finding nothing. All that remained was evidence of a day in progress that had simply and suddenly stopped.

"Where are they?" Eira kicked the dirt in frustration. There was no blood. No sign of a fight or smell of death lingering. And Eira knew well that death was a scent that hung in the air long after its occurrence.

Cian turned a slow circle, surveying the houses they'd rifled through in vain. "The village is gone."

Eira nodded at her sister's echo of the messenger's words. "But what does that even mean?"

"I don't know." Cian sheathed her sword. "But we won't find out today."

"You want to leave?" Eira frowned. "But we haven't learned anything."

Cian's laugh was dry. "We learned it wasn't a hoax."

"We should search the forest," Eira argued. "Search for tracks."

"No." Cian began to retrace their steps. "It's time to return to Tearmunn. We've passed the point where we can do this alone."

Eira gritted her teeth, knowing Cian was right. But she wanted to stay. To delve further into this mystery of a silent village.

"However the Circle decides to proceed, I'm not staying behind on the next mission," Eira snapped.

"I didn't say you were." Cian glanced over her shoulder and smiled mischievously at Eira. "And I didn't say I'm willing to stay behind either."

With a laugh, Eira ran to catch her sister. When they reached the edge of the meadow, where the trees leaned over the path, Eira looked back at the silent huts, watching smoke that still slunk into the sky from fires abandoned . . . when?

"The village is gone," Eira whispered to herself, but Cian heard her sister.

"We will find the cause of this," Cian said. "Together."

Eira took Cian's outstretched hand, clasping it tight. "Together."

SIXTEEN

THOUGH AT FIRST she'd welcomed Barrow's silence, as they rode into the keep, his stony expression unnerved Ember to the point that her blood felt like ice. Not once had Barrow looked at her nor had he spoken. When they reached the stables, he barked orders to the servants and they quickly assumed care of the steaming mounts.

Without a word he strode away, leaving Ember with no choice but to chase after him. Barrow kept walking until they reached the practice field. She felt a spike of relief that it was empty. Ember wouldn't have welcomed an audience for her first attempt at sparring, particularly when she'd be facing Barrow. She glanced at him, taking in his height, the massive blade strapped to his back, the broad set of his shoulders. She shivered but wasn't entirely certain that fear was the cause for the gooseflesh on her skin.

"Lora!"

After so much silence, Barrow's shout made Ember jump. He raised his hand in greeting as a figure garbed in a dark gray, hooded robe approached them. Ember's chest caved a bit. She would have a witness to what was sure to be a humiliation. When the stranger reached them, slender hands pushed back the hood to reveal a face with delicate angles and a head of pale blond hair.

"Ember, this is Lora." Barrow nodded to the blond girl. "Should you ever need to practice sparring on your own, she can assist you. Rarely is she away from the field."

Lora smiled. "To be away would be to shirk my duty."

Ember was puzzling over Barrow's words, for one surely couldn't spar alone. Lora's eyes were on her, so Ember forced herself to smile at the girl.

"I doubt this match will offer much entertainment," she said. "Barrow could probably beat me if he was blindfolded."

Lora laughed, but Barrow shook his head. "You won't be fighting me."

Ember looked from him to the pale girl. "Am I fighting Lora?"

"I'm not a fighter," Lora told her. "Just a simple cleric."

"As if such a thing existed." Barrow smiled at her and the back of Ember's neck grew hot. When she spoke, a part of her knew it was only to interrupt their exchange.

"If I'm not fighting you or her, then who is my opponent?"

Barrow took a step back, making a deferring gesture to Lora. The slender girl bowed her head. Her palms rested against each other as if she were in prayer. Ember shifted on her feet. Was this part of their regular practice? Should she pray as well?

She glanced at Barrow, who wasn't praying. He was still watching Lora. The heat on Ember's neck prickled onto her scalp. She forced her eyes off them and onto the damp ground.

She drew a sharp breath and scampered backward.

The earth at the cleric's bare feet was bubbling.

As Ember watched, the ground erupted. Earth stretched upward into a column taller than Lora. The mass of soil expanded and contracted, its shape changing as Lora maintained her contemplative pose. Limbs burst out of the block of earth. Arms and legs of mud snaked out of the lump. Hands with five fingers appeared. A neck. A head. But no face.

Lora raised her head and opened her eyes. The mud creature stood before her as if awaiting her command.

"That is your opponent," Barrow said.

Ember gazed at the strange form. "What is it?"

"Simply a shape called forth from the earth to which I've temporarily lent part of my spirit," Lora answered. "It has no name, for it is not a living thing. Not much more than a poppet for all intents and purposes."

When Ember turned to Barrow, he said, "I said you would face horrors because of your calling, but you will also witness many wonders. This is the first."

"And I am to fight it?" She looked at the mud man—if it could be called that. Its body was straight and lacked defining contours, giving no indication of sex.

Lora lifted her hand and the creature moved, its steps slightly halting. "It will engage with you when I command it. It will also learn from you. As your skill progresses, so will its abilities increase."

"The earth creatures make fitting opponents when you first begin to fight, or later if you're unable to find a sparring partner," Barrow said.

The cool steel of Silence and Sorrow whispered to Ember as she slid them free of their leather covers.

"Let the blades speak to you," Barrow murmured as Ember and the creature began to circle each other. "They were forged for you and you alone."

The weight of the weapons in her hands was reassuring. Grasping the leather-wrapped handles felt oddly natural. The perfect circle and interior half circle of the blades shone in in the daylight. Their gleam was subtle, reflecting the sublime quality of moonbeams. The thought sent prickles up her arms as if the energy contained within the blades had seeped into her skin and now traveled through her veins.

She began to move tentatively, sweeping her arms back and forth to become accustomed to the wheels. With each motion the blades hummed through the air, singing their own silvery melody. The strange, alluring sound began to lead her body's movements. As she flowed over the damp earth, Ember's arms and legs took on the pattern of a dance that was both surprising and familiar. The mud creature mirrored her movements though it bore no weapons. Behind it, Ember noticed Lora and Barrow watching her, waiting.

Ember struck out with her left arm, bringing the blade up and across the creature's chest. It feinted and the blade whistled through the air, missing its mark.

"Again," Barrow commanded.

She jumped forward, this time bringing both wheels up and criss-crossing them in swift horizontal strokes. The blades struck, catching the creature where a man's collarbone would have been and again at its stomach. Having no mouth, the mud thing didn't cry out, but the evidence of her blows remained in the chunks of earth missing from its body.

Lora raised her arms and the creature threw itself at Ember. She dodged, twisting around, and struck its back with a series of rapid blade strokes.

With each exchange the creature became more aggressive, its lumbering movements transformed into quick steps that matched Ember's dance-like combat. The fight continued, and Ember was surprised she didn't tire. The longer she battled the mud creature, the more connected to her body and the blades she became.

Finding herself crouched low after the thing had knocked her with a painful kick to her stomach, Ember drew on the coil of energy in her chest when it raised its arms to rain down a blow on her bowed head.

Ember sprang up, flying at the creature. She drew the blades in a blindingly swift motion that followed her own path, rising from the ground and tearing through the air. The wheels came up one after the other, connecting with the creature's upper arm and continuing without pause. Ember sailed past the mud man, hit the ground, and pivoted around, ready for its next strike.

The creature wasn't moving. It stood facing her but didn't strike.

A moment later Ember saw the reason for its—or Lora's—hesitation.

Its arm lay on the ground beside it. Though the mud thing had no eyes, it turned its head to gaze at its severed appendage.

"Uh . . ." Ember glanced at Lora, who calmly picked up the arm and went to the mud creature. It stood still while she held the severed limb to the stump below its shoulder. Earth flowed, drawing the piece back into the body, and the creature was whole again.

Barrow coughed and Ember could hear his laughter beneath the sound. "A point of instruction."

"Yes?" She didn't want to turn her back on the mud thing. Though she doubted it had emotions, she still worried it would seek retribution for her slicing its arm off.

"Your blade is sharp enough to take off any limb," he said. "But under combat conditions your adversary will have muscle and bone to contend with, which puts up much more resistance than clay."

Ember nodded, tightening her grip on the wheel's handle.

"And as a general rule you'll want to kill, not maim, your enemy," he continued. "If you want to cut something off, go for the head."

That made her turn, expecting that he was teasing her, but his expression was serious.

Seeing her surprise, he said, "Hesitation will get you killed."

Barrow's eyes moved off her. It was only the sound of the creature's feet squelching on the damp ground that told Ember he'd given Lora some sort of silent signal.

Ember wheeled around to find the mud thing lunging at her. Drawing a sharp breath, she spun around, lifting her blades in a sweeping arc. The wheels hit their mark, slicing through the creature's neck. Its head toppled to the ground and a moment later its body collapsed into a pile of slop.

She was still breathing hard when Barrow came to her side.

"You listen and you learn quickly," he said. "Well done. I think you're ready for more of a challenge. That will be all, Lora. Thank you."

Lora bowed and, after covering her head with the robe's hood once more, quit the field.

"Put your weapons aside," Barrow told Ember as he unstrapped his own sword belt.

When she hesitated, he said, "You're still acting on instinct, which is fine. But you'll need to use your mind in battle as well as your will to survive. Until you do that, we'll spar without weapons."

She frowned at him, which made him laugh.

"It's just that I don't want to lose an arm, Ember," he said. "We'll test our blades against each other when you've learned control."

The pride Ember had felt after decapitating the mud creature melted away. As she unbuckled her belt, her confidence wavered. Barrow was right. She might have overpowered that thing Lora had summoned, but she'd been nothing more than a wild thing—an animal fighting for its life.

She set her belt and weapons aside, exhaustion disheartening her as much as the weight of the lesson.

Barrow stood face-to-face with her, and Ember steeled herself for the next round of instruction.

Now that they were so close, she had to lift her chin to meet his eyes. He was a head and a half taller than she and built like a statue. Even if she'd had her blades, Ember doubted parting Barrow from any of his limbs would be an easy feat.

"The clerics can summon creatures of the earth to supply us with convenient practice partners," he said. "But they are mindless things and only offer limited challenge."

Ember nodded, rolling her shoulders back to free them of tension. She knew it was only a matter of time—probably minutes—before she'd be asked to fight again.

"In the field you'll face creatures that embody cunning and deceit," he told her. "They will constantly search for ways to exploit your weaknesses. To turn your skills against you. If you only lash out against these fiends, you will not prevail."

Cold fingers crawled over Ember's skin. "I understand."

"Know your strengths and use them." He looked her up and down. "Tell me how you can beat me."

She stared at him, waiting for him to break into a grin at any moment. He'd just finished lecturing her about how she relied on instinct alone to fight. She had no chance of besting Barrow Hess. He had to be joking. The smile she expected didn't come.

"Your strengths," he said again.

"I—" He wanted an answer and she had to find one. But what could he be thinking? She was armed only with the ceremonial dagger she'd been given the night she was called to the Guard. They were on a practice field so she could learn how to fight—but she had yet to gain any skills.

Barrow folded his arms across his chest. "Very well, then. Start with my weaknesses instead."

"But you don't have—" Ember bit her tongue, blushing as she realized she was about to proclaim his perfection.

The ghost of a smile passed over his face.

"I mean . . . how could you lose?" she asked while her pulse skittered anxiously.

"I rarely lose." He let his full smile appear then. She looked away, feeling unsteady, and not just because she still didn't know how to answer him.

"Let go of your expectations," he said, putting his hands on her shoulders and forcing her to look directly at him. "Forget anything you know of me. Look at me as a body—the body of an attacker, an enemy. Your enemy."

He stepped back to let her assess his frame.

"What do you see?" he asked.

"You're tall," she said. "Broad shoulders. I see strength."

He nodded. "How you do defeat strength?"

She ground her teeth, wanting to prove herself capable, but all she felt was her lack of experience. She didn't see a way to fight him and win.

"Let me tell you what I see." Barrow tilted his head, walking around her in a slow circle. "A girl. Sinewy but lithe. And she has fire in her eyes."

He was behind her when he suddenly lunged at her back. Without thinking she dove for the ground, tumbling until she came up in a crouch.

"What do you have that I don't?" His question was tinged with laughter.

He stood over her as Ember watched him. She was still coiled up like a cat ready to pounce. When she didn't answer, he lunged again, arms stretching toward her. She took advantage of her taut muscles and launched over him, pushing off his exposed back as he lunged at her. She landed on all fours and rolled to her feet, ready for the next strike, but was surprised to see Barrow sprawled face-first on the ground.

He swore, climbing out of the muck. "Speed. Instinct. That's what you have. You're even faster than I thought—that's why I ended up in the dirt."

She was relieved when he smiled at her.

"Again," he said, lunging before she could raise her guard. Her only choice was to flop onto her stomach, rolling over in the mud so Barrow's charge took him past her.

"What was that?" she shouted, but she was laughing as she looked down at her mud-covered tabard.

"Payback."

She laughed, but the sound became a shriek when Barrow rushed at her. Ember tried to scramble out of the way, but she didn't move quickly enough. Barrow's arms locked around her legs, dragging her on her stomach through the mud.

"Remember what I told you," he said as she struggled. "Your opponents learn your skills and adjust their tactics."

Ember squirmed loose and rolled onto her back, but in the next moment Barrow's body lay across hers, pinning her to the ground.

"Your advantages are speed and agility." His hands gripped her forearms, holding her down. "So I have to keep you still to win."

Breathing hard, Ember looked up into his face. He wore that infuriating expression of being on the verge of laughter.

"You're supposed to be teaching me," she said. "Not enjoying yourself."

"I believe I can do both." He smiled.

She gritted her teeth and tried as hard as she could to shove him away, but she might as well have been trying to lift a boulder.

"This is hardly fair." Ember glared at him.

"That's part of the lesson," he answered, still smiling. "Most fights aren't fair."

"Fine," she said. "Lesson learned. Are you going to let me up or make me spend the night in the mud?"

When he laughed, Ember took advantage of the distraction. She jerked hard beneath him, making him lose his balance. Rather than freeing herself, Ember only managed to cause Barrow to collapse into her.

"Points for effort," he grunted, beginning to right himself. "I think you may be part fox, Lady Morrow. You've got the coloring to support my suspicions."

Propping himself on one elbow, he reached out to brush a strand of auburn hair from her face. For a moment his fingers rested against her cheekbone.

"I'll take that as a compliment," she murmured, trying to catch her breath. She'd made an honest attempt to free herself, but now she couldn't focus on anything but the length of Barrow's body pressed against her. His face was very close to hers. She could see dark stubble beginning to peek out on his chin and jaw.

"It was meant to be one," he said quietly, and went very still. Without warning he pushed himself up and stepped away from her. "I think that's enough for today."

Ember sat up, surprised by his sudden change in mood. He offered his hand to help her up but released her fingers the moment she was on her feet.

"I've kept something from you and I can't continue to do so," he said.

"What is it?" Ember asked warily.

"I wanted you to fight so you knew your strength, your inherent skills," he said. "You are a warrior, Ember, don't doubt that."

"But—" She braced herself as if waiting for a blow.

The soberness of his expression did nothing to quell her growing anxiety. "You're going into the field tomorrow. Lukasz told me last night."

She swallowed the sudden thickness in her throat. "Tomorrow?"

"That's not all." Barrow sighed. "We're investigating what could be a serious threat in the Black Forest. It's a high-risk expedition, so Lukasz will lead the mission himself. Five of the Guard will accompany him."

For a moment she felt relieved, knowing the burden of her first foray into the world would be shared. But Barrow spoke again:

"Alistair will be there."

The sound of Alistair's name jolted through her.

Barrow put his hand on her shoulder. "You cannot let what has passed between you be a distraction. He made a terrible mistake by burdening you with his desire. But I will not let it endanger you."

Ember drew a long breath before saying, "I won't let it get in the way. I'm here for a purpose that has nothing to do with Alistair. He's a member of the Guard, which makes him my brother and friend. As you said, we live and die for each other."

"Very well," he said, though with slight hesitation. "When we're in the field, I want you to stay close to me. You've proven capable in combat, but that won't compensate for the shock of facing off with a beast that wants to kill you."

"The revenant wanted to kill me," Ember countered.

Barrow regarded her calmly. "Yes. It did."

He picked up his sword belt, wincing slightly as he did. "And I'll bear the bruises that witness to your skill. It still would benefit you to watch and learn from the rest of the group. Don't endanger yourself unnecessarily."

"Why would I?" Ember regretted the sharpness in her voice, especially when Barrow gave her a thin, cold smile.

"Because you may be a natural warrior, but you're human," he said. "You'll be tempted to make a point to Alistair. And perhaps try to impress Lukasz. Both choices would endanger you . . . and all of us."

Ember bowed her head, kicking the dirt as shame washed over her. How was it that this tall knight could look at her and see into her heart? Every word he'd spoken was true. She wanted to show Alistair she belonged among the knights, that she was as much of a warrior as he. And she wanted Lukasz to see her as a valuable addition to the Guard. Most of all, she wanted Barrow to have no regrets about choosing to be her mentor.

Barrow's light touch on her arm drew her eyes up.

"Come, Ember," he said. "It's time to restore the strength you spent today."

SEVENTEEN

TWO THINGS HAD ROBBED Ember of sleep. The first was Alistair. All through the night any sound reminiscent of footsteps had made her tense, one hand clutching the dagger beneath her pillow. She couldn't go on like this. As much as she'd spoken the words to Barrow that her commitment to the Guard was beyond any grudge she might bear toward Alistair, she worried that it might not prove true tomorrow.

Adrenaline building from nightfall to dawn's first light was the second reason she hadn't rested. And it was that still-churning source of energy that kept her from exhaustion despite her sleepless night.

Ember dressed and made her way to the barracks' main hall. Barrow, Kael, and Alistair were at their table from the night before. Taking the coward's path, Ember ducked her head and slid into a seat next to Sorcha.

Lukasz's deep voice rumbled, "Good morning, Lady Morrow."

"Good morning, sir," Ember said.

A servant placed a bowl of cooked oats before her. She forced the spoon to her mouth, though her stomach didn't want food.

Sorcha set down her spoon, fixing Ember with a puzzled frown. "Not that we object to your company, Lady Morrow. But it is customary that you are a constant companion to your mentor until your apprenticeship ends."

"Never mind that, Sorcha," Lukasz said. "If Barrow hasn't instructed Lady Morrow to join him for meals, then she may sit where she wills."

Sorcha shrugged and returned to her oats. Lukasz leaned back in his chair, regarding Ember.

"I'm told you fared quite well on the practice field."

Ember lowered her gaze. "Lord Hess flatters me with his praise."

The commander's laugh resembled a bear's growl. "Barrow is not known for his gracious manner! His fair assessment of your skill bodes well for us. You've been told of our mission today?"

"Only that I'm to join you," she said, gaining some confidence after Lukasz's pronouncement about her aptitude in combat.

"The others are used to encountering beasts of the dark," he said, smiling at Sorcha, who shrugged. "Let me offer you some illumination."

He turned his eyes back on Ember. "Our missions take us many places. Some near, some far. We respond to rumors of evil omens. Some of the missions lead us to baseless fears. Others pit us against those manifestations of evil we've sworn to defeat."

"What's happening in the Black Forest?" Ember imagined only a serious threat would compel the Guard to make the long journey from Scotland to the realm of the German princes.

"People are disappearing."

Sorcha stopped eating to listen, watching the commander closely.

"It's gone on for the past month," Lukasz continued. "At first only a few villagers went missing. But when children vanished, the rumors began."

"How many?" Sorcha asked.

"We're not sure," Lukasz said. "But enough to signal the presence of something unnatural in the forest and enough to create panic in the villages."

Ember stirred her oats, though Lukasz's story made the thought of another bite unappealing. "What could make people disappear?"

A sour expression crossed the commander's face. "Creatures first identified in my homeland. We call them striga."

"Night flyers?" Sorcha's mouth twisted. "Disgusting."

"Yes," Lukasz said. "And very dangerous."

"What are they?" Ember asked.

"Monsters," Sorcha said. "Monsters who feed on human flesh . . . especially that of children."

Lukasz nodded. "The stories of my homeland say that the striga were once barren women whose envy of other women's children turned them into these flesh-eating creatures: witches and cannibals."

"That's horrible." Ember's skin felt cold.

"It is," Lukasz told her. "In more ways than the obvious. The lore will eventually drive the forest people to search for a culprit."

Sorcha was shaking her head. "That always ends poorly."

"We need to hunt the striga and dispose of it," Lukasz told them. "According to our sources, rumors have begun to fester throughout the villages of the forest. Once accusations begin to fly, they'll surely find some poor woman, or more than one, to burn as a witch."

"The missions of the Guard are as often about saving innocent people from such fates as they are about destroying the real monsters," Sorcha said to Ember.

Ember's mind reeled. "None of the stories are true? Of witches in league with the devil?"

"Everything we've learned in Conatus would negate the verity of witchcraft as it is commonly understood." Lukasz stood up. "The evils we face are not of this world. Their true dwelling is elsewhere, a darker place still shrouded in mystery. We do all we can to learn of this spawning realm that plagues our world with its diseases, but our efforts have been for naught."

"And lately things seem to be getting worse," Sorcha muttered. She squinted at Lukasz. "What do you make of Eira and Cian's report?"

Lukasz shook his head slowly. "I wouldn't wager a guess as to what might have caused what they found. We'll find out soon enough, though. The Circle will send out another patrol to the village as soon as we've completed this mission."

"Something's happened to another village?" Ember asked, noting the deep lines of concern etched on the commander's face.

"A nearby settlement is gone," Sorcha told her. "Dorusduain."

"Gone?" Ember frowned.

"The structures remain," Lukasz answered Ember. "Houses, tools, carts. But all living things that should have filled the village vanished, according to Cian and Eira."

Watching Ember's face twist in puzzlement, Sorcha said, "A messenger arrived yesterday with news that Dorusduain was gone. That was the only message he carried, and the source of that information remains unclear. Eira and Cian took it upon themselves to discover whether the message carried any truth, and since they've returned, the Circle has been questioning the messenger in the hopes that we might learn more about what happened to the people of Dorusduain."

A thrill spiraled through Ember at the sisters' courage. That two women would ride out alone, hunting a terror that could empty an entire village, bolstered her spirit. Ember hoped she could muster that same bravery in the Black Forest.

Her thoughts were interrupted by the commander rising from his chair.

Lukasz raised his voice so it filled the hall. "Those embarking on today's mission should now assemble in the paddock. We'll leave Tearmunn shortly."

As the room filled with the sounds of knights finishing their morning meal and moving into the pattern of the day, Ember went to the table where Barrow, Kael, and Alistair were getting to their feet.

"There she is," Kael greeted her warmly. "These two were claiming that it's my conversation that kept you away this morning. Say it isn't true, milady."

Ember laughed. "Of course not. I wanted to speak with the commander."

Barrow's brow shot up and Ember quickly said, "He told me about the striga."

"So it's striga," Alistair said, and Ember noticed he avoided making eye contact with her. "I thought that might be the case when I heard about the disappearances."

"An unpleasant day is ahead of us," Barrow said. "We'll have to spend hours scouting and then wait for it to appear."

"Wait for it?" Ember frowned. "Aren't we hunting it?"

Kael answered her. "They're called night flyers for a reason. I'd guess Lukasz is hoping we'll find its roost and catch it sleeping. But considering the number of villages affected, it's a wide swath of forest we'll be searching. Odds of finding it before nightfall are against us."

"We won't find anything if we dally here," Barrow said, and took off in the direction of the armory. Kael was soon at his heels, leaving Ember to stand alone with Alistair at the table.

She had started to turn when his voice stopped her.

"Wait."

Ember's heart jumped into her throat and she almost ignored him, wanting to run after Barrow and Kael.

"Please, Ember."

She slowly turned and found Alistair's eyes on her, large and pleading.

"I'm a fool," he said.

"You are," she said, letting her tongue run ahead of her mind.

Alistair blanched but stammered on. "If you choose to hate me . . . if you wish to curse my name, I will not begrudge you the right . . . but I beg for your mercy and your forgiveness."

Ember held her breath, startled by the sudden change in Alistair. She couldn't remember a time in their shared childhoods when he'd apologized for anything. He'd often taken a beating from his father rather than admit he'd done wrong.

"Please, Ember." Alistair's voice dropped to a whisper. "I would still be your friend."

Releasing her breath, Ember said, "As would I."

"Good," he said with a nod, but he wasn't looking at her.

Ember followed his gaze and found Barrow waiting at the far side of the hall. He was watching them.

"Come, then," Alistair said, walking toward Barrow. Ember followed, and when they reached him, Alistair said, "I'm sorry to keep your student from you, Barrow. I simply wanted to wish an old friend luck on her first mission."

"She needs no luck," Barrow said.

"Of course." Alistair brushed past the taller knight into the hallway.

Ember began to follow him, but Barrow caught her elbow.

"Is all well?"

"Yes," she said truthfully. Alistair's admission of offense had freed the painful knot tied in her belly for the past day.

Barrow looked into her eyes for a moment, searching for proof that she'd spoken honestly, and then continued into the hall. She walked beside him in silence.

The paddock was located between the practice field and the stables. They came upon Ian and two stable hands holding six restless horses, Caber and Toshach among them.

An older man with a shiny, bald head, who was cloaked in the same dark gray robes worn by Lora, stood alongside the Guard's commander.

"When you're ready, Hamish," Lukasz said.

Hamish bowed. "Commander."

From within the folds of his robes, Hamish produced two slender metal spikes unlike anything Ember had seen. Stranger yet, the bald man began to stab the air with the spikes. His arms reached high and dipped low.

As he moved, the air began to change. No longer was Hamish striking at the air; instead he was pulling shimmering threads of light through the empty space before him. The spikes moved faster and faster. The bright threads twisted, layering atop one another. The horses began to paw the earth, shying away from the ribbons of light that flowed from Hamish's spikes. Soon a tall, gleaming rectangle appeared holding an image in its depths more vivid than a tapestry. Within the light-filled shape Ember could see a heavily forested slope.

Hamish spun to a stop. He bent over, panting. Sweat poured over his scalp and down his face.

Ember had taken several steps back.

"What is that?" she whispered more to herself than to anyone else.

But Alistair had made his way to her side. "That is how we can make it to Cornwall and back in a day."

"But how?" She gazed at the shimmering image, her heart battering her ribs.

"The mysteries of the clerics are many." Barrow approached her from the other side. She thought she noticed him shoot Alistair a warning glance. "One of the secrets they've unlocked is this: a means to open doors to far-off places."

Ember's breath was coming fast. Her first encounter with the wonders at work within Conatus had fascinated her, but the reality of their existence was finally settling in her mind. Magic. Conatus wielded powerful magic. Real magic.

The danger of their position made her sway on her feet. Hadn't Sorcha and Lukasz just spoken of how many innocents were burned for accusations of witchcraft? And there was no innocence to be found here. If others were to learn what went on behind the walls of the keep, surely they would all be tied to stakes and set aflame. It had already happened to the Templars. What was there to stop it from happening again?

Barrow's hand was on her shoulder. She looked up at him and saw him taking in the fear in her eyes.

"The path is here," he said quietly. "But you are free to walk it or choose another way."

As he spoke, Sorcha moved into the light, leading a roan gelding, and was gone. No, not gone . . . but in a different place. Through the wavering gleam of the doorway Ember could see her standing near a tall pine tree. Lukasz and his dapple-gray mare went after her, followed by Kael and Alistair with their mounts.

"What do you choose?" Barrow said, remaining at her side.

Ember ran her fingers over Silence and Sorrow, hanging in their leather sheaths at her sides. She answered him by taking Caber's reins from Ian and walking into the light.

Her skin prickled as she passed through the door, as if hundreds of butterfly wings brushed against her and then were gone. Caber pranced and snorted as they moved through the light but gave no other signs of distress.

Alistair was waiting for her on the other side of the door. "Incredible, isn't it?"

They stood in the midst of tall pines, the cover of the trees much denser than that of Glen Shiel. Sunbeams struggled to pierce the cloak of branches.

"Can it be real?" Ember murmured. "Are we truly in the German forest?"

"It's real." As Barrow answered, the light-filled door vanished, making her gasp. Toshach swished his tail as if nothing extraordinary had happened.

"Where did it go?"

"Hamish closed the door," Barrow said. "Leaving the portals open would expose Tearmunn to discovery. And the magic that Hamish wields is rare. We've found few individuals who can master the art of weaving portals."

While logical, his answer didn't speak to Ember's primary concern. "But how do we get back?"

"A door will reopen here at the appointed hour tomorrow, as the mission is likely to take us through the night." Barrow moved to Lukasz's side and Toshach pranced to impress the commander's mare, who eyed the eager stallion with disdain. The commander was gazing up into the tree cover, turning in a slow circle.

"It makes me miss my homeland." Lukasz gave a wistful sigh.

Kael swung into the saddle of his bay mare. "You're imagining the resemblance. We're much closer to France than Poland."

Lukasz threw him a cold glance. "Don't spoil my reverie."

Ember only half noticed the exchange. She was still mulling over the news that she'd be spending the night in a foreign land where flesh-eating monsters might be living in the trees. It wasn't a comforting notion.

"Don't worry, Em," Alistair said as he mounted his coal-black gelding. "If we find the striga early, we'll get to spend our night at a village tavern. The Germans brew incredible beer."

Ember returned his smile weakly. Caber nudged her shoulder, and she gratefully let him lip at her braid.

"At least you're here," she murmured, patting the stallion's velvet nose.

Alistair grinned at her. "My pleasure."

She didn't bother correcting him given that she'd pledged to restore their friendship.

When they were all mounted, Lukasz reined his mare around to face the group.

"Our work will be much less treacherous in daylight," he said. "Though also less likely to bring us success. Hamish brought us to the central point around which the disappearances have occurred. There's a village directly to the east. We'll fan out in pairs to the west, south, and north. Keep an eye out for evidence of the striga—its roosting site or remains of its prey. Should you find something, alert the rest of us with a horn blow."

Ember was about to ask about Lukasz's last instruction when she looked down at her saddle and found a small horn of polished ebony hanging from a leather cord.

"If we find nothing before sunset, we'll regroup here and proceed with our hunt." Without waiting for a response, Lukasz wheeled the gray mare around and set off to the south at a gallop. Sorcha clucked her tongue and her gelding took off in pursuit of the commander.

Kael stretched lazily. "North or west?" he asked Alistair.

"Does it matter?" Alistair asked.

"North is hills and woods," Kael said. "West is the Rhine."

Ember spoke up. "I'd like to see the river."

"As the lady wishes, then," Kael said. "Let's go, Alistair."

The two men set out at a trot.

"You want to see the Rhine?" Barrow asked Ember.

"The river is the closest I imagine I'll ever be to France," Ember said. "And soon my sister will make her home there. She's betrothed to the Count de La Marche."

"Is she?" Barrow nudged Toshach into a walk and Caber fell in beside the other stallion.

Ember nodded.

"Our work takes us to many places in the world," he said. "Even France. You may yet visit the French kingdom."

"That may be true, but I'll likely never see Agnes again, and since I have the opportunity, I would like to at least have looked on the land she now calls home," she told him.

"And why France?" Barrow asked. "Your sister had no suitors closer to home?"

Ember's laugh was abrupt. "She did! In fact, it was Alistair's older brother, Henry. I always thought her silly to be smitten with him. Henry's as hotheaded as Alistair. But when my father arranged the match with the count, Agnes gave no objection. He hopes gaining kin across the channel will bring him lands there as well. Even if she dislikes her new husband, Agnes would never cross my father."

And I wonder if that is the cause of her sorrow, Ember thought, surprised it had taken her so long to consider that possibility. She wished she could speak to Agnes. How many burdens did Agnes bear alone because Ember had been too consumed by her own worries about the future? She didn't know when she might find out. There had been no word from her family since they'd left Tearmunn.

"Mmmm." Barrow cast a sidelong glance at her. "And he had similar plans for you?"

"My father always has plans." She put her heels to Caber and the stallion leapt forward.

EIGHTEEN

THE COMMANDER'S prediction proved accurate. Though Ember and Barrow spent the morning winding through the forest and the afternoon traveling alongside the Rhine, they found no signs of the striga. In the course of their search they'd scared up a few deer and startled a peasant woman who was out gathering firewood, but otherwise they'd only had each other for company. No horn called them back. When the haze of sunset seeped through the pines, Barrow reined Toshach to the east.

"Let's return to the others."

By the time they reached their point of origin, the sun was gone. If a moon graced the night sky, its light wasn't strong enough to push back the forest's gloom. Ember squinted into the darkness, hoping at some point her eyes would adjust. She didn't know how she'd fight if she was blind.

Her fears were slightly allayed when Sorcha produced a lantern, which she hung from a wooden pole. The horn panes of the lantern were barely translucent, throwing only a bit of light into the shadows.

"So it's a hunt, then," Kael said.

"Yes." Lukasz passed a weary hand over his face. "We'll have to draw it out."

"And hope it's hungry," Kael added.

Sorcha shifted in her saddle and the lamplight flickered. "They're always hungry."

"And that works in our favor tonight," Lukasz said, swinging out of his saddle. "We'll leave the horses tethered here. The striga is no danger to them."

Kael jumped down from his mount and grinned darkly. "Horseflesh can't compare to human."

Barrow grimaced as he dismounted. Ember slid out of the saddle, leaning her forehead against Caber's neck and feeling regretful that she'd be leaving him behind.

When the horses were tethered, the knights walked a short distance into the forest and gathered in a tight circle.

"How do you propose we lure the striga?" Alistair asked in a hushed voice.

Ember didn't know if whispers were necessary, but the pressing darkness and thick silence of the Black Forest did make speaking in normal tones akin to shouting.

Kael kept his voice low as well. "I'd think that would be obvious. The striga will be looking for a meal."

Barrow nodded, and Ember's skin began to crawl.

"The villagers have begun to avoid the forest after dark," Lukasz said. "We should be the only prey available tonight. And with the forest folk hiding in their houses, the night flyer should be getting desperate for fresh meat."

"Ember is the obvious choice," Sorcha said. "She's the smallest of us, and if she rids herself of her weapons and tabard, she'll appear vulnerable."

Alistair bristled. "We're not using Lady Morrow as bait. I'll do it."

"I'm not afraid," Ember protested, though she had to push the words out of her closing throat. "I can make do with a dagger. Just tell me what to do."

"No," Barrow told her. "He's right. Revenants are vile foes, but a striga is a truly vicious and cunning monster. Your first mission is not the one in which to take such a dangerous role."

Lukasz nodded. "Alistair is as fine an option as Ember. He may not play the part of a helpless young woman, but he'll easily appear an overconfident fool."

"Thanks, Commander," Alistair said drily.

Lukasz grinned at him. "If the role fits . . ."

"Of course." Alistair unbuckled his sword belt and pulled off his tabard, handing both to Kael. "What now?"

"Take the lantern and start walking east," Lukasz told him. "We'll flank you, keeping to the shadows. I'd wager the striga will be hunting closer to the village, hoping it can catch someone who thinks it safe enough to step outside if they stay close to home."

Sorcha passed the lantern to Alistair.

"One more thing." Lukasz pulled a dagger from his belt, and before Alistair had time to react, the commander sliced open the side of his neck.

"What the—" Alistair clapped his hand over the shallow but bloody wound.

"It will find you more quickly if it can smell your blood," Lukasz said, wiping his blade clean.

Alistair pulled his hand away, gazing at the blood that stained his palm. "Wonderful."

"Stop complaining," Kael said. "You volunteered, remember?"

Alistair cursed under his breath, but he took up the lantern and moved into the forest. When he was a short distance ahead of them, Lukasz signaled for the group to follow. Kael took a path directly behind Alistair while Barrow and Ember moved into the darkness on his right. The commander and Sorcha followed to the left.

They stalked through the forest. As he'd directed, Ember kept close to Barrow. She took note of his carefully placed steps, each made with the intent to keep his presence silent, hidden from notice. Her mentor slipped from tree to tree, leaving no evidence of his passage. Her fascination grew as she watched him. Barrow seemed to embody calm and grace, the opposite of what she felt. Her heart slammed against her rib cage and her pulse roared in her ears, so deafening that she worried it alone would alert the striga to her presence. Her blood raced through her veins, aflame with fear. Each curving branch, shift in shadow, and any root that stretched out to snag her step made her pulse stutter.

Alistair, by comparison, created a ruckus as he moved. He yawned loudly and stretched, kicked twigs as he walked. Ember found it difficult not to laugh at his antics. Alistair did appear to be nothing more than an overconfident youth strolling through the night woods.

The flicker was so brief Ember wondered if she'd imagined it. Barrow came to an abrupt halt and she knew she hadn't. A shadow had passed through the lantern light. If Alistair had noticed it, he didn't give any indication but continued his jaunty stride without pause.

When branches of a pine to his right creaked, as if bowing beneath unusual weight, Alistair did pause. He maintained a calm repose, lazily glancing from side to side as would any person who heard a strange noise in the dark.

The striga made no cry as it attacked. It flowed from the shadows above, a dark shape falling toward Alistair. When the creature was nearly upon him, Alistair whirled, bringing the lantern around with a shout. The pole slammed into the striga, knocking it back. The creature wailed, its keening filled with surprise rather than pain.

Caught in the lantern's glow, the striga's features were made plain and Ember's stomach twisted at the sight. It had a human-like form, its skin leathery and the color of dust. Its wings were black and dwarfed its body.

The striga screamed at Alistair, revealing a mouth full of needlelike teeth. It slashed the air in frustration with taloned fingers as it hovered before him.

Three silver streaks sailed into view. The striga arched backward, its cry now one of pain. When it turned, Ember saw three daggers protruding from its shoulders. Kael rushed out of the shadows, throwing another dagger as he ran. Lukasz burst into the light, his claymore stretching toward the sky. Sorcha appeared at his heels, brandishing her short sword.

Barrow's sword slithered out of its sheath. Silence and Sorrow leapt into Ember's hands as she ran after her mentor to join the fight.

The work was done before they reached the others. The fourth and fifth daggers Kael had let fly tore through the striga's left wing, rendering it useless. The striga screeched and dropped to the forest floor. Before it could right itself, Lukasz was on it. With two hands gripping the hilt of his claymore he brought the tip of the blade down, piercing the striga's chest. The winged creature gave a violent lurch. Blood spouted from its mouth and then it went still.

It was a victory, swift and brutal. But a victory nonetheless.

Though she'd had no part in the creature's demise Ember felt a stirring pride in how easily her companions had achieved the night's aim. With a bit of regret, she slid her blades back into their covers.

"Gather kindling," Lukasz said, jerking his sword free of the corpse. "We'll burn the body and be on our way."

"Can we pass the rest of the night in the tavern?" Alistair called to Lukasz. "We're already on our way to the village."

Lukasz laughed. "Perhaps you've earned a drink."

"I've earned ten drinks," Alistair said.

Ember should have felt relieved, but the hair on her neck was still standing up. Alistair had propped the lantern pole against the ground and was lounging against it, a tired smile fixed on his face. He'd been very brave, and his courage made Ember wonder if she hadn't judged him too harshly. Beneath his bravado lay strength and dedication.

In the darkness behind Alistair and the lantern light, something moved.

She could barely make it out in the shadows, but something was there. It crawled down the tree trunk headfirst, claws digging into the bark, its wings folded like a cloak over its back.

Another striga.

"Something is wrong." Ember turned at Lukasz's alarmed voice.

To her left and right rustling sounds passed through the high branches, followed by an unnatural breeze. Wind born of enormous flapping wings.

Behind her Barrow whispered, "This isn't possible."

The noise grew. Gentle rustles transformed into buffeting winds bearing the promise of a gale.

Sorcha peered into the treetops. "No. It can't be. Lukasz?"

"It wasn't alone." Lukasz spewed curses before shouting, "Make ready your weapons!"

"Do not leave my side," Barrow said. And though she heard his command, she had no thought but for Alistair and the striga no one else had seen. It slithered down the tree and flattened itself to the trunk, camouflaged against the bark.

Alistair had straightened, but apart from the lantern pole he was unarmed. The striga behind him lifted its head, gazing at his unprotected back.

Ember shouted Alistair's name as the creature launched itself toward him. Alistair gazed at Ember in confusion when she threw herself at him. Her body crashed into his, taking them both to the ground. But Ember landed atop Alistair and it was her flesh that the striga found.

She gasped as its talons ripped into her heavy wool cloak. As she wriggled on the ground, desperate to crawl out of the striga's reach, the cloak tore away. The beast had no intention of letting its prey escape, and immediately it struck again. This time its talons sank deep into her shoulders. Ember shrieked as the skin and muscle of her back split apart.

Around her, shouts of confusion and panic rose from her companions.

Lukasz cried, "To me! Don't give them your backs. Form a circle here!"

In her peripheral vision she caught snatches of other striga dropping from the trees, falling on the knights. Two, three, four, five . . . the shadows of the forest had come to life, hurling themselves at her friends.

A triumphant screech made her ears ring. Ember braced herself for another blow from the striga that held her, but instead it buried its claws deeper into her and began to flap its wings. Ember groaned in pain as the striga lifted her from the ground by the long talons of its feet. Alistair shouted, jumping up and trying to reach her. But the beast had already risen to the treetops.

"Don't let it flee!" Sorcha called. "Kael, where are your daggers? Take it down!"

Ember heard something come whistling through the night air, but the striga zigzagged in its flight path, avoiding the attack. She twisted her head around. Already the glow of the lantern was fading as the tips of pines closed in on the rest of the Guard.

Barrow's voice chased after her: "Fight this beast, Ember! Free yourself and I'll find you!"

Ember's vision blurred and she struggled against unconsciousness as pain threatened to overwhelm her. The striga was bearing her away from the others, turning south as it flew faster and faster. She didn't understand why, but whether the creature wanted to feast on her without distraction or if it thought her easy prey while her companions were more likely to put up a fight, Ember knew she had to free herself—however impossible that seemed.

Her weapons still hung at her sides. She clenched her teeth, wrapping her fingers around the handles though she couldn't know for certain if she'd be able to lift her arms or if she might do even more, possibly irreparable, damage if she forced them to move. What she did know was that she would have only one opportunity to strike.

Taking a deep breath, Ember mustered all her strength and forced her arms to swing upward in a swift arc. She cried out as her arms crossed in front of her face and the blades hit their mark. Her scream one of agony as much as a battle cry, Ember felt her muscles tearing in the striga's grip.

The striga screeched and then groaned as its belly opened up. Viscera spilled out, raining gore on Ember's head and shoulders before slipping over her body and falling to the forest floor. The beast plunged out of the sky. Its grip on Ember slackened and was gone.

The creature, bereft of its life, was silent as it fell. But Ember screamed as the ground rushed up to meet her.

NINETEEN

THE COLD BROUGHT Ember back into the world. Her body shook and pain racked her shoulders, arms, and back. She pushed herself onto her hands and knees. The striga lay beside her, its split belly yawning toward the night sky. Ember began to retch, the cramps in her stomach nearly as painful as the wounds on her back. Though moving was agony, she crawled away from the dead striga, dragging herself along the forest floor. Her hands met the leather handle of one of her wheels. She felt in the dark until she found its partner, forcing back rising bile, unable to keep from imagining how easily she could have landed on top of the blades, spilling her own entrails only moments after she'd eviscerated the striga.

Having no idea where she was, she didn't know where she intended to go, only that she couldn't bear to be near the striga's corpse. Its presence was repulsive and some still rational part of her mind warned that rotting flesh might attract predators . . . or the other striga. She crawled until she could no longer bear the pain, then dropped to the ground, shivering and exhausted. Her cloak was gone, her tabard and kirtle shredded, leaving her bare skin exposed to the frigid air.

Where had the beast taken her? How far? And why had it carried her away from the others?

She knew she should try to stand up and find some way to

identify her location or at least make it identifiable to anyone searching for her. If anyone was.

The forest offered no clues—only eerie silence. She couldn't hear sounds of her companions or of battle. How many creatures had fallen on them? Ember thought she'd seen six or seven. Enough to overwhelm the warriors. What if they were all dead? What if the remaining striga came in pursuit of the one that had taken her?

Waves of exhaustion beat at her as she tried to kneel and slid her wheels back into their slipcovers. Her calves wobbled when she started to stand, giving out after only a few moments. She collapsed onto her stomach and then rolled onto her side, curling into a tight ball in the hopes that she might conserve some of the fleeting warmth in her body. The black swell of unconsciousness threatened to pull her back into its depths. Ember forced her eyes to remain open, knowing that falling into that darkness might mean she wouldn't wake up again. Between her wounds and the numbness overtaking her limbs, she knew she must fight to keep her body from succumbing to the cold and its weariness.

Though it was pure torment, she let her mind focus on her wounds because it kept her awake. If she started to go numb, she had only to move her arm or shoulder and the jolt of pain brought her back to the freezing night and her broken body. As time passed, even this tactic began to fail her.

She was slipping in and out of consciousness when she heard it: the soft thud of hooves against soil. At first she believed herself in a dream brought forth by desperate hope, but the loud snort, followed by a fearful whinny and shuffling noise of a shying horse, was sudden and close.

A moment later she heard Barrow's call: "Ember! Ember, where are you?"

Barrow and Toshach must have come across the striga's corpse, which likely startled the horse.

She tried to cry out, but only a croak slipped from her throat. A long moan of pain came when she tried to push herself up to crawl toward the sounds.

The hoofbeats were closer now and Ember began to drag herself along the ground. A tall looming shape emerged from the forest. Painted in darkness, horse and rider melded into a single shape and had she been a lost child, Ember might have thought she'd crossed paths with a centaur.

The image broke as Barrow swung out of the saddle and came to her side.

"You killed the striga." His voice was hushed. "That's remarkable. How badly are you injured?"

She couldn't answer. Any remaining strength had been spent in the short distance she'd crawled. Exhaustion and pain pushed her back to the earth.

"I'm sorry, Ember, but I have to see the wounds." She didn't even have the will to protest or cry out when Barrow rolled her onto her stomach. She did whimper, however, when he peeled back the tattered remains of her tabard and kirtle. Dried blood had pasted the cloth to her skin. She felt the warmth of fresh blood flow on her back.

Barrow swore. "These look deep, but I can barely see. I'll try to bind them as best I can."

He was gone from her side and she soon heard the rip of cloth. When he returned, he helped her sit up, then wound long strips of fabric around her body, covering her upper back and shoulders.

The pain was so horrible that Ember could barely stay upright. Her body was shaking and the night had gained strange floating colors that rose like fog as she gazed into the darkness.

"It's a poor job," he muttered. "But it's the best I can do."

He left again and soon another string of curses floated through the night air. When he returned to her, Barrow said, "The fates are cruel. I've found you, but the horn is gone. I can't call the others to us and I don't want to move you until there's light to guide us."

Ember didn't answer. She couldn't. She simply let her body fall to the ground as it wanted to. She heard her mentor whispering to himself.

"Damn! She'll freeze to death before the morning."

What happened next only came to her in snatches. The sound of a girth being unfastened. The soft, curious whicker of Toshach close by. The gentle tones of Barrow's voice as he spoke to the horse.

She was vaguely aware of the sudden welcome warmth as the stallion's huge body settled on the ground next to her and of her own form being carefully pushed up against Toshach's side.

"Don't think me a churl, Ember." Barrow stretched out next to her on the opposite side of Toshach. "If you aren't kept warm, you might not see the morning."

He moved closer, his body pressed against hers, his cloak covering both of them.

"Stay strong," he breathed into the crown of her hair. "Daybreak brings us aid. I swear it."

Through the haze of pain Ember smiled slightly. Part of her believed she had no chance of seeing the morning Barrow promised. But at least she would no longer die alone.

The morning did come, and at its first pale light, Ember's eyes fluttered open. She felt wretched, stomach-sick and still dizzy, but her mind was clear in a way it hadn't been the night before. At least she was warm. With a sharp breath she became aware of the cause for her body's sole comfort. Barrow still slept. His lips were slightly parted and his steady breath peaceful.

Ember watched his face, entranced by the opportunity to observe the warrior so closely without his knowledge. Her breath hitched the longer she looked at him, mimicking her uneven pulse.

She'd never been this close to a man, not even her father, who'd regarded affection toward his children as foolish coddling. Tucked against Barrow's chest, she breathed in his scent, earth and pine mixed with sweat and the warmth of skin. The heat of his body kept the chill of morning at bay. Unable to resist, Ember reached out and touched the bare skin where Barrow's shirt was open at his throat. Her fingers stroked the hollow above his collarbone and slid down until she could feel the rise of his chest muscles. Her hands were trembling, but she didn't want to stop. He was so warm.

Barrow's eyes opened and suddenly he was gripping her arms. She worried that lingering in his arms without waking him, and going so far as to touch him, had earned his disgust, but Barrow wasn't looking at her.

"Be still," he whispered. He rolled over and his gaze swept the forest.

She heard it then. A quiet rustle of cloth followed by a crooning, mournful sound.

"Can you move?" Barrow asked, voice low.

Ember tested her shoulders, wincing at the sharp pain in her back that answered the motion. But it wasn't unbearable. She nodded.

"I'll help you onto Toshach's back."

He leveraged her body carefully up and onto the horse.

Toshach flicked his ears, turning his head to look at his new rider.

"Slowly," Barrow told the stallion, and Ember wound her fingers in his mane as he lurched up.

Barrow stroked Toshach's nose, whispering too low for Ember to hear.

He turned and drew his sword. Toshach followed as Barrow crept with silent steps through the trees. When Barrow paused, she peered around the horse's long neck.

The body of the striga caught her attention first. Of course it would still be nearby, though she barely remembered crawling away from it in the dark. The sight of the thing in daylight was more awful than her first glimpses the night before. Devoid of life, it had a desiccated, hollow appearance and its mouth lay open, fixed in a final death cry—like something with a hunger that could never be sated. The crooning sound came again, drawing Ember's eyes to the right.

A figure was hunched over the striga's corpse. The head lifted and Ember saw it was an old man. He stood up, revealing a bony, thin body covered by tattered robes. His white hair hung in long, greasy strands around his face. When he looked at Barrow, he appeared neither surprised by nor afraid of the approach of a sword-bearing knight.

Instead he looked down at the body again and sighed. "You didn't have to kill her."

To his credit, Barrow took the strange comment in stride as well as the surprising fact that he'd spoken in English. "I'll have to disagree with you there."

"She only tried to lead you to me," the old man told him. "As she was bidden."

"And the others?" Barrow kept his sword at the ready. "Were they hoping to lead us somewhere else as well? If so, your beasts conveyed such an intention poorly."

A rasping cackle escaped the old man's throat. "My servants must eat. I cannot forbid them sustenance. I only needed one or two of you to find me."

Ember watched Barrow's grip tighten around the hilt of his saber. "I see."

"And the others you fought?" the man asked with a pained expression. "Are they dead as well?"

Barrow nodded. "How is it that you've come to this forest?" he asked. "Give me your name."

"My name does not matter." The man showed Barrow a toothless smile. "It has meant nothing to me or to the world for many years."

"Why is that?" Barrow asked.

The old man's smile vanished. Squinting, he tilted his head and peered at Barrow for a long while without speaking.

"You are not the one," he said.

When his eyes rested on Ember, she clung to Toshach's neck, pressing herself into the horse. The old man's eyes were much younger than his body and filled with a cold fire that made Ember shudder.

"Neither is she," he said.

"How is it that you summoned so many striga?" Barrow took a threatening step toward the man.

The old man's mouth twisted in disdain. "You are not the one."

"That's hardly important to me," Barrow told him, advancing another step.

"Kill me if you will, knight." The stranger's odd grin was back. "My corpse will answer you no sooner than I in this moment."

Barrow didn't respond, but Ember noted the quivering tension in his shoulders. The old man's eyes rolled up in his skull.

"Your friends approach."

The words were barely off his lips when rapid pounding hoof-beats sounded nearby. A moment later Lukasz, Sorcha, Kael, and Alistair were upon them. Caber was tied by a lead rope to Alistair's mount.

When the knights saw Barrow, sword drawn, facing the old man, they quickly formed a half circle behind the stranger, cutting off any path of escape—not that he'd shown any inclination to flee.

The man turned around slowly, looking at each of the warriors in turn. He shook his head with a weary sigh.

"Not here, not here," he muttered, and began shuffling anxiously in place. He continued speaking under his breath, carrying on some mad conversation with no one but himself.

While the others kept watch over the stranger, Lukasz guided his mount to Barrow.

"We've been searching for you all night," he said. "Why didn't you summon us?"

"The horn was lost sometime last night," Barrow told him. "I had no means to call for your aid."

Lukasz frowned but turned his gaze on Ember. "And, Lady Morrow, are you badly injured?"

Ember managed to straighten on Toshach's back though her own back flared with renewed pain. "I'm not sure."

"Are you in pain?" the commander asked her.

"Yes," she said, deciding there was no courage in a lie.

"I did what I could," said Barrow. "But my bandages are no substitute for the art of a healer."

"We'll soon return to the keep," Lukasz assured Ember. "And your wounds will be tended."

Ember smiled her relief and allowed herself to lean forward against Toshach's neck.

With Barrow at his side, the commander walked to the old man, who'd ignored their exchange in favor of turning in a circle while wringing his hands.

Lukasz's booming voice broke through the stranger's quiet ranting. "Are you the sorcerer who brought this evil upon us?"

The stranger's nod was bizarre, almost eager.

The commander's face grew troubled. "All of the night flyers we faced last night were summoned by your will alone?"

"Mine. Yes. Mine. Mine." The old man gave a few jerking hops, as if dancing in some twisted celebration.

"Bind him," Lukasz told Barrow. "His power is much greater than any we've encountered before. He must be brought before the Circle."

The stranger offered no resistance when Barrow tied his hands and feet. He made no sound nor did he struggle when Lukasz and Barrow slung him belly down over Caber's empty saddle, securing him to the horse in a way that would prevent him from putting the horse to his own uses. Caber pinned his ears and pranced, nostrils flaring at the strange scent of the old man bound to him. The chestnut stallion craned his neck and whinnied, turning his head in Ember's direction.

"I think he misses you," Barrow said, passing her and continuing into the forest.

He returned a few minutes later with Toshach's saddle. Lukasz stayed at Ember's side while Barrow saddled the stallion. They both helped her mount and Barrow climbed into the saddle behind her.

"Pardon my company, Ember," he said.

"I'm sorry to be such a burden." Ember fought the urge to lean against him. The memory of waking in his arms was close and startlingly vivid. She could too easily slip back into sleep, letting the security of his presence carry her away from the pain that held her body in its grip.

It was Barrow who pulled her against him. "A wounded warrior is never a burden. Rest now. You'll soon be in more able hands than mine."

Ember was grateful to relax against his chest. Her eyelids were heavy, eager to obey Barrow's command. As they dropped down, she saw Alistair watching her. When he caught her gaze, he lifted his hand and offered a tight smile. But she was already too far gone to return it.

TWENTY

BY THE TIME EMBER stirred again, the landscape that welcomed her from sleep was familiar. The steady motion of Toshach's gait slowed to a stop in Tearmunn's paddock. Ember sat up and immediately winced from the pain.

"You needn't move." Barrow's voice was at her ear. "We'll send for healers to bear you to your cell."

The thought of being carried in a litter from the stable to the barracks mortified her. "No, no." She straightened further without flinching to make her case. "I can walk. I don't think the injury is that serious."

"You've lost a lot of blood."

Ember gritted her teeth. "I can walk . . . please."

"As you wish," Barrow said. "But I hope you're not so eager to suffer that you'll refuse a bath and an elixir to ease your pain if I order them for you."

Ember smiled at the promise of hot water brought to her cell, and she would have eaten newt eyes if someone claimed they'd take the pain in her shoulders away.

She could feel blood and grime caked to her face and back, itching as it dried. Beneath the itch lay a steady, building pain nagging her like the drone of insects. Barrow's hastily wrapped bandages chafed at her wounds, but at least the sudden bites of pain kept dizziness at bay.

"If you insist," she said, and felt his chest rise and fall with quiet laughter. Unfortunately the motion sent pain shooting through her shoulders, but she worked hard not to show it.

He slid from Toshach's back and handed the horse's reins to a waiting stable hand.

Ember bit the inside of her cheek as she slowly pushed herself out of the saddle. If she moved carefully enough, she could almost ignore the pain. She felt strong hands grasp her waist, easing her to the ground. Despite her claim that she didn't need help, she turned with a smile to thank Barrow for his assistance. But it wasn't Barrow's face she found upon turning. Alistair still held her waist, though he dropped his hands from her sides when her eyes widened upon seeing him. From over Alistair's shoulder Barrow watched them. He didn't interfere, but his brow knit together as the pair stood awkwardly while the stable hand led Toshach out of the paddock.

"Thank you," Ember muttered, and moved away from Alistair. Though she felt unsteady, she managed to make her way toward the barracks. She could feel Barrow's gaze boring into her back with each painful step.

I will not falter. I will not falter.

"Let me help you." Alistair touched her arm and she jerked away before she could help it. His grimace was fleeting, though, replaced in a moment with a gentle smile.

"There's no shame in it, Ember," he said. "You did well. Killing a striga on your own is better than most initiates ever could hope to do."

Ember returned his smile, sorry that she should be so repulsed by his touch. She would have to make an effort not to shy away from him if she wanted to mend their friendship.

"Thank you, Alistair . . . perhaps you can assist me to the barracks?" It was a first step toward making things right between them.

Alistair hesitated but then offered his arm, which Ember took, letting some of her weight lean into him. Barrow, who had silently made his way to stand beside her, cast a wary glance at Alistair but didn't voice an objection. As Alistair led her forward, Barrow stayed at her shoulder, following like a shadow.

The rest of their group bustled ahead of them. Stable hands were already seeing to the horses while Lukasz and Sorcha gave orders. Kael stayed close to the sorcerer, who watched the flurry of action with a bemused smile even as Kael jostled him into motion.

Ember's eyes moved over the prisoner, who was being led by Lukasz a few steps ahead of them. The sorcerer walked proudly, back straight—a ridiculously dignified pose for someone whose clothes resembled badly deteriorated burial cloths. He was also calm for his predicament, acting more like an honored guest than a captive. Was he simply that proud? Or did he think showing fear before the Guard would only worsen his position?

"Stop!"

Lukasz raised his hand and all activity ceased. A woman was running across the courtyard, waving her arms and shouting at them. It took Ember a moment to recognize her. Eira was dressed in a silk gown dyed a deep blue that rivaled the night sky; its skirt dragged through the muddy ground as she ran. Her hair was piled atop her head in a carefully arranged mass of tiny braids and ringlets currently favored by noblewomen.

When she reached them, she spoke breathlessly. "You must take Lady Morrow and prepare her."

It was Barrow who stepped forward. The tall knight's body partially shielded her from Eira's view.

"What's happened?" he asked.

"The abbot is here and demands an audience with her," Eira told him. "He arrived an hour ago. Without announcement."

A ripple of tension swept over the Guard. Beside Ember, Alistair cursed under his breath.

"What's wrong?" Ember asked, but Alistair shook his head to silence her.

Lukasz frowned, glancing at the prisoner and lowering his voice. "But he was just here."

"I know," Eira said. The look she gave him was weary. "He received a letter from her father."

"Lord Morrow?" Lukasz shook his head. "He's interfering. He should know better."

"Apparently he doesn't." Eira searched the group until her eyes rested on Sorcha. "You know what to do. I've had the necessary items sent over to her room. Gather the servants you need and bring her back to the manor as soon as you can."

Sorcha nodded and grasped Ember's hand. "Come with me."

"She's injured." Barrow frowned at Eira. "Can't it wait? She must be seen by the healers."

Eira shook her head. "If the abbot has to see her in a sickbed, it will only make things worse. She'll have to bear the pain until he's satisfied."

Sorcha's grip on Ember's arm tightened. "We'll place a salve on the wound. It should give us a bit more time."

"But—" Ember's feet skidded on the ground as Sorcha began to drag her away from the group.

"Please don't argue," Sorcha hissed. "He can't see you like this."

"Who?" Ember said as Sorcha tugged her along, leaving the others behind. "The abbot?"

"Of course the abbot," Sorcha said. "We're lucky he insists on a large meal in the manor when he arrives. If he were in the courtyard to meet us, I don't know how we'd explain ourselves."

They entered the barracks and Sorcha began shouting orders to servants, who scurried to obey. Ember struggled to keep up as Sorcha took the stairs two at time. Waiting outside Ember's cell, Sorcha flung open the door and cursed under her breath as Ember stumbled inside. Even with the awkward, slow pace she'd taken to reach the barracks, her back and shoulders burned with renewed pain. She was trying to catch her breath when she noticed her room wasn't as she'd left it. Colors were strewn over her usually drab pallet—silk gowns in jewel tones had been laid out along with slippers and gem-encrusted hair combs.

"Hurry!"

Ember asked, "What am I supposed to do?"

Sorcha shook her head. "I'm sorry, Ember, I know this must be confusing. Time is against us. Once the abbot's belly is filled, he'll seek you out. You must be ready. Get out of those clothes!"

When Ember stood for a moment, staring at the other woman, Sorcha threw up her hands and then began roughly tugging Ember's tabard over her head. Forced to lift her arms, Ember swayed as a wave of nausea layered atop the searing ache of her wounds. Though questions battered her mind, Ember pushed them aside and let Sorcha strip her clothes away. Ember stood shivering in her kirtle when two women appeared bearing a copper tub.

"We didn't have time to heat it, milady," one of them said.

"It can't be helped," Sorcha said. "Scrub her down. Mind the wounds."

Resigned to whatever fate awaited her, Ember didn't fuss when the servants helped her out of her kirtle. They swiftly unwound the cloths that flattened her breasts tight against her chest.

Sorcha turned away to inspect the gowns. "Do you have a color preference?"

Ember glanced at the dresses: gold, pale blue, and rose were her options. She was about to answer when a wet, icy cloth against her back made her screech.

"Hush!" Sorcha chastened. "I'm sorry for the cold, but you must keep quiet."

Ember clenched her fists as the two women scrubbed her skin

clean with the frigid water from the tub. She was grateful when they took care to gently rinse the torn flesh of her shoulders. While one of the servants continued washing her limbs, the other opened a glass jar and smoothed a pungent concoction over her wounds. She flinched even at the woman's light touch, but as the mixture went to work, her pain was replaced by a cool tingling, then numbness.

The other servant had done a thorough job of ridding Ember of grime. Her body was shiny and pink from their efforts after a few minutes. No evidence of her wrestling in the mud of the German forest floor remained. She could no longer complain of pain in her shoulders, but she was so cold she was shaking.

"Here." Sorcha gestured for Ember to raise her arms. A clean, finely stitched kirtle descended over her head, followed by the gold gown. Sorcha straightened the gown on Ember's shoulders and then one of the servants tightened its laces. Ember's breasts, which had been hidden all day, now swelled against the press of the fabric. She blushed at the transformation, much preferring the androgyny of the Guard's tabard to this gown, which accentuated her womanly attributes.

Sorcha pulled the chair away from the small table and guided Ember to it.

"I have to ready myself," she said. "But Mary and Joanna will see to your hair."

The two servants got to work before Sorcha was out of the room. Ember held her breath so she wouldn't cry out as the women wrenched her hair free of its tight braid and began to comb out its length. She knew they weren't trying to be cruel, but their focus on speed made their hands rough. It took focus and will for Ember to stay quietly in the chair as her hair was divided into sections, half of it twisted atop her head and held in place by carefully positioned combs. The rest was left free, tumbling down her back like a crimson cloak.

"Oh, good." Sorcha reappeared in the doorway. Ember couldn't believe how quickly she'd transformed herself. No longer in her warrior's gear, Sorcha had donned a deep gray gown with an embroidered bodice. Her braid had been replaced by dark waves that tumbled over one shoulder. Taking in Ember's startled expression, the other woman laughed.

"I've had a lot of practice." She smiled. "And I cheated. The skin you can see may be free of grime, but if you looked beneath my kirtle, you'd think I took a bath in pig slop."

Ember laughed, grateful for a moment of levity after the rush of anxious preparation.

Sorcha stretched out her hands. "Come, Lady Morrow. It's time we present you to Abbot Crichton so he's assured all is well within Tearmunn."

When Ember rose, the two servants curtsied. She murmured her thanks and followed Sorcha into the hall. She wanted to squirm in her gown, which was odd given that she'd worn such clothing all her life and hadn't been bothered by it before today. The dress compared unfavorably to the freedom and protection offered by the warrior's garb she'd become accustomed to wearing. But something else scratched at her consciousness that was much more irksome than the gown. Walking behind Sorcha, she felt transfigured by this change in wardrobe, as if she'd been snatched back by the life she'd left behind.

Sorcha glanced over her shoulder. "I apologize for the costume, but we're forced to disguise ourselves any time the abbot visits."

"Why?" Ember asked as they descended the stairs. "I thought Father Michael fulfilled the office of the Church here."

The other woman tensed. "Father Michael lives with us and ministers to our souls as well as serving the village chapel. He is sympathetic to the demands of our mission and a true shepherd to his flock. But he's simply a priest—a good and humble man. Not the sort who rises to power. And as we are beholden to him, he is beholden to others."

They exited the barracks and crossed the courtyard. The sudden movement caused Ember's shoulders to seize up with pain, making her fully aware that the relief offered by the healer's mixture was only a temporary reprieve from her injuries, but she gritted her teeth and managed to keep up with Sorcha's determined pace.

"Abbot Crichton is Father Michael's superior and he controls the coffers of Tearmunn." Sorcha kept her voice low. "This keep—in the eyes of the Church—is actually an abbey, though obviously our order is nothing like those to which monks or nuns belong. Abbot Crichton is the head of this abbey, but he prefers the comforts of his own estate and doesn't make his home here. Father Michael was appointed to reside with us and see to the day-to-day spiritual matters of Conatus. The abbot visits us on occasion to be sure we're still submitting to the Church's authority."

"I don't understand," Ember whispered. "Abbot Crichton doesn't trust Father Michael?"

Sorcha laughed coarsely. "Trust has nothing to do with it. Tearmunn is hidden in this glen because it keeps us out of the world of men—for the most part. We have a few ties with the village on the loch. The clan lords of this region visit us, but only rarely. Abbot Crichton is the only one who makes himself a nuisance."

When they'd reached the manor, Sorcha paused. "You must take care with each word you speak to the abbot. He has as many nobles in his pocket as he can afford. His visits have nothing to do with ensuring we're upholding our vows and everything to do with keeping his pockets full."

"You bribe the abbot?" Ember gasped. She knew of priests who skimmed from a parish's alms or those who kept mistresses or even had children, but having spoken with Father Michael, she found it difficult to imagine that anyone who knew the truth about Conatus would abuse that privilege.

Sorcha nodded. "We have no choice." She took Ember's chin in a light grasp, forcing the girl to look directly into her eyes.

"Listen to me, Ember." She spoke softly but with intensity. "The abbot left Tearmunn the day you arrived. For him to have returned this quickly, asking to see *you,* means something has gone very wrong."

"My father—" Ember began, remembering Lukasz's words. *He should know better.* She shuddered. What had he done? Would he threaten Conatus to the point that they'd send her away?

"If he's bribed the abbot, I don't know what will happen," Sorcha said. "But if he's only complained and has yet to pay for Crichton's assistance, we may salvage this wreck."

Numbed by fear, Ember simply nodded.

"The battle you face now is as important as when you faced the striga." Sorcha's fingers brushed her cheek. "Courage."

"What do I say?" Ember asked.

"The abbot holds a limited view of what a woman's role in Conatus should be," Sorcha told her. "He tolerates Eira and Cian's presence on the Circle but wouldn't be so accepting of our calling to the Guard."

"He doesn't know?" If Abbot Crichton wielded as much control over Conatus as Sorcha claimed, it was hard to believe he could be so ignorant of their practices.

"If he does, he's elected to turn a blind eye to it," Sorcha said. "And we should be thankful he cares more about maintaining his own manor than interfering with ours."

"But if my father's written to him . . ." Ember's stomach twisted.

Sorcha nodded, confirming what Ember had left unsaid. "What you must do now is to convince the abbot that your father speaks lies to poison the Church against us. You cannot reveal anything about your calling, about the Guard."

"What will Eira have told him?"

"Even with Eira and Cian on the Circle we still know it is a risk to bring women into the Guard," Sorcha said. "Plans were already in place to counter a problem like this. There are many roles women can take in Conatus that could garner no objection from the abbot. Eira will have told him that you're training to become a healer and a midwife."

Ember gazed at Sorcha, letting her words sink in. She would have to lie to the abbot. And lie well. The only positive effect of how frightened she felt was that that her anxiety temporarily overpowered the pain of her wounds—a pain that had been mostly numbed by the salve but flared up if she moved too suddenly or without care.

Sorcha took her arm. "Keep breathing. It will do us no good if you faint before we reach the abbot."

Ember hadn't noticed she'd been holding her breath, but at Sorcha's urging she gulped air, which made her head spin. She let Sorcha lead her into the manor, through the long hall gleaming with candlelight. The heavy layers of their skirts rustled along the stone floor, filling up the silence between them in place of conversation. Sorcha guided her past the great hall and the door beneath the stairs that had taken her into the cellar. They turned a corner, heading into another corridor, and for a moment Ember thought they were going to the chapel or Father Michael's quarters. But Sorcha stopped in front of a door opposite the chapel entrance. The warrior woman bowed her head and closed her eyes. Ember wondered if Sorcha had paused to offer a brief prayer. Drawing a quick breath, Sorcha lifted her head and rapped on the door.

"Come!" a throaty male voice called.

Sorcha opened the door, and Ember stayed close to her as they entered the room. Her heart thudded against her ribs and she clasped her hands together to stop their shaking.

"There she is." The man who was seated beside Eira in the small but finely appointed chamber rose. He boasted more girth than height, and Ember couldn't guess his age. His slack lips complemented his jowls, which quivered with each step he took.

He stopped just short of Ember and Sorcha, extending his hand and revealing fingers covered in gold and gemstones.

"I was afraid the good folk of Tearmunn had misplaced you."

Ember curtsied, taking the abbot's hand—which was unpleasantly sticky—and kissed his signet ring. "Forgive me, Father Abbot. I didn't want to cut my lessons short. I shouldn't have made you wait."

"Your lessons?" The abbot fixed his watery gray eyes upon her.

She closed her eyes for a moment. If she spun too intricate a web of lies, she would surely end up caught in them herself. How to get through this without giving up the truth?

A polite cough made her eyes flutter open. Standing in a shadowed corner of the room was Father Michael. When Ember looked at him, she swore he gave a slight nod.

"I was learning what to do in the case of breech birth," she said. It was one of the only things about midwifery she knew. Women feared a babe that hadn't turned in the womb. Such cases too easily ended with a stillborn infant or a mother whose bleeding couldn't be stopped.

Abbot Crichton regarded her with a wan smile. "And you find this work fulfilling?"

Ember nodded. "To relieve the pain and suffering of the sick and weak is truly God's work."

"Your father expressed concern that you would find life within Tearmunn wanting." He returned to his chair, groaning as he eased his weight into it.

"My needs are few," Ember told him. "And they are all well met."

The abbot picked up a golden chalice and sipped the wine within it. "There are those who would argue that a young woman such as yourself might better serve God as a wife and mother, increasing the number of the faithful by blessings of your womb."

Ember's throat closed up. The pain in her shoulders was making itself known, protesting her stiff repose. Her dress was too tight, and she found breathing difficult. Heat prickled down her limbs. "My father thought perhaps that in time I would wed the son of a local lord; thus, I would serve Conatus and my father."

The abbot considered this and after taking another sip of wine spoke again. "It remains true that your father owes a great debt to Conatus. You are the payment for this debt. And it seems not unfitting that your marriage be delayed as long as we require."

Not trusting herself to speak, Ember nodded slowly.

"If you are amenable to your work here, I see no reason to interrupt your service." He ran his finger around the rim of the chalice. "Perhaps your father is simply overprotective. Or too eager to join his house with that of our lord Mackenzie."

Ember managed to force her voice out. "That may be true, Father Abbot."

"Very well," he said. "For now I shall inform Lord Morrow that his concerns are unfounded. You are dismissed, Lady Morrow. Go with God's blessing."

Given how unsteady her legs felt, Ember thought her curtsy enough of a miracle to prove she had earned God's favor. She was still a bit dazed from the episode when Sorcha guided her from the chamber.

Much to Ember's surprise Barrow was waiting for them outside the door. The three of them moved farther down the corridor, keeping their voices low.

"What happened?" he asked Sorcha.

"The crisis appears averted," Sorcha told him. "At least for now. We won't fully know what's transpired until we're able to speak to Eira alone."

They fell silent when the door opened. Father Michael closed the door behind him and came to join their huddled group.

"I'll ask you to come to the chapel, Lady Morrow," the priest said.

Ember frowned at him. Though pleased by how quickly and easily her audience with the abbot had gone, her mind was clouded and an ache was building in her head. She didn't want to go to the chapel, even with kind Father Michael. She needed her bed.

She threw Barrow a grateful smile when he said, "She's injured, Father. We should have the healers see her and then send her to rest as soon as possible."

Father Michael nodded. "Of course. But, my child, you must confess when you're able. I would be neglecting my calling if I didn't hear your contrition and offer what absolution I can."

"Confess?" Ember wondered if she was hearing the priest correctly.

"You did just bear false witness to Abbot Crichton," Father Michael told her.

For a moment a chill replaced the creeping heat that had been steadily draining Ember's strength, but she caught the sparkle in Father Michael's eye.

With a relieved breath she said, "I will give my confession soon, Father."

Father Michael's smile bordered on puckish as he made the sign of the cross and bid them good night.

Barrow cast a sidelong glance at Sorcha. "I take it she did well?"

"Remarkably." Sorcha laughed. "I think even Eira was impressed."

Barrow's rumbling laughter joined Sorcha's.

Ember wanted to laugh with them, but she was fighting to catch her breath. The heat that had been building beneath Ember's skin now beaded into sweat beneath her bodice and at her temples. Trembling spread through her arms and legs.

"I think we may have misjudged Ember's calling," said Sorcha to Barrow. "Perhaps we should send her out as a spy."

"That may be the case," Barrow said. "But we'd miss her in the Guard."

Sorcha nodded, smiling at Ember. "Where did you learn to act, dear girl?"

Ember opened her mouth but found she couldn't draw breath at all.

"Ember?" She could hear the concern in Barrow's voice, but she could no longer see his face, only a blur of colors. The floor beneath her feet tilted and she was falling. She barely felt Barrow's arms around her, catching her, lifting her up. Her skin was on fire, and the spinning before her eyes twisted her stomach into knots.

The sound of Barrow speaking was very far away. "She's burning up."

Darkness rose behind the chaos of colors, crashing down in a wave that swept Ember from consciousness.

TWENTY-ONE

ON THE OTHER SIDE of the closed doors Abbot Crichton swirled his chalice of wine, lifted it to his lips, and drained it in a long, single gulp. Then he poured himself another.

"Quite a lovely thing, our lady Morrow, is she not?" Wine dribbled from one corner of his wide lips. He wiped his mouth with the back of his hand.

Eira murmured her agreement, wondering when this boor of a man would leave her to the pressing work she was neglecting so he could linger in his cups.

"You'll understand, then, why I see it as such a shame that you would use her for such brutal work," he said.

"You find midwifery that brutal?" Eira asked.

With a groan, the abbot lowered himself into a chair, his girth spilling over the edges of the seat. "I never knew you regarded me as such a fool."

Eira had been worrying at the silk of her gown, thinking what a waste of time and effort it was that she and the other women were trussed up to deceive the abbot. His words froze her hands on her lap. Hoping her face was blank, she lifted her eyes to meet his.

"I'm sorry?"

"Dear, dear Eira," the abbot said. His smile reminded her of a coiling snake. "Must we play this game? The night grows long and I would seek my bed."

Refusing to take the bait, Eira said, "Forgive me, Father Abbot. I don't understand."

Abbot Crichton's smile vanished. "How long did you expect me to go along with this charade? I know about the Guard. Lady Morrow is simply your latest recruit. Hoping to establish your legacy, Eira? Is that the reason you took a nobleman's daughter and handed her a sword?"

Eira's jaw worked as her mind grasped for a response, finally settling on the truth.

"She was called to serve where she belongs."

"Are you so proud that you believe you can flout the natural order that our Lord established?" The abbot's words weren't angry, but languid and cruel in the way that a cat toyed with a captured mouse.

"This natural order you claim is foolish," Eira told him. "Why hinder warrior spirits because they're contained within a female form?"

"It sounds like you already have an answer for me." The amusement in his voice infuriated her.

"You know how vital our work is," she said. "Limiting the roles of those few who belong to Conatus endangers not only us, but those we've sworn to protect."

The abbot pursed his lips, nodding.

"If we had your blessing, we could train young women openly." Eira heard the fervor in her voice but pressed on. The abbot knew the truth about the Guard, which meant she had nothing to lose and she might even have the chance to sway him. "Nobles could send their unwanted daughters to us instead of hiding them in convents."

Abbot Crichton laughed. "You think the lords of England and

Scotland would prefer their daughters wielding swords instead of rosaries?"

"I believe many of the girls would prefer it," Eira said, lifting her chin.

"Perhaps that's true." The abbot shrugged. "But those girls don't tithe to the parish. They don't command their own personal armies. And they don't have the ear of any king."

Eira's shoulders wanted to crumple in defeat, but she forced herself to sit stiffly.

"Lord Morrow has petitioned me to return his daughter to him," Abbot Crichton said. "The accusations he makes are serious. Not only are you corrupting young women, but you are in league with the devil."

"Witches," Eira murmured, remembering the scene Edmund Morrow had made the night after Ember's calling.

"The Church must investigate such accusations," the abbot continued. "After all, we know the temptations of Satan can infect even the most stalwart of orders."

Eira felt blood drain from her cheeks as Abbot Crichton made the sign of the cross, saying, "We need only remember the Templars."

"You know what we do here." Eira couldn't stop her voice from shaking. "You *know*."

The abbot sighed. "Alas, I am often away and perhaps things have occurred in my absence that are unsavory. I make allowances for your unique purpose and know you must call upon strange forces to aid you in battle. Though you give me assurances, I know little of the mysteries your magicians employ. It may be these powers have led you astray . . ."

Eira stood up, giving the abbot her back. She didn't want him to see how frightened she was.

"What do you want?" she asked. "For the lady Morrow to be returned to her father?"

"The lady Morrow seems perfectly content here," he replied. Eira heard him slurp more wine. "She lies beautifully, which demonstrates her commitment to the Guard."

A dagger lay hidden within Eira's bodice. She wanted nothing more than to slide it from its sheath and give it a new home in the abbot's gut.

"Lord Morrow has only made a complaint," he went on. "He hasn't done enough to persuade me his cause is worthy. I believe the Circle might have a stronger position to take in this matter."

Eira turned to face him. "How much?"

Abbot Crichton dipped his finger into his wine, watched the liquid slide like a drop of blood onto his palm, and then licked it off. "Your tributes will be four times a year instead of two."

She clenched her fists. Though the Church supplied Conatus's treasury, the abbot already claimed a percentage of their funds to supplement his personal coffers. Now he wanted more. Her Guard had been brutally attacked by striga. An entire village was missing. But this man—who'd been appointed as the Church's authority over Tearmunn—cared only for gold.

Eira's hands were shaking, her lips tight and trembling with rage. She couldn't risk speaking for fear of what she would say.

"If you don't want to have this conversation again, I'd recommend that Lady Morrow be your last protégé," Abbot Crichton said.

"How do I know these new tributes will be enough?" Eira asked sharply. "Lord Morrow could offer you payment to retrieve his daughter."

"He could, couldn't he?" The abbot rose. "Only time will tell, I suppose."

Seething, Eira watched as Abbot Crichton finished his wine and waddled toward the door. He opened it, pausing to look over his shoulder at her. "I'll expect the first payment ready in the morning to take with me when I depart."

She didn't answer. She didn't have to. The abbot knew she could make no objection.

"*Deus le volt,*" he said. Then he smiled and closed the door.

Eira bowed her head. "No, Abbot," she whispered. "I do not believe God wills this."

Though her destination was the stockade, meaning another trip through the muddy courtyard, Eira couldn't bother with taking the time to trade her fine gown for a Guard's attire. At this point she would have delighted in seeing the gown burn. As a member of the Circle she had full access to any prisoner, and the warden stationed at the stockade simply placed the key ring into her outstretched hand and inclined his head in respect as she brushed past him and descended the stone steps to the cell block. Though it was unusual for a member of the Circle to question a prisoner alone, it wasn't unheard of. And Eira was desperate to free her mind of the abbot's arrogance. Interrogating the sorcerer would remind her of how important their mission was, no matter what petty abuses Abbot Crichton heaped upon them.

Conatus held few prisoners. Most of the sorcerers and black-magic dabblers they encountered were puffed up with pride enough to think they could best the Guard. As a result they died in the field, never having the opportunity to occupy one of these cells. At this time, the wild man from the Black Forest was the stockade's sole inhabitant.

Eira fitted the key into the lock and opened the thick wooden door. Though it still had the bleak, shadowed aura of a dungeon, the stockade could have been much worse than it was. The stone floors were dry and clean. Care was taken to prevent vermin from making their homes in the nooks and crannies of the building. Even so, the beatific expression fixed on the prisoner's face took Eira by surprise.

She entered the cell, locking the door behind her. The prisoner scrambled to his feet. As he gazed upon her his eyes widened; even in the dim light they took on an unsettling gleam.

"You." His whisper slunk through the air. "Yes. Yes. You."

"Do you think you know me, goodman?" she asked, keeping her voice pleasant. Lukasz had told her this man was mad. Perhaps if treated kindly, he would happily reveal the source of his power.

The man gibbered at her. She looked away when spittle flew from his mouth. "No. I do not presume, lady. I was only sent to find you."

The flesh along Eira's spine crawled. "You were sent here?"

I should summon the Guards, she thought. *Perhaps this man isn't mad but has set a trap for us.*

But she didn't call out. The silver gleam of the man's eyes flared and she was filled with the need to know more.

"What is your name?" she asked.

Despite the intensity of their roving gaze, the man's eyes couldn't seem to focus. They lolled about in their sockets, wild and constantly moving.

"I am but the messenger," he rasped. "Beloved and blessed." His English was clear but strange, devoid of any accent by which she'd be able to place him.

"Then give me your message," Eira said.

"You received the message. You came." He spoke almost reverently. "You and the other. But you didn't stay long enough. You didn't seek the source."

"I and the other . . ." Cold slipped along the back of Eira's neck. "Do you mean my sister? Are you speaking of Dorusduain?"

He crooked his finger at her, leaning in conspiratorially. "The village is gone."

Disgust twisted deep in her belly and Eira stepped back, regretting her decision to come here. She turned to leave him but was stopped by the man's anguished cry.

"No! Please!"

Eira looked over her shoulder and saw him on his knees, swaying in despair.

"Don't leave, great lady," he pleaded. "You must hear me. I've been sent to you."

"By whom?" Eira asked. She was unsettled but wanted to keep him talking. If she asked enough questions, surely she would garner useful information.

"My master." He lifted his hands toward the sky in supplication. "My lord."

"Tell me about your master." Eira had broken into a cold sweat. "Where is he?"

"Everywhere," the man told her as he scrambled to his feet. "Here and not here."

"He must have great power," she mused. "To be everywhere."

The sorcerer's wheezing laugh filled the room. "No one is greater. He is the harbinger of your greatest dreams and the nightmare of your enemies."

Eira was tempted to ask if the magician's greatest dream had been to wander the earth in dirty rags.

Before she could quip, the wild man spoke again. "He's shown you his power—the wonders he has wrought in your world."

Any humor kindling in Eira was snuffed out by his words. "Like making a village disappear?"

Revulsion filled her when he nodded and clapped with delight.

"He has been searching for you," he said, offering her a grin marked by blackened and missing teeth. "And now I shall have my reward."

"How can your master be searching for me when I know nothing of him?" Eira reached into the pocket of her skirt, fingers finding the hilt of the dagger secreted there.

"My master sees all. Knows all." The man's eyes rolled up into his skull. "He will reveal his secrets to you."

"Why would he do that?" Beneath her ribs Eira's heart jumped, reacting to the mixture of revulsion and fascination that pumped through her veins.

"You hold the answer in your hand," he said.

At first she thought he'd somehow read her mind, referring to the dagger her right hand gripped beneath the folds of her gown. But he cackled and pointed at her left hand, from which dangled the ring of iron keys.

The man clapped. "The door will open! Master, I have served you well!"

Eira's temper broke. "Old man, you are a prisoner and at the mercy of Conatus. You brought great evil upon this world and will be punished."

"You don't wish to seek him?" The man cocked his head. "He waits for you. He will honor you above all others. He has told me this."

"And if I don't seek him," Eira said. "If I give the order for your execution—which you surely know is your fate—what will your master do then?"

He bowed his head, shuffling his feet. Eira could hear him muttering but was unable to make out his words. When he lifted his head, his eyes were shining with tears.

"If you do not come to him, I have failed and will have earned my death."

"Your master won't come to save you? He won't seek you out here?" Eira still worried that somehow this man was only the first sign of a greater evil to come upon Tearmunn.

He shook his head. "You must go to him. He cannot cross over. The door remains shut."

Eira lifted the key ring; the iron keys jangled against each other. "The door you wish to open?"

"Not I. Not I." He gazed at the keys longingly. "Only you."

"Why me?" she asked.

"Only my master knows," he told her. "And I am not worthy of such secrets."

"What is this door you speak of?" Eira took a step toward him. He was harmless, she'd decided. And most likely insane. And yet . . .

"The door to the other side, the other world."

She froze. The other world. In sites scattered from Europe to the Holy Land to the Far East, clerics of Conatus had scoured ancient texts for evidence of the other—for that place from which Solomon had called forth strange spirits to build his temple. But all their searching led to naught.

It was hard for Eira to keep her voice steady. "Do you speak of the world from which you called the striga?"

He nodded eagerly. "But I did not call them. Only the master may do so. He called the striga and bid them serve me. No creatures of the other side may serve in our world without his permission. He is the ruler of all."

Eira rocked on her feet, hardly believing what she was hearing. "Have you any proof of this?"

"He will show you." The man scampered forward, reaching for her hand. Her dagger flashed out to press against his throat.

"Forgive me, great lady," he gurgled against the blade's edge. "I only wish to lead you to him."

Eira waited for him to back away. He groveled as he moved, muttering nonsense with each step.

"I have not agreed to seek your master," she told him. "If you value your life, you will keep your distance."

"Yes, my lady." He prostrated himself on the floor, making her stomach turn. "Yes. Yes."

The dagger shook in her hand and her pulse grew quicker with each moment. It was too much, so unexpected. This madman spoke of keys, but it was he who might be her key to everything.

"Have you eaten?" she asked.

From where he was crouched on the floor, the man peered up. "I need no sustenance, lady. I live only to serve."

She forced her lips into a smile. "I'll have food sent to you."

As she backed toward the door, the man moved to a squat. His eyes were huge and she worried he would burst into tears.

"Will you not come with me, lady?"

"We'll speak again soon," she told him. "You have my word."

"Great lady." He bobbed up and down, trying to bow even in his hunched position.

Eira rushed up the steps, pausing only to press the keys into the warden's hand. The Circle couldn't gather until Abbot Crichton departed in the morning. But when he and his gold were well away, she would call her peers together.

Cian didn't wake when Eira entered their room and stripped off her gown, leaving it in a heap on the floor. Though too occupied by thoughts to sleep, Eira slipped into bed to wait for the dawn. She stared at the ceiling with a smile playing over her lips.

How strange this world was, she mused, that good tidings were delivered from the mouth of a madman.

TWENTY-TWO

EIRA PACED THE FLOOR while the other Circle members milled around the long, narrow table. Claudio and Ewan represented craft; Thomas and Fionn hailed from the clerics in the office of knowledge. She and Cian, speaking for war, completed the Circle. Eira had invited the knights who'd been sent to the Black Forest to join them. The Guard received some unfriendly glances from Claudio, who believed Circle meetings should remain closed to even high-ranking members of Conatus. But Claudio and others of his ilk were the very reason Eira had requested the presence of the knights.

While Eira continued her restless passes through the room, Cian addressed Barrow.

"How fares Lady Morrow?"

Barrow, whose face was haggard from lack of sleep, said, "Still unconscious. Infection has set into her wounds. The healers are waiting for her fever to break."

Cian frowned. "Are they hopeful?"

"Yes." It was Alistair who answered her. "They've said a strong spirit will aid her. And no spirit is stronger than Ember's."

"That's true enough," Barrow murmured, earning a disdainful snort from Alistair.

Sorcha looked at the two of them, lifting her eyebrows. Barrow met her gaze and gave a quick shake of his head. Alistair ignored her.

Lukasz and Kael entered the hall. The commander's eyes were questioning. The summoning of the Guard to a Circle meeting was rare.

"Please be seated," Eira said.

The room quieted and all eyes turned upon her.

Offering a thin smile, she said, "We all know how quickly rumors spread through this keep. So I have no doubt most of you are aware of the nature of Abbot Crichton's visit."

Murmurs of affirmation answered her.

"The lady Morrow handled the abbot's inquiries better than we ever could have hoped," she told them. "Unfortunately the abbot seems to have found other ways to glean information about the inner workings of Conatus."

Claudio's eyes narrowed. "Are you saying he has a spy among us?"

Eira nodded. "I don't suspect it's any of our number, but a servant or a courier. Someone who has access but not loyalty."

"We must find the traitor!" Claudio half rose from his seat, but Cian grabbed his arm and pulled him back into his chair.

Eira smiled gratefully at her sister. "I'm sure we all share your indignation at this treachery. But I also hope you'll see the futility of weaseling out any such person."

"How can you say that?" Claudio snorted. "Let a fiend like that go unpunished?"

"She's right, Claudio," Cian said. "The abbot has deep coffers with which to buy informants. If we find one, he'll simply buy another. Our energies are better spent elsewhere."

Others around the table nodded their agreement, leaving Claudio to stew silently.

Eira waited until she was sure there would be no further comment on the matter.

Thomas, the eldest member of the Circle, folded his hands on the table. "I have no doubt we're all in agreement that avarice is the abbot's greatest sin. But what recourse do we have other than to submit to his demands?"

It was the youngest member of the Circle, Ewan, who added, "Thomas is right. We're under his thumb and he knows it."

"What of Lady Morrow?" Cian asked. "Did the abbot request that she be sent away?"

The members of the Guard who had joined the meeting shifted uneasily at the question.

Barrow and Alistair spoke simultaneously.

"That isn't an option," said Barrow.

"Sending her home would destroy her," Alistair muttered.

"Ember isn't leaving us," Eira said quickly as the two knights fell to silent glares aimed at each other. "And we will not sacrifice her for our own interests. She was called to the Guard and she belongs here. The abbot is simply using the girl for leverage."

"I was informed of the payment sent with him upon his departure," Fionn said. "But I would be a fool to think the issue ends there."

Eira nodded. "He's demanding an increased tribute. Four payments a year instead of two."

Quiet protests rumbled around the table.

"The threat he holds over us"—Eira lifted her hands, asking for silence—"is to reveal to the Church the presence of women in the Guard . . . and to lead his superiors to believe that we delve into dark magics."

Feeling her own anger building, she took a deep breath. "If we reject his conditions, we're facing accusations of witchcraft."

For a space of several beats no one spoke.

Then the room erupted.

"How dare he!" Claudio was on his feet while Ewan beat the table with his fists.

Thomas bowed his head.

"Does the man care for nothing other than himself?" Lukasz asked, shaking his head.

Alistair's face reddened with fury while Sorcha's paled.

"We'll all burn," she said. Barrow took her hand, scowling at no one in particular.

"Peace, my friends." Father Michael, who'd been sitting quietly in the corner of the room, stood up and came to Eira's side.

"Indeed this is deeply troubling," he said. "But God will show mercy to those who place their trust in him."

Sorcha laughed mirthlessly. "You're a good man, Father Michael. But your claims about God are quite empty when his agent schemes thus."

The priest's eyes were sad. "You speak the truth, Sorcha. We know too well that there are those who claim to serve God but serve only mammon. But the heart cannot serve two masters. The work you do here is God's work. Have faith and our path will reveal itself."

Sorcha returned his kind smile with a scornful stare. Hopeless expressions overtook the remainder of the group.

Keeping her voice quiet, Eira said, "There may be another way."

It took a moment for anyone to react to her words. Cian acknowledged her first.

"Another way?"

Eira took her time, choosing her words carefully. "After the abbot made his threats, I sought out the prisoner."

"Alone?" Thomas frowned at her. "This prisoner has powers we've never encountered, Eira. Any interrogation of him should not be taken lightly."

"Of course it was impulsive," Eira said. "And I beg pardon of the Circle. But I believe my desire to learn more of him may have proven fruitful. Vital, even."

Barrow's brow knit together. "The man is insane. I have a hard time believing he will be anything but a burden to us. How can we be aided by one whose words have no meaning?"

Swallowing her frustration, Eira smiled at the knight. "He spoke some sense to me, Barrow."

"Why would he gain clarity in your presence when he had none for us?" Barrow asked.

Eira opened and closed her mouth. She had been about to repeat what the wild man had said to her, that she was the one his master sought and only she. Something held her tongue—not a desire to deceive the others, but a twist in her heart that whispered to reveal that bit of information might hinder her from fully using it as she wished.

"Eira?" Cian was watching her sister with increasing concern. "What did he say?"

Quickly calculating how to share enough but not all she'd learned, Eira said, "He claims to know the source of the evils we've sworn to defeat."

"The source?" Lukasz straightened in his chair.

"Yes," Eira told him, then let her gaze sweep over the entire group. "The power of which you spoke, Thomas, this man claims it is no power of his own."

"He didn't call the striga?" Sorcha asked.

Eira shook her head. "He spoke to me of his master. One who commands all the creatures we've encountered. All we hope to destroy."

"That's not possible," Claudio said. "No such being exists."

Father Michael's voice was quiet. "As a member of the Circle, Claudio, you should know better than to speak of what is and is not possible. Is not most of our calling to defeat that which is impossible for most of our brothers and sisters in this world to fathom?"

Claudio dropped his gaze.

Encouraged by Father Michael's words, Eira pressed on: "If what our prisoner says is true, we might be able to hunt his master. If we can defeat him, it may mean we've cut off the path by which these monsters enter our world. Now we only hold these wicked creatures at bay; if we were to banish them forever, we would be honored above all others."

Barrow was shaking his head. "I don't believe it. Your hopes are understandable, Eira, but this man is raving mad. He's infatuated by his own power and making up stories to sustain his delusions."

"Have you another explanation for the six striga that served him?" Eira snapped.

"Eira's right, Barrow," Alistair said. "We were caught unawares. No sorcerer we've tracked has ever had more than one beast under his command."

Sorcha put her hand on Barrow's arm. "Even a madman sometimes speaks the truth."

Eira smiled, about to continue, when Thomas broke in. "Even if he is revealing truth to us, how does it change our standing with the abbot?"

Ewan nodded. "The abbot is our primary concern. Once we've determined how best to proceed, we can investigate the matter of this prisoner. We can keep him in the stockade as long as we need."

"We need more time to question him," Fionn added.

"That may be the wisest course at this time," Father Michael said. "I can pursue channels within the Church. Abbot Crichton has made enemies, and perhaps we can find a sympathetic ear among his superiors."

"Forgive my disagreement, Father," Eira said, feeling the tone of the room shifting away from her interests. "But even if such a friend in the Church hierarchy exists, the abbot need only begin a whispered campaign to spread lies about our order and we'll find ourselves subject to investigation. Too many fear heresy; we can't risk that. What I'm proposing would allow us to bypass all the corrupt channels of politics."

"How, Eira?" Cian asked. "Why will seeking out this supposed master help us in this matter?"

"Don't you see?" Eira struggled with her frustration. "If we find this master, we'll have the answers we've always sought. Our prisoner claims he serves a creature that opens the door to the other side. If we gain such secrets, how can the abbot oppose us? How could anyone oppose us? To manipulate our work would be to circumvent the very purpose of Conatus!"

Thomas, Conatus's quartermaster, blew out a weary sigh. "Dear Eira, what you're suggesting is a terrible gamble. You would make our work known to the public, which would invite chaos. The abbot already threatens to undermine our purpose. I find it highly unlikely that any new wisdom or secrets we might find would change the disposition of such a man."

"But—" Eira cast a pleading glance at Cian.

Cian spread helpless hands on the table. "I fear Thomas is right. The abbot has shown himself to be single-minded in all things."

"There's another concern as well." Lukasz rose, folding his arms across his chest. "If indeed this creature the prisoner calls his master exists, we know nothing of its capabilities."

"Go on." Claudio regarded the commander with interest.

Lukasz began to pace as he spoke. "The man we captured claims the striga weren't under his command but his master's. If that's true, who is to say that this being can't summon any number of monsters to his aid?"

Eira's hands balled into fists. She wanted to object, but she couldn't deny the soundness of Lukasz's words.

"What if this prisoner is here only to bait us?" he continued. "He offered no resistance to his capture. He sits in his cell without complaint."

"You think he means to lead us into a trap?" Barrow asked.

"I don't know," Lukasz said. "I'm only pointing out what's possible."

Eira bowed her head. Hadn't she suspected the same thing?

She looked up in surprise when Alistair said, "But we could at least send a scouting party. It would behoove us to seek out evidence of this creature, would it not?"

"Yes," Eira said a little too quickly, gaining a sharp look from her sister.

Eira returned the look steadily. "The Guard should send a party to hunt for the sorcerer's master."

"The Guard is riding to Dorusduain." Lukasz offered her a quizzical glance. "You'd have us split our force. We don't know what we're riding into."

"Forgo the mission to Dorusduain," Eira told him. "Our prisoner claims that the village is gone *because* of his master's power."

"How could you keep this from us?" Sorcha asked, drawing a sharp breath.

"I'm telling you now," Eira said. "What truth lies in this claim, I know not. But the wild man says he was the source of the message about Dorusduain."

"That's impossible." Lukasz scowled. "We captured the sorcerer in the Black Forest. The messenger who brought news of Dorusduain said he was stopped by a stranger on the road from Cluanie."

"I can't explain it." Eira straightened, refusing to give ground. "But how would he know of the message?"

Thomas scratched his beard. "Perhaps a coven of warlocks has risen. Our prisoner could be in league with others."

"Then we must force our prisoner to reveal the identities of his brothers," Sorcha said. "And we will hunt them down."

Barrow nodded. "If they've been working together, it could explain the large group of striga. They'd have more power in greater numbers."

Eira kept quiet. Though she couldn't pin down why, she knew the sorcerer wasn't part of a coven. The impossibility of his claims, his very madness, made her believe him incapable of the plot Sorcha was suggesting.

"And if it isn't a coven?" Cian asked. "Summoning striga is one thing—but what of Dorusduain? Have we encountered any warlock or sorcerer capable of emptying a village with no trace of bloodshed? If this creature the sorcerer calls master is real, what will that mean for us?"

"I fear it would mean war," Lukasz said quietly. "And a type of war the world has never seen."

Thomas was watching the commander. "I think you're right, Lukasz. Even if not a war, any unnatural skirmishes of a greater scale than those we are accustomed to, any larger number of these creatures, could draw attention to Conatus in a dangerous way. If their territories go up in smoke or are suddenly overrun by demons, we'll be answering to the armies of kings as well as our usual foes."

"Which would be just as bad as what Abbot Crichton threatens." Cian nodded.

Sorcha gritted her teeth. "Such a course could be our own undoing."

"I disagree." Eira spoke, suddenly desperate to regain control of this discussion. "If we're going to seek out this 'master,' we should not delay."

"You seem to feel strongly about this issue." Thomas turned to her. "Why?"

"Because Eira is always for war," Fionn grumbled.

"It's the perfect time." Eira ignored Fionn, answering Thomas. "Now that France is giving aid to the Welsh rebellion, the English are too distracted to pay us mind. And the French are too worried about England to notice what we're doing."

Kael thumbed the edge of his dagger. "If the English and French can't sort themselves out, this war will go on for a hundred years."

Barrow laughed roughly, nodding. "Indeed it will."

"What about the Scots?" Claudio asked. "Considering the location of this keep, it's them we'd best keep an eye on."

"They're mired in the succession, plotting ways to kill all the heirs apparent," Ewan said, earning a cold laugh from Fionn.

"And the Church is focused on the schism," Eira said. "As long as we keep Abbot Crichton happy with his payment for now, we won't have trouble with the Church. He's playing the same game we are, trying to stay out of the mess made by Rome and Avignon. And he's using the distraction of their squabble to increase his own fortunes. The more land and influence he claims, the more sway he'll have over whoever claims the papacy. The abbot is now the only one watching us. We have time to work with, but who knows how long that will last."

Cian folded her hands, resting them on the table. "I don't trust the soundness of this strategy, sister."

Eira's face went blank. "How so?"

"The prisoner is clearly unstable," Cian said. "We have no way of knowing if he speaks anything other than madness. Why waste our energies?"

"Then what harm could come from investigating his claims?" Eira smiled. "That's all I ask."

"Any time we send the Guard into the field there is a risk," Ewan said. "I'm not certain that this search for a source of the darkness we fight is wise. Particularly with the abbot looking over our shoulder. At any moment he could cry heresy and all our lives would be forfeit."

"But it is the only chance we have to find the source—the greatest mystery of all," Eira argued. "Why wouldn't we take it?"

"If it were that simple, it would indeed be a worthy mission," Cian said. "But I can't believe it's that simple."

"Cian speaks true," Ewan said. "We need more time. The prisoner is ill and his testament unreliable."

"Any delay is a mistake," Eira whispered, trying to mask her anger. "A terrible mistake."

Ewan shook his head. "Your petition remains under consideration, Eira. I only ask patience until we gain more wisdom on this matter."

"The Guard will investigate Dorusduain as we'd planned," Lukasz said. "After we've learned what happened to the village, we'll be better able to plot our next move."

Eira bowed her head. "As you wish." But her heart had already chosen another path.

TWENTY-THREE

EIRA URGED HER MARE, Geal, into the thick mist high atop the hillside, searching for the cairn. She'd visited this place before. As an ancient grave marker, the pile of stones had attracted the attention of a warlock. They'd captured him but not before he'd slit the throat of the foolish girl he'd lured to the site. Though she'd viewed it as a tragedy at the time, today Eira counted the girl's death as good fortune. A rightful end for an empty-headed ninny, so easily led to her doom.

A place where blood had been shed. That's what the prisoner told her to seek if she wanted to find his master.

She'd visited the prisoner each day since the Circle had gathered. Making her trips to the stockade when her peers had already sought their beds, she'd taken care that her conversations with the wild man were witnessed by no one.

His words were always strange, sometimes frightening. But the more she spoke with him, the more convinced she became that investigating the truth of his claims herself was the only course of action possible. That conclusion had led her here, to a lonely hilltop where a wicked man had taken an innocent life in the hopes of coaxing an evil creature into his service. Such incidents were often those that incited the Guard's trips into the field. More often than not, they arrived too late to prevent bloodshed, using the evidence of nefarious deeds to pursue the sorcerer who'd perpetrated such evils.

Conatus punished those who summoned darkness into the world, but they'd found no way to stem the flow of nightmarish beasts. That was why Eira made her way through the thick swirls of mist, seeking the lonely cairn.

Her mare, silver-white like the mist, snorted, pawing at the earth. Eira reined in Geal and dismounted. Animals always sensed the presence of evil, even the echoes of wicked deeds long past. The warlock had taken his victim's life more than two months prior, but Eira's steed still tossed her head and shied when Eira tried to lead her toward the pile of stones cloaked by the damp, gray air.

Geal suddenly reared, giving a piercing whinny of protest. Muttering a curse, Eira searched the hillside until she found the bone-white trunk of a dead pine on the ground a short distance from the cairn. She tied the horse to the dried wood and returned to the cairn on her own.

She gazed at the stones for several minutes. Her pulse was uncomfortable, drumming through her veins, reminding her that despite her decision to come here, she remained unsettled by the choice. What she had to do next didn't ease her mind.

Gritting her teeth, Eira drew her dagger and laid it against her palm.

He is waiting. Your blood will call him forth.

She'd questioned the wild man incessantly on this point. How could her blood bring forth anything? From what Conatus had learned of dark magics, at the least she'd expected to sacrifice an animal and chant an invocation, but the prisoner had laughed at her doubts.

Your blood will call him.

Eira turned the edge of the blade on her skin. With a single, swift stroke she opened her flesh. Crimson liquid welled up, spilling over her hand. She watched her blood drip to the earth in front of the cairn, half wondering if some hideous creature would burst from the soil in the hopes of devouring her.

Nothing happened. Eira heard Geal stirring where she was tethered. The mist continued to swirl around her. Doubts built in her mind, eroding the confidence that had driven her here. Why had she listened to the words of a man so clearly mad? It was no wonder the others had rejected her pleas at the Circle's meeting.

Eira pulled a length of clean linen from where she'd tied it on her belt. She was about to bind her sliced palm when a voice filtered through the mist.

"You won't need to do that."

She spun around, dagger held low. "Who's there?"

A tall figure loomed, its features obscured by the mist. "I thought you were expecting me."

Eira shuddered. Whatever she'd anticipated, it hadn't been this. The voice that addressed her was rich and smooth and spoke with far too much confidence.

"May I approach?" The speaker sounded amused.

Taking a few steps back so she could use the cairn as a shield if needed, Eira called, "Show yourself."

As if it had been commanded, the mist parted to reveal a tall man. He was dressed in simple but finely made garb: a heavy, dark cloak over a plain linen shirt and leather chausses. From what Eira could see, he bore no weapons.

He tilted his head, regarding Eira with a slight smile. His face wasn't unpleasant, but Eira wouldn't have called the man handsome. There was too much haughtiness carved into his aquiline features, and the turn of his lips hinted of disdain. His hair fell to his shoulders, sleek and darker than the richest earth.

"My lady." He addressed her with the semblance of respect but in contrast to the groveling prisoner offered no bow or even the slightest inclination of his head. Eira had the sense that this man deferred to no other.

When she didn't respond, his smile twisted. "Will you hide behind those stones all day?"

Eira grimaced. "You speak as if we're not strangers. As if you weren't summoned by blood."

"Blood is natural as water," the stranger said. "It's simply more personal. How would I have known it was you waiting for me without such an intimate offering?"

"It was no offering." Eira shuddered at the suggestion. "I'm only here to learn who or what you are."

"Very well." He shrugged. "But your hostility is unwarranted. Here—let me see to your hand."

When he spoke, the cut in Eira's palm throbbed. She glanced down only to see fresh blood welling from her sliced flesh.

"A gesture of goodwill," he said softly. "Come to me."

Her eyes ran up and down the stranger once more. She was still unable to see any weapons, nor did she sense imminent attack. Danger, yes. Danger hung in the air around her, thicker than the mist. And yet she moved slowly toward him, keeping her dagger ready.

If he attacks, she told herself, *I'll have no trouble slicing his throat. Closeness means equal risk for both of us.*

When she was within striking distance, she paused.

"Your hand," he said, offering his own to her.

With her right hand gripping her dagger tight, Eira extended her left hand toward him. She fought the instinct to jerk back when he touched her, though his skin was warm and he handled her injured palm gently. For a moment he simply looked at the wound, watching as blood pooled in her cupped palm.

His sigh sounded regretful as he dipped his fingers into the blood, tracing the line of her sliced flesh. His touch caused her no pain, but heat spread through her hand, tingling up her arm and into her chest.

When he let go of her hand, Eira gasped. The blood was gone. As was the deep cut. No evidence of the injury remained, not even the hint of a scar.

"Who are you?" Eira breathed, gazing at her unmarked flesh.

"An ally," he said quietly. "One who would aid you in your cause."

She frowned, tearing her eyes from her palm to peer at his face. "Do you have a name?"

"In my own lands I go by a name that your tongue cannot utter," he told her. "Here I am called Bosque Mar."

"Lord Mar," Eira said, betting the stranger's air of self-importance would mean that addressing him with respect was likely to elicit the most information. "I am Eira. A servant of Conatus."

As she expected, his eyes lighted at the form of address. "I know who you are, Eira. And I would hardly call you a servant. You are a warrior. A leader of men. Destined for greatness."

Her skin prickled. "How do you know me?"

"I have many eyes in this world," Bosque told her. "And I've learned much. All of which has led me to you."

"Why?"

"I would prefer to show you," he said. "Will you ride with me?"

Out of the mist another shape took form. A tall horse approached Bosque on silent hooves. Eira took a step back from the creature. To all outward appearances it looked like a stallion, but she knew it was no true horse. The beast's sleek black coat was alive, moving as if born of shadow. Its eyes were black as coal, but within their depths burned a sickly green light.

"Where are we going?" Eira asked.

"A place familiar to you," Bosque said. In a single, smooth motion he was astride the shadow horse.

Eira glanced into the mist. Somewhere behind this gray veil, Geal was tethered. She considered the weight of the dagger in her hand. With one blow she could dispatch this man called Bosque, ridding the world of whatever threat he might pose. But he'd yet to show any intent to harm her. Through some unknown magic he'd healed her wound.

"Very well." She went to find her mare.

Bosque's voice trailed after her. "You'll need to calm your steed. It will likely find both me and my horse . . . unsettling."

Eira had already anticipated such a reaction from Geal, but the horse had an obedient disposition, and while the mare balked as the tall rider and his dark mount emerged from the mist, she didn't offer unmanageable resistance. As long as Eira permitted Geal a wide berth from Bosque's shadow horse, the mare heeded her commands.

Bosque led the way, guiding his horse even deeper into the mist along the ridge of the hilltop.

"You speak of your lands." Eira spoke carefully. "Where are they?"

"My world lies behind the shadows of yours," he said. "Separate, yet tied to it."

"How is such a thing possible?" she asked.

He reined his horse closer to hers, which made Geal snort nervously.

"There are many worlds, many lands," he told her. "Some call to one another. Such is the case with my world and yours."

Eira frowned. "Call to one another?"

"When the needs of one world could be met by another, the two are drawn together." His voice was reverent. "Like attracts like."

The mist swirled around them, giving birth to haunting shapes that Eira tried hard to ignore.

"My home is sundered by war and death, much like this world is," Bosque continued. "I am but one of many who long for order over the ruling chaos." He turned in his saddle to look directly at her. "I am like you. Alone and in need of allies."

Though her heart stuttered out of its rhythm, Eira feigned scorn. "You'll understand my doubt of this claim. The man who sent me to you. Your servant. It was his forays into the occult that allowed striga to plague the Black Forest. Those creatures feed on innocents. On children."

Bosque watched her, giving no indication of surprise.

Eira pulled her eyes from him. "I have sworn to rid this earth of such monsters. You and I are not alike."

She was surprised when he laughed. "Oh, we are, Eira. You simply misunderstand me and the creatures I command."

When she didn't answer him, he said, "The monsters you seek out and kill to protect your people are sent here only by necessity."

"And what necessity is that?" Eira glared at him.

"You are a warrior and a commander of warriors," he answered. "As am I. The creatures you hunt are my soldiers."

"Then why are they here?" she asked. "Is not the war in your own world, or has it spilled into mine?"

Bosque shook his head. "You're right to question me. The war is being waged in my own lands, but the spaces by which I can bring my warriors into this world give me an advantage against my enemies."

She cast a sidelong glance at him. "How so?"

"The creatures of my world take their sustenance from things other than flesh," he said.

"The striga feed on flesh," she countered.

Bosque offered her an indulgent smile. "Human flesh is only a small part of what striga need to survive. It is their victims' terror upon which they truly feed."

"Fear?" Eira's chest tightened.

"Hence the reason they prefer to hunt children," he told her. "Their fear is much stronger, purer. The fear of a grown man or woman is tainted by their mind's attempts to rationalize the attack."

She bristled at the casual way in which he discussed the murder of children.

"But striga are among the basest creatures I can command."

Bosque shifted in his saddle. "For this same reason they are more easily summoned by your feeble magicians, as are the spirits that revive corpses or the mischievous imps that gain strength from cruel tricks. They enter your world by my leave, and by my leave they serve men here."

"Are you saying that the only reason these monsters cross over to our world is because they prefer the food here?" She wanted to gag. For the entire mission of Conatus to be reduced to a matter of predators and prey seemed like sacrilege.

"Perhaps it's too much of a simplification," Bosque said. "But in some ways, yes."

"Is that what happened to the people of Dorusduain?" Eira asked. "Has an entire village filled the bellies of your beasts?"

Bosque smiled slowly. "No. Dorusduain is a lesson . . . and an unfinished one at that."

"I tire of your riddles." Filled with disgust, Eira reined in her mare. "We have nothing more to discuss. How dare you insult me by rendering the world I've sworn to protect into cattle for your wolves to slaughter!"

He pulled up his mount. "Please, Eira. You misunderstand me. I only offer this poor explanation in order to reveal to you how it might end."

Her resolve to quit this meeting slackened. "End?"

"You and I contend with each other when we would do better to unite our efforts," he told her. "The truth is we want the same thing."

"And what is that?" Eira asked.

"To win our wars."

"My war seeks the destruction of your minions," she countered.

"Does it?" He smiled. "Or is there another war better suited to your nature?"

Bosque waved his hand and the mist parted. She couldn't help but gasp at the impossible sight before her. No longer riding on the ridge in the hills above Tearmunn, she saw the last curls of mist floating above a sun-drenched field. Peasants were at work in the soil, preparing for the spring planting. Their horses stood on a wide path that curved up to an imposing manor.

Eira gripped the reins, trying to calm herself. A ride that should have taken all day had somehow passed in less than an hour.

"I apologize if I've shocked your senses," Bosque said. "I merely wanted to save us the trouble of a long journey."

"You travel through the threads of the earth?" Eira asked slowly. "As we do?" She hadn't seen the shimmering light of a woven portal, but perhaps its presence had been shrouded in the heavy mist.

"No," Bosque answered. "I cannot open such doors. But there are other doors available to me. Sadly, my talent for travel is limited. I can only pass through them with the one who has called me here, as my presence here is tethered to that person. Conatus has the power to move armies at a moment's notice. An enviable skill indeed."

She didn't answer, unsure if she was more unsettled by the incredible power he'd just demonstrated, his observations about Conatus, or where he'd taken them.

"What are we doing here?" Sensing her rider's anxiety, Geal tossed her head. Eira was relieved to turn her attention to controlling the horse. Handling a restless mount was much preferable to considering the consequences of being in this place in the company of the mysterious Bosque Mar.

"Have I brought you here in error?" he asked, smiling. "Is this not the home of your enemy?"

Having gotten control of her mare, Eira nodded. Then she turned to look again upon Abbot Crichton's estate.

TWENTY-FOUR

"WOULD YOU LIKE to admire the manor for much longer?" Bosque asked Eira with the trace of a smile.

The look she threw at him was sour. "You speak to me as though you've offered a satisfying explanation of why you've brought me here."

Bosque laughed. "Why I've brought you here must be shown, not explained. Shall we pay our respects to the abbot?"

He urged his mount into a trot, leaving Eira's mare to follow a short distance behind. As they approached the ornately carved doors of the abbot's house, suspicion crept into her mind. What if all of this—from the prisoner to the strange appearance of Bosque on the hillside—were some elaborate plot orchestrated by the abbot himself? What if he sought a way to accuse her of treachery?

Eira shook off her doubts. Though he benefitted from overseeing Tearmunn, the abbot kept his involvement with their work minimal. He cared not for the arcane knowledge housed in their libraries or the magic wielded by their clerics. Sometimes she wondered if the abbot even believed that the evils Conatus faced were real. She also doubted he was imaginative enough to create such an intricate trap.

When they reined in their horses near the manor, servants hurried to meet them. Bosque murmured softly to his mount. The shadow horse shifted its weight and seemed to gain more substance.

The movement beneath its glossy coat became less pronounced. The strange green light in its eyes dimmed.

One of the servants took their horses to be watered and fed at the abbot's stables, which Eira had heard he'd filled with fine steeds from the far reaches of the earth—not to put to use, but simply to admire. The other servant led them into the house.

They were taken to the abbot's study. He sat at a wide table of polished ebony.

"Eira!" The abbot set down his quill. "What a pleasant surprise. I was just finishing up my correspondence with Rome."

Eira offered him a thin smile. "I hope you have good tidings to share."

"Tidings fair enough for now." Greed filled his eyes. "I was pleased with my agreeable parting from Tearmunn. I assume you've come here to ensure our good relations continue."

She didn't answer, glancing at Bosque. Why were they here?

The abbot rose and came around the table to face them. His eyes narrowed as he looked over Eira's companion. Bosque returned the abbot's gaze steadily. He stood a full two heads taller than the squat clergyman.

"And who is your companion?" Abbot Crichton frowned. "A guest from one of Conatus's outposts abroad? An emissary from the Holy Land?"

"I've traveled far greater distance than that to be here," Bosque murmured.

Abbot Crichton's mouth turned down sourly, but he lifted his hand. "I am the abbot of Tearmunn. Tell me of your origins and perhaps I will grant you the Church's blessing. You'll find it worthwhile to be in my favor."

Bosque eyed the abbot's proffered hand with disgust. "I need not your blessing."

The abbot stared at Bosque. His cheeks purpled and he spluttered. "What blasphemy is this? Do you know whom you address?"

"I do." Bosque smiled. "And I am here to make an offer."

"What dealings would I have with the likes of you?" Abbot Crichton spat. "You have no authority over me."

Eira watched the exchange with increasing fascination. The satisfaction of seeing Bosque insult the abbot made her toes curl inside her boots.

"It is not your place to say if you will or will not deal with me," Bosque answered. "You have caused my friend great pain."

"Your friend?"

Bosque gestured to Eira. "She makes great sacrifices to protect her world, and yet you dishonor her and her order."

"How dare you!" The abbot's eyes bulged. "I'll see you rot in my dungeon for your insolence."

"My lady." Bosque looked at Eira, ignoring the abbot's strangled protests. "May I show why I led you to this place, and to this man?"

With a shiver of anticipation, Eira nodded.

Bosque smiled and returned his attention to the fuming abbot. "I offer you this choice. Submit to Eira's will and plague her no longer with your petty quests for wealth and power. You are not worthy of her time or worry."

"Submit?" Spittle collected in the corners of the abbot's mouth. "Tearmunn and all within it defer to me."

"That may have been true," Bosque answered. "But it shall be so no longer."

Though he glared at Bosque, the abbot wasn't foolish enough to advance on a man who projected such pure physical power. Instead he lunged at Eira.

All Bosque did was wave his hand. The abbot flew back, toppling head over heels across the table and onto the floor.

"You would be wise to heed my warnings," Bosque murmured as the abbot struggled to his feet. His red-faced fury had whitened into shock.

"Who are you?" Abbot Crichton's voice trembled.

"The one who will change all things." Bosque lifted his hand, tracing a shape in the air. The path his fingers drew filled with flames in their wake, suspended in the air, blazing but giving off no smoke.

The abbot gave a strangled cry and made the sign of the cross. Eira took several steps back, but was more fascinated than frightened.

The flaming symbol hung before Bosque. It shuddered and pulsed and then burst outward. Where the fiery shape had been something new, something dark and strange loomed. Its substance moved constantly, not unlike the strange appearance of Bosque's horse. But this thing was no horse. It billowed like a plume of smoke and gave off the scent of burning hair and flesh. Eira swallowed hard so she wouldn't choke on the stench.

"Behold." Bosque smiled at Eira. "A soldier of my army."

"What is it?" Eira whispered.

"A wraith," he told her. "Capable of wonders you have never witnessed."

He pointed to Abbot Crichton and the wraith slithered toward the quivering man.

He shrieked, flailing his arms as the creature's shadow form poured over him. His fearful cries became screams of pain as the wraith snaked around him. The abbot writhed and screamed.

Eira knew she should be horrified, but watching the pompous man's torment sent a thrill up her spine.

The abbot's cries drew alarmed servants to the study. Seeing their master twisting on the floor, assailed by some dark force, they called for his guards. Bosque winked at Eira and summoned three more wraiths, which met the guards who stormed into the room. Their swords passed through the wraiths like sticks through water. Within seconds the guards, like the abbot, were on the floor screaming as the wraiths consumed them.

"Can the wraiths be killed?" Eira whispered.

"Not by any weapons known to you," Bosque told her.

Eira faced him, frowning. "If you have such soldiers, why do you seek my aid?" She shivered, gesturing to the helpless guards. "It would appear you are invincible."

"My power is limited here," Bosque said. "I can only give as much as is asked of me. I came at the beckoning of your blood. I remain only at your will."

"At my will?" Eira gazed at him, reveling in the promise of power held by his words.

"As I've said," Bosque said softly. His hand came up to touch her cheek. "You and I are the same. Let us help each other. This is merely a demonstration. Every nightmare you and your order have fought, every single one enters this world at my bidding. Imagine if they were here to do your bidding in my stead."

The abbot's screams became desperate moans. She pulled her eyes away from Bosque's penetrating gaze. His eyes were silver, full of a brightness that promised endless possibility.

"Eira, please," Abbot Crichton called to her. "Have mercy!"

Eira regarded the squirming abbot calmly. As he crawled toward her with the wraith still wrapped around him, her nose wrinkled, reacting not only to the shadow creature's scent but also repelled by the pungent odor of the abbot having soiled himself.

"Help me," Abbot Crichton sobbed. "I submit to you. I submit."

Behind Eira, the guards were still screaming. "You submit . . . to me?"

"Yes!" The abbot clawed futilely at the shadow tendrils that snaked around his limbs.

"Enough?" Bosque cast a sidelong glance at her.

Eira paused, watching as the abbot stretched pleading hands toward her. He thrashed on the floor, his agony terrible. And beautiful. Something new and alive with pleasure raced through Eira's veins.

"Not yet," she whispered.

The abbot shrieked again and Eira began to smile.

TWENTY-FIVE

THE WATERS WERE so dark that Ember didn't know if she was swimming to the surface or if she was struggling ever downward, sealing her own doom. She kicked hard, hoping that her efforts would win her light and air. The cold, watery prison clung to her, trying to hold her back. With all the strength she could muster, Ember pushed herself up, up, up.

She was gasping when her eyes opened. Squinting against the sudden light, she tried to sit up but groaned when pain shot through her shoulders and back.

"You're awake!" A woman in gray robes rushed to the bed where Ember lay. She put her hand on Ember's forehead. "And the fever is gone. It must have broken in the night."

"Where am I?" Ember asked. The room was small and well lit, but it wasn't her cell. Morning light streamed in through tall windows, washing dull stone walls in a buttery hue.

"The manor," the woman told her. "You've been battling an infection for the past two days. We were quite worried, but you pulled through. Your constitution is enviable—many people wouldn't have overcome the fever you were stricken with."

Ember's vision slowly adjusted to the sunlight. She glanced around the room.

Misunderstanding her searching gaze, the nurse said, "Don't

worry, my lady, you haven't been neglected. I've been stretching your arms to keep you from losing a full range of movement. You'll soon need to use your weapons again, lest you lose all the strength you'd gained."

Ember began to thank the nurse, but the woman went on. "And *he's* watched over you day and night. In fact, I was surprised to find you alone when I arrived this morning."

"Who, Alistair?" Ember asked. It was a thoughtful enough gesture for him to stay with her through her illness, if a bit possessive.

The healer shook her head. "No, no. I meant Lord Hess. Of course, Lord Hart has visited you too, but it's Lord Hess who's most often here."

"Barrow?" Ember frowned at the healer, more than a little startled by her words. Of course Barrow would be concerned for her welfare, but surely he had better things to do than sit at her sickbed.

At that moment Barrow entered the room, halting when he saw Ember awake.

"And there he is now," the healer said.

Barrow looked like a rabbit cornered by a fox, unsure whether to fight or flee.

"Does she need attending?" he asked the healer. "I don't want to disrupt your care."

"I was just leaving," she told him. "No walking yet, but she'll need to stretch her arms and back. She may need your help with that."

The healer collected the used bandages and her medicines. Barrow waited until she'd left, then came to sit in the chair beside Ember's bed. She noticed he had a thick, leather-bound volume tucked beneath his arm.

"What's that for?" she asked, feeling awkward. The knowledge that Barrow had watched over her daily since she'd fainted made her light-headed and her skin strangely warm.

Barrow seemed equally ill at ease. He rubbed the back of his neck, shifting his gaze away from her.

"I've been reading to you."

"Reading to me?"

He set the thick book in his lap. "Herodotus: *The Histories*."

Ember frowned at him, which at last garnered his smile.

"I'm supposed to be teaching you," he told her. "Herodotus has excellent accounts of the Greco-Persian wars. I considered Sun-tzu's *Art of War* but thought a narrative better than military philosophy for the moment. And even if you were unconscious, I thought you might . . . be able to hear."

Her throat closed and she looked down at her hands.

Silence filled the small space between them.

After a few minutes Barrow coughed. "Shall I leave you?"

She shook her head, forcing herself to look at him though her face felt strangely hot.

"I'm grateful for your company, but wouldn't you rather be out on a mission?"

He sighed. "Our missions are on hold while the Circle determines our best course of action."

"Our best course of action regarding what?"

When he balked, casting his eyes toward the door, Ember sucked in a sharp breath.

"My father . . . what did he do?" She was desperate for Barrow to look at her again. "What happened? Am I being sent away?"

Her chest cramped at the thought and she couldn't stop the anxious moan that slipped from her throat.

Barrow's eyes finally met hers. "Please, Ember—if the healer thinks I've caused you pain, she'll flay me."

"I won't go back," she said. "This is where I belong."

He didn't touch her but rested one hand on the edge of her bed. "You're not being sent away. The abbot has rattled the Circle, something he takes great pleasure in."

Ember slumped against her pillow. "But it was my father's complaint that brought the abbot here. He saw through my act."

"He knew about your calling to the Guard well before your father petitioned him," he said. "We believe he's bought off a servant to spy on our order. It's not surprising, but inconvenient."

"Maybe I should return home." She sighed. "If my father will bring this burden on Conatus, my presence risks too much."

"If it weren't your father, it would have been something else," he told her. "Rumor has it that the abbot believes himself worthy of a grander home—and he needs the funds to build a new manor. He took advantage of your father's complaint because it hits the sisters where they feel most vulnerable. Eira and Cian were the finest knights Conatus has seen. They want to ensure that other women can follow the same path they did, even women of noble birth. You're the first of what they hope will be many."

"Will the Circle meet the abbot's demands?"

Barrow rubbed his temples. "I don't know. They've been closed up in meetings and I've only been in attendance at one. I know little, but from what I've heard, they're split over the issue."

"Is there a choice other than submitting to Abbot Crichton?" Ember asked.

"Eira seems to think so," he said with a grimace.

Ember frowned. "What's wrong?"

He shook his head. "I'm not sure. Eira wants to resist, and I'd be the first to choose that path if I thought it viable . . . but something doesn't feel right about this."

"I don't understand." Ember didn't like the way Barrow's voice had tightened.

"The man we came upon in the woods," he said, leaning forward so his folded arms rested on his thighs. "He's imprisoned in the stockade. We've been questioning him day after day, but he speaks only madness."

"He looked mad," Ember said.

"For all intents and purposes he is mad," he said. "But he was able to call half a dozen striga into the Black Forest to serve him. Such a thing isn't possible—at least we didn't believe it to be."

"And Eira thinks he could aid us against the abbot?" Ember worried at the deepening strain on Barrow's face, so his quiet laughter came as a surprise.

"I suppose this is as good a lesson as Herodotus." He set the book on the foot of her bed. "We fight creatures that are unnatural, beasts that corrupt our world. We've learned bits and pieces of the ways they can be summoned and more importantly how to kill them."

He leaned back in his chair. "The aims of our clerics have been focused on drawing on the elemental magic held by the earth to combat those evils that don't belong here. The powers we employ in this war against darkness are natural repellants to the creatures we fight."

Ember lay very still, rapt by the tale.

"But Eira believes our energies misdirected," he told her. "She wants the clerics to shift their study to our adversary—the supposed master of those wicked beasts that surface from the mysterious dark."

"That doesn't seem unreasonable," Ember said quietly.

"No, it doesn't." Barrow drew a long breath. "I can't explain why I'm troubled by her request. It's that man we captured. He shows no fear despite being our prisoner. And he should be afraid. Any person we find dabbling in black magic does not see the light of day again. Because he allied with darkness, his life is forfeit."

"But he's what Eira wants the clerics to study?" Ember asked as pieces of Barrow's story fell into place.

"Yes," he said, frowning. "Eira believes this sorcerer has tapped more deeply into these dark mysteries than any other magician we've captured. And she's right."

He looked into her eyes. "Tell me if you think me a fool, Ember."

She opened her mouth to object, but he kept speaking. "Eira thinks our prisoner may have found the source of all that is evil. Every beast we kill. She wants to seek that source out and destroy it."

Ember held his gaze when he paused, gathering his thoughts.

"It follows that our enemies come from somewhere or something, but for reasons I can't explain, I don't want to seek it out, though Eira claims to do so might afford us the only opportunity to rid this world of these evils forever."

"I could never think you a fool," Ember whispered. The thought of a source that brought things like the striga and the revenant into being made her shudder. "What will happen now?"

Her mind was split, some of her attention still held captive by the thought that her father would continue to demand her return while the remainder cautiously mused over Eira's proposal. No matter how frightening the source might be, if these horrors could be banished from the earth, how could Conatus fail to attempt that mission?

Barrow shrugged. "It's in the hands of the Circle. Tomorrow the Guard returns to Dorusduain. Perhaps we'll find more answers to guide our steps."

"You're riding out tomorrow? I want to be ready," Ember told him. "I've already been lying about for two days."

She started to sit up but winced as tight skin over her healing wounds objected.

"You're not going back into the field until you've fully recovered. And you've already done enough in the fight with the striga." Barrow was on his feet, his hand on her shoulder as if to press her back into the pillows. "Don't strain yourself. You'll be fighting alongside me soon enough."

Ember lifted her hand, pushing his away as she gritted her teeth and wormed her way up the bed until she was upright. "The healer has told me if I lie here much longer, I could lose all the strength in my arms."

He nodded slowly. "The healer said you might need help."

"She did." Ember frowned. "I don't know what she meant."

"I think I might." His voice trailed off. He took a few steps away from her, looking at the door. For a moment she thought he was about to leave, but he turned around and came to her side.

"Try lifting your arms," he said.

Without hesitation she raised her arms. Pain made her gasp before they were level with her shoulders.

Barrow leaned over, taking her forearms in his hands and looking her in the eye. "This will hurt."

Slowly he lifted her arms. Her breath became shallow and she bit her lip, trying to will away the sensation that Barrow was about to tear her arms from their sockets.

"Breathe," he murmured. He drew her body forward so her chest folded over her thighs, stretching the muscles in her back in addition to those of her shoulders and arms.

Despite all her effort to swallow it, Ember choked out a sob.

"You're strong, Ember." Barrow held her, keeping steady tension in her outstretched arms. "Remember that."

"What are you doing?" The outraged question came from the doorway.

Ember started to lift her body, but Barrow kept a tight grip on her arms. "Sit up very slowly."

Her body protested as she retracted from the stretch. When her head was upright, she saw Alistair coming across the room. Barrow paid the younger man no heed, easing Ember back against her pillow.

She brushed a tear from her cheek, not wanting to look at Barrow and wishing she could have been stronger.

"It will get easier," he said, cupping her chin in his hand so she had to meet his gaze. "I can read to you for a bit and then we'll try again."

She didn't know what was worse, that she'd now cried twice in front of him or that she was going to have to go through the painful exercise again. And probably soon.

Alistair shoved Barrow away from the bed. "I asked you what you're doing, brute!"

"Alistair!" Ember glared at him. "What is wrong with you?"

Alistair's face was white with rage. "What's wrong with *me*? Look at you. He hurt you."

"He's helping me," she said, furious again that her face was tear-streaked. "It's not Barrow's fault that my recovery isn't pleasant."

He didn't reply but stood staring at her, breathing hard.

Barrow cleared his throat.

"What?" Alistair threw him an unfriendly glance.

"I was just waiting."

"For what?" Alistair asked.

"An apology." Barrow smiled at him.

Alistair's answering smile was cold. "Does a farmer apologize to his jackass for the sting of the switch?"

"Alistair!" Ember wished she could get out of bed and kick him.

When he turned back to her, his eyes were pleading. "He's baiting me. Can't you see it? Why do you trust him?"

"Why wouldn't I trust him?" she threw back. "And why would Barrow ever bait you?"

"Why indeed?" Barrow murmured, but the teasing lilt of his words had vanished.

Alistair ignored him. "Shouldn't the healer be ministering to you? I wasn't aware Barrow was qualified."

"Any one of us could aid Ember with these exercises." Barrow gestured to her. "Perhaps you'd like to take over?"

Ember's eyes widened. She stopped herself from protesting, but not before a pained expression cut across Alistair's face. Barrow looked at Alistair and then at Ember, his face suddenly troubled.

"I'm sorry I interfered." Alistair stared at the floor rather than meeting her eyes. "I wish you a swift recovery."

He walked away.

"You don't have to leave!" Ember called after him.

Alistair didn't look back.

Barrow's gaze followed Alistair's abrupt departure. Ember expected him to make a derisive remark about Alistair's ill temper, but instead he slowly backed away from her bedside. Avoiding her questioning eyes, he murmured, "I should leave you to your rest."

Ember frowned. "I thought you were going to read to me."

"So did I." His answer seemed directed to himself rather than to her. He didn't look at her when he said, "I'll send the healer to assist you with your exercises."

"Barrow—" she began.

He cut her off. "I'm glad you're awake, Lady Morrow. And I wish you a swift recovery."

Before Ember could begin to puzzle out his odd change in behavior, Barrow was gone.

TWENTY-SIX

EIRA WAS VAGUELY aware that Cian kept stealing glances at her. No doubt her sister was worried, but Eira couldn't shake herself out of a dreamlike state as they rode eastward. Today the sisters returned to the village with twenty of the Guard, nearly the full company, all armed to the teeth. Though only four knights remained at the keep—including Barrow, who'd requested to stay in case the lady Morrow's condition took an unexpected turn for the worse—Tearmunn remained well protected. The keep had defenses beyond its knights that were invisible to the eye.

On the road to Dorusduain, the restless mood of the soldiers permeated the air, stiff and edged with fear. But the cloud of apprehension that hung heavy over the rest of the Guard didn't touch Eira.

Eira's distracted state of mind kept flipping between two puzzles. The first was the night of dreams that held her entranced. While sleeping, she'd dreamed of the abbot's estate, of standing over the abbot with Bosque Mar at her side. They'd laughed, watching as Crichton begged for mercy.

It should have been a nightmare. But the scene she'd lived and then relived in her sleep filled her with a sense of delight. She wondered at her proclivity for taking joy from his pain but pushed aside her fears of moral corruption whenever they crept into her thoughts.

Hadn't Abbot Crichton earned his punishment? And Eira had shown him mercy by commanding Bosque to spare the man's life. The abbot was a prisoner in his own estate, but he was alive because of Eira's will.

Eira's heart bloomed at the memory. A single phrase uttered and this man—if she could call him a man—Bosque Mar had served her. She still couldn't comprehend what he was. And she remained wary of his assertion that they could work toward the same purpose, yet his power appeared immeasurable. As an enemy, Eira would have viewed Bosque as the worst kind of threat. Still, he claimed he wanted not to fight, but to help her. But how?

Her musing flipped to the second riddle of the day: what had happened to Dorusduain. *"Dorusduain is a lesson . . . and an unfinished one at that,"* Bosque had said.

The lesson was meant for her, Eira had no doubt. But what he intended for her to learn sent alternating spikes of fear and exhilaration through her limbs.

Lukasz's shout forced Eira out of her own thoughts. The soldiers had reached the edge of the forest, where the path disappeared among trees before revealing Dorusduain. The commander turned in his saddle, beckoning to the sisters. Cian and Eira rode forward. When they reached him, he asked, "Are you certain we must leave the horses here?"

"Eira and I are skilled riders," Cian told him. "And I was nearly thrown by Liath. Something in the place creates terror in the horses. We're better off on foot."

"Leave two knights here to watch over our mounts," Eira added.

"Fitch, Mercer," Lukasz called out. Eira watched as two of the younger knights of the Guard brought their horses forward. She let her eyes roam over the soldiers, feeling her own age in contrast with their rosy-cheeked youth. She recognized Fitch, whose face was as pointy as a rodent's, and lanky, tow-headed Mercer, but she barely knew them. Joining the Circle put her at a distance from new recruits to the Guard. This was the first time in months that either Eira or Cian had joined the Guard on a mission. Eira's chest pinched, signaling how much she missed the camaraderie.

"Yes, Commander." Fitch stole a curious glance at the sisters as he approached, making Eira tense.

We're little more than mythical creatures to these boys, Eira thought. She knew of the nickname "the weird sisters" that passed the lips of the younger ranks of Conatus along with stories of their exploits in battle before they'd joined the Circle. Though the name wasn't meant to be cruel, Eira felt pangs at the aloofness that had grown between herself and the people she led.

When Mercer reined his horse alongside Lukasz, he too gaped at Eira and Cian before turning his attention to the commander.

"The sisters have informed us that the horses won't tolerate whatever magics have been at work in this place," Lukasz told the men. "You'll remain here with the horses. Sound the horn if you're set upon."

Fitch was already dismounting; he seemed happy enough to stay behind, while disappointment was written across Mercer's face.

"Yes, sir," Mercer said, though his shoulders slumped a bit.

Lukasz stood up in his stirrups, calling to the Guard: "We'll continue on foot."

While Fitch and Mercer rounded up the horses, Lukasz led the rest of the company into the forest. Cian and Eira flanked the commander.

"Was it this quiet when you were here?" Lukasz asked Eira.

"Yes," she answered. The sound of the knights' chain mail and the clank of their weapons against armor was shocking amid the heavy silence.

Nothing had changed since their visit. Wildlife hadn't returned to the forest. Not even a breeze stirred the leaves of the trees.

When they reached the village meadow, Lukasz raised his hand, bringing the company to a halt.

"Three groups," he ordered. "I'll lead the first group with Eira and Cian in a sweep of the village itself. Sorcha and Kael, pick your men and take point for the second and third groups. Sorcha, take the planting and grazing fields. Kael, head into the forest that borders the village on the east. At the first sign of trouble—or any evidence of what's happened to the villagers—sound your horn."

Lukasz nodded to the sisters. With weapons drawn they moved into the village. Like the silent forest, the village appeared exactly as Eira and Cian had found it. Everything abandoned. No signs of life. The only change Eira noted was that the fires had finally died, leaving gray ash in their wake.

The trio emerged from the first hut and Lukasz heaved out a long breath. "All the houses were empty like this one?"

"They were," Cian said. "Every one of them."

"Let's make a quick job of this, then," Lukasz said. "If nothing has changed, I doubt we'll find anything here. We should separate to continue the search and rendezvous at the far end of the village. We're likely better off searching the forest with Kael's team."

"I agree," Cian said, moving off to the next thatch-roofed hovel.

Eira glanced at Lukasz. "Do you still think a warlock responsible for this?"

"I fear I don't want to know what could do this," Lukasz murmured. He left Eira standing beside the hut.

She hesitated, caught in the question couched in his words. She believed she knew exactly what had done this, though she didn't know how or why.

A lesson.

Uneasy, Eira gripped her sword tightly and passed by the houses Cian and Lukasz searched. She opened the door to another hut, finding exactly what she'd expected. A dead fire. Bread that had gained spots of blue-green mold since she'd last seen it. There was nothing to see. Nothing to learn from this place.

Eira started to turn, but something stopped her. A flicker in her vision. Movement. Keeping her sword low, Eira pivoted, her back to the open door. Her gaze roamed the small space. Nothing was moving. Dim light filtered into the house, barely piercing the shadows. Eira frowned and then choked on her breath when one of the shadows moved.

She could barely make out its shape. It hung in the corner, camouflaged by the darkness of the house. She knew it was watching her. And when it moved again, she knew it was aware she'd seen it. It moved again and she became certain the shadow creature had wanted her to see it.

A wraith. One of Bosque's minions. The very thing that had filled her dreams with cruel, wonderful laughter as it tormented Abbot Crichton.

Eira kept her eyes on the wraith. Now that her sight had adjusted to the low light, she could clearly make out its shape, a billowing cloud of smoke. Her pulse jumped in her throat, but the wraith didn't approach her. It remained in the corner.

Slowly Eira backed out of the house into the light of day. Her heart thudded against her ribs as she closed the door, waiting. Nothing happened. The wraith didn't emerge, didn't follow.

Had it been there the first time? With Eira not knowing that such creatures existed, had it floated in silence in the corner of the house, escaping notice?

A disgusted grunt made Eira start.

"I thought we'd find something this time," Cian said as she walked up to her sister, shaking her head. "But it's all the same."

Eira stood frozen while Cian surveyed the silent houses.

"I can't bear this," Cian said. "Will you finish searching the village with Lukasz? I want to get into the forest."

"Of course," Eira answered stiffly.

Two quiet voices were whispering to Eira. One urged her to tell Cian that something was horribly wrong. That they'd missed a vital clue because they hadn't known how to see it. But the second voice compelled Eira to keep her secret, at least until she knew more about why Bosque's wraiths were here.

"Thank you," Cian said. She peered at Eira. "Are you all right?"

Eira nodded, still feeling every heartbeat like a hammer in her chest.

Cian laid her hand on Eira's shoulder. "The emptiness. The silence. I know how horrible it is. We will make this right. I promise."

Eira forced a smile and Cian went to tell Lukasz that she was forsaking her search of the village to join Kael's team in the forest.

Suspicion pooled in Eira's mind as she opened the door of the next house. With only slight variation, rotting leeks on a table instead of moldy bread, this home was a twin to the last. Eira forced herself to draw deep breaths as her eyes adjusted to the dim interior. Remaining near the door, she searched the corners of the room with her gaze until she found it. Tucked in the eaves like smoke that hadn't escaped through the chimney was another wraith.

Without pause Eira slipped from the house, closing the door behind her. She would have wagered all her possessions that every hut in the village was now home to one of Bosque's shadow creatures. And she was sure the wraiths had been there when she and Cian had first come to Dorusduain.

But what was the lesson? Did Bosque mean to show Eira his benevolence? Death had lurked above the sisters but had been held in check. Or was the lesson's intention something else? Perhaps he wanted Eira to see the devastation he could unleash at will. Fifteen houses in the village. Sixty-some souls snatched from the village without warning.

A horn blast sounded from the forest. Lukasz burst from a doorway.

"With me!" he called to Eira as he ran. In an instant she was at his heels. They plunged into a forest as silent as that on the village's western border. Eira listened as she ran, twigs crunching under her feet. She expected to hear shouts and noise of battle. But nothing had followed the single horn blast.

They came upon Kael, Cian, and the five knights accompanying him standing amid the tall trees, wearing confused expressions. But they weren't fighting. Some of the knights didn't even have their weapons raised.

Eira whirled at crashing sounds barreling through the forest toward them, but she lowered her sword when Sorcha appeared with her team.

Sorcha glared at Kael. "You're supposed to blow the horn when you're in trouble, not when you get bored."

"I wasn't bored; I was lonely." Kael grinned at her. "Look at all the friends I have now."

"Kael." Lukasz didn't join in the quiet chuckling of the other warriors.

Kael smiled slyly at the commander. "You said to sound the horn if we found any clue as to what's happened. We may have found one."

"It's true," Cian said. "Two creatures ran into the forest ahead of us. And they don't belong here."

"Did you recognize them?" Lukasz asked. "Creatures we've fought before?"

Kael coughed, glancing at Alistair, who stood beside him, scowling.

"They were hobgoblins," Alistair growled.

"Are you certain?" Lukasz asked. "Hobgoblins aren't enough to frighten away a village."

"They were hobgoblins," Cian told the commander. "Why they're here I couldn't say."

"Hobgoblins point to warlocks," Sorcha offered. "Perhaps after they'd gotten rid of the villagers, they sent the hobgoblins in to steal."

"I didn't notice evidence of stealing," Lukasz said.

Sorcha shrugged. "It's my best guess."

"I sent Alan and Philip ahead to track the hobgoblins," Kael told Lukasz. "Unless you've found something else, I'd suggest we follow them."

"Sorcha?" Lukasz turned to her.

"Nothing in the fields but abandoned plows," she said. "I agree with Kael—we should track the goblins."

Lukasz nodded. "Fan out, but not too far. Make sure you keep a line of sight to Kael; he'll lead the way."

The Guard spread into a loose line and threaded through the forest behind Kael. Eira sensed the mood of the knights was both perplexed and sour. The continued, unnatural silence of the forest only heightened the tensions running through their company. Though each knight had been trained to move through the wilderness as quietly as a cat, the absolute stillness in this strange place made every rustle of fallen pine needles and gentle footfall deafening. Whatever lay ahead would surely hear them coming.

They'd encountered hobgoblins often enough. But these creatures were more nuisance than threat, dangerous only in large numbers and only if they caught you alone. When Eira snuck glances at her companions, she saw their furrowed brows as they tried to work out how hunting goblins could be connected to the missing villagers.

The Guard didn't know the secret that thrummed in Eira's veins. That village wasn't empty; it was full of wraiths. And now goblins were sneaking through the forest.

Dorusduain is a lesson . . . and an unfinished one at that.

Eira's skin prickled. Her lesson hadn't ended. She was beginning to fear what Bosque wanted to teach her.

A short, sudden scream rose from the forest a short distance ahead of them. Kael gave a sharp whistle and the line of Guards broke into a run. A second shriek pierced the air and then ended abruptly.

"Alan! Philip!" Kael shouted. "Signal us!"

No answer came.

"Stop!" Cian cried. "Stop now!"

The line broke as some warriors responded to her call and others plunged on, hunting for their missing peers.

"Halt!" Lukasz's deep voice pulled the still-running soldiers back to their commander.

Cian was turning in a slow circle, looking up into the trees. Both hands gripped her sword hilt.

"Be ready!" Lukasz called. The knights formed a tight ring around the commander and Cian, backs to Lukasz and weapons pointed out toward the forest.

"What is it, Cian?" Lukasz asked.

"The trees have changed," she whispered. "Look at the trees."

Eira followed her sister's gaze, at first seeing only the dense clusters of pines tall and broad enough to blot out the sky. Looking more carefully, Eira noticed that some of the trees differed from the russet bark of the evergreens. Dead tree trunks, leeched of color, were smattered among the healthy pines. Spindly white branches at awkward angles sprawled through the air, grasping at nothing. The dark, vine-like foliage that hung limply from a few of the branches looked sickly as well—though Eira had a hard time believing that any tree so clearly devoid of life could sustain leaves of any kind.

"Disease?" Kael asked. "Is there a blight in this forest? It could have been spreading toward the village and the folk worried it would kill their crops."

"Those aren't trees," Cian said.

"Stay here," Lukasz ordered as he pushed his way out of the ring. Ignoring his command, Eira went after him as he walked to the nearest dead tree.

Lukasz stopped alongside the dead trunk and Eira heard him make a choking sound. Reaching the tree, Eira saw that the trunk wasn't solid. And Cian had been right. It wasn't a dead tree.

Bleached bones had been built into the shape of a tree trunk. Eira looked up. The branches were bones too. Bones of all shapes and sizes. Something glopped onto her shoulder. What Eira brushed away was thick and slimy. When she looked at her wet, sticky fingers, they were crimson. Blood. Blood had fallen from the bone tree.

Eira forced herself to look up at the branches. The heavy, roping foliage drooped toward her, dripping blood. She looked away before she could recognize too many of the parts that belonged inside someone's body.

Lukasz gripped her arm, pulling her back to the ring of knights.

"How many trees?" he asked Kael.

"I can see five or six," Kael answered. "There could be more deeper in the forest."

"Five or six accounts for the village." Lukasz's face had drained of color. "And more."

"Where are Alan and Philip?" Alistair asked quietly.

His answer came in the form of a bellow followed by a shape hurtling from high among the pine trees.

Philip's limp body thumped on the ground and rolled over once. His chest was split open.

Another shape descended, but this one landed on its feet. When it rose, it loomed over them, half again as tall as Lukasz and twice as broad. Its skin matched the ruddy brown of the pine bark and its eyes shone like garnet. The tall creature wore a ragged shirt, and a hat was perched between its long ears. Red liquid slid off the hat onto the sides of the creature's face.

Eira had encountered a redcap once before and she wasn't pleased to meet another. Most sorcerers knew that while the idea of summoning the much larger and more vicious cousin of hobgoblins might be appealing, it rarely went well in practice.

Redcaps wielded powerful magics of their own and easily broke the binding spells used to call them to their would-be masters. Eira had come upon her first redcap just after it had decapitated its summoner and was kicking his head around like a ball.

Beside Eira, Kael spewed curses.

"Steady," Lukasz murmured.

The redcap gazed at them, raised its arms in triumph, and let out another bellow. Two more redcaps lumbered out of the forest. Their hats dripped fresh blood. Alan's head decorated the long pike carried by the third goblin.

"We can take them down," Lukasz said in a low voice. "They have size and strength, but we have skill."

"Where did they come from?" Cian asked.

"That's a question to be answered after they're dead," Lukasz answered her. He raised his arm, shouting an order. "Arrows, now. We have the best chance if we can blind them."

Seven of the sixteen knights bore ranged weapons. Projectiles whistled through the air, revealing the marksmen's skill. Arrows and bolts lodged in the closest redcap's face, several slicing through its eyeballs.

The redcap screamed, clawing at shafts.

"Kael, take your team and cover the archers. Keep the other goblins off us." Lukasz pointed to the other two redcaps. "Sorcha's and my men will hack this one apart. Don't call out if you can help it. If it hears you, it will have a better chance of grabbing you and breaking you in half."

Kael dashed into the forest with the archers, seeking to outflank the redcaps still in possession of their sight. The blind redcap stomped around madly, roaring and swinging its pike.

"A redcap's bones are like iron," Lukasz told the remaining knights. "If you try to strike a blow to its heart, you're likely to break your blade. Slashing wounds, deep cuts that sever. When it falls, cut its throat. Now go."

The knights rushed at the flailing redcap, but Lukasz stepped in front of Eira and Cian, blocking their path to the fray.

"My ladies, you must stay out of this," the commander said brusquely.

Cian laughed at him. "Don't be ridiculous."

Lukasz looked at her somberly. "I know well your skills as warriors, but this is a fight my soldiers are prepared for. It's not worth risking two members of the Circle. You are needed there. You are the voice of the Guard."

"We are warriors of the Guard," Eira snapped. "Don't ask us to stand by while you fight and bleed."

"You risked enough bringing us here," Lukasz said. "Trust that if the battle goes awry and we need your swords, I will call on you."

Eira was about to argue, or even strike the commander to prove her strength, when Cian answered. "Very well."

Lukasz nodded at Cian and with a battle cry stormed at the blind redcap.

"How could you?" Eira hissed at Cian.

Cian leveled a cool gaze on her sister. "There was no time to argue. Lukasz needs to be with his men more than we need to be in that fight."

"We are not doddering old fools or helpless maids," Eira spat. "We're warriors. More skilled in combat than most of the knights here."

"They are skilled enough," Cian said quietly. "You bring shame on yourself to belittle them so."

Bile came up Eira's throat with her anger. Too furious to speak, she turned her gaze on the unfolding battle. Kael and his archers had blinded the second redcap, but the third had learned from the others' folly. The clever redcap had torn a large branch from a pine tree, swinging it before his face to deflect arrows.

A roar from the closest redcap drew Eira's attention. Lukasz hadn't exaggerated his advantage over the blinded goblin. The Guard's axes, swords, and polearms struck relentlessly at the redcap, shearing flesh from its arms and legs. Following Lukasz's commands, the knights attacked without a sound, leaving the redcap to wield its pike in vain. Desperate and maddened by pain, the redcap threw down its weapon and turned to flee. It trampled over two knights as it stumbled into trees.

"Finish it!" Lukasz called as he led his warriors in pursuit.

As Lukasz's company disappeared into the forest, shouts of triumph rose from Kael's team. The blinded redcap, not able to aim its thrusts, had mistakenly impaled the other redcap with its pike, killing it. The dead redcap collapsed and the blind redcap tripped over the corpse. Without hesitation Kael's men leapt onto the fallen monster, raining fatal blows on its exposed throat.

Eira knew both redcaps were dead when she heard Kael shout, "To the commander!"

Leaving the gigantic corpses behind, Kael and his men raced into the forest, following the trail of blood that would lead them to Lukasz and the final goblin.

"I don't think the commander will be calling for us," Cian said with a dry laugh.

Eira bit her tongue, too wearied by anger to fight with her sister.

"We should see to Philip's body." Cian returned her sword to its scabbard and walked toward Philip's broken corpse. "He can receive proper burial at Tearmunn."

Resigned, Eira followed her sister but stopped when she heard a strange snapping sound behind them. She twisted around, searching for the source of the noise. Without warning an object buzzed past her, its speed creating a stiff breeze that kissed her cheek.

Cian screamed.

Whipping around, Eira saw her sister hunched over. Something slender and white projected from her left side. Another buzz, another breath of wind, and a second white spear pierced Cian's body just below her left shoulder. Cian screamed again and fell to her knees.

Eira rushed to Cian, crouching beside her. Trying to shield her sister as much as she could, Eira searched the trees for their attacker. High-pitched cackling brought her gaze to the branches of a bone tree. Among the draping gore perched a hobgoblin, its beady red eyes fixed on Eira. It cackled again before it launched itself into the high branches of a nearby pine tree and disappeared. Whether satisfied with its attack or unwilling to risk a fight once it had been spotted, Eira didn't know, but the small goblin seemed to be gone.

Cian began to cough, spitting blood onto the ground. One look at the wounds snatched Eira's breath. The hobgoblin had created its weapons by snapping limbs from the bone tree. The jagged, razor-sharp points of splintered bone had been thrown with enough force to render Cian's armor useless. Both of the makeshift spears had entered her back and spiked out of her lower-left abdomen and upper-left chest.

"Lady Cian!"

Eira looked up and saw Alistair running toward them. Reaching the sisters, he stared at Cian, horror overspreading his face.

"What happened?"

"A hobgoblin was in the bone trees." Eira's voice shook. "It ambushed us and disappeared."

"Hobgoblins don't attack like this," Alistair whispered hoarsely. "They never attack like this."

Eira could only nod. She'd never known a hobgoblin to wield weapons or to demonstrate such deadly accuracy in an attack. But then, the Guard had never faced a band of striga or discovered a village devoid of its residents. The rules of their world were changing quickly. Too quickly to see what was coming next. Too quickly to save Cian. She drew a breath to speak, but only a sob came out as Cian collapsed on her side.

"Lukasz sent me back to tell you we're pursuing the goblin toward the river," Alistair said. "We were to follow . . ."

Eira cradled Cian's head in her lap.

"I'll go for help," Alistair told her. "There are elixirs in the saddlebags."

"There's no elixir that will save her," Eira answered. "These are fatal wounds."

Alistair tugged at his dark curls, frantic. "There must be something. In all that we study there must be something that can save her."

Eira shook her head. "Nothing we've learned—"

Dorusduain is a lesson . . .

Forcing her breath to slow, Eira held up her palm. It was dirty but unmarked. Skin that had been cut open, that blood had poured from, was whole again.

"I know what can save her," Eira whispered.

"Tell me how I can help." Alistair crouched beside her. "I'll do everything I can."

"I need you to leave," Eira told him.

Alistair stood up, frowning. "I'm not going to leave you like this. What if the hobgoblins return? What if there are more redcaps?"

Eira's jaw clenched, but she couldn't waste time arguing.

"Will you swear to me that what you witness here, you'll not speak of to anyone?" she hissed. "Swear on your life."

Alistair paled, but nodded.

"If you forsake this oath, I will kill you myself." Eira waited until he nodded again. "Hold my sister; try to keep her still. If the bone splinters move, it will cause more damage."

Eira and Alistair slowly traded places. Alistair's eyes were wide. He looked frightened, not of his oath but of Eira herself. He probably believed she'd gone mad with grief. He'd be sure of it when he saw what she was about to do.

But she couldn't worry about Alistair's assumptions. Drawing her dagger, Eira sliced open her palm and waited for her blood to hit the ground. She began to chant, but her mind was racing as she spoke the incantation the prisoner who called Bosque Mar master had taught her.

Blood has been spilled here. Cian's blood. Philip's blood. The redcaps' blood. He must come. He must.

Eira kept her eyes closed as she chanted. And hoped. Her eyelids snapped open when Alistair gave a cry of alarm.

"Don't move, Alistair!" Eira snapped.

"But—" Alistair had one hand on his sword hilt, the other holding Cian. His eyes were fixed on the place where Bosque Mar had materialized.

Paying no attention to Alistair or Cian, Bosque came to Eira, taking her hand and kissing it.

"My lady Eira."

When Eira drew her hand back, the wound was gone. She pointed at Cian's crumpled form. "Can you save her?"

Bosque glanced at Cian, then returned his gaze to Eira. "Do you want me to save your sister?"

"My sister is dying," Eira snarled at him. "Of course I want you to save her. Show me the power you claim to have."

"I've offered many demonstrations of my power," Bosque said quietly. "And you require yet another?"

"Please." Eira's anger broke and she bowed her head. "Please save Cian."

Bosque reached out, lifting Eira's chin. His silver eyes bored into hers. "Your will."

He moved to Cian's side, kneeling on the ground. Alistair stared at him in disbelief, but Bosque calmly regarded the knight and said, "Open her mouth."

Eira didn't see Bosque's weapons, but in a moment he'd opened the vein at his wrist and held it over Cian's lips. His dark blood trickled onto her tongue. Eira watched as Cian swallowed reflexively. Still keeping his wrist to Cian's mouth, Bosque reached out and grasped the bone splinter at her shoulder and with one jerk pulled it free. Without hesitation he reached for the other spear, sliding it out of Cian's abdomen. Alistair gasped when blood didn't gush from the puncture wounds, but Eira knew what was happening. The wounds were closing, Cian's flesh mending.

Withdrawing his wrist from Cian's lips, Bosque leaned over and whispered in her ear. He stood up but glanced down at Alistair's ashen face.

"Thank you for your assistance, young knight." Bosque's silver eyes searched Alistair's face. "Give me your name."

"Alistair Hart," Alistair whispered, gazing into Bosque's strange eyes without blinking.

"I hope we'll meet again, young Alistair." Bosque smiled at him before returning to Eira's side. "She'll sleep now. And she won't remember the attack . . . I thought the memory might pose some difficulties for you."

Eira stared at him, unable to speak. Her mind stormed with joy and fury.

"You're angry," Bosque murmured, stepping close to her.

"Was this your lesson?" Eira asked, glancing at Cian's resting body and the blood-covered bone pieces that lay beside her. "Are you so cruel a teacher?"

"The lesson is that you need me," he told her. "As I need you."

"The redcaps, the village," Eira said. "All of this was your doing?"

"It was."

"How could I need you?" Eira kept her voice low. "I'm grateful that you healed Cian, but your redcaps killed two of the Guard. My sister was nearly killed by spears made from the bones of villagers. Innocent people."

"As I said." Bosque spoke gently. "I need you. Without you I'm forced to this . . . to acts of desperation for my cause."

"You still need to feed your army," Eira countered. "Isn't that why your beasts are here, hunting those I've sworn to protect?"

"Yes," he said. "But I'm also here because I am subject to the foolish whims of feeble-minded magicians with delusions of their own power. That is why striga and redcaps terrorize small villages. I am a beggar, scavenging for what scraps I might find."

Bosque leaned in, murmuring to her. "You can change my fate. I would be subject to your will alone, where only those deserving punishment receive it from my warriors. Men like Abbot Crichton. Men you deem corrupt."

His breath was cool as it brushed her cheek. "I can save those you love . . . and I will destroy your enemies."

He stepped back, smiling. "Think on my words. I must leave you now as your companions are returning. You know how to find me when you've made your choice."

Eira nodded.

Bosque glanced at Alistair. "The boy has potential. His heart's desire has been denied. Keep that in mind and he could be an asset to you. Very soon you will need strong allies."

Eira's brow furrowed and Bosque laughed, the sound fading as he slipped into the forest shadows. From behind her, Eira heard the shouts and calls of the returning Guard. Their imminent arrival propelled her to Alistair's side.

"Remember your oath," she said to Alistair.

"I will," he answered without pause. "And we should tell everyone that Cian suddenly took ill."

Though slightly taken aback by his easy acceptance of the lie they would share, Eira still smiled at his quick thinking.

"I only ask one thing of you." Alistair looked at her and there was hunger in his eyes.

"What?" Eira asked warily.

"Tell me who that man was. Tell me everything."

TWENTY-SEVEN

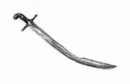

EMBER WOKE, SKIN flushed, but not because her fever had returned. She scooted up in bed and tried to catch her breath. She'd been dreaming, caught in an illusion so vivid it still clung to her mind.

The dream had felt real because it had occurred in the same place she'd woken. Barrow had been reading to her as he'd told her he'd done each day while she recovered. But in this dream he hadn't read to her from a chair pulled up next to her bed. Instead she'd been curled up against the length of his body, her head resting against his chest. She not only heard but felt each word he read as it rumbled from his throat.

She could still hear the deep, steady tones of his voice. She could feel the warmth of his skin. His bare skin against hers beneath the bed linens.

Ember's fingers curled around the blanket as an unexpected shiver passed through her limbs. What madness was this? She'd never had such a dream, but it wasn't the surprise of its impact that worried her. The allure of a maiden's fantasy was nothing she dared succumb to—particularly when it involved her mentor. Barrow deserved her respect and surely would view doe-eyed infatuation with nothing but disdain, or at best a weary indulgence.

Her discomfiture was made worse by the fact that Barrow hadn't visited since the day she regained consciousness. Alistair had come to see her on several occasions, making apologies for his earlier outburst. He'd also recounted the horrible events of Dorusduain. Philip and Alan had been the only Guards lost, but others had suffered grave injuries, and the sickening fate of the villagers cast a pall on all the souls at Tearmunn. Even Lady Cian had taken ill.

Ember was grateful for Alistair's company. He was her link to the outside world. Every time he appeared, bearing news of the Guard or other business of the keep, Ember hid her disappointment that he'd become her regular companion while Barrow had for some unknown reason given up his daily visits to her sickroom.

"I have good news." The healer's cheerful smile was a welcome relief from Ember's tumble of thoughts.

Ember sat up, noticing with satisfaction that doing so no longer took effort nor caused her pain. She brightened further when she saw that the healer was carrying her clothes.

"Am I free?"

The healer laughed. "I truly hope your stay here hasn't felt too much like a prison. But you are free to return to your own quarters and to move about Tearmunn as you wish."

Ember rolled from bed, snatching the clothes from her.

"Before you flee . . ." The healer clucked her tongue. "You must continue to exercise your back and shoulders and I don't want you to leave the keep for another five days."

Ember's face fell. She'd wanted to escape Tearmunn on Caber's back, hopefully with Barrow and Toshach as companions. But even with these restrictions it would be wonderful to leave her sickroom. While the healer continued to fuss over her, checking her healed-over wounds one last time and reminding her not to exert herself too much, Ember pulled up her hair, securing it with the ringed braid Sorcha had taught her. She exchanged her sleeping shirt for a clean chemise and chausses and belted on her tabard. Even if she couldn't leave Tearmunn, she was eager to return to a semblance of normalcy. She might not be able to perform all her duties with the Guard, but she could at least look like she belonged with them.

She looked about, frowning. "Where are my weapons?"

"Have you not listened to anything I've said?" the healer scolded. "You'll have no need for them until Sunday."

"Not to use," Ember said. "I want to be sure they haven't been lost."

The healer laughed. "If I know anything about the Guard, it's that they do not allow any weapons to be lost. I'm sure they're in the barracks, awaiting your return."

Her words reassured Ember, but only slightly. She'd feel better with Silence and Sorrow hooked to her belt where they belonged.

After thanking the healer for her care and making several more promises not to return to the field too soon, Ember escaped the sickroom and hurried from the manor. When she burst through the doors, she gulped the spring air. The day was warm and further lightened her already buoyant spirit.

Despite her promise to remain within the keep, Ember walked quickly to the stables. Even if she couldn't ride, she wanted to see Caber, and she hoped she might encounter Barrow with the horses too. His sudden absence chafed at her, making her worry she'd done something to offend him.

"Lady Morrow!" Ian was leading a frisky dun colt from the stables. "It's good to see you well again. The rumors about your battle with the striga are impressive."

"It's good to be well. And I'm sure the rumors are much embellished from the truth," Ember said, though she was pleased to think that her first foray into the field might have bolstered her reputation throughout Conatus. She smiled at him and then looked at the prancing colt. "Who is this?"

"A troublemaker," he said. "We've just started his training and he's due out on the longe line today."

The colt reared, jerking Ian back. He swore, examining the fresh rope burn on his palm.

"Looks like you've got your hands full," she said as Ian calmed the skittish young horse.

"It's going to be a long morning." Having gotten the colt under control, he stroked the dun's bowed neck. "But well worth it. He has a fine spirit and will make the best of horses once we understand each other. Speaking of which, Caber will be happy to see you. He's been in quite a foul temper since you took ill."

Ember sighed. "I've been ordered not to ride yet."

"That's a shame," Ian said. "When Caber's unhappy, he likes to bite."

"Oh, dear." Ember spared the stable hand a guilty smile.

"No worries, my lady." He laughed. "We were accustomed to Caber's moods long before you arrived. The only difference now is that his temper is tied to you."

Ember couldn't help her smile, which Ian returned warmly. "It's always good to see a strong bond between horse and rider."

She nodded, more eager than ever to visit the stallion.

"Are you looking for Lord Hess as well? Or just Caber?" Ian asked.

Not expecting his question, Ember looked at the ground, hoping Ian didn't see the heat creeping into her cheeks.

If he noticed, he gave no indication, only saying, "I think he's getting ready to take Toshach out, but you can probably still catch him."

Keeping her head ducked, Ember murmured her thanks and hurried past Ian into the stables. The rich scent of hay and sweet bite of grain eased her frantic pulse. As she walked along the stalls, horses poked their heads out, ears flicking in curiosity as she passed. When a familiar well-shaped chestnut face appeared, Ember called out.

"Caber!"

The stallion bellowed in return, craning his neck out of the stall and tossing his mane. When he began knocking his front hoof against the stall door, she ran forward. Caber gave another high-pitched whinny and banged on the door again.

"I'm coming!"

When Ember reached the horse, he blew into her face. She stroked his velvet cheeks and scratched his ears. He leaned over and gave a firm nip to her shoulder, enough so that it hurt but didn't break her skin.

"Hey!" She rubbed her shoulder and he snorted, pinning his ears back to show his disapproval. Then he lifted his head and tried to chew on her braid as usual.

She twisted her head away but stroked his neck when he bowed his head close to her. "Will I be forgiven if I sneak a handful of grain to you?"

He answered with a hearty, low sound. Laughing, Ember planted a kiss on his nose. Approaching hoofbeats turned her head. The sound stopped as Barrow came to a halt with Toshach just behind him.

Ember's heart jumped into her throat. It only took a moment of looking at Barrow's dark hair and the gap where his shirt opened below his throat, giving the slightest hint of his chest, to plunge her back into her dream. She looked away as her skin heated up.

"Ember." Barrow sounded as uneasy as she felt. "Have you recovered?"

Still not sure she could bury her embarrassment, Ember returned her attention to Caber, who had begun banging on the stall door again now that Toshach was near.

"Almost," she answered him. "I've been told not to fight or over-exert myself. But I feel well enough."

"Good," he said.

She glanced at Toshach. The stallion was saddled and bridled.

"Are you going out for the Guard?" she asked. "Or just for a ride?"

Barrow shifted his weight. "I'm just taking Toshach into the glen. We both could do with a bit of exercise."

Ember nodded, wondering if he would go to the hidden waterfall he'd shown her. She half expected an invitation to join him even though she knew she'd have to decline. But Barrow stood quietly, leaving Ember to deal with the hollowness that carved out an empty space beneath her ribs.

Caber kicked the stall door again and she forced a smile. "He'd like to go with you. But I'm not allowed to leave the keep yet."

"That's probably best." Barrow led Toshach a few more steps along the stalls. "If you're feeling up to it, the healers could use your help. There are many injured after the Dorusduain mission."

Ember stared at him, disbelieving that their conversation would end so abruptly.

"I was relieved to hear that you weren't injured at Dorusduain," she said quietly.

He was silent for several moments before saying, "I wasn't there."

Ember didn't know what to say. She'd simply assumed he'd been with the Guard. Alistair hadn't mentioned Barrow in his accounts, but Ember knew Alistair didn't like talking about her mentor, so she hadn't asked him. She'd waited to ask her nurse if Barrow was among the injured. Part of her was shocked that Barrow would miss such an urgent and dangerous mission. Another part was disappointed because Ember had somewhat assuaged herself by imagining that the attack on Dorusduain and subsequent plotting within the Guard had kept him from visiting her.

Before she could speak again, Barrow stopped Toshach and turned to face her. "There's another matter I must discuss with you."

Ember didn't know why her stomach twisted, but she suddenly felt sick.

"After much consideration . . ." Barrow's jaw was tight, as though he had to force his words out. "I've decided that I'm not the best person to serve as your mentor."

"What?" It was the last thing she'd expected him to say.

"Strange things are stirring. Dark things. I don't know what is coming, but I fear it and I can't suffer distraction. I must focus on my own role in the Guard rather than yours." Barrow twisted Toshach's reins in his hands. "Sorcha will take my place. I'm sure you'll find her an exceptional teacher."

Casting her eyes downward, Ember blinked hard. Was that all she'd been to Barrow? A distraction? The tears that burned in the corners of her eyes were as unwanted as this news. She wanted to ask him why, to demand an explanation. But she was too frightened of the reasons he would give. If Barrow no longer wanted to guide her steps as she progressed to full status in the Guard, it meant that somehow she'd failed to meet his expectations.

What had it been? Where had she fallen short? She bit her lip, wanting to do anything to keep from crying in front of him. Her tears would surely only earn more of his disdain. All she could guess was that their trip to the Black Forest had somehow provoked this new poor opinion of her.

And hadn't she disobeyed him?

Barrow had instructed her to watch the other knights, to be cautious on her first mission and not enter the fray. But she'd done just the opposite, throwing herself at the striga when it attacked Alistair. As a result she'd been carried off while the rest of the Guard were embroiled in their fight against the remaining creatures. And hadn't it been Barrow who'd spent an entire night searching the forest for her?

What she'd thought had been concern and devotion to her must have instead given Barrow reason to doubt her skills. Now he wanted no more to do with her.

From where he stood, still holding Toshach, Barrow said quietly,

"If you should need my assistance, I will always help you, Ember. I am still your friend."

Ember didn't answer. She couldn't bear to look at him. His attempt at pacification only made things worse.

Toshach's hooves clopped on the ground, slowly fading away. Caber gave a shrill whinny, calling after the other stallion. Feeling rather numb, Ember searched out the grain bins. She returned to Caber, opening his stall door and slipping inside.

The stallion greedily ate the grain from her palm, swishing his tail in contentment. When the grain was gone, Ember brushed off her hands and began rubbing down Caber's fine coat. He submitted happily to her ministrations, occasionally flicking his ears in curiosity at her silence. No longer able to contain it, Ember choked out a sob. When she twisted her fingers into Caber's mane and let her tears drip onto his withers, the stallion craned his neck around and bent his head, snuffling comfort into the crown of her hair.

TWENTY-EIGHT

EIRA BID THOMAS good night, closing the door as she left his room. The meeting had gone as she'd expected. Ever the philosopher, Thomas would spend eternity wringing his hands over Conatus's dilemma: obedient to the Church yet enmeshed in those dark mysteries it abhorred. She'd doubted the eldest member of the Circle would be amenable to her suggestions, but she had to try. She expected she'd earn the same result when she spoke with Fionn. The scholars were tediously predictable.

Claudio had been a surprise. With his cautious nature, Eira had expected him to reject her offer outright. Instead he'd peppered her with questions, his desire for security proving to outweigh his sense of loyalty to the Church.

Next she would work her way through the Guard and the clerics. Gaining supporters among the knights and magic workers was essential. Time urged her to haste, while the need for secrecy held her back. If her bid was to be successful, she couldn't delay forever. Now was the perfect time for this shift in power to occur. If all went well, it could happen swiftly and without too much disruption. One by one they would fall into line. Even those who doubted her initially— when they saw what she'd seen, understood how much their lives would change for the better if they followed her—surely then all resistance would fade.

Stopping only to retrieve her heavy riding cloak from her room, Eira made her way from the manor into the courtyard as the sun vanished behind the hills of Glen Shiel. She was halfway to the stables when a shout stopped her.

"Eira!"

She turned to see her sister running across the courtyard. Like Eira, Cian was dressed for a night journey—heavy cloak covering her riding garb.

Cian smiled when she reached Eira's side. "I'm glad I caught you."

"Why?" Eira's sharp tone made Cian step back.

"You've made so many of these night trips alone," Cian said, keeping her tone gentle. "I thought you might need company. And after Dorusduain—"

"You think I need you to watch over me?" Eira laughed. "When was the last time you bested me on the practice field?"

"I meant no insult." Cian's brow furrowed. "Only that with the reports we've been receiving, it seems unwise for you to scout on your own."

Knowing an argument would only make Cian more stubborn about accompanying her, Eira worked her mouth into a smile.

"Forgive me, Cian. You didn't deserve my harsh words. I only worry because you were so recently ill."

"But I'm well now," Cian said, blushing. She'd been startled and ashamed when she'd woken in her bed and was told she'd succumbed to fever in the midst of battle. "Let me come with you."

Eira took her sister's hands. "Please. I shouldn't have snapped at you. The truth is I've been unable to sleep since the abbot's visit. I use the night rides to clear my mind. It's hard to stay within the keep when I feel so often like it's a prison and Abbot Crichton holds the keys."

She squeezed Cian's fingers, waiting for her reaction.

"I think we all feel that way right now," Cian said carefully. "But it doesn't give you leave to behave recklessly."

Dropping Cian's hands, Eira took a deep breath as she struggled to keep her temper in check. "Of course you're right, Cian. But you have my word that my patrol is merely an excuse for a night ride. I need time alone and away from here."

She began to turn away, but Cian ran past her, blocking her path.

"I know you still see me as a child," Cian said.

"A child?" Eira laughed. "Neither of us are children—we haven't been for a long time."

"Then stop dismissing me like I'm only your younger sister and listen to me as you would another member of the Circle," Cian said. "As I am."

"Cian, please hear me as your elder sister, as your friend." Eira felt desperation creeping into her voice. "I need this time alone."

Cian gazed at her, frowning, and suddenly Eira thought she was looking at the little girl who'd been at her side every day of her life. Within the depths of her sister's eyes she saw trust, and guilt tried to worm into her heart. Eira broke eye contact.

"You have to let me go," she said. "Alone."

Stepping to the side, Cian said, "You know I won't stop you."

Eira began to walk away without looking at her sister. Her chest cramped when Cian's voice followed her:

"Be careful."

Though her heartbeat had set off at a gallop, Eira kept Geal at a slow pace for the duration of the climb into the hills. Her mind was too full of thoughts, questions, and doubts. She needed time to think, to be sure that she remained in control of this odd arrangement she'd entered into with Bosque Mar.

Spring showed its true tempestuous nature this evening. Gales shrieked over the slopes, burning Eira's cheeks and whipping her cloak about. She rode on, impervious to the elements that attempted to deter her from this journey.

When she arrived at the cairn, she tethered her horse. Despite the many visits she'd made to this place, Geal had never adjusted to

Bosque's presence. She couldn't trust that her mount wouldn't flee upon his arrival.

Eira drew her dagger, gazing at her palm. The pale flesh was whole, unmarked. No matter how many times she cut into her hand, drawing the blood that was necessary to summon Bosque, his healing power left her palm perfectly intact. No scars. No pain. His power had saved Cian's life.

The ritual of calling him with her blood only to offer up her hand for him to heal had settled deep in Eira's bones. While she wouldn't describe it as trust, she did sense a change in her regard for him. She felt an assurance in his company, a stilling of the restlessness she suffered behind the walls of Tearmunn. An easing of the worries that had plagued her for so long.

As the blade sliced her flesh, she noted the way her pulse slowed. Her breath eased.

"I've missed you." Bosque's long form slipped from the cover of mist.

Eira didn't answer but lifted her palm, which he took into his hands.

"How is your work progressing?" he asked as he closed the wound.

Though the cut was healed, he continued to press her hand between his. Eira didn't try to pull away.

"As I expected," she told him, "there are those who will easily be swayed. And those who will not."

With a brief smile, she asked, "And how are you finding your new home?"

"Quite pleasant." He laughed. "The abbot spared no expense appointing his manor."

Eira cringed, saying, "I'm too familiar with that truth."

He shrugged. "I'm happy enough to reap the benefits of his greed."

"How is the abbot?" she asked.

"Still groveling." Bosque released her hand, and Eira was startled by the sudden cold that poured over her. "He will never pose a threat to you again."

She felt the same thrill that lit her blood when the abbot had been in the throes of torment, held captive by Bosque's wraith. "Good. And his household?"

"Those who resisted have been dealt with," he told her. "The rest have wisely submitted themselves to my service."

She nodded. "We can't afford for anyone to know things have changed for the abbot. Not yet."

"I will act as you see fit," he said. "But the longer you delay, the less likely you'll be able to maintain the element of surprise."

"I know." Eira frowned.

Bosque walked around her in a slow circle. "Those of your people who are resistant . . . what would it take to spur them to action?"

She licked her lips, thinking. "A greater threat than what the abbot represented. Something more immediate."

"Something like Dorusduain?" Bosque asked, smiling slowly. "Or perhaps something even more frightening?"

Eira's pulse skipped into a faster rhythm. "An attack?"

He didn't answer, but continued to smile.

"It would create alarm," she mused. "Urgency that might out-weigh caution."

"What about an enemy they cannot defeat?" Bosque was behind her, murmuring into her ear. "Save for your assistance?"

Shuddering, she whispered, "Your wraiths?"

"No man can destroy them," he said. "And I can place them at your command. To use as you see fit."

Her breath was coming hard. "Yes."

"It should be soon," he said quietly. "And costly enough to pro-voke them—only true sacrifice births the hunger for retribution."

"True sacrifice." Eira closed her eyes.

"And if we make this pact, it requires something of you." He rested his hands on her shoulders. "Something more than what you've already given."

She tensed and his laugh was low, with a cutting edge.

"My lady, it is not what you're thinking," he told her. "My wants are not like those of other men. I desire your love and loyalty, but I do not ask for your body."

Eira turned to face him. "What must I do?"

He took her chin in his hand. "If you wish to command my servants, which is to truly share in my power, you must be loyal to me and only to me. Swear your allegiance and I will serve you always. Each decision you make will be supported by all I have at my command. Any who oppose you will fall."

Despite the darkness Bosque's eyes were bright as molten silver.

"Tell me how I can bind myself to you." As she spoke the words, Eira thought she heard Cian's voice.

Be careful.

But what other choice did she have? Eira knew this creature called Bosque Mar was dangerous. But if his existence on earth was tied to her, he would only do *her* bidding. All she was doing was opening a door of opportunity for her allies. Yes, she stood to gain from the arrangement. But if she had such power at her command, she would use it to punish evildoers. She would establish a new order. A better way of life for Conatus. A life in which they led rather than served, where none would have to accommodate the vices of men like Abbot Crichton.

Bosque stepped back. "A blood oath. And these wounds must remain—a mark on your body that symbolizes your fealty. I will not heal you."

"I understand," she told him, though she'd begun to tremble.

"There is another matter." He brushed his hand along the length of his body. "This is merely a suitable shape for me to take in this world. But it is not my true self."

Eira drew a shaky breath. "Are you a man?"

"You know I am not," he said, holding her gaze. "The oath, if you swear it, must be made when I have taken my true form. Made to the world that is my home. Only then can you draw on its power."

The wind screamed as Eira spoke. "Can you tell me what you are before I swear my allegiance?"

"You have no word for what I am," he told her. He took a step closer, lowering his voice. "If you are afraid to look upon me, you may turn the other way when you speak the words. I am from another world, one that would be strange to you. I take no offense if you wish to see me only as the man I appear to be now."

It meant a willful act of self-deception. Eira knew that. If she made the blood oath to the man who was not a man, she would remain blind. But she clung to his offer out of the fear that seeing what lay on the other side of his human mask would drive her from this path. Too much was at stake. She'd glimpsed a future that she couldn't bear to let go.

"Thank you," she said.

He smiled, the silver of his eyes flaring like a lightning bolt. "Kneel."

Eira turned her back to Bosque and knelt.

"Remove your cloak and your shirt."

With the wind tearing over the hill, Eira expected to find herself shivering as she exposed her bare skin to the elements. But instead she felt warm, as though she was cocooned by Bosque's presence, protected from the cold.

When Bosque spoke again, she recognized his voice, but the words were clipped by a strange clicking noise.

"Have you called me here of your free will?"

"Yes," Eira said. She gasped when something sharp, but not metal, pierced her skin.

"Do you invite me into this world, binding me to you with your blood?"

"Yes." Tears slipped down her cheeks as a cut slowly opened from her shoulder to her lower back.

"Do you swear your fealty to me, by the blood spilled today?"

"Yes." She dropped onto all fours as another diagonal wound sliced the length of her back.

The wind suddenly ceased its howling, leaving an eerie silence. Shaking, Eira curled over. Her back burned with pain. Rain took the place of the wind. The cool water mingled with the hot blood running down her skin.

"Rise, Eira."

She was afraid to lift her head, but the hand that touched her shoulder was warm. Human.

Moving stiffly due to her wounds, Eira donned her shirt, tabard, and cloak. When she turned, Bosque—looking just as he had the first time she'd seen him—gazed at her with sympathetic eyes.

"I am sorry I have to leave you in pain."

With a tight smile, she said, "It was my choice."

His silver eyes flared again. "Yes. It was."

"What happens now?" she asked.

"We incite your companions to action," he told her. "It is time to reveal to them what is truly at stake. Gather your allies. When and how we move forward lies with your will. I exist only to serve you."

Eira nodded, lifting her face so the rain washed away the last of her tears. She stared up into the dark heavens, where stars were masked by clouds.

"Eira?"

She blinked away the raindrops and looked at him. "I know what must be done."

Hours later, while most of Tearmunn slept, Eira stole into the barracks. She climbed the stairs and crept past the cell doors until she reached the room she sought. Knocking as quietly as possible, Eira waited a few minutes before the door creaked open.

Bleary-eyed, Alistair peered at her as though he were dreaming. "Lady Eira?"

"I'm here to keep my promise, Lord Hart," she told him.

His blue eyes sharpened, and he stepped back, ushering her into his cell. She sat in the wooden chair beside his pallet. Alistair glanced at his unmade bed and rumpled sleeping shirt.

"I can dress . . ."

"There's no need," Eira said, gesturing to the pallet. "Please sit."

Alistair obeyed, and Eira smiled when the young knight sat straight and at attention as if he were wearing his Guard uniform.

"I will tell you all you wish you know," Eira said. She lowered her voice. "But first I have a question for you, Alistair."

He blushed when she used his Christian name. Eira took that as a good sign.

"Ask me what you please, my lady," he murmured.

"If I could give you anything in the world," Eira said softly, "what would you want?"

TWENTY-NINE

EMBER'S HEART JUMPED at the knock on her cell door, as it had gained a habit of doing, but her pulse slowed again as it was also wont to do when she opened the door and didn't find Barrow.

"May I come in?" Alistair asked.

"Of course." She stepped back so he could enter. His visits had become frequent since her recovery. Ember was surprised to find she welcomed his company—their relationship had eased back into the familiar patterns of their childhood. The light banter and teasing they shared helped alleviate the dull ache that had made its home in her chest.

"I have a surprise and a gift," Alistair said. "Or rather, it's a gift that's also a surprise."

"I don't need any gifts, Alistair." Ember smiled. *Or surprises,* she thought.

"It would be a shame to let your recovery go uncelebrated." Alistair winked at her. "Besides, if you say no, you'll only feel left out. Everyone else will be there."

Ember peered at him suspiciously. "Be where?"

"Open this and see if you can guess." Alistair brought his hands around from behind his back, revealing a cloth package bound with twine.

With a puzzled glance, Ember took the parcel from him. She

371

drew her dagger and cut the twine. When she pulled back the cloth covering, a soft green fabric peeped out at her. Ember shook out the dress that had been folded within the plain cloth. It was the color of faded grass. Lovely, but simple—its fabric smooth and light, lacking the finery and weight of the gowns she'd worn at home and had donned for her audience with the abbot. It reminded her of something that female servants wore when they gathered in the manor for the annual Yule celebration, when her father distributed gifts.

"Do you like it?" Alistair asked.

Ember nodded but asked, "Why have you given me a dress?"

"The village on the loch is celebrating the spring planting with a ceilidh," he told her. "I'd like to take you."

She hesitated and he quickly said, "As your friend, Ember, nothing more. You'll see when we get there that everyone from Tearmunn is in attendance. The village festivals never fail to impress. Food, dancing, drink. Surely you want to go?"

"Of course," she said, and Alistair's eyes brightened. "I've been hearing about it. But aren't we required to be here for the ritual of Fidelitas tonight?"

"We are," he said. "But the ritual takes place at midnight. There's plenty of time for festivities before the ceremony."

She smiled at him. "Then I would love to go."

"Wonderful," he said. "Change your clothes and I'll be back to fetch you soon."

When he'd left her, Ember stood holding the dress in her hands. The ceilidh did sound appealing, but despite what she'd told Alistair, part of Ember was reluctant to go. If all of Tearmunn would be at the celebration, that meant Barrow would also be there. And Ember had made a habit of avoiding him. Not that it took much effort. Her former mentor seemed to be avoiding her as well. She saw him at meals and occasionally on the practice field when she and Sorcha had sparring matches.

As Barrow had predicted, Sorcha was an exceptional teacher and Ember had made significant progress. But she didn't fully credit her new mentor's skill for her swift advances in combat. After Barrow had disowned her, Ember had thrown herself into training relentlessly. She was determined to fill the void in her chest with an unparalleled commitment to her training. For the most part this strategy had proven successful. It was only when she saw Barrow, or when he acknowledged her with a polite but restrained greeting, that she felt like he'd punched her in the gut.

It was all foolishness, she thought as she unbraided her hair, letting it fall in waves down her back. Had she not let herself become overly admiring of Barrow, she wouldn't be in this predicament. She might have more relief if her overactive imagination would spare her nightly visits from the tall knight. In her dreams Barrow recanted his words from the stable. He asked her forgiveness and promised never to leave her side. But the worst of it was that her mind didn't stop at a simple reconciliation. Instead it pressed her into his arms, showed her the shape and strength of his body in far too intimate ways, and made her wake breathless and bathed in sweat.

Ember shed her usual clothing and found a clean kirtle. She slid the dress over her head. It buttoned up the side so the waist and bodice hugged her curves. Though she didn't quite know what to make of Alistair supplying a dress so perfectly tailored to her size, she was grateful for its lovely shape and the way the skirt swirled around her ankles, flaring out if she turned in a circle or twisted side to side.

After a soft knock at the door and Ember's invitation, Alistair reentered her room.

He looked at her for a moment and she saw him swallow. "You're lovely."

"Thank you," Ember said. "You look quite the dashing knight yourself."

And he did. Alistair had traded the Guard's uniform for finely woven chausses, a fitted linen shirt, and a dark vest. He was clean-shaven and he smiled at her, his face full of the boyish charm that so many women would surely find irresistible. But not Ember.

For a moment she wondered what could be wrong with her that she would reject the professions of love from one so desirable as Alistair. He was her lifelong friend, a proven warrior, and inarguably handsome.

Though she might muse about her own heart's failings, she knew it was no use to speculate about Alistair. She could think of him as nothing other than her friend.

His brow furrowed. "Has Eira spoken to you yet?"

"Eira?" Ember shook her head. "Does she need to see me?"

"She'll seek you out, I'm sure," he said. "When she does, please listen to what she has to say, Em. Eira is a great leader. She can do so much for us. For all of us."

He drew something from his vest pocket. "In the meantime I know she wanted you to have this."

Dangling from his fingers was a pendant suspended by a thin gold chain.

"Why?" she asked.

"I don't know," he said with a weaseling smile. "Perhaps she thought you'd be suffering without the fineries of home."

"Ugh."

He looped the chain around her neck. "You should wear it tonight."

"I don't know," she said as he fastened the clasp. "It's a fine gift. What if I lose it?"

"Don't lose it."

She cupped the pendant in her hand. It was rimmed with gold, its surface delicately carved to reveal a rose crossed by two swords.

Alistair leaned over her shoulders. "The Bloodrose. It represents the love and sacrifice required of a true warrior."

He took the pendant from her fingers, turning it over. "See."

"*Sanguine et igne nascimur.*" Ember read the inscription. "In blood and fire we are born. And Eira's name is here as well."

"She has great faith in you," Alistair said.

"I don't know why," she murmured. "I've done little since I came here."

"Little?" He snorted. "You killed a striga that led us to a prisoner who may be more important than any we've ever taken."

She tilted her head, peering at him. "Is there news about the prisoner?" She'd heard little other than that the wild man was still confined in the stockade.

He looked away. "Only rumors."

"What rumors?" she asked.

But Alistair smiled, ignoring her question. "Remember what I said. Listen to Eira."

"I will," Ember said, distracted by her own thoughts.

"Please, Ember," Alistair said. "I want you to understand how much I trust her."

She looked at him, surprised by the seriousness of his words. But the solemn moment had passed.

"Shall we go?" He offered his hand and Ember took it. "Ian's readying our mounts."

They rode from Tearmunn at a leisurely pace, watching the sun set over Loch Duich as the horses picked their way down the hillside. Alistair kept Ember laughing by admitting to her all the mistakes he'd made during his trial with the hobgoblins.

"It's a miracle I'm not dead," he told her.

Ember doubted that all the faults he'd heaped on himself were true but thought them instead created for her entertainment. "I saw you bait the striga. You were incredibly brave."

"All fools are brave." His eyes twinkled in the rosy twilight.

The sounds of the planting festival drifted toward them from the village that squatted at the edge of Loch Duich. Bonfires began to dot the hillside behind the village, ringing its perimeter with flames that leapt toward the heavens. But it was the music that tugged at Ember's spirit. Pipes, flutes, and drums wove complex melodies bursting with life.

They left their horses tethered at the village border, giving coins to the pack of boys who'd been assigned to watch over the mounts. Alistair led the way into the center of the festival, and with each step Ember's senses were assailed by sight, scent, and sound. The music roared in her ears; her heart pounded with the frenzied drumbeats. Venison, beef, and pork roasted on spits, filling the air with savory odors. Local artisans called out to them, hawking wares ranging from pottery to potions. At the center of it all was the dance. Bodies flew about in a broad circle, dipping, twirling, bowing—partners changed, hands clasped. Laughter and shrieks of delight became part of the ceilidh music.

"May this planting grant us a blessed harvest." Father Michael smiled warmly at them. "And the ritual of Fidelitas prepare us for the work to come."

"Have we missed anything?" Alistair asked him.

The priest gestured to the musicians. "Only the chance to dance with your commander. He talked his way into the performance as soon as he arrived."

Ember tracked the spot to which Father Michael pointed, and gasped. Lukasz was seated amid the village musicians, beating furiously on a bodhran.

Alistair was laughing, but Ember turned a questioning gaze on the priest.

"Music is a great love of the commander's," he told her. "And he rarely is afforded the opportunity to play."

He looked past the dancers at Lukasz, whose eyes were closed as he lost himself in the fierce rhythms he created. "He's very talented," Father Michael observed.

"Don't tell him that." Sorcha materialized from the crowd with

Kael at her side. "If you do, no one in the barracks will sleep again because Lukasz will be drumming all night."

"She's right." Kael tipped his wooden cup to his lips. "I know you love to build up our spirits, Father, but in this case have mercy."

"Any other surprises?" Alistair asked.

"I think we're about to be surprised by rain." Sorcha glanced up. The sunset had vanished behind a cluster of threatening storm clouds.

"It's a planting festival. Rain is welcome." Kael grinned, casting a sidelong glance at the ring of dancers. "I'll tell you what *would* surprise me: if our Barrow manages to get through this night without a betrothal. I think I've observed a dozen maids vying for his attention. The poor man hasn't had a chance to eat, or even sit, since we set foot in the village."

Though her chest was burning, Ember couldn't resist searching the blur of moving bodies. Finding Barrow was too easy. He was taller than most of the villagers. She watched as he lifted a girl up at the waist, twirling her around and releasing her. The girl laughed as her golden locks bounced, gleaming in the firelight.

Ember pulled her eyes away, suddenly wishing she were back in her room. Or blind.

"Hold your tongue, Kael," Sorcha said. Ember glanced at her and was surprised at the sympathy in her gaze. Sorcha smiled briefly at her before shoving Kael playfully. "You've had too much whisky. You know Barrow has no interest in these girls."

"I've hardly had too much!" Kael turned over his cup, empty. "Look, my cup is empty. Does anyone want to assist me in righting this wrong?"

Alistair laughed and turned to Ember. "Whatever you please, my lady."

"I see your true nature, choosing the pretty girl over your handsome mentor," Kael said to Alistair. "Turncoat."

Sorcha took Kael's arm. "I'll help you, poor fool."

"A good woman, this one." Kael laid a noisy kiss on Sorcha's cheek. As they walked away, Alistair asked, "Do you want to go with them?"

Ember shook her head. "I want to dance."

Though her chest was still burning at the sight of Barrow's hands on that girl, Ember knew indulging her jealousy would prove as empty as Kael's cup. She loved to dance and dance she would.

Alistair regarded her with surprise. "Dance?"

"Yes, Alistair," Ember answered, taking his hand. "I can dance with my oldest friend, can't I?"

She saw disappointment flicker briefly in his eyes as her words drew a firm line between them, but he answered, "You can. And we shall."

He took her hand, leading her into the throng of dancers, who moved around the bonfire with rapid twists and twirls. When the song ended and the partners made their bows, Alistair tugged her into the line.

"See you in a bit!" he called as the music rose again.

She laughed. The dance began, and after only a few turns she was out of Alistair's arms and in those of another man. The joyful abandon of country dance had her spinning and flying down the line as the men of the outer circle moved clockwise and their female partners moved counterclockwise. Dizzy but ecstatic, Ember reveled in the flare of her skirts, letting the music carry her feet in steps so fast and turns so quick she felt as though she barely touched the ground. Her partner caught her forearms, whipping her around and sending her with gales of laughter on to the next man.

Her laughter stopped when she recognized him.

She could tell Barrow was as surprised to see her standing before him as she had been to suddenly encounter him as her next dancing partner. But of course she would—Scottish country dances always involved changing partners and hadn't she known that Barrow was in this dance circle? Had she hoped for this without admitting it to herself?

They both went still for a moment. Barrow coughed then, stepping toward her. Ember bit her lip, offering him an uncomfortable smile. His arm encircled her waist and he clasped his hand in hers. They began to whirl in time with the pounding drums.

The world slowed. The music and the other dancers faded, leaving only her and Barrow moving together. She could see each spark leap from the bonfire, escaping from the flames to dance toward the night sky. Her pulse drowned out the drumbeat, jumping through her veins. She could feel Barrow's heartbeat too, as if her own heart were racing alongside his.

They were dancing, feet flying as they followed the pattern of the circle. But Ember moved like one mesmerized, her eyes never leaving Barrow's steady gaze. With each step their bodies drew closer, hands gripping each other's fiercely. Soon the dance would force them apart, throwing them into the arms of the next partner. That knowledge made Ember's chest tighten.

Barrow was still holding her eyes with his. They were dancing so close now that each step, twist, and turn had them brushing against each other. Ember could feel the heat of his body contrasting with the chill of the spring night.

The melody rose and a downbeat struck, signaling each dancer to relinquish his partner for the sake of another. For a moment, Barrow's fingers dug into the fabric of her dress as if he wanted to cling to her rather than let her go. That was when the sky opened up.

Rain fell in swollen drops that exploded on Ember's head and shoulders, soaking her within moments. The deluge scattered the crowd. Dancers, musicians, and spectators ran shrieking, desperate for shelter. Sheets of rain blinded Ember, plastering her hair to her face and neck.

"This way." Barrow's hand slipped around her wrist. He tugged her away from the fire, which spit and sizzled its protest as the rainfall attempted to extinguish the flames. Barrow was running, and Ember was pulled along with him into the dark forest. She wiped at her face, struggling to see. Between the shadows and the heavy rain, she might as well have been running blindfolded.

Barrow slowed and then stopped, releasing her wrist. She squeezed her eyes tight, trying to shut out the rain. But somehow it was no longer raining, or at least the initial torrent had stopped. A scatter of drops hit her at irregular intervals, but she no longer felt as if she were standing beneath a waterfall.

Where had Barrow led her?

Ember looked up and found herself beneath one of the largest trees she'd ever seen. The branches of the ancient oak spread above them, offering temporary shelter from the deluge, but Ember's clothes had been soaked during their flight. Barrow leaned against the tree's broad trunk.

"We can linger here until the storm passes," he said, brushing his still-dripping hair off his face.

Ember twisted her own heavy, wet tresses in her fists, wringing out the water, and then pushed them back behind her shoulders. The sensation of having the full length of her hair covering her back was odd, but not unpleasant.

The sounds of music, dance, and revelry had vanished, drowned out by the steady beat of rainfall. She wondered if the villagers had fled to their homes or if, like Barrow and her, they had stolen to nature's harbors for protection from the downpour.

"Are you cold?" Barrow asked.

Lost as she was in the rhythms of the storm, his question startled her. Despite being slick with rain, her skin felt warm. Her heart only now began to slow after pounding with their flight from the ceilidh. She shook her head, but found herself shivering. It wasn't from the night's chill, but because of the path his eyes were taking from her face along her neck to her chest.

Ember glanced down and saw that her sodden dress clung to her body. A few raindrops that found their way through the barrier of tree branches chased each other from her collarbone over her skin, disappearing into her bodice. She looked up at Barrow and met his gaze, though she didn't recognize his expression. Had she not known better, she would have thought he was in pain.

He reached out, lightly grasping her arms. Ember shivered again and her pulse quickened.

"Come closer," he said. "You're trembling."

She stepped toward him, wanting to speak, but her throat had closed up. Her eyes were on his face. She was close enough to see droplets collecting on his eyelashes. She wanted to be closer. Her heartbeat outpaced the downpour, its speed stealing her breath, leaving her dizzy. When Alistair had drawn her into his arms and pressed his mouth to hers, she'd been breathless, but only in a way similar to being punched in the gut. The sensation had made her sick with fury.

But now she was tracing the shape of Barrow's mouth with her gaze, wishing she could touch him with more than her eyes. With each moment she felt warmer, drawn to him in a way she didn't understand. Barrow moved one hand to her waist. He was frowning, as if his confusion matched her own. His hand slid over the curve of her hip. With more than a little hesitation he drew her closer. He moved her slowly, steadily, until her rain-soaked form was fitted against his.

"Ember," he said. Her name was like a siren song on his lips. She leaned into him. Her hands came up to his chest. She grasped his shirt, wanting to hear him speak again. As if he'd pulled the thought from her mind, he bent his head closer, whispering her name once more.

"Ember." When he spoke, she could taste his breath, subtly sweetened by spiced wine. "Forgive me."

She opened her mouth to answer and his lips touched hers. As she fell into the kiss, she understood for the first time what her sister had spoken of when she warned against the celibacy of the Guard. No sensation could match that of Barrow's mouth moving against hers. Ember twisted her fingers through his damp hair, pressing into him and parting her lips further. His tongue slipped into her mouth. When Alistair had grabbed her, smashing his face into hers and invading her mouth with his thrusting tongue, she'd never imagined that a kiss could provoke anything but disgust from her. Now she knew better. The heat coursing through her veins was intoxicating.

Ember clung to Barrow because all she wanted was to be closer to him, but also because she feared what would happen when they finally parted. His hand moved up her rib cage, and his thumb traced the outer curve of her breast. Her body quaked and a small sound emerged from her throat.

He pushed her away, gazing at her face. The fear building in her chest was mirrored in his eyes.

His skin had gone pale. As he dropped his hand from her side, Ember realized he'd taken her soft cry as an objection to his touch.

"Barrow." She grabbed his wrist, closing her other hand over his fist. She placed their joined hands against the damp skin above her breastbone. "I—"

She wanted to tell him that her lips were still warm from his kiss. That her body craved more than the skimming caresses he'd barely given it. Ember stood looking up at him, clutching his fist to her chest, unsure how to voice the tumult of revelations that filled her mind.

He returned her gaze, freeing his hand but only to twine his fingers through hers. They stared at each other, breathing hard, neither of them speaking. His other hand came up to stroke her cheek. Then he slid his fingers to the nape of her neck, drawing her close. She lifted her face, lips parting to welcome his kiss once more. But the kiss never came.

A piercing scream ripped through the heavy veil of rain. Barrow and Ember jumped apart. In the next moment they were running through the blinding downpour toward the sound, pushing through brambles and brush as another scream and then another rose in the night.

THIRTY

"HURRY!" BARROW CALLED over his shoulder as he stormed toward the village. Ember was falling behind, though her lungs felt about to burst from the effort she put into her pace.

The screams were horrible. Agonizing. Unceasing. Despite her shrieking instincts, which begged her to turn and flee, Ember ran toward the sounds of torment. Shadows were closing in around her. Torches and campfires that had kept the forest lit with the subtle glow of flame had been drowned by the rain.

Barrow's long legs carried him through the woods faster than Ember could manage. She could barely see him through the maze of trees and blinding downpour. Each moment seemed darker than the last, as if night itself manifested into a living thing bent on smothering her.

She was almost to the village, she thought, but she'd now completely lost sight of him.

"Barrow!" she shouted. "Sorcha! Alistair!"

Whatever was happening, she hoped it was something they'd face as a united front, particularly since her only weapon was a dagger she'd secreted into her dress pocket. Out of the corner of her eye, Ember saw a tall shadow rise up, slithering from behind a tree trunk. Though her sense told her it was only her mind playing tricks, her body jolted to a stop and turned.

As she stared, the shadow continued to come toward her. Ember couldn't move. Couldn't breathe. What was this thing?

The creature had no flesh. Its form was utterly composed of shadow, or perhaps ink-black smoke—it gave off an acrid odor of burning and decay. In the darkness it was nearly invisible; only the constant movement of its ephemeral body gave away its presence.

Ember drew her dagger, already questioning whether something not made of flesh and bone could be injured by a blade. The sinister form slunk closer, dark tendrils snaking out to grasp her. She had lifted her hand to strike it when the shadow creature suddenly billowed up, as if it were hesitating.

"Ah!" Ember grasped the pendant that lay against her chest. It was hot, burning her skin.

The thing backed away, its form turbulent like boiling smoke. And then it vanished.

She stood still, breathing hard and using a light touch to probe the tender skin beneath the pendant. The gem was no longer hot in her fingers, and if weren't for the sting of the burn on her chest, she might have believed she'd imagined the incident.

Where had it gone? Each shadow now seemed a menace. She had to find the others. Warn them.

"Lady Morrow!"

Ember whirled around to see Eira coming toward her. Unlike her companions who'd attended the festival, Eira wore full battle garb.

"Are you hurt?" Eira asked her. "You're trembling."

Ember shook her head. "Something's happened."

"I know," Eira said. "That's why I've come."

"I thought the villagers weren't supposed to see women among the Guard," Ember said, frowning.

"That's why I have this." Eira donned a helmet. "Come with me. Stay close."

Eira didn't run, but walked at a fast clip toward the village. The screams hadn't stopped, though some had weakened, becoming wails of despair. They reached the edge of the forest, and though Ember would have rushed into the fray, Eira grabbed her arm.

"Wait. You're hardly ready for battle."

Ember squinted through the rainfall, still hearing the screams but unable to see what was happening. "We have to find the others." She brandished her dagger. "I'll manage."

Eira looked at her. Ember thought she noticed Eira's gaze drop to the pendant that hung from Ember's neck before she nodded.

"Yes," she said, releasing Ember's arm. "Stay by my side."

At a cautious pace that Ember found infuriating, Eira led the way into the village. They wove between clusters of thatch-roofed homes. The screams were close now. Their sound made Ember's throat close.

"There." Ember choked on the word as she pointed to a man who writhed on the ground. His body had been engulfed by the same sort of shadow creature that she'd encountered in the forest. The man screamed, his hands clawing at the earth as his attacker held him, its shadow body pulsing like a leech sucking blood. It seemed not to matter that the creature had no weight or substance; its grasp appeared inescapable.

Eira began to move away.

"But—" Ember was still watching the man in horror.

"Our purpose is to find our companions," Eira told her. "We can't help him."

Though Ember's stomach churned, she followed Eira farther into the village. The rainstorm at last gave them reprieve, but Ember couldn't be grateful for the sights a clear view afforded her.

The shadow beasts were everywhere in the village, their victims chosen without regard to age or sex. Some lay limply, whether dead or unconscious Ember didn't know. Others still flailed, desperate to escape their torment. Those she spotted were all strangers, men, women, and children from the village. With each new sighting Ember feared she would come upon someone she knew.

"What are they?" Ember asked, her voice shaking.

"Hush," Eira said. "Don't draw their attention."

They reached the bonfire circle. Burning wood still spit and hissed, smoke and steam rising together into the night sky.

"Ember!"

The sound of Barrow's shout brought tears to Ember's eyes.

"Here!" she cried out, earning a stern glance from Eira.

He wasn't alone. Lukasz and Sorcha were with him, both bearing daggers like the one Ember had carried in her dress.

Lukasz regarded Eira with alarm. "Why are you here? And in uniform?"

"I heard there was trouble," Eira answered coolly. "And most of the Guard was absent. I thought it prudent to take precautionary measures."

"Where are the others?" Ember asked. Alistair and Kael were still missing, as was Father Michael.

Lukasz shook his head. "I don't know. Hopefully well away from the village. If we're lucky, the rain drove them back to Tearmunn."

"What is this evil that's come upon us?" Sorcha hissed.

"We must return to the keep," Eira said. "We can do no good here."

"I wish I could argue with you." Lukasz laid the blade of his dagger flat against his palm. "I threw my other dagger at one of beasts. It was like attacking a cloud."

Eira turned and gestured for them to follow. "That's why we mustn't wait. Our only choice here is retreat."

"I don't know." Lukasz hesitated. "Even after my attack, the creature didn't turn on me. They seemed intent on attacking the villagers only."

"That doesn't matter now," Eira told him. "Follow me."

She led them toward the forest. Now that the rain had stopped, Ember could see huddled figures in the woods. Some of the villagers had climbed trees. Others crouched in groups, gazing grief-stricken as they listened to their neighbors' cries.

"Why don't they run to the keep?" Ember asked Lukasz. "Wouldn't we offer protection?"

"We would," he told her. "But you'd be surprised at how much it can take to drive a man from his home. Some will stay even in the face of certain death."

This very case proved the truth of his words, Ember thought.

Sorcha suddenly shouted, pointing to her right. One of the shadow creatures had abandoned its victim. It now flowed over the rain-soaked ground, moving away from them toward the center of the village. Sorcha turned and rushed after it.

"Where are you going?" Ember cried, and then she saw it.

A child, barely old enough to walk, tottered through the mud. It wailed, soaked by rain and full of fear, likely searching for its mother. The shadow creature kept its inexorable pace, bearing down on the toddler. Ember's glance moved from the child, seeking any sign of hope for its salvation. Her gaze settled on a figure only a short distance from the toddler. A tall man leaned against the side of a house. His pose was casual and his head tilted as if watching this tragedy unfold were somehow amusing.

"Who is he?" Ember whispered. But no one heard her as Lukasz swore and started to go after Sorcha.

"No!" Eira stepped in front of him. "I'll go after her. You must get the others to the safety of Tearmunn."

"You take them," Lukasz growled. "I should fight with Sorcha."

"I'm ordering you, Commander," Eira said, drawing her sword. "I'm more ready for a fight than you are. You've already lost one dagger today."

Lukasz glared at her but nodded. "We'll see you in the keep."

Eira nodded. "Godspeed."

When the others were out of sight, Eira broke from her run, instead walking calmly into the village. Ahead of her, Sorcha dove between the wraith and the child. Rolling to her feet, Sorcha scooped up the toddler and whirled to face the wraith.

With only a dagger to defend herself, Sorcha spat on the ground. "Go to hell, you fiend."

Eira lifted her hand and the advancing coil of shadow stopped. Its nebulous form undulated, gave a sudden shudder, and then vanished. Sorcha stared in shock at the empty space where the wraith had been. With the child still wailing in her arms, Sorcha went very still, uncertain of her next move.

Behind her Bosque Mar straightened. "The menace is past!" he called in a voice that reached across the village. "See to your families."

Creaks and whispers filled the air as hidden villagers emerged from within houses and beneath carts or piles of straw.

"Gather here! I have the fiend who brought this sorrow upon us!" Bosque seized Sorcha from behind, which made her drop the child. It sat in the mud, screeching.

Sorcha battled to free herself and shouted, but Bosque's arms were locked around her, stronger than iron.

"Eira! Help me!"

Bosque looked at Eira, giving a slight nod. Sheathing her sword, Eira turned a regretful glance upon Sorcha. She'd known the night would end here, but she was sorry for it.

A true sacrifice.

Eira wished it hadn't been Sorcha, but she also knew that the villagers were much more likely to accuse a woman of witchcraft than a man. And Sorcha had proved resistant, hostile even, to Eira's call to arms. That made Sorcha an enemy. Once their plan had taken shape, its target had been an obvious choice.

At least I saved the girl, Eira thought, *and Alistair believes she'll join us.*

With a sigh Eira pulled her eyes off Sorcha and slipped away. She wove her way between houses and finally stopped, crouching out of sight so she could watch and listen without being spotted.

Curious, frightened villagers began to cluster around the tall man who held a struggling woman fast.

"Jamie!" a woman cried, and rushed forward, sweeping the crying, mud-covered toddler into her arms.

"By the grace of God alone your child lives," Bosque told her. "This witch would have taken your babe to sacrifice."

Murmurs flew through the gathering crowd, punctuated by sobbing and grief-filled wails.

Sorcha ceased her struggling and her face blanched with disbelief.

"I am no witch," she whispered, but as she began to fight against him once more, her voice became a shout. "I am no witch!"

"She is a witch." Bosque tightened his hold on her. "Only the work of the devil could bring such sorrow here."

Affirmative rumbles filled the air. The distraught crowd pressed closer, men and women jostling each other to get a look at this man and his captive.

"We all know the devil must find agents to do his bidding," Bosque told them. "Witches are the servants of the devil. They are his whores!"

This shout earned Bosque nods and calls of "aye!" from the mob.

Bosque raised his right hand, able to keep Sorcha imprisoned with only one arm. "I swear to you that I saw this witch command the demons that attacked us. When she tried to steal that child, she bid the creatures leave."

"You saw this?" the mother of the child asked.

"Indeed I did," Bosque told her. "And are not the demons gone? Have they not left us in our sorrow to bury the dead?"

"I saw it too!" a man called. He stepped from the crowd and turned to address his neighbors. "From where I was hidden under my wagon, I saw her command the demons to leave. She's a witch!"

Wails rose from the villagers that blended with angry shouts.

Bosque shook his head. "And this is not all. I know this woman. She is not one of us but one of them." He pointed northwest to the road that led from the village to Tearmunn.

"She belongs to Conatus. To the people of the keep."

A man called out, "But the knights offer protection!"

"Is this protection?" Bosque asked. "Where are the knights now? Have they done anything to stop this?"

Sorcha thrashed in his grip. "These are lies!"

Bosque pressed his other arm against her throat, choking off her words. She scratched at his arms as he strangled her.

"Have we not long borne the rumors of their heresy?" he asked the crowd, who answered with shouts.

"I've heard they use the Saracens' magic!"

"They steal women and children!"

"They should have burned with the Templars!"

The mood of the villagers shifted, their grief abandoned in favor of rage.

Sorcha's face was turning blue. Bosque shoved her forward, and she fell to her hands and knees, gasping for air.

"And what message shall we send to Conatus? How shall we repay those who sent a witch into our midst?"

The mob swarmed over Sorcha.

Eira bowed her head and stole from the village, carefully making her way back to the road and taking care not to draw notice. Alistair pushed back the hood of his cloak at her approach. He'd been waiting at the edge of the road, holding the reins of two horses.

"Is it done?" he asked.

"Yes." She took her horse's reins from him and mounted. "But this night is only the beginning."

"He told us that someone must die. That death begets life," Alistair said reverently. "The old must collapse so the new can rise."

"Bosque Mar is as wise as he is powerful," Eira said. "And you've been listening carefully to his words."

Alistair nodded, watching plumes of oily black smoke rise into the sky. He shook his head regretfully. "Sorcha was a fine warrior. I'm sorry to lose her."

"So am I," Eira told him. "But her mind clung to the old ways. She closed her ears to my pleas."

"She couldn't be saved," Alistair murmured.

"No," Eira answered. "She could not. But she was only one. After tonight the others will seek the shelter we offer from the coming storm . . . including Lady Morrow."

"Yes, my lady." Alistair smiled at her as he swung into his saddle. They set off at a gallop, bearers of urgent news for the knights of Tearmunn.

Much later—long after the fire had died and the woman's charred corpse was taken down—the villagers would not be able to recall the name of the man who'd discovered the witch, nor how he'd known she hailed from Tearmunn—proving at last that the rumors of Conatus consorting with evil spirits, even the devil himself, were true. They all agreed, however, upon their good fortune that such a wise man had been sent among them so that they might be delivered from God's wrath.

THIRTY-ONE

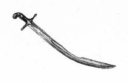

BODIES KNOCKED INTO Ember as she made her way toward the manor's great hall. Conatus had assembled to celebrate the ritual of Fidelitas, but Ember couldn't imagine any ceremony taking place in this mob. The packed corridor was abuzz with whispers.

Ember might not have been able to reach the hall, but she was following Barrow, keeping so close she almost trod on his heels. His tall, strong figure parted the crowd, and Ember took advantage of the path he cleared before the throng closed in again.

Barrow pushed people aside until they stood before those members of the Circle who'd made their way here: Claudio, Ewan, Fionn, and Cian. The great cedar loomed behind them, waiting for its annual tribute. Still absent were Eira, Thomas, and Father Michael. Ember's chest contracted. If Eira was still missing, it meant she and Sorcha both could be in danger. Ember hadn't spotted Alistair anywhere in the crowd either. Looking up, she saw that the gallery was filled with anxious observers as well. They were all waiting, speaking in hushed tones that flooded the room with a steady drone. Her eyes continued to search for her friends; she hoped to catch a glimpse of them.

"This is no way to sober up." Kael came up beside her, rubbing his head. "What's going on?"

"I don't know yet," Barrow said. "Did you hear of the attack?"

"Bits and pieces," Kael told him. "I made my way home when the rain hit; finding my bed seemed like the best option at that point. It was all the commotion that woke me up."

"Did Alistair go with you?" Ember asked.

"No," Kael said. "I haven't seen him."

Her skin went cold.

"Don't be afraid for him," Barrow said quietly. "The creatures were attacking villagers, not us. We may not know why, but it's enough to know that Alistair should be unharmed."

Ember nodded but knew she wouldn't shake her fears until she saw Alistair.

The mood of the crowd was growing restless. What had been whispers transformed into muttered complaints and soon grew into shouts demanding answers.

"Ugly room," Kael said. "It's not helping my headache."

New cries poured in from the corridor beyond the great hall that sent ripples of motion through the gathered mass. The crowd parted and two people came striding into the hall.

Ember threw herself at them. "Alistair!"

"Are you all right?" he asked, catching her in his arms.

"Yes, yes." She embraced him tightly. "When you weren't here, I feared the worst."

She released him, stepping back. "Where were you?"

"When the downpour started, I took shelter in the woods," he told her. "I met Eira on my way back to the village. She told me what happened."

Though Alistair had stopped at Ember's call, Eira had continued on to the Circle. She turned, raising her arms.

"Peace, friends! You mustn't be afraid. We will soon be free of this menace!"

Shouts answered her:

"What are they?"

"Is it true they cannot be killed?"

"It's said they are living shadow!"

"How many villagers are dead?"

Eira raised her voice again. "You will have answers, but now I must beg for your patience. The Circle must convene. Leave us to deal with this matter. Go about your business and keep the work of Conatus under way!"

The crowd stirred restlessly, unsatisfied with her words.

Another voice from the back of the hall called out, "Obey the words of your wise councillor."

Ember rose on her tiptoes and saw Father Michael weaving through the crowd. Lukasz's massive form loomed behind him, warning off any who might think this crisis somehow undermined the priest's authority. "Return to your tasks or seek your bed. Pray for deliverance from this evil if you will, but do not remain here where you will only stir up fear—the tool of Satan. Have faith in your elders."

Though the murmuring continued, the crowd began to disperse. Slowly the room cleared.

"I shouldn't have gotten up." Kael groaned. He turned to go.

"Hold, Kael." Eira came toward them, lowering her voice. "There is news you must hear."

The relief Ember had felt upon seeing Alistair began to drain away. Eira was here, but Sorcha was not.

When the great hall was empty save the Circle and the members of the Guard Ember had seen at the ceilidh, Eira nodded to Alistair. He left them to close the broad doors, sealing off the hall.

"Eira, what's happened?" Cian asked her sister. "Are the rumors true?"

Eira nodded. "And there is more to tell that is much worse."

"Where is Sorcha?" Lukasz frowned at Eira.

"Dead." Eira turned her back to them, walking a few steps away.

"Dead?" Kael lurched on his feet. "How?"

When Eira faced them, her features were drawn. "After you left, the creatures vanished. I don't know why or how, but they disappeared."

"What does that have to do with Sorcha?" Lukasz stood rigidly, his eyes full of rage.

"When she tried to save that child, she threw herself in front of one of the shadow creatures," Eira told him. "And when she did so, it disappeared. All of them did. Some of the villagers witnessed it . . . and took it to mean that they were under her sway."

Cian drew a sharp breath. "Are you saying they thought she was a witch?"

"Without question," Eira said. "They burned her."

The group went quiet, all eyes fixed on Eira in disbelief.

Slowly Lukasz said, "Why didn't you stop it?"

"I couldn't," she answered. "They overwhelmed her before I could intervene. They were mad for blood. It would have been suicide."

"You should have tried," Lukasz hissed.

She glared at him. "You don't know what they were saying. They knew she was one of us. They burned her with cries of heresy. Our heresy."

"May God have mercy on us." Father Michael made the sign of the cross. "And protect us from this evil."

Ember had begun to cry softly. Sorcha, burned? She felt sick with grief.

Beside her Alistair stood stiffly, his face betraying no emotion.

Lukasz kept an unrelenting gaze on Eira. Barrow and Kael's faces mirrored their commander's.

Claudio stepped between Eira and the knights. "This is a great tragedy, but we must look to the future. What can be done?"

"Her death must be avenged," Kael said.

"Make war on the village?" Claudio's eyes widened. "That would serve only to confirm their fears. We claim to be here by God's will. We are supposedly their protectors."

"The sword is not the answer," Fionn added quickly.

"They burned her." Lukasz turned his glare on Claudio and Fionn. "Will you do nothing?"

Father Michael sighed. "Sorcha's death is a horrible blow, born of an unknown evil. But to seek vengeance begets only more wickedness. We must forgive."

"There can be no forgiveness for this outrage." Lukasz's voice shook. "She was one of us."

"If we attack the village, we bring about our own destruction," Claudio said.

Cian nodded, though her eyes were bright with tears. "We cannot do anything for Sorcha now other than pray for her soul. The true cause of her death was the attack—the arrival of this new enemy."

"Cian speaks true," Eira said. "We must fight our true enemy."

"An enemy that manifested from nothing and then vanished without warning?" Lukasz said through gritted teeth. "How are we to find, much less fight, such an enemy?"

"We have a way to seek them," Eira told him. "We can find the source of this evil."

Barrow frowned at her. "You mean the source the prisoner speaks of?"

She nodded.

Thomas rubbed his short white beard. "We've agreed that pursuing that route is futile."

"Do you still believe that?" Eira asked. "Given what's transpired this eve?"

Thomas's brow furrowed, but he didn't answer.

"We know nothing of this source if it even exists," Barrow said. "That search could lead to nothing."

"I agree with Barrow," Lukasz said. "We must grieve our fallen companion, but the wisest course is to wait this out. The villagers have sated their bloodlust. We have the resources to pull behind our walls and defend against any assault. Their anger will abate with time."

"Unless there is another attack," Eira countered. "Will you risk that?"

Lukasz glowered at her, but Claudio answered, "I believe you to be right, Eira. Perhaps this incident is a punishment for our failure to act on the prisoner's bidding."

"You believe God sent Sorcha to the stake to teach us a lesson?" Barrow growled.

Claudio took a few steps back and Father Michael placed a gentle hand on Barrow's arm. "A poor choice of words, perhaps."

Fionn quickly came to Claudio's defense, saying, "He only meant that we must consider the course Eira suggests more seriously than we once did. I agree."

"Is there another option?" Ewan, who had hung back, pacing beneath the Conatus crest, finally spoke. "Can we not call for aid?"

"From whom?" Cian asked. "We cannot ask our brothers and sisters of the order. We've all sworn to deal with domestic conflicts on a local scale in order to keep our connections secret. To bring foreign knights into Tearmunn would violate that code."

"From Rome, then?" Ewan said, turning to Father Michael.

"What say you, Father?" Claudio asked.

Father Michael shook his head. "There will be no aid from Rome, for there is no Rome to call upon. As long as the schism divides our Church, we have no one to turn to."

"Let me speak with the prisoner," Eira said. "If he does not reveal the source of the attack, if he can give us nothing of use, then we shall follow Lukasz's plan and seal ourselves within these walls until the danger is past."

Claudio nodded. "I see no other way."

Thomas and Ewan murmured their assent, though they exchanged a worried glance.

"Father Michael?" Cian asked. "Fionn?"

The priest smiled sadly. "I am no warrior. I defer to the will of the Circle."

"I agree with my peers," Fionn answered. "We must seek the cause of this tragedy. And Eira has offered the most plausible means to do so."

Cian turned to Lukasz. "I won't agree to this course of action without the support of the Guard."

Lukasz sighed. "If it must be so, I will consent."

"And the rest of you?" Cian's gaze swept over the other knights.

"We serve at the will of our commander," Kael answered.

"Thank you," Eira said. "I am humbled by your trust."

She looked at Lukasz. "By your leave, Commander, I would take Alistair with me when I interrogate the prisoner. It would be wise to have another sword at hand."

"As you wish," Lukasz murmured. Though he faced Eira, his gaze was somewhere distant.

"For now we must protect our order from the wrath of the villagers," Cian told them. "Spread the word that none are to leave Tearmunn until further notice. Any person from the village who begs entry must be unarmed before being given leave to pass through our gates."

"Will our defensiveness aggravate their fears?" Thomas asked.

"I will send messages of goodwill," Father Michael said. "It is my hope that we may use words rather than weapons to settle this matter."

Thomas nodded.

"May we take our leave?" Lukasz asked roughly. "I must inform the rest of my knights that we have lost a sister."

"Of course," Eira said.

"I will accompany you," Father Michael told him. "To share in your grief and offer prayers for her eternal soul."

Cian took the priest's arm. "As will I."

Lukasz bowed to the Circle and left the room with Kael trailing after him. Father Michael and Cian moved quietly to the door, speaking to each other in low tones. Barrow followed, but Ember hesitated. She glanced at the departing knights and then at Alistair.

"Will you come with us?" she asked him.

It was Eira who answered her. "I don't want to delay our new mission, Lady Morrow. I'm afraid I must ask Alistair to remain with me."

Alistair nodded, taking Ember's hands. "I'll speak with you soon, Ember. Be well. I thank God for your safe deliverance from this terrible night."

Ember offered him a weak smile, finding his formality strange and out of character.

With a much more confident smile, Eira said, "Indeed, Ember. We rejoice in your health and safety, for in the coming fight you will be greatly needed."

Frowning in confusion, Ember forced herself to murmur, "Thank you, my lady."

Alistair squeezed her fingers and pulled her closer, leaning down to whisper in her ear. "Remember, Eira is coming to speak with you soon. Our world is changing and you must be ready. Eira's way is the only way."

He straightened and dropped her hands.

Unsettled by his words, she stepped back, wanting to run to the door. Instead she forced herself to depart at a dignified pace. Alistair walked with her, bidding her good night and closing the doors to the great hall behind her. As she stood alone in the corridor, Ember heard the doors' massive bolts slide into place. The groan of metal against wood echoed around her and Ember was gripped by a sudden, cold sense that something had gone awry in the way a tiny fissure in a lodestone could bring down the greatest of buildings.

THIRTY-TWO

THOUGH HER FEET were moving, Ember wasn't conscious of walking. Tears stained her face, yet crying had also become an involuntary reflex. Grief numbed her as she trudged from the manor to the barracks, but she walked on. There was nothing else to do.

Once inside the barracks she hesitated. Where to go? Conatus was an order steeped in history and ritual—and they'd just lost one of their own. Were there preparations to be made, actions she should take?

These were questions to ask her mentor. Of late her teacher had been Sorcha. Now Sorcha was gone. When Ember closed her eyes, she saw flames leaping toward the sky, heard the crackle and hiss of kindling being consumed by fire, and gagged as the tendrils of smoke curled upward, encircling Sorcha like the ropes that bound her to the stake.

Ember's mind too quickly fixed on these horrible visions. She couldn't face them alone.

If she went to Barrow, what would he do? Not only had he relinquished the role of mentor, but after what had happened in the forest . . . Thinking of his touch, his warmth offsetting the cool rain, made her head spin. She didn't know what any of it meant.

Silent tears were coming again, these brought on by frustration as well as sorrow. Needing to clear her thoughts before facing any of the Guard—even to mourn—Ember climbed the stairs. She would seek her cell and solace, weeping for Sorcha alone before she joined the others.

Before she reached her cell door, the sound of a ragged sob, very close, pulled her up short. The door to the cell on her left was ajar. Ember crept up to the door. She could see the narrow pallet and Kael sitting on it with his face buried in his hands. His shoulders shook.

Though muffled by his hands, his mourning filled the room with a broken sound that made Ember's throat tighten. She watched him, wondering if she should go to him. No one should be left to drown in this depth of sorrow. As she decided to slip inside and sit with Kael, someone else—someone who'd been hidden by the partly closed door—came into view.

Ember pressed herself against the door frame as Lukasz knelt in front of Kael. The commander took Kael's hands in his own, pulling Kael's fingers away from his face. Lukasz's strong jaw was outlined by the glistening of tears, but he wept silently. He placed his hands on the sides of Kael's face, running his thumbs along Kael's sharp cheekbones.

"We will endure this. We must," Lukasz said.

"How?" Kael asked him.

Lukasz slid his strong arms around Kael's shoulders, drawing him down until their lips met.

Ember lurched back into the hall, heart ramming against her ribs.

She'd known Kael had a lover; Barrow told her as much. But the commander? She wondered if Barrow knew of or even suspected this relationship.

But Barrow hadn't jumped into her mind only because of what he'd said about Kael and the Guards taking lovers of their choosing. The sight of that kiss, tender but edged with pain, made her own lips burn—remembering the touch of Barrow's mouth on hers.

She had to find him.

Ember hurried to the stairs, making her way to the barracks hall. Most of the Guard had gathered there. The majority of the knights were clustered around Cian and Father Michael, some weeping openly, others silent and grim-faced. A few had broken away from the larger group to grieve on their own.

Though she took care to search the faces of the assembled, the one she sought proved absent. She turned around, walking as quickly as she could without breaking into a run. Once back in the courtyard, Ember did begin to run. Splashing through puddles, she rushed to the stables. She slowed once she was inside. In the damp, dark night the sweetness of the grain seemed stronger. She hesitated at the edge of the long, dark corridor that ran between the stalls. Within the shadows she could hear the horses breathing, the swish of their tails, the occasional snort or soft whicker.

Taking a few steps forward, she peered into the darkness but found no evidence that anyone other than the horses was passing the night there. Even so, she pressed on, walking carefully and listening for any signs that she wasn't alone.

A lantern would have been helpful, but Ember was compelled to move forward without the security of a light for her path. She'd come in search of raw truth, the kind perhaps only revealed beneath the cover of darkness.

She was grateful that she'd come to know the stables well. If it had been otherwise, she might have fled from the massive shapes that rustled behind stall doors. A few of the horses stirred, watching as she passed.

Ember walked on, and darkness cocooned her with each step. She paused only when she caught the murmur of a man's voice. Turning in the direction of the sound, she stole forward, treading lightly so as to approach without notice. Even after several minutes in the stables, her eyes could make little out in the darkness, but she could tell as she approached one of the last stalls in the corridor that it was occupied by two distinct shapes instead of only one—the shadow of a horse, and that of a man. Her heart felt like a stone, much too heavy in her chest.

"Barrow," she whispered.

One of the shapes behind the stall door moved, coming toward her. Behind him, Toshach whickered quietly.

"Ember?" Barrow unlatched the door, letting it swing open. "What are you doing here?"

His question stung, but she said, "Looking for you."

He didn't answer her but stood silently, only a shadow that rose before her.

"Please." Ember's voice broke. "I don't know what to do."

Barrow stepped out of the stall and closed the door. She didn't know what else to say. Even if she'd had words to speak, she wasn't sure she'd be able to get them out. Her breath was ragged.

"I'm sorry to have left the barracks without finding you first," he said slowly. "I didn't know . . . I thought it might be best if we spent time alone."

Ember's stomach clenched. "I shouldn't have come here."

"No." Barrow moved closer, reaching out to take her hand. "It was wrong of me to leave you . . . but after . . ."

His fingers closed over hers, squeezing them so tight it was painful. Ember didn't know if he was speaking of Sorcha or of their kiss, but she took a step toward him. He lifted her hand to his face. Her fingertips touched his cheek and jaw, becoming wet with what remained of his tears.

"I should have stayed behind." His voice was rough.

"Eira ordered us to leave, and even Lukasz defers to her authority," she told him. "We followed the commander as we were bidden. How could we have known?"

"I've lost companions in battle," he whispered. "Such is our lot, our calling. But not like this. Never like this."

Ember nodded, letting her hand move from his jaw to his neck. She rested her head against his chest and let her tears come quietly, but freely.

"I fear what it means," he said.

Closing her eyes, Ember could hear Alistair's whisper. *Our world is changing and you must be ready.*

Barrow wove his fingers through her damp hair, cradling her head. "I will not ask anything of you, Ember."

Ember lifted her face, trying to make out his familiar features in the dark.

"What do you want to ask of me?"

"Too much." He drew a shuddering breath. "I thought myself strong, but discover I am weak as the next man. Perhaps weaker."

"And if I wish to give what you ask," she whispered. "What then?"

He bent down, brushing his lips over her forehead, the bridge of her nose. He kissed her cheek and she felt his breath on her lips, his mouth close to hers but not touching. Sensing his hesitation, Ember gripped his shirt and pulled him to her.

When her mouth opened against his, he groaned. His tongue slipped between her lips to lightly caress hers. Her body pressed into him, the damp chill of the night fleeing before the sudden heat of her skin.

Barrow's arms came around her back. He lifted her up, turning her so she was pinned against the stall door. His mouth left hers to trail down her jaw and neck. Her breath caught when his kiss followed the line of her bodice.

When he pulled away, she tried to bring him close again. He gently kept her apart, saying, "We shouldn't linger here, Ember. Anyone could come upon us."

"Where?" she asked, only caring to find a place quickly so she could feel his body against hers once more.

Barrow took her hand and began to lead her toward the stable entrance. "Are the Guard assembled in the barracks?"

"Most of them," Ember said, feeling her chest hollow out at his question's implication. "Must we join their vigil?"

He shook his head. "Tonight Lukasz informs our brethren of Sorcha's death and of the disruption of the ritual of Fidelitas. A ceremony to honor her will take place in a few days after the appropriate preparations have been made."

When they reached the courtyard, Barrow paused, drawing them into the stable's shadow. His lips found hers, lingering, tasting before he broke away to ask, "What do you want, Ember? I won't go any further until I know your mind."

She was afraid to speak. To be honest was to lay bare her heart. "I don't want to pass this night without you."

He cupped her face in his hands. "And I do not think I could bear this grief if not for you."

Ember laid her hands over his. "Will you stay with me?"

"I will." He kissed her softly. "Go to your cell and I will come to you . . . if that is truly what you desire."

"Not only what I desire, but what I need," she whispered, and he kissed her again.

"Go now," he told her. "I'll follow shortly."

She hurried across the courtyard to the barracks, shivering in the absence of Barrow's warmth. The Guard's quarters were subdued, wrapped in silence. Ember didn't know if her companions had sought their beds or were still gathered in the hall, mourning Sorcha. She climbed the stairs, passing Kael's cell on the way to her own, and wondered if Lukasz would spend the night with Kael—the two of them finding solace in each other's arms behind closed doors. The same solace she longed to share with Barrow.

Taking a candle from the hall lantern, Ember stole into her cell, keeping her movements quiet for fear of stirring any of the Guard.

What lay ahead for Barrow and her remained a mystery she wasn't compelled to solve . . . at least not yet. Should anyone witness Barrow coming to her room at this late hour, it could raise questions she didn't want to answer. She lit the candle that sat on the small table and restored the hall light.

In the soft glow of candlelight Ember unbuttoned her dress. She half wondered if she should wait for Barrow before disrobing. But her dress was mud-covered and still damp through to her kirtle. The fabric of the two garments seemed almost melded together, lying heavy on her chilled skin. As she was pushing her loosened gown and kirtle off her shoulders, Ember heard the door open behind her. Her pulse jumped but she continued to let the dress drop. It skimmed over her breasts, baring them, as she turned.

Alistair stared at her, eyes wide.

Ember gave a small cry and jerked her kirtle back up, pressing the fabric to her collarbone.

"Ember." He breathed her name, taking a step toward her. "Oh, Ember."

She backed into her pallet. "Wait, Alistair. What are you doing here?"

"Eira asked me to find you. She's unable to come herself tonight, but what she wants to tell you is urgent. I'm here on her behalf," he said. His eyes had fixed on the place that she'd just covered with the still-damp kirtle. "We need to talk."

"But . . ." Ember groped for a way to get Alistair out of her cell before Barrow arrived. "It's so late and I'm tired. Can you come in the morning?"

He shook his head. "It can't wait."

"Then let me dress again," she said. "I can't speak to you like this."

Alistair came to her before she could object. His hands gripped her bare shoulders.

"Listen to me," he whispered. "Hear what I have to say, please."

He hurried on without waiting for her assent. "I understand now, Ember. I'm so sorry. I should have seen it before."

"Seen what?" Ember glanced toward the cell door. When would Barrow arrive? What would he think when he found Alistair here?

"Why you felt you had to reject me," Alistair told her.

His words drove thoughts of Barrow from her mind as her blood went cold.

"You came to be with me," he continued. "Like we'd always spoken of since we were children. But of course you could never take me as a lover. And as a husband I have nothing to offer. No lands. No fortune."

"Alistair."

He pressed his fingers onto her lips.

"Let me finish. There's another way."

Ember couldn't breathe. What was he talking about? Her pulse had become a steady drumbeat, low and hard, that echoed in her ears.

"Lady Eira is a great warrior and a leader like no other," he said. His eyes had grown bright with excitement. "She is sympathetic to our plight. The life of the Guard is brutal. We give up so much and for what?"

His fingers dug into her shoulders. "We protect the world without acknowledgment. We give up wealth, happiness . . . love." He lifted his hand to cup her face. "It doesn't have to be so."

"What are you talking about, Alistair?" Ember's voice was shaking.

"A new order," he murmured. "A world where we are honored as we should be. Where we are not subject to the avarice of men like Abbot Crichton or the dumb bloodlust of a peasant mob."

Her skin prickled. "Tell me more."

He smiled, encouraged. "Eira wished to speak to you of these matters herself. But things have progressed too quickly. Just know that when the time comes, you must ally yourself with her. To do otherwise would be the greatest folly."

She didn't understand, but the sharp, knife-like twist in her belly told her that something was horribly amiss.

A soft knock came at the door and Alistair turned around. "Who is that?"

Ember felt as though an invisible hand was strangling her. She opened her mouth, but only a croak came out.

"Ember?" Barrow's murmur reached them.

Alistair's face darkened as he strode to the door.

"Alistair, no." Ember choked the words from her throat, but it didn't stop him. He opened the door, glaring at Barrow.

"How dare you come to Lady Morrow in the middle of the night, you cur." Alistair spat at his feet.

With a drawn face Barrow gazed at him and then at Ember, who still clung to her loose kirtle.

She shook her head. "Barrow, please, it's not . . . He surprised me."

The pale cast of Barrow's skin became a white rage. "I told you to stay away from her. And yet you burden her still with your childish obsession."

"I love her, you brute!" Alistair snarled.

Barrow grabbed Alistair by the shirt and towed him into the cell, kicking the door shut behind them.

"I would not bring shame on Lady Morrow by drawing our companions to witness this scene," Barrow said. "But I will not tolerate your presence here."

"I have far greater claims to Lady Morrow than you." Alistair shook himself free of Barrow's grip.

Barrow's hands fisted. "No one has claim on her."

"And I suppose you're here to comfort her now that her mentor is dead . . . the mentor she gained once you abandoned her." Alistair smiled cruelly. "Do you think to wile your way into her bed, promising to guide her to womanhood?"

Barrow lunged at Alistair, but Ember reached him first. Her fist cracked against Alistair's jaw.

"How dare you claim to love me and speak of me so?"

Alistair stared at her, rubbing his face. "I'm sorry, my lady. This barbarian's rudeness infects me."

"Barrow has done nothing wrong," Ember told him. "I asked him to come here because I don't understand what is required of the Guard after Sorcha's death."

Alistair's eyes roamed over Ember's bare shoulders. "And you thought to receive his advice in your nightshirt?"

Ember stiffened. "I thought he had decided the hour too late to come. His appearance is a surprise to me. Just as yours was."

Behind her, Ember could hear Barrow breathing hard, but he didn't move toward Alistair again.

"Then perhaps the honorable thing to do is for both of us to bid you good night." Alistair glanced at Barrow. "Ember spoke true. The hour is far too late and we needn't keep her from sleep with our quarrel."

Barrow was silent for a moment but then said, "Agreed."

Ember turned, casting a pleading gaze on him. How could she object without making things worse? He gave a slight shake of his head.

"After you," Barrow said to Alistair, gesturing to the door.

Alistair bowed to Ember and said, "Think on my words, Ember."

Barrow lifted his brows but followed Alistair to the door without speaking.

He turned in the door frame. "Sleep well, Lady Morrow," he said. Then he closed the door.

THIRTY-THREE

EMBER STARED AT THE ceiling, unable to sleep though she lay on her pallet in a clean, dry nightshirt. She'd listened so hard for any sign of Barrow's return that her ears ached. But he hadn't come back. She toyed with the idea of going to him but couldn't help but think that his absence was a sign of anger toward her. The thought of seeking Barrow's cell and his bed only to be turned away made her feel as if she'd be sick.

Her mind remained divided because of another matter as well. What did Alistair mean about a new order? Did Eira have a plan that only the Circle knew? But if that were the case, why would Alistair know about it and not the rest of the Guard?

In the woods, that shadow creature had manifested in front of her, but when the pendant had burned, it had vanished.

The pendant that Alistair had given her. Eira's pendant.

And what had Eira told them about Sorcha's death? She'd said that the villagers believed Sorcha to be a witch because the shadow creatures had vanished instead of attacking her. And they'd burned her for it.

Ember's throat went dry. Why had the creatures vanished? Had Eira given Sorcha a pendant as well?

She climbed from her bed, groping in the darkness for the necklace, which she'd left on the table.

Her hands shook as she lifted it, trying to make out its details despite the lack of light to see by. In the shadows she could see nothing other than a pendant dangling from a chain, but the longer she gazed at it, the faster her pulse pounded.

Could she have been taken in Sorcha's place? Did Sorcha burn only because she'd been caught in the village where Ember had not?

The knock at her door made Ember jump. The pendant slipped from her hand, its gold edges tinkling against the table when it fell.

Ember's throat went dry. Why had the creatures vanished? Had Eira somehow been connected to it? She'd been the only one to witness Sorcha's demise. Could she have stopped it but didn't?

Before she could answer, the door opened and Ember's chest tightened. She was certain Alistair had returned. But the figure that entered her cell was much too tall to be Alistair.

"Ember, you must wake." The sound of Lukasz's voice startled her more than the knock at her door.

"I'm awake, Commander."

"There is an urgent matter," he whispered. "Dress and come to the stables. Make haste, for time works against us."

"I'll hurry," she said.

Without another word he was gone and she was once again alone. Ember slid a fresh kirtle over her shoulders and pulled on chausses. After she'd belted her tabard, she hooked the leather covers for her weapons into place, haunted by the feeling she would need them. She donned her heavy cloak and drew its hood over her head.

When Ember reached the stables, she found a small group huddled around a single lantern held by Father Michael. She glanced over the half dozen men and women, seeking familiar faces. Lukasz and Kael were both there along with knights she recognized but didn't know other than from sharing meals with them in the hall. The only person present who wasn't one of the Guard was Thomas, the eldest member of the Circle. She continued her search, and her eyes burned when she realized she'd been expecting to see Sorcha among them.

"Ember."

She whirled to find Barrow standing behind her. Fighting the impulse to embrace him, she let her fingers brush over his before letting her hand drop to her side.

His smile was fleeting. "I'm sorry . . ." His words trailed off, but she knew he couldn't say more.

"It doesn't matter."

He joined her in the small circle, standing close enough that their arms touched.

Lukasz, who'd been speaking quietly with Father Michael and Thomas, looked over the group and nodded.

"This completes our number." He sighed, shaking his head. "We are few, but I can't claim surprise at that."

A weasel-faced knight, who Ember remembered was named Fitch, asked, "Are the rumors true?"

"I am sorry to say that they are," Lukasz answered, looking around at the huddled group. "You are here because you came to me after Eira visited you with promises of power, of a new hierarchy in Conatus."

While the people around her nodded, Ember frowned. When Lukasz saw her furrowed brow, he smiled and said quietly, "Or you are here because someone I trust believed you to be incorruptible."

Ember felt Barrow's hand rest on the small of her back. She nodded at the commander, but her head was spinning.

Promises of power. A new order. Alistair had come to her tonight, speaking of Eira's greatness. *I want you to understand how much I trust her.*

He wanted me to join them, Ember thought as bile rose in her throat. *Did he know what Eira planned for Sorcha? Did he do nothing to stop it?*

"You promised a witness to back up your words, Commander." Fitch cast a suspicious glance around the dimly lit circle. "Where is he? I want to follow you, but I need proof."

"Lora." Lukasz beckoned someone from the darkness of what Ember had thought was an empty stall.

The cleric who summoned sparring partners from the clay appeared, supporting a rickety man whose eyes were wild with fear.

"You said you'd protect me." He clung to Lora.

"These are friends, Goodman Sawyer," Lora said gently. "None here will offer you harm."

"You don't know, you don't know." Sawyer's limbs shook. "They all turn. They all choose him."

"Who is this man?" Barrow asked Lukasz.

"A servant of Abbot Crichton," the commander told him. "He arrived at the keep yesterday and Lora was the first to speak with him. She had the good sense to keep him hidden."

"Hidden from whom?" Fitch asked.

"My fellows in the Circle," Thomas told him. "I am afraid they cannot be trusted."

Restless shuffles stirred the group.

"What do you mean, the Circle can't be trusted?" the knight called Mercer asked.

Father Michael raised the lantern so its light rained down on his head. "A great evil has come upon us. A darkness that corrupts the very core of our order."

Lukasz nodded, gesturing to Sawyer. "This servant brings a tale of woe from the abbot's estate."

Mercer snickered. "Since when is woe for the abbot woe for us?"

"In this case the abbot's downfall could very well be our own." The commander didn't smile.

"What's happened, Lukasz?" Barrow frowned at him. "What has befallen the abbot?"

"Tell them, Sawyer." Lora nudged the shuddering man.

Sawyer's eyes roved over the group as he spoke. "I was there when they came. The lady Eira and the strange man."

Ember's breath became shallow. Barrow took her hands in his, hiding their clasped fingers in the folds of his cloak.

"They met privately with my master," Sawyer said. "But soon the abbot's screams filled the halls of the manor and spilled out into the gardens. We all heard him crying for mercy. He found none."

"Who caused the abbot's torment?" Lukasz asked, though the set of his jaw suggested he already knew the answer.

Sawyer's mouth quivered. "H-h-him. We didn't know what they were. The things he called to his service. The monsters. The shadows."

"The shadow creatures?" Barrow asked with alarm. "The same beasts that attacked the village?"

"So it would seem," Thomas answered quietly.

"And Eira was there?" Fitch's hand was on his sword hilt, as if he expected an attack at any moment. "She went to the abbot and no one knew of it?"

"We knew nothing before Sawyer arrived," Lukasz said. "Go on with your tale, goodman."

"They slaughtered the soldiers who tried to help the abbot," Sawyer said, half sobbing. "They are invincible! No weapon can harm these demons."

"Do you believe they truly are demons?" Father Michael asked.

Sawyer nodded. "They serve their master, who is but the devil. What other creature could manifest such evil things at will?"

"What happened next?" Mercer's brow knit together. "After the soldiers were killed."

"There were a few left who surrendered." Sawyer drew a shaking breath. "Eira offered amnesty to any who swore their allegiance to her and to the stranger."

"Does he have a name? This stranger?" Barrow asked.

"His name is Lord Mar," Sawyer said. "Lord Bosque Mar."

"Is this demon known?" Mercer turned to Father Michael.

The priest shook his head. "I have never heard this name. Nor of any being who can call up demons in such number and with such powers."

Barrow drew a sharp breath. "And Eira was a witness to all of this?"

Sawyer's voice dropped to a whisper. "They say she delighted in the abbot's pain . . . They say she laughed."

"What of the abbot?" Fitch demanded. "Is he dead?"

"No," Sawyer told him. "He is a prisoner in his own home. At Eira's orders he signs what letters and documents she wills, and if he resists, the stranger brings his demons to torment the abbot further."

"This is our doom," Fitch murmured. "By her own will Eira let Sorcha burn . . . She will destroy us."

"Hush," Lora said as Sawyer wrung his hands and wept.

"And how can we trust this man?" Mercer glared at her. "What if he's come to us with this story only to elicit our own allegiances? He could give all our names to Eira."

Sawyer looked up, tears dripping off his chin. "No, Lord Knight, no. I was only able to escape because I am a woodcutter. When I went to my work in the forest, I ran away."

"You weren't pursued?" Barrow frowned.

"The abbot has many servants," Sawyer said. "I think Eira had little care for a simple woodcutter."

"She wouldn't want any to learn of what's happened at the abbot's estate," Mercer argued.

"Yes, Lord Knight." Sawyer nodded. "But who would believe me other than someone of your order? I came here in the hopes that Lady Eira would think it impossible for any of the abbot's servants to seek your aid. For the lady herself lives here, and if she were to discover me, I would surely be killed."

Father Michael laid his hand on Sawyer's forehead. "You are a brave man for bringing us this news. God bless you, my son."

Sawyer began to cry again.

"What will we do?" Fitch shifted on his feet, uneasy. "Confront Eira? If her allegiance with this fiend is revealed, perhaps we can expel her from Conatus and then seek a way to defeat her new ally."

"I'm afraid it's too late for that," Thomas said in a strained voice. "Eira has gathered followers. Many within Tearmunn have been swayed by her promises that colluding with this foul creature somehow befits our mission."

"How has her mind become so twisted?" Kael asked suddenly. "How could we have been so deceived?"

"It is indeed troubling." Father Michael bowed his head. "Perhaps even more troubling that she so easily gains the support of our fellows."

Mercer's gaze swept over their group, his eyes widening. "Are you saying everyone within the keep, save we few, have thrown their support behind Eira?"

"No," Lora answered him. "The clerics and servants know nothing of this. Only when I'd found Sawyer and heard his tale did I learn what was happening."

"Eira has laid her case before the Circle and the Guard, but not the whole of Tearmunn," Thomas said. "For that is where she believes the power of Conatus exists. The clerics will be the next to gain her attention."

"Even so." Fitch coughed, trying to cover the trembling in his voice. "Of twenty-five knights, we alone would resist?"

"So it would seem," Lukasz said wearily. "Eira was once the commander of the Guard. There are still many loyal to her. Before tonight I would have counted myself among that number."

Ember closed her eyes. Alistair's face haunted her. Unbidden, his words echoed in her mind once more. *I want you to understand how much I trust her.*

"B-but the Circle?" Fitch stammered. "All of them as well?"

"Not myself, obviously." Thomas offered him a weak smile. "Cian and Ewan are with us too."

"Then where are they?" Fitch asked.

"Cian stayed with her sister," Lukasz told him. "To keep her occupied while we met and decided upon a course of action. Ewan keeps watch for us. If we were to be discovered, this would end before it begins."

Mercer asked, "Before what begins?"

The commander and Thomas exchanged a troubled glance.

"Whoever this Lord Mar is, we must find a way to expel him from our world," Lukasz said. "Even if it means searching the ends of the earth for the means by which he can be defeated."

The gathering became very still as the implications of Lukasz's words sank in.

Barrow spoke first. "When do we leave?"

"Immediately," Lukasz answered. "As soon as the horses are saddled."

"You want us to abandon Tearmunn now?" Fitch shook his head. "Where will we go?"

Thomas frowned at him. "There is no other choice. If you delay, you risk revealing yourselves to Eira or any of her allies."

"As to where we'll go," Lukasz said, "we may have few allies within Tearmunn, but Conatus lives beyond these walls. We'll seek passage to Krak des Chevaliers."

"Syria? You would put us in the hands of the Mamluks?" Fitch gaped at the commander. "Their sultan, Faraj, is spoken of as a cruel man."

Father Michael said, "The Mamluks have been allies of Conatus no matter who rules them, and we will be offered refuge at Krak des Chevaliers."

"How can you be sure?" Fitch asked.

Lukasz's eyes narrowed. "I didn't know you to be such a coward, Fitch."

Fitch dropped his gaze, shamefaced.

"Peace, friends," Father Michael said gently. "These desperate times weaken our faith and make our hearts quail. Let us lift each other up."

"Father Michael is right," Thomas told them. "We can't afford to quarrel among ourselves. Fitch, the reason Krak des Chevaliers offers sanctuary is that it will take longer for Eira to affect such a keep that is within Conatus but outside Christendom. From what we've gathered, she's relying on the channels available to Abbot Crichton. That means she'll focus on the Holy Roman Empire and a few points east before broaching the lands of the Ottomans and Mamluks. At least we hope so."

"And hope is all we have," Lukasz finished.

"I am no coward," Fitch said, his voice low. "But surely we needn't take a ship. That voyage will cost us weeks. Have Hamish weave a door to Krak des Chevaliers that we might travel there with all the speed we command."

Lora sighed. "You can't risk bringing Hamish into this mess. We don't know where his allegiance will fall. If he proves sympathetic to Eira, he'll give away your hiding place."

"You came here this night of your own free will," Father Michael told them. "And you must now choose your path. Remain here to submit, or stay hidden, or else flee from these walls until we find a way to resist the rising dark."

Mercer asked the priest, "What do you mean hidden?"

"Cian, Thomas, Ewan, and I will stay in Tearmunn," Father Michael said. "You must have a way to know what happens here."

"That's a great risk." Barrow frowned. "What if you're discovered?"

"The cost would be greater if we left with you," Thomas told him. "If Cian and I went missing, Eira would know her opposition extends beyond a handful of the Guard and she will become much more dangerous. The more confident she is, the more likely we'll be able to exploit her pride."

Father Michael nodded. "And I must remain here and attempt

to uncover the origins of this creature who calls himself Bosque Mar. Without knowledge we cannot send him whence he came."

"Take Sawyer with you." Lora gently pushed the woodcutter toward Kael. "He can't be found here. Hide him in a town along the way if you must, but make sure he's beyond Eira's reach."

"Of course," Kael said.

Lukasz's command came in a hushed tone. "Those who choose to leave, ready your horses. We'll take our leave of the stable and leave two at a time by the way of the shepherd's door at the rear of the keep. Father Michael, Thomas, and Lora will keep watch, alerting us if any of our pairs garner unwanted attention."

Wordlessly the circle broke up, leaving in a rush, others stumbling away as if in a drunken stupor.

"Go to Caber now," Barrow said quietly. "There's little time."

Ember nodded, but Barrow was already walking away, leaving her to find her own way to her horse. After gathering her tack and empty packs to tie onto the saddle, Ember went to Caber's stall. Though the saddlebags were empty, Ember hoped that she might find the means to fill them along their journey. She kept her mind blank, focused only on readying Caber. Too much had happened in a small space of hours. Events that threatened to break her heart and shatter her mind. She couldn't think about Sorcha. Or Alistair. Any crack in her emotional wall and she would collapse into a rubble of grief. There was no time to let that happen.

Caber greeted her with a hearty snort. His attitude contrasted to her brittle spirit. A midnight ride presented the stallion with a much welcome adventure as opposed to the frightening flight that it posed to Ember. She saddled and bridled Caber quickly, despite his attempts to frolic in the confines of the stall. The horse's eagerness to be out of the stables helped to lighten Ember's mood; at least she'd have one companion in good spirits.

"Ember." Barrow stood on the other side of the stall door. In the darkness Toshach was a massive shadow behind the knight. Caber whinnied a greeting to the other stallion.

"Hush." Ember clicked her tongue at Caber as she stepped out of the stall. "Don't you know we're embarking on a clandestine journey?"

Caber snorted, shaking his mane.

She turned back to Barrow. "Are you leaving?"

"Soon," he told her. "But not without you. We should lead the horses to the back gate."

"We're riding together?"

Barrow quietly said, "Unless you'd prefer another's company."

"No," she whispered. "Of course not."

Ember reached her hand toward him. He took her fingers and lifted them to his lips. The gentle touch sent a quivering through her limbs. Feeling her throat close, Ember pulled free of his light grasp. She couldn't let emotions wash over her, even those she would welcome. It was too dangerous.

Barrow led Toshach forward, giving Ember room to bring Caber out of his stall. She brought the stallion alongside the other horse, and they walked together from the stables. Through the quiet night the two knights and their mounts passed the training field and the rear side of the barracks and the manor.

Lora was waiting by the shepherd's door.

"Lukasz and Kael are away," she whispered, opening the door for them. "Fitch and Mercer will follow you soon. Godspeed."

Ember took Caber through first and then Barrow went with Toshach. Lora closed the door, leaving them between the outer wall of Tearmunn and the cold wind that swept through the glen. They stood quietly, neither moving to mount the horses.

When Ember sighed into the night wind, Barrow reached out and touched her face. The warmth of his hand on her cheek drew out her fear.

"What will happen to us?"

He dropped Toshach's reins and pulled her close. "I don't know. None of us do."

"Would you think poorly of me if I confessed that I've never been so frightened as I am now?" she whispered.

"Would you think ill of me for offering the same confession?"

A sound, part laugh, part sob, welled from her chest.

Barrow kissed Ember's forehead, then leaned down and brought his mouth to hers. She grasped his shirt, pressing her body into his, letting his warmth briefly drive away the wind's frigid breath.

When they parted, he said, "The road ahead is unknown to all. I cannot offer you wisdom or guidance. Only the promise that I will never leave you."

Ember pulled his face to hers, kissing him again before she said, "Your strength gives me courage."

He smiled gently. "No, Ember, that is all your strength and none of mine." She balked, but he kissed her, murmuring against her lips, "And that is why I love you."

Still wearing a smile, but one that now hinted of mischief, Barrow left her speechless as he swung into the saddle.

"We must away, Lady Morrow."

Though her limbs had been rendered unsteady by his words, Ember lifted the reins over Caber's head and climbed into the saddle.

They set off at a dead run, and their horses were soon lathered from the pace. Two riders flying over the earth as if trying to escape the very night.

Ember turned to look over her shoulder, watching as Tearmunn shrank with distance. Looking away with a twinge of regret, she urged Caber forward and set her mind to the east, to a world unknown and a future unwritten.

ACKNOWLEDGMENTS

I am deeply grateful to the many people who worked tirelessly to bring *Rift* to life. The intuition and kindness of my agents, Richard Pine, Charlie Olsen, and Lyndsey Blessing, never ceases to amaze me. My publisher, Michael Green, renews my spirit with his enthusiasm and faith in the worlds I want to build. The incredible team at Penguin Young Readers makes all aspects of a book's life enjoyable, and I'm beyond fortunate to have so much talent and energy surrounding me.

Rift delves into the human past, and while it is a work of fiction, my colleagues and students at Macalester College always remind me that history is full of magic. My writing benefits from the support of amazing readers and friends: Lisa Desrochers, Kiersten White, Casey Jarrin, Heather Brewer, and David Levithan. I'd also like to thank the readers, librarians, and booksellers who welcome my characters, and me, into their lives with such graciousness. My family continues to remind me that living a dream is not only possible, but often necessary. And for my editor, Jill Santopolo, to whom this book is dedicated: thank you for giving me courage on the page and on a trapeze platform.

Turn the page for sneak peek at

RISE

the sequel to RIFT

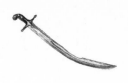

ALISTAIR COULD REMEMBER screaming only once before, at least since he'd become a man. The shrill cry had forced its way from his throat when he'd been pinned to the floor of the wine cellar. Three hobgoblins held him down, cackling, while a fourth stretched its long, clawed fingers toward his eyeball. That scream had been a brittle, strangling yowl of horror.

The sound escaping his lips now was brighter than shattering glass, jagged shards of pain and loss. Ember was gone.

Less than an hour earlier, restless after the events of the day— and of the night—Alistair had gazed at the stone ceiling in his cell. His pallet was unsympathetic to his pains, offering no ease or comfort to lull him into slumber. With eyes open, Alistair didn't see the rough-cut gray blocks above him. Neither did he see darkness when he closed his eyes.

An image had burned itself upon his vision. Skin revealed as linen slipped from Ember's slender but strong shoulders. Weeks with Conatus had chiseled her arms, making them hard as a man's, but Alistair remembered the softness he'd glimpsed. Her hair was fire, flames licking the snow of her naked body, its sudden curves appearing as her garment fell.

It was a scene stolen from his very dreams. Ember baring herself to him. Wanting him. Alistair would have given his soul to relive the moment. And change the way it had ended.

No matter how often he turned in bed or summoned other thoughts—for there was much to think on: Lady Eira's plans had been set in motion and everything was about to change in Tearmunn—he failed. Ember's bare skin, captured in the glow of candlelight, held him hostage.

Unable to bear the torment another minute, Alistair rose from bed. He hadn't bothered to change from his uniform into a sleep shirt. With Conatus reeling from Sorcha's death and Eira taking control of both the Circle and the Guard, the night portended chaos. Alistair had even kept his sword belted to his waist. Should a fight arise, he would be ready to assure Lady Eira's successful ascension to sole ruler of their order.

As he left his cell, Alistair briefly considered seeking out Eira. Perhaps she had need of his help maintaining order. But he readily dismissed that thought. Should she desire, Lady Eira would have no qualms about summoning him. Having given this brief attention to duty, Alistair succumbed to the siren song that called him through the dim corridor.

Passing the few doors that separated his cell from Ember's, Alistair paused in front of her door. What took place within this chamber once he entered would determine the nature of his relationship with Ember. Alistair knew this truth. He leaned against the door, letting the image of her half-clothed figure slide into his mind's eye, coaxing him to action.

Ember must have known he was the one at the door earlier that night. Only a trusted friend would intrude upon her at such a late hour. She hadn't dropped her gown in surprise. The chemise had been falling, released with purpose by Ember's own hand. She'd been waiting.

Alistair refused to believe Ember had anticipated the arrival of another. How could she?

Despite the sick twist of his gut the thought provoked, Alistair couldn't stop the needling doubt following his question. Barrow had come upon them. The knight had disrupted what Ember's skin promised Alistair.

Could Ember have been waiting for Barrow?

Alistair's roiling stomach tangled itself into a hard knot. No. It wasn't possible. Barrow had abandoned Ember. He'd cast her off, forsaking his role as her mentor. And hadn't Alistair restored his own friendship with her in the wake of Barrow's rejection? Hadn't he and Ember grown ever closer, slowly returning to the intimacy and trust they'd shared as children?

That history, the knowledge that he knew Ember better than anyone else, assured Alistair of what he'd always believed. Ember was bound to him, and despite her characteristic stubbornness, she loved him. They would marry, and she would be his. Alistair could imagine no other role for Ember in his life, and his loyalty to Lady Eira had secured his future with Ember. Eira had promised to bring changes to Conatus, which Alistair would soon take advantage of. No longer heralding ties to those monk warriors, the Knights Templar, the Conatus Guards' vows would be of fealty to Lady Eira and Lord Bosque Mar and nothing more. The new order offered Alistair all he desired.

Fortified by this thought, he rapped lightly on the door. And waited. He knocked again, daring to use a bit more force. With Sorcha's sudden death, most of the Guard would be away from their cells, holding a vigil in the hall below. Waking someone was of small risk, and since Ember had kept away from the gathering of knights when he'd sought her out earlier that evening, Alistair wagered that she'd remained secluded in her bedchamber.

Even after more insistent knocks, Alistair couldn't hear Ember stirring within. Perhaps her sorrow over Sorcha had driven her into deep sleep. Or still grieving, Ember might be weeping in her cell, too ashamed to share raw emotion with another. Alistair thought Ember all too concerned about showing a brave face to the world. She was strong enough. Maybe a bit too strong. Ember could be a knight of Conatus if it suited her. But she was still a woman.

Convinced that Ember was most likely hiding her feelings, as she was wont to do, Alistair slowly opened the door. As her dearest friend, it was his place to comfort her. He thought of pulling her into his arms, of stroking her auburn tresses to soothe her. His body tightened when his mind pushed its musings further, making him imagine his hands pushing the loose neckline of Ember's chemise over her shoulders. Watching it fall as it had a few hours before. This time Alistair would catch her hands in his own if she feigned modesty. He would clasp her fingers tightly and look upon her body as he longed to.

In the darkness of Ember's cell, Alistair clenched his jaw so he wouldn't groan. The idea of offering solace to Ember as she mourned had been muscled out by desire that felt as old as his bones. He moved forward, slowly through the black.

"Ember," Alistair whispered.

She gave no answer.

He started toward her pallet, hands outstretched. As he reached to rouse her from sleep, clouds peeled back, uncovering the moon. Translucent beams stretched through the narrow window, giving light to the cell.

Alistair stared at the pallet. The wool blanket lay in a crumpled heap at its center. The bed was empty. He was reaching toward nothing.

The shock of embarrassment was trampled by sudden rage. Where could Ember be?

At the vigil? Her presence there would make sense. After all, Sorcha had taken up the role of Ember's mentor after Barrow had forsaken it. But if Ember intended to spend the night hours honoring her dead friend, why had she been readying for sleep when Alistair last saw her?

Ember wasn't one for complacency. If she hadn't been able to sleep, she might have left her cell. But Alistair doubted she'd joined the knights' vigil. Ember would be more inclined to contend with her sorrow directly. She could be out walking the grounds. Or riding that horse she loved.

Twin spikes of fear and agitation lodged in Alistair's chest. Foolish girl. Lady Eira hadn't yet been able to bring Ember into her fold. That made the young warrior vulnerable. It would take time for Eira to quell the panic in the village, to reassure them that Conatus had been cleansed of its wicked elements and a new reign of justice was about to begin.

A sudden, unwelcome vision crowded out Alistair's fantasies. An unwanted sound filled his ears. Ember's screams. Her pale skin blistering and blackening, splitting open like old, dry leather. Her hair engulfed in real flames. Villagers dancing as they reveled in bloodlust, having captured and punished another witch. For what woman but a witch would ride out alone in the blackest of night?

Alistair was running before he reached the courtyard. Once outside, he sprinted to the stable, praying he wouldn't find what he suspected. Rushing along the stalls, Alistair pulled up at Caber's holding pen. Seeing that the stall was empty, Alistair bent over, spewing curses and trying to determine his next move. How could she be so reckless?

But Alistair knew Ember's wild nature would compel her to gallop off without thoughts of safety. He craved nothing more than to tether and tame her.

Frustrated, Alistair resigned himself to saddle his own horse and go out in pursuit. He couldn't risk Ember falling afoul of witch-hunters.

Before he'd reached the tack room, Alistair abruptly halted, going silent and perfectly still. A flicker of movement had slipped into his peripheral vision. Alistair drew his sword, turning to face the shape that cowered in shadows.

"Show yourself," Alistair said.

"Begging your mercy, my lord," a quaking voice answered.

"Fitch?" Alistair peered at the hunched figure. "Is that you?"

"It is, Lord Hart!" Fitch gave a cry of relief.

Alistair kept his sword at the ready. "Why are you skulking in the stables?"

Fitch crept forward, grunting with the effort. In the dark, his body appeared wide and misshapen. When he walked, his feet scraped across the dirt—or so Alistair thought. A moment later, Fitch was close enough for Alistair to see why Fitch had been hiding.

He was dragging a body.

With a hiss of breath, Alistair jumped back. "What is the meaning of this?"

"Please, Lord Hart." Fitch let the body go and dropped to his knees.

Alistair grunted in disgust to see a knight of Conatus groveling. He jerked away when Fitch reached as though to grasp Alistair's tabard.

"What I've done was to serve Conatus. I swear!" Fitch shook his bloodied fists at Alistair. "They've gone mad. They'll destroy us!"

Making sure his blade was between the cowering knight and himself, Alistair took a closer look at the unmoving man beside Fitch.

"Mercer." Alistair breathed the knight's name. Mercer's face was bloodied, his flesh swelling as it took on violet and gray hues. It was well known that Mercer and Fitch had long been friends. What could have provoked Fitch to attack a fellow knight?

As if sensing Alistair's scrutiny, Mercer groaned. Fitch lifted a hand to strike.

"No!" Alistair's command stopped Fitch's blow. They both watched Mercer, but the knight remained unconscious.

"You did this?" Alistair forced the tremor out of his voice.

"I had to." Beads of sweat stood out on Fitch's brow. "He's a traitor, Alistair. They're all traitors."

Alistair didn't know whether to take Fitch's use of his familiar name as a good sign or not. But the word *traitor* made his knuckles whiten as he gripped his sword hilt tighter.

"Speak quickly, Fitch," Alistair said. "Or I shall deal with you only as a cur who dishonors his companions with unprovoked violence."

"Take me to Lady Eira," Fitch pleaded. "She favors you. She'll grant me an audience if you ask. When Mercer wakes, he can be questioned and my words will prove true."

Alistair grimaced. "I'll take your confession and pass it on to Lady Eira. I'd sooner see you wait in the barracks for her judgment."

"No." Fitch fell over in the dirt when Alistair took a menacing step toward him. Fitch lolled on the ground like a beaten dog showing its belly. "Begging your pardon, Lord Hart, but I fear that I might be implicated in this treachery. I only wish to tell Lady Eira myself so she can see my contrition and restore me to my station. I risked my life to overpower Mercer so I would have proof of this conspiracy against Conatus. Please consider that."

Alistair found it difficult to feel anything but contempt for this man. Yet his bloodied hands and Mercer's limp form promised an intriguing tale. And if this treachery he spoke of was true . . .

"Very well," Alistair told him. "Lady Eira will hear your words. Now get up and stop shaming yourself with this pitiful display. I need your help to carry Mercer."

Fitch scrambled to his feet, casting a fearful glance at Mercer as though the unconscious man might revive and grab him.

Alistair grabbed Fitch and gave him a rough shake. "Act like the Guard you're supposed to be, Fitch. Take his feet and lead the way. I'll carry him at the shoulders."

Fitch turned away from Alistair and kicked Mercer's legs apart. Tucking a calf on either side of his waist, Fitch lifted the unconscious man's lower half while Alistair took care of his torso.

"That's good," Alistair told Fitch. "Head into the courtyard. And be quick about it."

A man twitching and quavering the way Fitch did wasn't someone Alistair wanted at his back. The two knights, one tall and wary, the other bent over as if on the verge of being sick, made their way across the courtyard.

"She's likely in the great hall," Alistair said, directing Fitch to the manor. "And if the Circle is with her, all the better. If traitors are in our midst, it's a matter to be addressed without delay."

Fitch muttered something unintelligible in response, but Alistair didn't bother asking him to repeat himself. He was already questioning his decision to bring Fitch to Eira. What if the man had taken ill and the madness of fever had turned him on his friends?

Still proving his worth to Eira, Alistair detested the thought of raising alarm without reason. It was the cool touch of fear, light on his skin, that kept Alistair moving at a swift pace toward the great hall. No matter how unstable Fitch might appear, something real lay beneath his words. Something real and very wrong.

The corridors of the manor were still. The Guard would be occupied with their vigil, and the staff must have sought their beds for the night. All for the best, Alistair thought. Too many questions were bound to chase after a pair of knights carrying the broken body of one of their fellows. With Sorcha's death raising alarm only a few hours earlier, further bad news could incite panic throughout the keep.

When they reached the thick double doors, Alistair pivoted to the side, bracing Mercer against him while he freed his other arm and pulled the door open. He took care to leave space only wide enough to carry the body inside.

"This is a private session!" Claudio's shout stopped Alistair in the doorway, leaving Fitch and the other half of Mercer still in the hall.

Despite his many years as one of two Circle members hailing

from craft, Claudio still bore the strength of years working with his hands. He strode toward Alistair.

"Peace, Claudio," Lady Eira called to him. "Lord Hart is welcome here."

Claudio hesitated, but didn't counter Eira's words, and Alistair quickly pulled the rest of Mercer, and Fitch along with him, into the room.

"What's this?" Claudio gaped at Mercer.

Alistair glanced back at Fitch. "Let's put him down. And then shut that door."

They laid Mercer on the floor while the other occupants of the hall gathered around. Fionn, per his office as a cleric, carried a scroll in his hand. He gazed calmly at Mercer as though the unconscious man were a puzzle to be solved.

Lady Eira spoke first. "What happened to Mercer?"

Before Alistair could answer, Fitch blurted out, "Have mercy, my lady. I swear I'll confess all."

"What do you have to confess, Fitch?" Eira asked, her voice cool.

"I've done wrong. I thought to betray the cause. But I know I was misled now. I seek to make amends." Fitch gulped, but when he opened his mouth to speak again, he suddenly yelped.

A hand had wrapped around Fitch's ankle. Mercer's eyes were open. With a jerk of his arm, Mercer pulled Fitch off balance. Fitch tumbled to the ground, and Mercer was on him, snarling like a wildcat.

Claudio shouted in surprise and backed away from the struggling pair. Fionn ran across the hall to take cover behind the sacred tree. Eira didn't move, but neither did she try to interfere.

"Traitor," Mercer spat as he struck Fitch. "I'll see you in hell for this."

"I'm no traitor." Fitch grasped Mercer's tabard, trying to shove Mercer off. "You're mad for believing them. They'll be the death of us."

"Stop!" Cian's clear voice rang out.

Alistair, who'd been about to grasp Mercer from behind and wrestle him away from Fitch, wheeled around. He hadn't noticed Lady Eira's sister in the hall. Cian leapt from the far corner of the room and closed the distance between herself and the tangled knights in a few long strides.

With a movement of such grace and strength that it stunned Alistair, Cian took hold of Mercer and Fitch—one in each hand—and threw them in opposite directions. Mercer rolled over once before jumping to his feet. He had no weapon to draw, but his fists were raised. Fitch, either reeling from Cian's sudden intervention or still shocked that Mercer had regained consciousness, fell back onto his hands and heels.

Cian's sword hissed out of its scabbard. "What is this talk of treachery?"

Mercer stared at her, and without breaking her gaze, he pointed at Fitch. "There is your traitor."

When Cian glanced at Fitch, his eyes bulged. He began to crawl backward like a crab. "You . . . you—"

"Yes, traitor." Cian moved toward Fitch. "You should fear me."

When Alistair realized Cian's intention, he rushed at her. "No! Wait!"

He didn't reach her in time. Cian brought her blade down in a clean arc, and Fitch's head toppled from his body.

"Damn your impatience!" Alistair watched blood pour out of Fitch's severed neck. "He was the one who came to me seeking aid. Why would you kill him?"

Unruffled by Alistair's fury, Cian said, "Your companion claimed he had a confession to make. One must sin to require confession. Fitch's face spoke to me plainly of his guilt. I've no doubt that his sins were great."

Alistair was shaking with outrage when she walked away from him.

Mercer stood still, face pale and fists raised. His expression was resigned, as though he expected to meet the same end by Cian's sword.

"You've seen how we deal with traitors." Cian spoke slowly to Mercer, holding his gaze. "Perhaps you would like a chance to confess, and if your contrition proves genuine, you'll be shown mercy."

Drawing a sharp breath, Mercer said quietly, "You cut him down like a common thief. I desire none of your mercy, and I have nothing to confess."

"Very well." Cian raised her sword.

"Put down your sword, Cian," Eira commanded. "When did my sister become a barbarian?"

Cian paused, glancing at Eira. "Death is the penalty for traitors."

"Of course it is," Eira answered. "But we've yet to learn the cause of these accusations."

"Lord Hart brought the men." Cian turned to Alistair. "I assume he has the answers we need."

Alistair jumped forward, speaking as quickly as he could. "I found Fitch in the stables. He'd beaten Mercer senseless and claimed there was a conspiracy against Conatus."

"Is there any truth to his story?" Eira asked him.

Alistair looked with regret at Fitch's headless body before he answered. "I don't know, my lady. Fitch desired to make a full confession to you personally. That's why I brought him here."

"You shouldn't have killed him," Eira told Cian. "It was reckless."

Cian returned Eira's stare without flinching. "To my mind, they're both traitors. The only difference between the two is that Fitch was clearly the coward. I took his head to make a point. A necessary one."

"You let your temper get the best of you, and you dishonor yourself by making excuses for it." Eira regarded her sister coolly.

"Go with Alistair and take Mercer to the stockade. Secure him there until we know the truth of this."

Cian gave a curt nod and then said to Alistair, "Wait here. I'll bring irons to bind him before we go to the stockade."

Alistair nodded. The chaos in the room gave way to an uneasy quiet. Alistair heard Fionn retching behind the tree.

Claudio approached them cautiously. He eyed Mercer, gauging whether any threat remained.

Mercer stared blankly ahead, giving no sign of worry that Alistair stood close by with his sword drawn in case of any trouble.

"You're going to question him, then?" Claudio asked Eira.

"I know one more suited to the task than I," Eira answered. "I'll ask Lord Mar to join us shortly."

Eira walked in a slow circle around Mercer, looking the knight up and down. Her smile made Alistair shiver.

Turn the page for the first chapter of

NIGH†SHADE

the book that began it all

I'D ALWAYS WELCOMED WAR, BUT IN BATTLE

my passion rose unbidden.

The bear's roar filled my ears. Its hot breath assaulted my nostrils, fueling my bloodlust. Behind me I could hear the boy's ragged gasp. The desperate sound made my nails dig into the earth. I snarled at the larger predator again, daring it to try to get past me.

What the hell am I doing?

I risked a glance at the boy and my pulse raced. His right hand pressed against the gashes in his thigh. Blood surged between his fingers, darkening his jeans until they looked streaked by black paint. Slashes in his shirt barely covered the red lacerations that marred his chest. A growl rose in my throat.

I crouched low, muscles tensed, ready to strike. The grizzly rose onto its hind legs. I held my ground.

Calla!

Bryn's cry sounded in my mind. A lithe brown wolf darted from the forest and tore into the bear's unguarded flank. The grizzly turned, landing on all fours. Spit flew from its mouth as it searched for the unseen attacker. But Bryn, lightning fast, dodged the bear's lunge. With each swipe of the grizzly's trunk-thick arms, she avoided its reach, always moving a split second faster than the bear. She seized her advantage, inflicting another taunting bite. When the bear's back was turned, I leapt forward and ripped a chunk from its heel. The bear swung around to face me, its eyes rolling, filled with pain.

Bryn and I slunk along the ground, circling the huge animal. The bear's blood made my mouth hot. My body tensed. We continued our ever-tightening dance. The bear's eyes tracked us. I could smell its doubt, its rising fear. I let out a short, harsh bark and flashed my fangs. The grizzly snorted as it turned away and lumbered into the forest.

I raised my muzzle and howled in triumph. A moan brought me back to earth. The hiker stared at us, eyes wide. Curiosity pulled me toward him. I'd betrayed my masters, broken their laws. All for him.

Why?

My head dropped low and I tested the air. The hiker's blood streamed over his skin and onto the ground, the sharp, coppery odor creating an intoxicating fog in my conscience. I fought the temptation to taste it.

Calla? Bryn's alarm pulled my gaze from the fallen hiker.

Get out of here. I bared my teeth at the smaller wolf. She dropped low and bellied along the ground toward me. Then she raised her muzzle and licked the underside of my jaw.

What are you going to do? her blue eyes asked me.

She looked terrified. I wondered if she thought I'd kill the boy for my own pleasure. Guilt and shame trickled through my veins.

Bryn, you can't be here. Go. Now.

She whined but slunk away, slipping beneath the cover of pine trees.

I stalked toward the hiker. My ears flicked back and forth. He struggled for breath, pain and terror filling his face. Deep gashes remained where the grizzly's claws had torn at his thigh and chest. Blood still flowed from the wounds. I knew it wouldn't stop. I growled, frustrated by the fragility of his human body.

He was a boy who looked about my age: seventeen, maybe eighteen. Brown hair with a slight shimmer of gold fell in a mess around his face. Sweat had caked strands of it to his forehead and cheeks. He was lean, strong—someone who could find his way around a mountain, as he clearly had. This part of the territory was only accessible through a steep, unwelcoming trail.

The scent of fear covered him, taunting my predatory instincts, but beneath it lay something else—the smell of spring, of nascent leaves and thawing earth. A scent full of hope. Possibility. Subtle and tempting.

I took another step toward him. I knew what I wanted to do, but it would mean a second, much-greater violation of the Keepers' Laws. He tried to move back but gasped in pain and collapsed onto his elbows. My eyes moved over his face. His chiseled jaw and high cheekbones twisted in agony. Even writhing he was beautiful, muscles clenching and unclenching, revealing his strength, his body's fight against its impending collapse, rendering his torture sublime. Desire to help him consumed me.

I can't watch him die.

I shifted forms before I realized I'd made the decision. The boy's eyes widened when the white wolf who'd been eyeing him was no longer an animal, but a girl with the wolf's golden eyes and platinum blond hair. I walked to his side and dropped to my knees. His entire body shook. I began to reach for him but hesitated, surprised to feel my own limbs trembling. I'd never been so afraid.

A rasping breath pulled me out of my thoughts.

"Who are you?" The boy stared at me. His eyes were the color of winter moss, a delicate shade that hovered between green and gray. I was caught there for a moment. Lost in the questions that pushed through his pain and into his gaze.

I raised the soft flesh of my inner forearm to my mouth. Willing my canines to sharpen, I bit down hard and waited until my own blood touched my tongue. Then I extended my arm toward him.

"Drink. It's the only thing that can save you." My voice was low but firm.

The trembling in his limbs grew more pronounced. He shook his head.

"You have to," I growled, showing him canines still razor sharp from opening the wound in my arm. I hoped the memory of my wolf form would terrorize him into submission. But the look on his face wasn't one of horror. The boy's eyes were full of wonder. I blinked at him and fought to remain still. Blood ran along my arm, falling in crimson drops onto the leaf-lined soil.

His eyes snapped shut as he grimaced from a surge of renewed pain. I pressed my bleeding forearm against his parted lips. His touch was electric, searing my skin, racing through my blood. I bit back a gasp, full of wonder and fear at the alien sensations that rolled through my limbs.

He flinched, but my other arm whipped around his back, holding him still while my blood flowed into his mouth. Grasping him, pulling him close only made my blood run hotter.

I could tell he wanted to resist, but he had no strength left. A smile pulled at the corners of my mouth. Even if my own body was reacting unpredictably, I knew I could control his. I shivered when his hands came up to grasp my arm, pressing into my skin. The hiker's breath came easily now. Slow, steady.

An ache deep within me made my fingers tremble. I wanted to run them over his skin. To skim the healing wounds and learn the contours of his muscles.

I bit my lip, fighting temptation. *Come on, Cal, you know better. This isn't like you.*

I pulled my arm from his grasp. A whimper of disappointment emerged from the boy's throat. I didn't know how to grapple with my own sense of loss now that I wasn't touching him. *Find your strength, use the wolf. That's who you are.*

With a warning growl I shook my head, ripping a length of fabric from the hiker's torn shirt to bind up my own wound. His moss-colored eyes followed my every movement.

I scrambled to my feet and was startled when he mimicked the action, faltering only slightly. I frowned and took two steps back. He watched my retreat, then looked down at his ripped clothing. His fingers gingerly picked at the shreds of his shirt. When his eyes lifted to meet mine, I was hit with an unexpected swell of dizziness. His lips parted. I couldn't stop looking at them. Full, curving with interest, lacking the terror I'd expected. Too many questions flickered in his gaze.

I have to get out of here. "You'll be fine. Get off the mountain. Don't come near this place again," I said, turning away.

A shock sparked through my body when the boy gripped my shoulder. He looked surprised but not at all afraid. That wasn't good. Heat flared along my skin where his fingers held me fast. I waited a moment too long, watching him, memorizing his features before I snarled and shrugged off his hand.

"Wait—" he said, and took another step toward me.

What if I could wait, putting my life on hold in this moment? What if I stole a little more time and caught a taste of what had been so long forbidden? Would it be so wrong? I would never see this stranger again. What harm could come from lingering here, from holding still and learning whether he would try to touch me the way I wanted to him to?

His scent told me my thoughts weren't far off the mark, his skin snapping with adrenaline and the musk that belied desire. I'd let this encounter last much too long, stepped well beyond the line of safe conduct. With regret nipping at me, I balled my fist. My eyes moved up and down his body, assessing, remembering the feeling of his lips on my skin. He smiled hesitantly.

Enough.

I caught him across the jaw with a single blow. He dropped to the ground and didn't move again. I bent down and gathered the boy in my arms, slinging his backpack over my shoulder. The scent of green meadows and dew-kissed tree limbs flowed around me, flooding me with that strange ache that coiled low in my body, a physical reminder of my brush with treachery. Twilight shadows stretched farther up the mountain, but I'd have him at the base by dusk.

A lone, battered pickup was parked near the rippling waterway that marked the boundary of the sacred site. Black signs with bright orange lettering were posted along the creek bank:

NO TRESPASSING. PRIVATE PROPERTY.

The Ford Ranger was unlocked. I flung open the door, almost pulling it from the rust-bitten vehicle. I draped the boy's limp form across the driver's seat. His head slumped forward and I caught the stark outline of a tattoo on the back of his neck. A dark, bizarrely inked cross.

A trespasser and trend hound. Thank God I found something not to like about him.

I hurled his pack onto the passenger seat and slammed the door. The truck's steel frame groaned. Still trembling with frustration, I shifted into wolf form and darted back into the forest. His scent clung to me, blurring my sense of purpose. I sniffed the air and cringed, a new scent bringing my treachery into stark relief.

I know you're here. A snarl traveled with my thought.

Are you okay? Bryn's plaintive question only made fear bite harder into my trembling muscles. In the next moment she ran beside me.

I told you to leave. I bared my teeth but couldn't deny my sudden relief at her presence.

I could never abandon you. Bryn kept pace easily. *And you know I'll never betray you.*

I picked up speed, darting through the deepening shadows of the forest. I abandoned my attempt to outrun fear, shifted forms, and stumbled forward until I found the solid pressure of a tree trunk. The scratch of the bark on my skin failed to repel the gnat-like nerves that swarmed in my head.

"Why did you save him?" she asked. "Humans mean nothing to us."

I kept my arms around the tree but turned my cheek to the side so I could look at Bryn. No longer in her wolf form, the short, wiry girl's hands rested on her hips. Her eyes narrowed as she waited for an answer.

I blinked, but I couldn't halt the burning sensation. A pair of tears, hot and unwanted, slid down my cheeks.

Bryn's eyes widened. I never cried. Not when anyone could witness it.

I turned my face away, but I could sense her watching me silently, without judgment. I had no answers for Bryn. Or for myself.